Richard Pierce is a writer, poet, and painter. His debut novel, *Dead Men*, was nominated for The Guardian First Book Award. He lives in Norwich, and walks a lot.

www.tettig.com

Also by Richard Pierce

The Immortality Chronicles
The Immortality Clock
The Mortality Code

Aggie's Art Of Happiness
Dead Men
Tettig's Jewels
Bee Bones
The Failed Assassin

A FEAR OF HEIGHTS

Richard Pierce

NoPapyrus Press

First published in 2024 by
NoPapyrus Press
79 Cromwell Road, Norwich, NR7 8XJ

ISBN: 978-1-0686452-0-4

Front cover photograph:
Heaven Himalaya, CC BY-SA 4.0, via Wikimedia Commons
Page URL:
https://commons.wikimedia.org/wiki/File:Sunrise_at_the_tip_of_Mount_Everest.jpg
File URL:
https://upload.wikimedia.org/wikipedia/commons/b/bd/Sunrise_at_the_tip_of_Mount_Everest.jpg

Back cover:
Richard Pierce

For the sherpas.

For Tibet.

ACKNOWLEDGEMENTS

My thanks and unconditional love, as always, to Marianne, Oscar, Charlotte, Kara, and Alex. The truth is that without the safe space of your understanding of me and love for me I'd not be here right now.

I've been obsessed with the mountains ever since I first read Heinrich Harrer's *The White Spider* as a boy (in its German original *Die Weisse Spinne*). Shocking and sad, exhilarating and addictive. I remember, too, sitting on the edge of a glacier in Liechtenstein with Trudi, one of my sisters, our legs dangling out into the void. Trudi did get all the way to Kathmandu, but illness forced her back many years ago before she even saw Everest.

This novel has come from that obsession. I first put pen to paper on 8th June 2011, always with the thought of not releasing the novel until the 100th anniversary of the last time those two men were seen.

I am very grateful to Jochen Hemmleb for the generous amount of time he gave me when I started writing the book. Any errors in climbing technique or imagination are mine alone. Historical notes are at the end of the book.

And now, on that 100th anniversary and beyond, it's time to halt the desecration of Chomolungma, and to give the Goddess Mother Of The World back to her people.

Richard, April 2024

There are mountains hidden in treasures.
There are mountains hidden in swamps.
There are mountains hidden in the sky.
There are mountains hidden in mountains.
There are mountains hidden in hiddenness.
This is complete understanding.

Chuanzi Decheng

Chapter 1

8th June 1924, Mount Everest

An empty sky.

Mallory, in the oxygenless haze, asked his friend to take the first last step.

'You sure?' Irvine shouted

'She's all yours.' Mallory nodded against the gale, stretched out an arm.

Irvine moved his legs slowly, weighed down by the lack of air, and a long moment later held a hand out to Mallory, pulled him up onto the summit.

Arms draped around each other's shoulders, they looked out at a world above the clouds, the sun reflected from their goggles. They'd left their tent at five that morning, just before sunrise, had melted snow all night, impatient of waiting, irritated by the oxygen masks around their faces. The artificial air ran out a few hours before they'd reached the summit.

'Did you remember the camera?' Mallory said.

Irvine fumbled with his jacket, pulled the camera out. 'What's the plan?'

'One of you with the flag first. Then one of me.' Mallory took the camera, waited for Irvine to get the flag out and unfurl it, took a step back. 'Hold it up.'

Irvine did, and grinned.

They changed places.

Mallory, unshaven, smiled, eyes ablaze. 'We did it, Sandy.'

'You did it.'

'We. The two of us with our flag.' He held the camera at arm's length, fingers freezing, took one last photo, handed the camera back.

'And now?' Irvine said, and fumbled the camera back into an inside pocket.

Mallory said nothing, kneeled down, reached into his tweed jacket, and took out a photograph of his wife. The wind tore at it, but he wouldn't let go. 'I promised Ruth,' he said.

Irvine started to make a hole in the snow and rock with his ice-axe, the harsh sounds carried away by the hungry wind, part of the snow plume blown out into the blue sky. 'Hang on.' The sound of the axe all of a sudden dull, no longer hard and solid.

'What is it?'

'I don't know.' Irvine carried on, dug, scratched, scraped.

Mallory put his wife's picture back in his pocket, started digging at the other side of the hole, paused to look at his watch. Half past three. 'We've got to go,' he said.

'Not now,' Irvine said. 'We need to find out what this is.'

'D'you think someone's been here before?'

Irvine shrugged. 'Keep digging.'

Both men struck at the ground between deep, painful breaths. The sound changed again. Wooden. They both saw it now, used their hands to uncover it. Mallory lifted it out.

'Impossible,' he shouted.

'Open it.'

Mallory pulled at the top of the smooth, brown box, finally wrenched it off.

'Let me see,' Irvine said.

'It's a prayer flag.' Mallory pulled the material out, ragged, torn and faded. 'Looks ancient.' He stopped. 'There's something wrapped inside it.' He lifted it out, weighed it in his hand.

'Bronze?'

'Could be. It's really heavy.'

'It looks like those singing bowls at the monastery in

Rongbuk.'

'Wouldn't the monks have told us?' Mallory said.

'I don't know.'

'Take a picture of it.'

'Shouldn't we take it with us?'

'That would be wrong.' Mallory sighed, a glassy breath. 'Someone got here before us. Simple as that.'

'But who?'

'We'll ask the monks.'

'And if they won't say?' Irvine took two pictures.

'Then it'll stay a mystery.' Mallory put the bowl and prayer flag back in the box, and, as an afterthought almost, slipped in Ruth's photo, fixed the lid tightly into place, and put the box gently back where they'd found it. 'Come on. Let's cover it up and go.'

'Aren't you disappointed?' Irvine said.

'No time to be. We need to get back down to tell everyone.'

'I don't understand it.'

'Neither do I. There must be a reason for keeping it secret.' He tried a deep breath. 'Let's go home. I'm tired.'

They reached the base of the summit pyramid quickly, despite the lack of oxygen, despite the wind, despite the increasing cold. The next stage was the most difficult. They climbed down the nearest promontory easily, although the gales battered them, and their fingers froze through their gloves. When they reached what they'd christened the Second Step, the wind suddenly dropped.

'Thank God for that,' Irvine said.

'I don't like it.'

'D'you want to try to find a way round it?'

'There isn't time,' Mallory said. 'I'll rope you down and climb down after you.'

'Isn't there anything to fix a rope to?'

Mallory shook his head. 'I looked on the way up. Nothing but loose rocks and scree.'

'Fine. Let's do it.'

Mallory checked the knots on the rope around Irvine's waist, then his own. 'Ready?'

Irvine nodded. Still no wind.

Mallory checked his watch. 'Six. We're making good time.'

'Then we might just get back before the moon goes.'

'I hope so.' Mallory braced himself, leaned backwards, watched Irvine disappear below the edge. After a few minutes, the rope went slack. Mallory walked towards the sheer drop. 'Sandy?' he shouted.

'I'm down.' A dry echo.

'On my way.' Mallory, the rope still around his waist, lowered himself onto his knees, stretched his legs out into the brief void, and started to climb down the rock, its warmth gone.

Irvine, close to the face, stared up, watched Mallory almost swim down the mountain, arms and legs moving so quickly they were nothing but a blur. He kept hold of the rope, to give Mallory the security of knowing he was somehow still holding him. Then the wind started again.

Mallory, halfway down the wall, had started to relax when the wind hit him. 'Dammit,' he grunted, clutched at the mountain with his fingers, felt his belly scrape against sharp outcrops of stone. But still he was in control, still he maintained his almost magical ability to stay glued to surfaces no-one else could master. He stopped, and breathed the thin air deep into his lungs, started again, inch by inch, foot by quicker foot. The wind dropped again. Nearly there. He looked down, couldn't see Irvine. 'What the hell?' he muttered. And then he slipped, his feet out into empty air, his fingers scratching at the impenetrable, in slow motion, falling,

falling, falling.

Irvine heard the curse, the screech of Mallory's hobnailed boots skidding off the mountain, saw the falling man, tried to gather the rope to himself quickly, was still grabbing at it when Mallory hit him, knocked him over, and bounced away from him, out onto the snow platform at the foot of the Step. Irvine lay in the snow, the pain blinding him, coursing through him from his head down his back and out into his left foot. He couldn't move, barely perceived the bundle of flesh and bone Mallory had become, just a yard from the ten thousand foot drop into emptiness, didn't see Mallory bleeding from his mouth, his face, his nose, didn't see him roll over, back towards safety, snatch at the empty snow, open his eyes and slowly get up.

'That was close,' Mallory said. 'Come on. Wake up.'

'We should be dead.' Irvine shook his head, a blond mane turned white.

'But we're not.' Mallory reached out to Irvine, grabbed his hand. 'We'll get there. Not far now.' He wiped his face with some snow. 'Just a flesh wound.'

Irvine, on his feet by now. 'You sure it's nothing worse?'

'I'm fine. Let's keep going. Are you alright?'

'Bit of pain. You should lose some weight.'

Mallory laugh was hoarse as he put his arm round his friend. 'I promise I will, as soon as we get home.'

They moved forwards, gingerly, until the pain left their bodies and the bleeding stopped. They cleared the First Step without any problems, the sun now almost gone, the yellow stones just below them stretched along one of many gullies leading down to safety, to the relative warmth of their tent, and then further on down the mountain to their comrades waiting for them.

'Which one?' Irvine said.

'Any.'

'You sure?' Irvine looked at his friend.

'Of course I am. I'm just exhausted. If we had time, I'd rest here, just until …'

'You die?'

Mallory smiled. 'No, not that. I just wish we'd brought more gear so we could set up a tent here.'

'Without oxygen?'

Mallory shrugged. 'Maybe.'

'We need to get down as quickly as possible. Maybe not even stop at Camp Six, but get down to where Odell's waiting.'

Mallory shook his head, cleared his mind. 'You're right, of course. I don't know what I was thinking.'

'You're just tired. You've been doing all the hard work.'

'Not really. Just thinking about that bowl.'

'I still can't believe it.'

'Let's see what they say when we develop the film.'

'That'll be a bombshell.'

'We have to tell the truth. There's no point hiding what we found. It wouldn't do to lie.'

'No.'

They carried on down the gully, were brought up short when it ended suddenly, nothing but sheer cliff, down to the next layer of the mountain. And the moon starting to cast blurred shadows.

'Hell,' shouted Mallory. 'We took the wrong one.'

'Better turn back,' Irvine said.

Mallory shook his head. 'No point. It's not that difficult. I'll lower you and you can belay me again.'

'You sure?'

'Yes. I've wasted enough time already. Come on.' Mallory took off his goggles, the wind tugging at his dark hair. *We're out of time.*

'See you in a minute.' Irvine started downwards.

Mallory fed the rope slowly through his hands, took

Irvine's weight over his shoulder, revelled in his own strength, despite his tiredness. *Slack. Call. Check. Sandy down safely.* He started the descent, hands and feet finding holds in the wall, second nature, part of nature, George Mallory at his best, at one with the mountain, in control, on the way home, a streak of dark in the moonlight. *Ruth.* The wind hit, a crashing, howling, final blow, threw him clean off the wall and out into space. He fell a long way before the rope stopped him, stopped him so hard it crushed his waist and chest, almost broke him in half, ribs cracking. *Ruth.* He crashed into the side of the mountain, bounced, stopped briefly, heard the shearing of the rope even above the screeching of the wind, tumbled further down the mountain, the umbilical cord to his friend severed, fell, faster and faster, his stomach scraping along the ice and rock, grabbed at the moving ground with his left hand, brought his ice axe round with his right hand, tried to force it into the ground, harder and harder, muscles aching, eyes closed, trying, trying. *Ruth.* The awful scream of his leg breaking, shattering, bending the wrong way. The pain. The ground too hard. The ice axe rebounded with a force he couldn't control, slammed into his skull and away down the cliff before he felt it, brought darkness to him before the mountain stopped his fall.

Chapter 2

20th February 2011, Christchurch, New Zealand

She's leaving again.

'Do you have to?' I say.

'I don't have a choice.'

'You always have a choice.'

'You know that's not true.'

'Stay. Please.'

'No.' She zips up her bag.

'You'll have to choose, one of these days.'

She looks at me, down at me, her long black hair alive with anger. 'Never.'

'You can't be bound to two men.'

'He's my brother, for God's sake, not my lover.'

'Does that matter? Is it any different? I don't think it is.'

'Why can't you ever understand?' she says.

'It's a whim of yours.'

'No, it's not. He needs me.' She stares at me, her momentary silence a cloak. 'You've never liked him.'

I hate her when it's like this. 'That's not true. He's just …'

'What?' A knife of a word.

'He's better than me. You're always there for him, when I want you to myself.'

'We're twins,' she says. 'We're different. We always have been.'

'I know.' I sit down on our bed. 'I don't like being without you.'

She sits down next to me. 'Listen, James,' she says. 'How long have we been married?'

'Forever.' My anger makes new words. 'Too long.'

'Be serious.'

'I am.' I shrug. 'Ten years?' I drag in an involuntary

breath. 'And it's always like this. It never changes.'

She sighs, grinds her teeth, too used to this. 'And how often have I gone away?'

'I can't remember.' *Just go and don't come back.*

'It's always worked out, though, hasn't it?'

I nod. Even my gestures tell lies.

'He's in trouble,' she says.

'He's always in trouble. And you're always too ready to help him.'

'It's serious trouble this time.'

'That's not the point.' *What is the point? There is no point any more.* I'm too afraid to say it.

She gets up, rips her bag from the bed. 'But it is.'

'Maybe I could come with you.'

'You say that every time.' She turns and walks away. 'And then do nothing.'

I shake my head. 'You think I'm weak.' I know I'm weak. I should have left a long time ago. I'm tired of this.

'I think you're you.'

'Tell me what I should do.'

'Stop hating Simon,' she says softly.

'I don't.' *Oh, but I do.*

She glowers at me. 'What then? Try to explain it this time. But you never can, can you?'

I shrug. 'I don't know. Maybe I envy him.' Every syllable pushes her further away. It's best that way.

'I'm going,' she says. 'I need to get to the airport.'

'Where is he?' Why don't I ever think it's another man she's running to?

'I don't know,' she says.

'Then how do you know where to go?' I wish there was another man to take her away from me, away from my unspoken doubts and rage.

'I'm guessing. That's all I can do, all I've got left.'

'Have you tried to call him?'

'Do I look stupid?' she says.

We're downstairs by now.

I say nothing. I can't think of anything to say that won't destroy us.

'I've tried his mobiles, his land line, tried email, facebook, twitter. Nothing.'

'So where are you going?' Not that I really want to know. Where was love? It disappeared when her body became the stranger.

'Where I know his things are, in Cambridge.'

'It's halfway across the world,' I say.

'Well-spotted.' There's no smile in her voice, none of the light-heartedness married people should share. Because we don't share anything any more.

'I thought you hated England.'

'I'm not planning on staying. I'll be back before you know it.'

'You'll be gone for ages.' *With any luck.*

'Only for long enough to find him or find a trace of him.'

'It's winter over there. You'll miss your New Zealand summer.'

'Not as much as I'll miss him if something bad happens to him,' she says.

'Aren't you exaggerating?'

'I don't think so.' She turns to me, as tall as me, more fragrant, more gentle, and much much more determined. Perhaps I do still love her, perhaps she does still mean something to me, although I find it harder and harder to find that something.

'You can cry, you know,' I say. I can always find the right words to comfort someone else, but never the right ones to comfort me. I should go to a brain doctor.

'You silly man,' she says. 'I love you, you know. That's why I can go away. Because you'll always be here.'

I put my arms round her. And it's true, every time I

touch her, I'm in love with the way she feels, with the way she smells, with who she is, and what she is. The only woman I've ever loved. The only woman I'd have left my England for. 'Always here,' I whisper into her ear. 'For you, just for you. I'll miss you.' Lies can be the truth, when we don't know which is which.

'Same.' She lets go of me, opens the door into the warmth of the Christchurch February. There's a taxi waiting.

'I could've driven you,' I say.

'It's easier this way.'

'Who for?'

'Both of us. I hate airport goodbyes, and you'll just find more words to put doubts into my head.'

'What do you think you'll find?'

She shrugs. 'I'm always afraid it'll end badly with Simon.'

'Take care, then. Call me.' One of these days it'll end badly for all of us. This is such hard work.

'I will. Promise. Bye, James.'

'Bye, Alice.' I kiss her, take a breath of her.

I watch her clamber into the taxi with that effortless grace which attracted me to her in the first place, her long hair shining in the sun, her legs swinging from the street into the car in those black combat trousers she favours. She waves at me, smiles. And then she's gone.

It's always like this. She goes away, and the house seems smaller, devoid of the spirit that made us buy it in the first place, empty, useless, and not even the memories keep me hoping. I rattle around the rooms, pick up things, her things, put them down again, in exactly the same place she left them. I open the back door, look across the small garden, find nothing to keep me interested, close the door again, start my pacing again. A travel writer who doesn't travel; now there's something.

When I met her, I hadn't planned for it to be my last trip; it was supposed to be the beginning of doing more and more. It was the big one, the reward for all those years of running round Europe and the States writing travel guides for students, a reward for the hard slog, something I really wanted to do, to write about my passion. But then it all went wrong, all fell to pieces. I haven't been on a plane since then, since that last unconscious trip back here, back to her country, after she'd saved my life, somewhere on Everest, somewhere in a whiteness I try to forget, surrounded by a panic and fear I try not to remember, curled up next to a dead man, waiting for my own death. And then her face over me, an angel with ebony hair, a warm breath on my eyes, fresh oxygen. She abandoned her attempt at the summit for me. And all we'd done was to talk to each other in the few weeks of the walk in to Base Camp, all we'd done was drink mineral water with each other, and a glass of wine one evening when we'd heard some of the others had summited, including her brother.

I've got a picture of the two of us; Alice, on her feet walking out from the mountains to Kathmandu, holding my hand, and me, frostbitten and half-dead on a stretcher. It's over my desk here, framed, suspended on the white wall, to remind me, not of Everest, but of her devotion to the unknown me, to the English stranger who became her husband. To remind me of how she asked me to marry her, because it was then, with the cameras clicking, and the questions being shouted at us, that she said, matter-of-factly, *You'll marry me now, won't you?* I had no choice, either way. Neither my heart, nor circumstance, allowed me to refuse. And now? Why regret something that was meant to be? I don't know. I don't understand why I try to throw it all away. It's a disease.

I sit at my desk. The words won't come. All I get now are the dregs, the stories no-one else wants to touch, the ones that mean I don't have to leave this sanctuary, this haven, this hermit's cave. I thud out a few words, stop, hit backspace, delete the ill-chosen phrases, start again. I can't do this. I never could. I can't do anything. Once the self-doubt starts, nothing can stop it. And then you start doubting everyone.

The thing is, the press back home in England blamed me for the death of my best friend, the man I was curled up next to, the one we had to leave up there on Everest, the one who's still not buried, whose family haven't had what the Yanks call closure, the man I miss most of all men, my Graham, my cornerstone, the white to my black, the smile to my frown. But it wasn't my fault, it wasn't my doing, his death, his going, his passage into darkness. Mountains take lives. We knew the risks. I sometimes wish Everest had taken both of us.

The next day, evening close, the phone rings.

'Hello?' I say.

'I'm in London,' Alice says.

'Good.' *Oh God, I miss you, despite everything.* Why can't I just say it?

'Are you ok?' she says.

'I'm the same as always. Nothing changes, and probably never will.' I stare at the wall. Nothing moves.

'Not good then.'

I shrug, although she can't see me. 'I wouldn't say that.'

'Don't lie to me.'

'I miss you.' And it's the truth this time, although my voice is as monotonous as always, and I don't say enough.

'I miss you, too.'

‘Why did you have to go?’ *Stop it, stop it now.*

‘Because he needs me.’

‘I need you, too.’

‘You’ve always got me.’

‘Not now.’ It’s selfish, I know.

‘You know what I mean,’ she says.

‘There are so many things I’d like to change, so many things I wish for.’ Newness, excitement, a way out of these dark days.

‘And they’ll all come true,’ she says. ‘Just give it time.’

‘There’s never enough time. You’ll run out of patience one of these days.’

‘No, I won’t. There’ll always be enough time. I promise.’ I hear the airport tannoy behind her voice. ‘Gotta go. Luggage is here. I’ll call you when I get to Cambridge.’

‘D’you think you’ll find him?’

The line’s dead already. She always moves more quickly than I ever could.

I’ve been in bed for an hour when the phone rings again.

‘He’s not here,’ she says. ‘What should I do?’

‘Are you booked into a hotel yet?’

‘No. It’s the middle of the day.’

‘Do it now, anyway. Then go back to College and try to get a key to his room.’

‘You should have come with me. You know better how this place works.’

‘I will if you want.’

I hear her shake her head. ‘Don’t. I shouldn’t have said that. I’ll work it out.’

‘Perhaps,’ I say into the dark. It’s so very dark.

‘What?’

‘Perhaps he doesn’t want to be found. Maybe he’s fine and just doesn’t want anyone around. You know he’s not exactly reliable.’ I make it up as I go along.

'I wouldn't be feeling this way if he was ok.'

'Ok.' I grit my teeth at her obsession with him. 'Get a hotel. Now. You're going to need some big-time sleep tomorrow. And make sure you eat.'

'I'll be fine.'

'Just do it, and let me know where you are.' *Because I need to know where you are all the time. Because I need to be in control. Because I'm out of control.*

'Anything you say.' I can hear her tolerating me.

'Call me when you know more.' *Don't ever hang up.*

'I will.'

'And don't go anywhere else without letting me know.'

'Why?'

'I don't want you disappearing as well.'

'Don't be silly. You worry too much.'

'Never.' *All the time. I want rid of you, but I don't want to lose you either.* God, my head hurts.

'Later.' She hangs up.

I sleep until ten the next morning. I try her mobile. No answer. I wander down into the kitchen, make myself some toast, chuck on some ham, wish myself a full English, although it's bad for me, and I have neither eggs nor bacon. Eat, shower, wander into the office, turn on my laptop, pace the rooms, look out into the garden, pour myself a coffee, back into the office, one hundred meaningless words. Must be time for lunch by now.

No notifications on facebook, no mentions on twitter. It gets late. A quiet day, obviously. I don't care. I just want to know what she's doing, what she's found. If she's found anything. The screen flickers. Odd. I walk out of the back door again. There's a silence in the air, and unreal stillness. Just like last September. Shit. The air growls and the ground shifts.

I can't stand up without holding on to anything. I hear the clatter of something, everything, in the kitchen falling. I stagger back into the house, through the carnage, arms outstretched, lean against anything solid I can find. The roar of the tremor is endless. Just as I get to the living room, there's a crash, and the wood burner tears itself away from the chimney and towards me. I jump out of the way. There's a cloud of dust, and the fireplace fills with bricks and ash and soot. I know I shouldn't, but I find my way into my office, reach for my laptop and grab it from the desk, just pull it to me, cables and keyboard and all, and race for the front door. I can't open it at first, almost wrench it from its lopsided frame as the earth's motion weakens. It scrapes open, and I'm finally outside, one hand above my head, the other full of computer and whatever else I've dragged with me.

I feel sick. My legs tremble and shake. It's like I've been at sea in a storm for days, or on one of those fairground rides I hate. The ground feels like it's still moving, like it's never going stop. There's a massive crack along the road, tarmac split, and rock and sand bubbling out of the gap. I turn and look at the house. The chimney's gone, and there's a long, jagged crack up and along the front side of the house, and not just where the bricks join; the force of the quake has split the bricks. All the windows have blown. It's gone, all gone. What now?

I pull my mobile out of my pocket. No signal. Only to be expected. There are people rushing along the road, some in cars; and clouds of smoke, maybe dust, rise and drift across from the city centre. I start running that way. The silence has given way to chaos, confusion, noise. The closer I get to the centre, the madder the traffic gets. Cars drive up onto the pavements, weave illogical patterns on the illogical roads. Everything's broken, everything. It's like the apocalypse; screaming, crying, shouting; running, dazed walking, limping. Empty faces.

I keep checking my mobile, even though I know there's no chance of getting any reception. I want to hear Alice's voice, want her to tell me what to do. I'm wandering past all these people who look like they need help, but I can't give them any, except the odd word, or smile. Most of them just shrug at me. I keep walking, get to the river, follow along its broken path to where the damage just gets worse and worse. Rubble, collapsed buildings, dust, smoke, crowds. I hear screams. They're under the rubble. I can help here, because what's needed needs no explaining. I just sling my laptop bag over my back, scramble up to the top of one of the piles and start ripping up bricks and slabs, pass them to the bloke who's followed me up, and he passes them on to the chain that's formed in half a minute. The police are here, and they help us. No-one tells us not to do what we're doing, no-one tells us to stop, because all that any of us want to do is to get the people out from under here, to keep them living.

There's some cloth; looks like a dress. I rip up the bricks even more quickly, my chest and shoulders aching, sweat pouring down the back of my shirt. In the sunless grey of this shattered day, I'm digging for life. My hands are bleeding. What if? I can't think. No, no, no! By the time we've uncovered her, we can tell she's dead; a young woman, and a baby in her arms, under her, shielded by her, saved by her, lost by her. And a bag full of new baby clothes.

That's it. I can't do any more. What's the use? How many dead this time? We were so lucky in September. How many friends gone – again? And not even in the mountains this time. I wander from one road to the next in a daze, pass the emergency shelters they're building from nothing in Hagley Park. And then it gets dark and starts raining, and I don't know what to do, and I know I shouldn't, and I walk back to the house, and I know I shouldn't, and walk into *our* house, and find, amongst the creaking, swaying memories, a rucksack, a sleeping bag, some waterproofs, and some empty water bottles.

My phone rings.

'James? James?' She's screaming. 'Is that you? Are you ok?'

'I'm fine, Alice, I'm fine.' And I am, somehow.

'I couldn't get through.'

'I should have kept checking the signal, but got bored of staring at the same dead phone. I hadn't realised the signal was back.'

'I've been trying for hours. I was really worried. I thought the worst.'

'Everything's bust,' I say.

'Are you safe?' She's sobbing now. 'Where are you?'

'At home.'

'Is it really safe?'

'Yeah.'

'You're lying.' She could always see through me.

'It's wrecked,' I say.

'Then get out.'

'I was just about to. I've got my bag all packed ready to go.'

'Where will you go?'

'I dunno.'

'I wish …'

'What?'

'Come to me,' she says.

'I … I …'

'Try.'

'I will.'

'Promise.'

The phone goes dead before I can promise. I pick up the rucksack, put my head torch on, and set out in the direction of the airport. It's only six miles away.

Chapter 3

The city's become a no-go area. The government's set up an exclusion zone because there's so much damage. People I pass tell me the cathedral's spire's fallen into Cathedral Square, that it might have killed at least twenty people. Over two hundred people have died, they say. It's a massacre. I'm not used to walking anymore, and it's getting light by the time I get to the airport, via various detours and stops to help people, and the weight on my back. How could I ever have got as far up Everest as I did? Maybe that's why I didn't get to the top. I'm just too unfocussed and out of shape.

The airport's chaos. It's closed to all but military flights and flights coming in with Search and Rescue teams, but it's still heaving, people clamouring to get away from New Zealand, to get to somewhere they think is safer, to leave all the destruction, pain and heartache behind. I keep myself to myself, wander into the toilets, where, by some miracle, there's still running water and electricity. I wash, of sorts, fill up my water bottles, and find myself a hidden, dry corner outside, sit down and wait.

I watch people, I hear sirens, nearly all the time. I think about Alice and her brother, about the mountains, about my fear of them, about my ten-year-old fear of heights, listen to the sounds of the planes, my heart beating faster, my instinct to run away, walk back home, creep into my destroyed sanctuary, and wait for whatever might happen. But I can't. I have to go to her, now, can't give in to myself and my fears as I've done so often before, can't let her down again, when she's never let me down, not now when she's finally called me to her.

Two days pass. I use the airport like a youth hostel. No-one asks me to leave. My beard, my mountain beard, starts to sprout again, scratches, makes me look fiercer than I could have imagined. When I close my eyes, I still can't close out the noise of this manic place, of this panicked, frightened place, and feel myself being dragged back to the stillness of the mountains, the deserted places I used to love so much before Everest nearly killed me. I've never had it in my heart, since then, to call that thing what the Tibetans call it, because, to me, it's not the Goddess Mother of the World; it's the heartless, evil beast which stole my best friend from me.

On the third day after the quake, the airport re-opens. It's pandemonium. The plane operators from Australia and New Zealand are offering dirt-cheap flights to the North Island or to Australia as part of the support effort. I add myself to the crush of people, start to shake as I get nearer the desk, breathe deeply to stop myself, hands in pockets, fists clenched against the cold of my fear, eyes wide open to stop myself thinking of the fiery storms of plane crashes, of the white space between planes and the earth.

'Can I help you?' she says when I get to the front of the queue.

'Have you got any flights to England?' I hear myself sounding like someone who's never bought a plane ticket before.

'Just about everything except First Class has gone. But I can put you on standby.'

'Any idea when?'

'There's a flight late tonight we might get some no-shows for,' she says. 'But I wouldn't hold my breath.'

'I'll take the chance.'

She takes my credit card. 'How should we contact you?'

'By mobile if the network's not too flaky,' I say. 'But I'm not going anywhere. I'll come and check now and again.'

'The queue's not going to get any shorter. Where can I find you?'

I tell her where I'm holed up.

'And no-one's told you to go away?' Her eyes are wide open under the red fringe. She might have been my type before I met Alice.

I shake my head.

'I'll come and find you if something comes up while I'm still on shift.'

'You're very kind.'

She smiles at me. 'No worries.'

And she does come and find me, when she's out of uniform, jeans and leather jacket, sits down next to me.

'There you go,' she says, and hands me a ticket and boarding card.

'Thanks a million.' I'm tempted to hug her, to hold her close for comfort, but I let the momentary impulse slide and glance at the ticket. 'But it's Business Class.' I look at her, my eyes hoarse with lack of sleep.

'I managed to upgrade you. You looked like you were desperate.'

'Oh, this?' I stroke my 4-day old beard. 'I'm just too lazy to shave.'

She shakes her head. 'No. Your eyes. Someone special?' There's something like regret in her voice.

'My wife. She flew out the day before the quake.' I have to be honest.

'Oh. My good deed then.' She smiles, a sad, lonely smile.

'Sure is. What's your name?'

'Fiona, but people call me Fi.'

'I'll look you up when I get back, Fi,' I say. 'Buy you a thank you drink.' Another place, another time, and it might have been different.

'That'll be nice.' She gets up. 'Better get home.'

'Where's that?'

'Just outside the exclusion zone.'

'Much damage?'

'It's not too bad, actually.'

'Is there anyone special there?' I can't help asking.

'My parents.' That smile again. 'I haven't quite managed to fly the coop yet. No-one'll have me.'

'I can't believe that.' And I can't. 'I bet you'll have someone by the time I get back.' I hope she will have.

She reaches out. 'You're on.' Her hands are cold. 'See ya.'

I watch her until she disappears from view, then look at my watch. Three hours to go. My first flight in over ten years. My palms are sweaty. Better go check in now so I don't change my mind. I don't call Alice. I'll let it be a surprise. I know where she is, after all. Because some crazed deity decided that Simon should go to my old college two years after I left, and years before I even knew of Alice's existence. And that's where she's gone to look for him.

I pick up my rucksack, walk into the terminal. Look up at the Departures board. There – London Gatwick via Singapore. I remember looking at the board at Gatwick before that trip to the mountain, all excited, shaking with the excitement of it, full of adrenaline at the loneliness of travel, that headiness of youth, immortality in my flesh. The letters blur in front of my eyes.

At Passport Control, the officer looks at me. 'You know your passport runs out in a couple of months, do you?'

I nod. 'I'll get it renewed back home.'

'You've been here for a long time.'

'I married a gorgeous Kiwi girl.'

'Lucky man,' he says and hands the passport back. 'Have a good time.'

'I'll try.'

The lounge at the gate is cool and full of relieved-looking people. I sit down, drink some water. I've started shaking again. Wonder about changing my mind. I can't help it. The older we get, the more we fear, the more we have to be afraid of. Being near death didn't make me want to grasp life as if there was no tomorrow; it made me scared of tomorrow not being there, of everything being worthless, without reason. I grab a magazine, look at the words without absorbing their meaning.

When we board, I start to feel dirty. The folks in Business Class look so clean, so spruced up in their suits and dresses, so normal, so superior to me. I wonder what they'd say if they realised who I was, the man who killed his friend on Everest, the man who should've been left to die along with the man he betrayed. Because he was just chasing a dream no-one had a right to chase, because he was doing what he'd told everyone not to do, to take part in the cheap free-for-all for a mountain polluted by tourism, because he wanted to prove a point. As soon as I sit down, I close my eyes, ignore them, ignore myself, grab the armrests as hard as I can. I think my heart stops when we take off. And when we're up and cruising, I go to the toilet and throw up more than once, until there's nothing left. I realise I'm afraid of seeing Alice again, too, because all my hurt's out there in the open again now, and my hate, and her trying to cure me will just make it worse. And liking that red-haired girl for just one brief moment already feels like infidelity.

Singapore's an irrelevant four-hour stopover. I wander, buy some cigarettes, although I've not smoked since *then*. I stare at men, at women, feel the humidity making me even sweatier, look at the clock every five minutes, wish time would pass more quickly, wish I could be certain I'm doing the right thing, remind myself why I'm doing this; because, for a change, she's said she needs me, because, for once, I'm not leaning on her. Is that why we've not had children yet, because she thinks I'm not strong enough? That my scars will never heal? We've never really talked about it. Maybe it's time we did.

And then I fall asleep. We land into the cold damp of the bleakest English month, too early in the morning. I shiver as soon as I leave the plane, carry on shivering all the way down to the railway station, and in the Tube. On the train from King's Cross to Cambridge, I look out, first at the old brick arches on the outskirts of the old London, then onto the bare fields of the countryside. It's all unfamiliar to me now, like I've never seen it before, like I'm here for the first time. I'm tired.

Familiarity returns when I get out of the train at Cambridge, when I walk away from the station and start trekking down the long straight road to the War Memorial. It's only one or two miles to where I'm going, and I need to walk to wake myself up. I remember the first time I came here, to be interviewed by two eccentric men, one a Welsh tutor, who was meant to be in charge of the college's pastoral care, and the other a professor of French who had the longest arms I ever saw. Dr Jones was more interested in rugby than languages, and Dr Edwards was more interested in the written than the spoken word. And, after ten minutes, when I'd said I didn't like rugby, and that I thought the spoken word was just as important as the written, all three of us found we were more interested in cricket than in my potential studies, and spent the rest of the time talking about how the Australians were bound to thump England in the Ashes. God, how naïve and young I was then, how sure of myself, how full of undiluted and unshakeable certainties and principles.

By the War Memorial, I turn right. The town's already alive. Crowds of students scatter by on bikes, the cloud lifts a little to let in that Siberian cold we always complained about, that wind driving down the east-facing streets all the way from the Urals, although someone later disproved that theory. The further into the centre I walk, the more I realise Christchurch isn't so dissimilar to Cambridge, that it is, or was, one of the most English towns I'd ever come across abroad. Maybe that's why I ended up there, why nothing made me want to leave it until now. I wonder how my friends there are, how many dead there really have been, and if we know any of them. But I haven't the courage to phone them to find out.

In the centre, near the market place, I stop and have a coffee and a croissant at one of the many coffee houses that seem to have sprung up since I was last here. I even smoke another cigarette. It's almost like I need a variation of Dutch courage to face my wife again, like we've become total strangers in just under a week. How will she be?

Just by Jesus Lane, there's a cut-through on the left, a small passage down which used to be the barber's shop I visited faithfully once a month for my Number One haircut. It's a cheese shop now. I follow the path until I'm opposite the Great Gate of my old college, gold paint glittering weakly in the misty morning, the tall wooden gates closed, and only a small door in them open. And a sign outside tells passers-by how much they have to pay to get in and have a look round. I take my alumni card out of my wallet, walk in, turn for the Porter's Lodge, but it's not there. The main one's been moved, they tell me, across to Chapel Court, sir, would you mind dreadfully going round that way?

Back out, and to the left, past the butt-end of the

chapel, in through the high railings, and there it is, a shiny new, almost all- glass Porter's Lodge, under the arches where there used to be nothing, just free air under the block my room was in during my final year. I push open the door, ask for Simon by name.

'He's not here, sir,' the porter says.

'I wasn't actually looking for him. I was assuming his sister was here.'

'And might I ask who you are, sir?'

'I'm her husband,' I say. 'And I'd rather you didn't ring up to the room. I want to surprise her.'

'Have you some ID, sir?'

I show him my passport.

'I see, sir,' he says, raises an eyebrow. 'We haven't seen you for some time.'

'It's been too long, yes.'

'Maybe so, sir,' he says. 'You know where Dr Young's room is?'

'In Third Court, isn't it?'

'Yes, sir.'

'Thanks for your help.'

'You're welcome, sir.'

Chapel Court connects to Second Court, where I spent many happy hours in the College bar. I turn right, follow the paving stones through to Third Court, turn left again opposite the steps up to the Bridge of Sighs. Nothing changes. The steps to F staircase are still uneven, the wood of the doors still dark with the patina of unretouched age. The outside door to Simon's set is open, the small brass knob of the inside door bright in the gloom. I turn it slowly, quietly. The room's warm. The scent of old books and passing time hasn't faded. I close the door behind me.

There she is, at the far end of the room, behind a desk covered in a mountain of papers and books. The brass light is on, shines brightly onto her. She's suddenly so pale, looks ill, drawn, tired. Her hands are a frozen white, clasping at a book. She doesn't notice me. Her electricity reaches me, nonetheless, sharp, stark, shocking.

I don't move, just watch; then, when she still doesn't look up, I walk towards her, my boots sliding across the floor, hardly making any noise at all. I reach the ancient desk, stand in front of it. 'Alice,' I say, quietly, my heart beating too fast.

Now she puts the book down, looks up at me, jumps up, and pushes the chair away from behind her. 'James!' She comes round the desk, rushes me, puts her arms round me, kisses me. 'I didn't think you would.'

'Neither did I.'

'Why didn't you tell me you were definitely coming?'

'I didn't want to disappoint you, and I thought we might talk me out of it if I did call you, even once I'd got to Singapore. And I wanted it to be a real surprise.'

'I've so much to tell you,' she says, without letting go of me.

'You look ill, you know, really ill.'

'I've not much felt like eating. I was thinking about you and Simon, nothing else.' She looks at me as if she expects me to contradict.

'You needn't worry about me.'

She kisses me again. 'But I do.'

I let go of her. 'What is all this stuff?' I let go of her and look at the desk.

'It's just as Simon left it, as if he's only walked out this minute.'

'He's not shown up since yesterday then.'

'No,' she says, and sighs. 'No-one knows where he is. He had dinner at High Table two weeks ago with a couple of guests, and then just disappeared.'

'What sort of guests?'

'They weren't women, if that's what you're thinking.

Two blokes, apparently.'

That makes a change, I think. 'Were they climbers?' I say, unasked questions on my lips, questions I'll never ask.

She shrugs. 'I've no idea. Nor do any of the people I've asked. I've been making myself a bit unpopular, I think.'

'I doubt it,' I say. 'Who could resist you? But, more to the point, what have you managed to find?'

She points to the desk. 'All this. I've been reading it since I got here. And I think I know where he is.'

Chapter 4

The night before Mallory's and Irvine's attempt at the summit, Noel Odell, with a couple of porters, climbed up to Camp V with fresh supplies. He stayed there overnight, on his own, in the mess Mallory and Irvine had left before they pushed onwards up to Camp VI. But there was no stove. Mallory had left him a note telling him it had rolled down the slope and off the mountain. Odell shrugged. Cold food would have to do, and the weather wasn't too bad. He wouldn't freeze in the night, wrapped up in the two sleeping bags he'd found. His only concern was that he'd have no water, nothing to melt the snow with.

He slept well that night, on the platform of stones dragged together against the slope of the mountain. Even the wind seemed to have disappeared, gone into hiding from those who wished to conquer the mountain, as now they would surely do. He liked it here, in the quiet upper reaches of the mountain. His only regret was that his body had acclimatised so slowly, too slowly for him to be considered for the summit party. He felt so fit now, so well, could cope much better than any of the others with the lack of oxygen, with the thin air. He woke when the sun audibly hit the tent just after five in the morning, cracked the overnight frost with its sudden warmth, even this high up.

'No rush,' he mumbled to himself, settled back into the sleeping bag. 'No snow to melt.'

An hour later, he finally unwrapped himself from the bag, made himself a breakfast of dried cereal and jam, ate as much jam as he could, because it was the only thing with any liquid in it. He wiped his mouth with the back of his hand, smacked his lips. 'Not bad at all.' His eyes lit up, and he smiled at the green of the tent.

'Better get going.'

He packed a bag full of provisions to take up to Camp VI so Mallory and Irvine could be sure of having enough to eat when they returned. He wondered if they would get to the summit. 'Nothing I can do about it now.' He put his stone hammer into the pocket of his coat. 'Mustn't forget that.' He closed up the tent, left into a morning that wasn't as cold as past ones had been, and headed on up towards the Northeast Shoulder, his eyes on the ground, looking out for geological samples he could take home with him. That's what he was really here for, after all.

As he walked, slowly, steadily, he resisted the temptation to look back down towards the other camps, stopped himself from looking up towards the summit, didn't want to tempt fate. There was so little wind for once, he decided to explore away from the ridge, followed tracks between the rocks on the great North Face, picked up stones, turned them over and discarded them, as if he were on a Sunday afternoon outing back home, on the foothills, plodding the usual well-worn paths.

It was only when he sat down for a rest that he noticed the gathering mist and clouds. He shivered in the breeze, tucked his jacket tighter around him, leaned back and looked up. The sun was still there, behind the clouds. 'Must be low,' he muttered. 'Probably clear up top.' He sighed. 'Would've been nice to be up there with them. Oh well.' He stood up, carried on his survey of the ground. He loved being here on his own, felt as if he were the only man on the mountain, as if the mountain were his, would tell him all its secrets. He took a deep breath, felt the energy flow through his body, wondered why he was suddenly so strong when they'd all, including himself, thought he might be the weakest of the lot. He shook his head and smiled. So what if he didn't get to the top? There might be another chance, some time. 'Don't have to be the first to be brave enough.'

His eyes fixed on the ground again, the clouds forgotten, Mallory and Irvine forgotten. There had to be fossils somewhere round here, in the limestone that had once been at the bottom of the ocean. He didn't want to leave without finding any. He moved closer to the ridge, fixed his gaze on the bottom-most layers where the ridge petered out into the face of the mountain. There, a jagged horizontal edge. He tapped it with his hammer, bent double to get close to it. A slice of the mountain came loose, fell down with a soft sound. He picked it up, turned it over, held his breath. Something about the shape. He tapped it again, his hand firm around it. It cracked open slowly. 'Got you.' He was holding a perfectly-formed ammonite, dark and matte in the subdued light. 'Yes,' he hollered. 'Yes, yes, yes.' He put the fossil in his pocket, sat down, pulled a biscuit and some raisins from his bag, ate and rested. It was just after noon.

He got up, stretched and yawned. Time to head for Camp VI now he'd found what he wanted. He scrambled up an outcrop, arms and legs stretched with unspent effort. When he got to the top, the clouds suddenly lifted, and his gaze was drawn upwards, towards the summit, now in sun. He scanned the mountain for movement, stood still to allow his eyes to focus. And then he saw it, saw them, what he'd hoped to see. First one small black dot, and then a second, on a small patch of snow. He watched them approach the headwall of a high step just below the final summit pyramid, saw one disappear into the wall and reappear at the top. The second did the same. It had to be Mallory and Irvine. He snatched his diary out of his pocket, ripped it open, scribbled in pencil *12:50 – saw*

M&I on ridge, nearing base of final pyramide. By the time he looked up, they had gone, hidden by the returning clouds. He scratched his head through his cap, sighed, and carried on towards the next camp.

It started to snow just as Odell reached the tent, the wind grown strong and bitter. 'The mountain's warning them off,' he muttered into the loneliness, dropped his gear inside, amongst the chaos of oxygen cylinders, clothes and food, sat down in the one free spot he could find, zipped up the tent and waited. 'Maybe they'll come back because of the storm.' The wind battered the tent, slicing up across the ridge.

After an hour he got bored. He shook his head. 'Better go see if they're coming back.' He ducked out into the wind and the horizontal snow, walked west along the leeside of the North Face, shouted out and whistled so they'd know where he was if they were coming back early. No response but the shriek of the gale. After another hour, he turned back. It was getting late.

The sun was out now. He picked up his bag from inside the tent, looked one last time at the summit, and saw nothing, no movement. He shrugged, turned back down the mountain, picked his way through the rocks evaporating snow, avoided Camp V, and raced down the mountain to Camp IV in a succession of controlled slides. He was met there by Hazard.

'Did you see them?' Hazard said.

'I think so. They were going for the top alright.'

'Where were they?'

'At the top of the Second Step.'

'When was that?'

'Almost one o'clock.' Odell said.

'They were a bit late, weren't they?'

Odell shrugged. 'George knows what he's doing.' He was tired of talking about it, wanted nothing but rest.

'Can you make me something to drink, please? George managed to lose the stove from Camp V.'

'Typical.'

'I'll forgive him his messiness this time. All he wants is to get to the top.' *Like we all wanted to*, he thought.

Hazard mumbled something Odell couldn't hear, served up cup after cup of tea, soup, other liquids.

'That's good, thanks ever so,' Odell said. 'I'm parched.'

'I think we'll watch the ridge in case we can see them come down,' Hazard said.

'That's a good idea. I just hope they do come down soon. I don't like this waiting.'

By the time darkness came, they'd seen nothing, so they kept watch until the moonlight disappeared. Still nothing.

*

Silence. Irvine, alone on the mountain, on his knees, the rope slack around his aching ribs, blood dripping from his face, freezing, congealing, bleeding, freezing. 'George?' he screamed. His throat hurt, had been hurting for days. No echo. The pain endless. He lifted his hands, stared at them. Gloves in pieces, the rope burns raw, the blood black in the moonlight.

'George?' He tried to get up. Nothing. The pain was everywhere. He let himself fall over sideways, ripped the rest of the gloves from his hands, buried his ragged palms in the little snow there was, the frozen cold a relief. Every breath hurt, in his throat, in his chest, down into his gut. The snow delicious on his sunburned face, too delicious. He looked down at the mountains opposite, so close, so close, so far away.

'George, we need to get to Camp VI,' he said to the clustering shadows. 'Come on, get up.'

'Can't.'

'Yes, you can.' He was talking to himself, knew it,

denied it. They were still together, up here, in the thin air, the moon still up, hope still there, a chance still of making the tent, not far away now, time standing still to save them, to make it all better.

'They're waiting for us.' He pushed himself up onto his elbows. Then another push, past the wheezing, past the howl of the wind, up onto his knees. He reached out for something, anything, felt the rock next to him, solid, unyielding, sharp, pulled himself upright, his legs shaking, shivering, a sharp stab up one of them, thought of lying down again, dragged himself one step at a time to where he thought the east was.

'We'll be fine,' he shouted. 'We got up there; we'll get down again.' He sobbed before he could stop himself.

'Not the first, not the first.' His breath clattered against his teeth.

Pull, drag, pull, drag. The dry sound of his hobnailed boots through snow and across rock. The sky so clear.

'Why did we leave it so late?'

He shrugged, stopped for breath. 'Where's the oxygen?'

'Oh, all gone, used up.'

'We should've left sooner, George.'

'That damn bowl.'

'Go back and get it then.'

'Can't, not alone.'

'You're not alone.'

He started moving again, his eyes closed; half-lying, half-standing, rubbing against the loose rock.

'The moon's going now.'

'Turn round. Go back up. Better up there than here.'

'No. Need to get home. Need to tell them about what's up there.'

'Turn round. Go west. To the Great Couloir.'

Wheeze, pull, drag. Wheeze pull, drag.

'Too steep. Camp VI. Here somewhere.'

Cold now, everywhere. In the wind, in the empty sky. Irvine lay down again. No feeling in his hands.

'You'll never find it.'

'You're lying!' He pushed himself up again, scrabbled further along the ridge.

'Try it, just try it.' He rolled over, started to move back towards where he'd fallen, less pain stumbling along this way.

The light flickered, grew dimmer, the white of the snow covered in the almighty shadow of night, the darkness complete and absolute. Irvine stopped, swaying, couldn't see his hand in front of his eyes.

'Can't go on. Can't.'

'Feel your way. There's safety above.'

'Cold, too cold.'

'It'll pass.'

'Why not just stay here for the night?'

'No shelter. Keep going. Lots of crags west. Out of the wind.'

'Too dark.'

'Just a little while longer, a bit further.'

'George!' He screamed into the wind, gesticulated furiously into the dark, thumped his chest with his broken fists. 'George!' He dropped down onto the rock, slid westwards on his belly, his hands above his head, more scraping, more tearing of the frozen flesh he could only hear, not feel, and his feet parallel, boot toes digging into the slope, and heart pounding, much faster than his breath came, much too fast.

The last of his energy was gone, and his movements automatic now, without thought, without thinking. His limbs stiff, he dragged himself a few more yards across the face of the mountain.

'I can't.' His lips parched and splitting.

'I know.' He didn't recognise his own voice.

'Sleep.' He curled up on the hard ground.

'You won't wake.'

'Don't care. I want it to stop.'

He closed his eyes, took one deep breath. The stars disappeared.

Chapter 5

The fire hisses. I pull her away from the desk, ignore the papers, and lead her over to the sofa, sit her down, sit down next to her, her hand in mine. I don't care where Simon is. I want us to stop being strangers.

'Did we ever talk?' I say. 'Really talk?'

'We've always talked. Probably more than most couples.'

'What about?'

'Things that didn't matter, things that swirl around the periphery of our lives, inconsequential things.' Her smile is tired.

'Why not about things that matter?'

'Because I've always been afraid of your pain,' she says, and squeezes my hand.

'But I always thought you married me because of it, because you wanted to heal it.'

Her laugh tastes bitter. 'I married you because I loved you from the moment I met you.' She looks at the fire and then back at me. 'Do you really think I could have married you out of pity?'

I shrug. 'You took pity on me. You saved me.'

'Anyone would have.'

'You know that's not true,' I say. 'Not on that mountain. Not on any mountain where no-one lives for long without oxygen.'

'Any real climber would have,' she says.

'But it was you, not just someone else.'

She stares at me. 'You'd have done the same, wouldn't you?'

'Yes, I would have.' I stare back at her. I'm guilty of forgetting how beautiful she is, of taking her beauty for granted. Why do we let the everyday steal from us, make even our deepest feelings seem mundane? We throw away so much. Why wouldn't I want to hold on to her?

'The thing is, you're my shelter,' she says. 'You always have been, no matter what you may think.'

'How can I be?'

'You're so scared of being scared,' she says. 'When it really doesn't matter. You're there when I need you, you protect me. I know you don't think you do, but you do. I'm safe with you, and I miss your arms when I'm away.'

'Then why go away?'

'I need the mountains. To test me, to be on my own with something none of us understand.'

'But they'll kill you.'

'Mountains don't always kill. I need to be up there, out on the rocks, far away from the normal world. Not climbing would kill me.'

'Aren't you exaggerating?' I say, those doubts coming back.

'You know I'm not.'

I bow my head. 'No.'

'I know what you're thinking,' she says.

'Do you? I don't want to lose any more friends. I don't want to lose you.'

'You won't lose me. Ever.'

'What if …?'

'What if what?' she says. 'What if I'd been killed in the earthquake?'

'Don't.' It's too painful even to think about.

'But it's true,' she says. 'Any of us could die at any time. You could have died.'

'I know.' I wish I were dead. Then all this would stop.

She smiles, a sour smile. 'The book was supposed to cure you of all this, not make you keep it inside, not make you prolong your own agony.'

'It didn't work, though, did it? It just made it worse.'

'I'm sorry.'

'Don't be. The thing is, when I was writing it, I did feel much better, even writing about Graham dying, all that stuff; it lifted the burden, until …' Until the book was published, that is, to howls of derision from the English climbing community, to accusations of desertion and betrayal. *Falling and Freezing* we called it, Alice and me. She wrote some of it, the story of how she found me, how she'd fallen in love with me before we even got to Base Camp, and how useless Englishmen are at recognising love when it hits them in the face, and how deadly all mountains are. It was her idea, the title, because Graham and I fell and froze, and because she fell - for me. Inexplicably. Is there anything left of that?

'Until what?' She rips me out of my memory.

'Oh, everything,' I say. 'And it didn't do what it was supposed to do, didn't discourage people from becoming Everest tourists. More people ended up going there than ever before.'

'Maybe we should've thought of that. Maybe we should have been more explicit and written that the danger doesn't come from the mountain but from who's on it.'

I laugh. 'The accidental bestseller, because people are bloodthirsty bastards and want to go to the scene of the wreck?'

She blows a raspberry. 'You care too much about what others think. Shame you're no good at ignoring them.'

'That's what you're good at.'

'Only because I'm not a repressed Englishman.'

'That's flippant,' I say.

'Not really.' She moves closer to me. 'Listen, James, stop taking this all on your shoulders. You being here; that's a good start, isn't it?'

'After all these bloody years? I suppose so.'

'Ah, you admit it, then? You're glad you came?'

'I threw up all the way here. It was awful.'

'It's still a start, a base to start from, all over again.'

'I didn't want to be on the plane. I kept seeing things.'

'That's something else,' she says, reading my memories.

'What?'

'The plane crash,' she says.

'What about it?' I grit my teeth, grab the arm of the sofa with my left hand, squeeze it until my knuckles turn white and ache.

'That wasn't your fault either. Plane crashes happen, specially in countries that do things on the cheap.'

'That's not the point, though, is it? People died.'

'But it is the point.' She puts on her fierce face.

'Not to me it isn't.'

'Maybe you'll see it differently now.'

'Maybe. But I lost more friends.'

'They weren't on the plane because of you,' she says. 'They were on it because they wanted to climb Everest.'

'So it's the mountain's fault. Like everything else is. I hate it, wish I'd never gone anywhere near it.'

She waits for the echo of my raised voice to fade. 'If it hadn't been for *that* mountain, we never would have met.'

My heart misses a beat. I can see the path to self-destruction so clearly ahead I could easily avoid it. But I don't, I can't. 'Maybe that would've been better. For both of us.'

She says nothing. I can feel her breath stop.

'You'd be happy with some other climber by now.'

She still says nothing, still doesn't let go of my hand.

'He'd be on the mountains with you, instead of being a coward in some crappy, broken house in Christchurch.'

She sighs, holds on to me, for some mad, obscure

reason. 'But you're not in Christchurch now. And we chose that house together and made it our own. What if we can't live there again, ever?'

I hear her voice, but I don't take in what she's saying. Just shake my head, let go of her hand, run my fingers through my hair.

'So,' she says after God knows how long. 'Are you going to help me?'

'Why haven't we had any children?' Is that it, is that really all I can say?

'Ah, the really serious stuff now,' she says and blushes.

'If you say so.'

'You think it's because I think you're weak.' Her voice tails off.

'You said that, not me. I've never thought about it before now. On the flight, anyway.'

'It's not the reason. And you're not weak, in any case. You're much stronger than you give yourself credit for.'

'What then?' I say, too loudly. 'Our love life's not exactly been energetic lately, has it?'

She reaches out to me, grabs my hand, pulls it forcibly back onto her knee. 'That's because both of us think too much, analyse too much, and don't just go with the flow. But that's not the point - what do you hate most about me?'

'Nothing.'

'You're a liar.'

'I don't understand. You always ask me questions I can't answer.'

'Has it ever crossed your mind I might be trying to get climbing out of my system before I have children?'

'You've never mentioned it,' I say. 'I know you're addicted to it, like I was, but you've never said anything about wanting to stop. You never really talk to me about it.'

'That's because it's so borderline, so potentially destructive, to talk to you about climbing. I don't want to hurt you.'

'I don't think you could hurt me.'

'That's a double-edged sword of a comment,' she says quietly.

'You know what I mean.'

'Do I?' she says.

'Of course you do.'

'Tell me what you mean. Look at me and tell me.'

'I love you too much.' And it's true, despite everything, despite this self-hate that boils over into hating her, despising the way she is, that unthinking confidence, that southern hemisphere swagger.

'For me to hurt you?' she says. 'Then why, why have you always shied away from talking about this?' For once, she looks surprised.

'I have no idea.' Maybe I'm getting old. Is reproduction a need that grows with a man's age?

'You know, until now, I thought we'd never talked about it because we were happy they way we were. Really, honestly.'

'Then what's changed?' I say. Am I any different to what I was a week ago? I don't feel it.'

'But you are,' she says. 'Your eyes are different now. Clearer, somehow, and I can see right into you. All this is my fault.'

'That's stupid, Alice.'

'Is it?'

'Yes. You're the strong one, not me.' Any minute now she'll take her cue and tell me to fuck off.

'But I'm not. That's the point, you idiot.'

'What?'

'You don't get it, do you? Still, after all these years.'

'Don't get what?' I say.

'That you're the one who saved me, really, then, when

we met. That you're the only one who keeps me in touch with the real world now. That I'd probably be lying on some mountain somewhere if I didn't have you to come home to.'

I'm speechless, swallow hard. I hadn't expected this.

'The world isn't what you think it is,' she says.

'Does that mean you want children?' Why do I always have to push things right to the edge?

'Let's find Simon first.' She gets up, goes back to the desk. 'You've got to have a look at this stuff.'

I sigh, and walk over to her. 'Why?' I shake my head, stare at the mess. 'Where've you been staying?'

'Here,' she whispers.

'You didn't get a hotel?'

'I didn't want to.' She's got black rings under her eyes.

'That's ridiculous,' I say. 'Come on, let's get a few things sorted. We'll come back later.'

'But I want to get on with it.'

'It'll keep. A few more hours won't make any difference.'

She hesitates. 'There's something odd going on. I don't want this stuff to go walkies.'

'It won't.'

'How can you be so sure?'

'I can't, I suppose. But there's a lock on the door.'

'Big deal,' she says.

'It would've gone missing before you got here if someone was after it. Though I don't understand why anyone would be.'

'There's a double bed. We don't need a hotel.'

'You've not left this room since you got here, have you?'

She shakes her head.

'So what have you eaten?' Why am I always so weasly, so boringly practical?

'I bought some stuff on the way here. It's in the

fridge.' She has this way of avoiding having to answer questions she doesn't like.

'Have you eaten any of it?

'A bit.'

'And have you had anything to drink?' I say.

'Of course. That's the first rule of the mountains – stay hydrated.'

'But you're not on a mountain.'

'I might as well be.'

'Eh? Stop speaking in riddles.'

'I'm far away from anything and everything.' She sits down in Simon's swivel chair again.

'You're not going to leave here, are you?'

'No way,' she says. 'Not until we've been through this again.'

'I give in,' I say. 'I'm going to go and get you something warm to eat, and then we'll go through this rubbish together.'

'You don't want to know where I think he is?'

'No. I can imagine anyway. I want to know why you think it, though.' I bend down to kiss her. 'Give me half an hour.'

On the way out I stop at the Porter's Lodge again. 'Has my wife really been in that room since she got here?'

'Yes, sir. Created a bit of a fuss, she did. Domestic Bursar gave in in the end. She got really cross when he called her an Aussie.'

'Are you worried about Dr Young?' I say when I've stopped laughing.

'He's always off on his little jaunts, sir, so it's not unusual for him to disappear.'

'I'll take that as a no. Don't his students get pissed off with him not being here?'

'He's too popular for that.' He bends towards me. 'Master's not happy, though, sir, between you and me.

If he's not back in a week, I think there'll be consequences.'

'And how do you know that?'

He stands up straight again, taps the side of his nose with his finger, and winks at me.

'Oh,' I say. 'Does anyone know anything about the two blokes who were with him at High Table the last night he was here?'

'Your wife asked the same. He just signed them in as guests. No names.'

'Isn't that a bit unusual?'

'Not really, not if there's no plans for the guests to stay overnight.'

'Oh, right. I didn't know that.'

'You should spend more time here.'

I shrug.

'No one here blamed you for what happened, sir,' he says. 'For what it's worth. All that rubbish in the papers. You should've come straight back here. You'd have been amongst friends.'

'That's … er … very kind of you.' I blink back some unbidden tears. 'Although the one friend I've been with is the only one I need.'

'I can see that,' he says. 'And very lovely she is, too. Though we all need more than just the one friend. You know what I'm saying.'

'I do,' I say, grab his hand for a brief handshake. 'That means a lot to me.'

'No problem, sir.'

Someone else comes into the Lodge, and he turns round to deal with them.

I walk out into the greyness, my boots heavy on the cobbles, and turn right into the town centre. A little later I'm laden with goodies of all sorts; fresh bread, warm soup, cured meats, real butter, wine. I stagger back through the streets which seem suddenly warm to me, like I've come home after a long time. I even catch myself smiling. Unusually.

'Has she got a key?' I ask the porter on my way through.

'Yes, she has.'

'Would it put the DB's mind at rest if I went to see him?'

'It might be a good thing to do,' he says.

'D'you think he'll let us stay in Dr Young's room for a while?'

'Can't see any reason why not. He might make a small charge, though.'

'I'm sure I can cope with that,' I say. 'Right, I'd better get on and feed that wraith of mine.'

Back in the room, I dump everything in the tiny kitchen, then carry the soup and bread out to the table by the sofa. 'Come on, Ally,' I say. 'Let's eat something.'

'Smells yummy. See, I told you I can't cope without you,' she says, her mouth full, and her cheeks finally with some colour in them.

'It's not as if I'd cooked it, though.'

'So? I could never be that organised.'

'That makes me sound very boring. Now shut up and eat.'

'Nom nom nom,' she says, and laughs.

The more I eat, the more I realise I'm starving. The cold takes its toll, even just this mild damp cold of the English winter. My eyes feel heavy, time difference catching up with me, making me groggy and hazed. We don't speak.

She's obviously ravenous, rips the bread to shreds impatiently, dips it into her soup, stuffs the drenched fibres into her mouth, hardly stops for breath, totally absorbed, oblivious to me watching her. Bread gone, she rips another piece from the loaf, bends forward, spoon in hand, shovels the red liquid into herself, slurps, downs another spoonful. How utilitarian our bodies are, how well-adapted to the need to take in fuel. When her bowl's empty, she licks her lips, wipes her mouth with her forearm, leans back and belches. Here, now, it's impossible not to love her, impossible not to ask myself how such a perfect body can consume such vast quantities of food without bloating.

'Are you done?' she says, at last.

'I suppose so.'

'And are you tired yet?'

'A bit. I can't feel any jetlag yet, though. Maybe it's because it's been such a long time since I last travelled.'

'Maybe.' She drags another chair to behind the desk, pats the seat. 'We'd better get on.'

The mountain of papers and books looks even bigger when I'm sitting behind it. I pull the chair closer to the desk. 'So, where do you think he is?'

'Sort this first, and we'll see what you think.'

'I already know.'

'That's what you think.'

'It's obvious, isn't it?'

'Look through this first and tell me then if you think it's still obvious.' She pushes her chair back from the desk and gestures at the pile. 'Go on. Be my guest.'

Chapter 6

'Hang on,' I say. 'I thought this was all going to be about the mountain.'

'See,' she says, legs stretched out, so so long, onto the table. 'You thought I'd say he was on Everest.'

I snort. 'How predictable I am.'

'Not really.'

I wade my way through the papers, up to my elbows in brittle words and pictures. I throw them to each side, part a Red Sea of mysteries. The paper scratches me, scrapes at my already blistered skin, draws blood from the imaginary invalid.

'None of this makes sense,' I say.

'Really?' She's making fun of me.

'You can bugger off.'

'You men are always so sure. You always think you're right, when you hardly ever are.'

'Oh, just we men, is it?'

'You know what I mean.'

'Sometimes I do, sometimes I don't. You're a mystery to me most of the time.'

She smiles and says nothing. She doesn't need to.

There are books here, on Buddhism, I'd never have thought would be Simon's style. He's one of these typical mountaineers; beer, women, risk. Doesn't hold back; makes life seem easy. Curls his fingers round every opportunity, makes each moment count – for him. Alice was right; I don't really like him, hate the ease with which he skips through life, how he makes everything look simple, how lucky he is. He's a magnification of her, exploded into arrogance.

'I know what you're thinking,' she says across the cooling room.

'What exactly am I thinking?'

'How ironic it is that my lucky reprobate brother has

disappeared without leaving any clues.'

'That's not it.'

'I can read you. You're no good at telling lies.'

'Have you thought about what this stuff is?'

'It's just one of his weirdnesses,' she says.

'Oh, yeah, of course it is. That's why you flew round half the globe.'

'So tell me what you see,' she says.

'Nothing yet. Just things I wouldn't expect of him.'

'You don't know him or like him.'

'But I understand him.'

'Ha!' Her tone cuts me.

'Just because I'm envious of him, just because I wish I wasn't the failed climber, doesn't mean I can't empathise with him.'

'Go on,' she says.

'Let me go through the whole pile first.'

'Come on. Hurry up.' She's getting cross.

'Ok, ok.' I drop the handful of paper I'm holding. 'I'd have expected all this to be about climbing, about what I thought were his obsessions.'

'So what if it isn't?'

'What did you think you'd find?' I say, intrigued.

She curls up, trousers tight around her hips. 'The same as you,' she says, reluctantly.

'So why are you taking the mick out of me, and pretending to know more than I do?'

'You're not his twin sister. I'm supposed to understand everything he does.'

'I'm no-one,' I say. 'But sometimes I see things clearer than you.' Perhaps that why I analyse my feelings too much, instead of just feeling them.

'Come climbing with me again.' That's out of the blue.

'I can't.' My heart's racing. I miss the open spaces, but fear the heights.

'You got here, didn't you?'

'Is that the point? And, anyway, that wasn't climbing.'

'One fear is much like the other,' she says. 'That's the point. If you overcame one, you can overcome the other.'

'What about Simon?'

'I think we're going to have to climb to find him.'

'So that's why you asked me to climb again,' I say, and shake my head. 'And where exactly?'

'Keep reading. I'm going to have a bath.' She gets up, stretches.

'It's a bit cold for that, isn't it?'

'There's a radiator in the bathroom,' she says.

'There never was in my day.'

She shrugs, ruffles my hair, pulls my face to her belly. 'Poor little you,' she says.

I smile into her shirt, nip at her muscles through it, push her away before she has time to react. 'Go on then.'

'If you hadn't been here, I'd not have moved from that desk, you know.' She walks away.

'I know.' Something feels different. I feel like living again.

The door closes quietly. I descend into another world, leaf through Simon's stuff slowly, carefully, don't want to miss anything. I flick through the books about Buddhism. Only a couple of them are about the monasteries in Tibet, but at least that's some sort of link to Simon's obsession with Everest. The others are about the faith in general, about how to be a good Buddhist, how to meditate effectively, how to achieve perfection in faith. I put all these books in one stack to the right side of the desk. I haven't got time to read every word of them. I scratch my head. Weird.

Ah, here are the books about the mountain. General stuff, as well, about its geology, about how it grew from being the sea bed to be the highest mountain above sea level, how there was controversy when, a few years ago, lots of people reckoned K2 was actually the tallest, how it's not the tallest if you start measuring from the sea bed upwards, all those sort of dry facts I get bored with too quickly. I build a new pile of books on the floor. It's odd, I think, that there are no notes in any of them, because Simon's an inveterate scribbler into books. That is one thing I've learned about him.

Here's the stuff I was expecting, all about Mallory and Irvine and the 1924 expedition to Everest on which they disappeared. Holzel, Salkeld, Hemmleb, all those books of theories that can't be proved or disproved, arguments for them reaching the top before Hillary and Tenzing, arguments against. The book with pictures of Mallory's bleached white body in it, the body they found in 1999, on the first day of a search expedition up into the Yellow Band below the summit. The body they at first took to be Irvine's, until they found Mallory's name tags in all the ripped clothes, and letters from his wife, and all those other things that identified him as being someone they'd never expected to find. A third pile of books grows in height, one after the other. There's even a copy of *Falling and Freezing*. Why's that here? I shiver, put it back onto the desk and stare at it.

Why do Mallory and Irvine still exert such a grasp on people's imagination? Is it because they disappeared, gone from one moment to the next, at least until they found Mallory's body seventy-five years after he'd gone? Or is it because there's still no certainty as to whether or not they reached the summit of the world's highest mountain? We become obsessed with the oddest things, do the strangest things. Why risk life and limb climbing up a dumb piece of rock, a growth on the face of the earth, why? Why risk climbing at all? I know everyone thinks Mallory said *Because it's there*, but most of us climbers know it's just something an American journalist made up, a sound bite from the 1920s, to hype Mallory's US lectures, to increase newspaper circulation. But it's a motive that applies not just to climbing, not just to climbers, but to everyone who tries to carve something extraordinary from the ordinary, who focuses on one goal to the exclusion of everything else. And when we fail, we become obsessed by our fears.

I grab the book from the desk, open it. *For Simon, with all my love, Alice.* I throw it down again, lean back and look out of the window. It's getting dark already. I frown. Where the hell is he? I hear her humming from the bathroom, a familiar tune from when we got married. What does she really think? About me? About Simon, about where he is? Is this another artificial mountain we're building? What if he's lost forever? Where the hell is his laptop?

The desk's clear of books now, and just the papers remain. I chuck them all together into a half-neat sheaf, no order to them, just random bits in a random sequence. Then I stare at the inarticulate patterns of Simon's scrawl, lift the first sheet from the others and try to read them. Why on bits of paper rather than in the books? Odds and sods of thought, lots of question marks, lots of crossings out, the signs of an untidy mind. Typical him. What do I care how he summarises Buddhism or geological events? They don't tell me where he is. They don't tell me if he's gone of his own free will, or if he's been taken away. It's madness. A puzzle. And she's a puzzle, too, Alice. Why not just tell me what she thinks? She's always been like this, slightly patronising, refusing to give me solutions to problems I'm too lazy to solve, always pushing me to try harder to find answers she already has. Is that why I love her and hate her? Is that why she loves me, because I'm so incomplete, so helpless, so lazy?

And then, on crumpled, wrinkled paper, throwaway scribbles. *Mallory – NOT MALLORY!! Enlightenment. IRVINE! Only he knows. Young enough. Not what's said – what's left unspoken.* And that's it. I turn the piece of paper over and over, read the words again.

'Doesn't make sense, does it?' she says, makes me jump.

'No,' I say. 'You nearly gave me a heart attack.'

'Sorry.' She's wrapped in a towel, another one round her hair. 'So, what do you make of it?'

'I don't know. It's gibberish. He can't mean the Mallory they found was really Irvine. They proved it. One of them says he looked into his face and recognised him, too.'

'What then? What else could there be that he thinks he knows and no-one else has a clue about?'

I shrug. 'Mallory wasn't exactly old. That's the bit that puzzles me most. What's Irvine young enough to know?'

'Mallory was old for the mountain at the time,' she says.

'He was only thirty-seven. Younger than I am now. And that's not the point. Why's Simon going on about Irvine?'

'Because they haven't found him yet?' she says.

'Maybe they'll never find him. It was pure luck they found Mallory.'

She laughs. 'The guys who were there might argue with that.'

'The found a needle in a haystack,' I say. 'No matter how many calculations they'd done.'

'That's all irrelevant.' She jabs her finger at the scrap of paper. 'What's he saying?'

'That Irvine was actually the driving force?'

She raises an eyebrow. 'Meaning?'

'Everyone's always banging on about how Mallory was the one who could climb and that Irvine was just there because he was good with the oxygen gear. What if it was Irvine who actually got them to wherever they got to?'

'But Mallory's a god.'

'To us maybe. We don't know what he was really like, or how Irvine compared to him. Everyone just assumes Mallory was the best.'

'That's heresy,' she says.

I shrug. 'I'm not saying Mallory wasn't brilliant. I'm just saying maybe Irvine was much better than people think he was, and his strength carried them much further than anyone accepts. He was exceptionally strong.'

She rubs her chin. 'Mmmm. I'll have to think about that one.'

'It's the only thing I can think of.'

'Hang on,' she says, crouches down by the piles of books, the towel falling open from her shoulders. 'There's something here about Irvine climbing.'

'I thought you knew where he was.' I try to keep my eyes off her.

'Irvine?'

'No. Simon.'

'I was making it up to get you fired up,' she says.

'You mean you don't know.'

'I mean I don't know. Shush!'

'You're such a tease.'

'I know. It's just the way I am. To get the best out of you.'

'That's mean.'

'But fair,' she says. 'Ah, here we are.' She grabs a book from the tumbling pile.

'What is it?' I can't take my eyes off her.

'A book about Irvine by his great-niece.'

'You can't have read it, surely.'

'I have read some of it,' she says. 'But Simon read it all.'

'So you think.'

'There's something in here about Irvine doing a really difficult climb after he'd been to Spitsbergen with Odell,' she says.

'Where? It's spurious.'

'It's not spurious at all. It fits in with what you said.'

'How's that?'

'Shush,' she says again, sits down on the floor, legs akimbo under the towel. 'It's here somewhere.' She turns over the pages quickly, too quickly.

'You'll never find it.'

'Will,' she says, child-voiced.

I sigh.

'Ha,' she says. 'Told you so.' She holds the book up in mock triumph, like Moses the Ten Commandments.

'Show me,' I say.

'No. I'll read it to you.'

I listen to her, say nothing until she's finished. 'So he led a really difficult climb to almost five and a half thousand feet. So? That's not exactly Everest.'

'Wait, wait,' she says. 'This Jaegerrasstind from the book, where is it?'

'You tell me. You've got the book.'

'Can't you google it?'

'Spell it.' I get out my smartphone, search. 'Nothing. The only thing that comes up is the bit you just read.'

'Bugger.' She gets up. 'Nothing else?'

'Hang on.' The connection's not great, pages take ages to load. 'Here we are. I reckon it can only be this one. Jiehkkevarri. This site reckons it's the highest mountain in the Lyngen Alps.'

'Are there any photos?' she says.

'Hang on. Why the hell's the connection so crap?

Here we are.' I hand her the phone.

She scrolls through the pictures in silence. Gasps. 'Look,' she says.

I sit down next to her. 'What?'

'It's almost a mini-Everest.'

'I suppose it is.' I'm not convinced.

'But look.' Her long index finger points at the right-hand side of the photo. 'That feature; it's like the Second Step, like the one Odell saw them climb up.'

'Or thought he did,' I say.

'He only changed his mind because people tried to change his mind for him. He saw them go up there, alright.'

I lean back against the wall. The room seems much warmer now. 'And this leads us to Simon, how?'

She shrugs. 'Maybe he's there.'

'It doesn't make sense. Why would he be there?'

'To try that climb, to prove that Irvine could have proved himself there.'

'Simon's done the Second Step on Everest anyway.' Free-hand, for God's sake, unroped.

'We'd do it to prove Irvine practiced it,' she says, and I know she'll not give up till she's persuaded me to go.

'We're going round in circles.'

She sits up, pulls the towel back tight round her shoulders. 'There are three options, I reckon.'

'And what would they be?'

'He's either gone to Oxford to go snooping round Irvine's old college, or he's gone to Norway, or he's in some Buddhist monastery in Tibet.'

'What about those guys he was last seen with?' I say.

'Maybe they were climbers. I can't imagine him asking anyone else to dinner.'

'Were they English?'

'It doesn't sound like it, from what anyone's said.'

'So where's the danger?' I say. 'It all sounds perfectly

innocuous.'

'Except that he disappeared the day after the dinner.' She sighs. 'There's danger everywhere, at least where Simon's concerned.'

'You said he was in big trouble, but I don't get that feeling.'

'There is, though, there is,' she says, insistently. 'It's got to be the mountain then.'

'Are you sure? You don't think he's been kidnapped any more?'

'I don't know.' She sounds desperate.

'We'll find him. Honestly.'

'I know we will.' She gets up, reaches for my hand, helps me up. When I'm on my feet, she drops the towel and kisses me like she's not kissed me for ages. 'Come to bed,' she whispers. She takes my hand, leads me into the bedroom. 'Fresh sheets, specially for you.' She pulls me down onto the bed.

'Eh?'

'I knew you'd come,' she says. Starts undressing me. 'You're my husband, after all, and I need you.'

'What about Simon?' My hands are around her naked, narrow waist.

'Tomorrow,' she says. 'We'll go find him tomorrow.'

Chapter 7

The rain wakes me. It clatters against the tiny window, its drops stones in the wind. Alice is asleep, on her back, arms thrown wide, breaths deep, oblivious. This is the way she's always been. Nothing can stop her sleeping if that's what she's decided to do, no matter how worried or excited she is. I've always envied how easily she falls asleep. I've wandered our house so often, in the middle of the night, alone with my demons, padded along the dark corridors until I've comforted myself with another glass of wine, or something to eat, until my heart and brain have slowed down to manageable speeds, until I've managed to separate myself from the part of me that's always running away.

There's a noise in the main room. I stop my breathing. Did we lock the outer door before our reawakened passion ran away with us? I hear a rustling, clamber out of bed as lightly as I can, bend my knees to find a discarded t-shirt on the floor, my feet on the cold floor, the boards for once silent. I grab it when I find it, slip it over my head, feel for my boxers, find them, climb into them without stumbling, creep to the door.

It's almost pitch black in there, a dark, grey light filtering in from the court, the shadow of the old library opposite. There is movement in there. I tiptoe across the threshold, breath shallow, pull the bedroom door closed behind me, reach for the light switch before thinking, flick it on. The brightness blinds me.

'What the fuck are you doing here?' The familiar voice and its arrogance take me by surprise.

'I could ask you the same,' I say, my eyes recovering from the sudden light. 'How did you get in?'

'It's my room,' he says. 'I've got a key.'

'She's worried about you.'

'She's here then, is she?'

'Of course she is. She said you were in big trouble.'

'I am.'

My eyes are finally back to normal. I look at him. Jesus, he looks awful. His face is bloody, and so's his shirt.

'I need to sit down.' He limps to the chair behind the desk, drops down into it, and exhales, in obvious pain.

'You need a doctor.'

'Impossible, I'm afraid. I can't let anyone know I'm here.' He flashes his smile. 'It's just a flesh wound.'

'Don't be a smart-arse.'

'I can't think of any other way to be.'

'What the hell's going on?'

'I wish I knew.' He lights a cigarette.

'The alarm'll go off.'

'Stop being so damn boring, James,' he says. 'I disconnected it ages ago. Bloody stupid anti-smoking brigade.'

I open my mouth to say something.

'Oh, give it a rest. How the fuck she ended up with you, I don't know.'

'Keep your voice down.'

'She'll sleep,' he says. 'She's not expecting me to be here.'

'How do you know that?'

'I know, that's all. This imagined bond between twins is just that. She'd have been here sooner if it really worked.'

'Are you going to tell me why you're here?'

He inhales deeply, flicks the ash onto the floor. 'Just to get something. Then I need to go again.'

'Didn't the porters see you? There's talk that you're in trouble with the Master.'

'The porters are on my side. And the Master's the least of my worries.' He laughs. 'I'm always in trouble with him, or with the faculty.'

'Don't you care?'

He shrugs. 'Why should I? They're just a bunch of idiots obsessed with imagined tradition and things I don't give a toss about.' He's still bleeding. It's so typical of him not to care.

'Where've you been?' I say. 'And where are you going?'

He holds up his hands, yellow fingers in the smoke. 'Too many questions, old boy. None of which I can answer, and none of which are your business.'

'It is my business when it drags my wife away from me. On a wild goose chase.'

'So I thought you'd given up flying?' There's the arrogance again.

'I didn't plan …'

'Oh, poor little Jimmy missed his little Ally, did he?'

'You're such a bastard.' I'd hit him if I had the courage.

'That's me.'

'She's tried calling you, texting you, everything.'

'I know,' he says. 'It's nothing new. I just ignore it, like I always do. She should stop trying to interfere.'

'Don't you care?'

'I haven't got time to care. Anyway, they've got all my stuff.'

'Who's they?'

'I wish I knew.'

'You're not making sense.' I'm tired of this.

'It doesn't matter.' He grabs the papers from the desk. 'This is what I need.'

'You're looking for Irvine, aren't you?'

He looks at me, his eyes on fire. 'No.'

'What?'

'I've found him.'

'That's impossible.'

He shakes his head. 'That's why they're after me.'

'You've not been to the mountain for years.'

'Oh, do stop with that pathetic *the mountain* stuff. It's Everest and it beat you. Accept it. And you don't know where I have and haven't been.'

I blush, face hot. 'You …'

'Go on then. Rearrange my face some more. It can't hurt any worse than it already does.'

I shake my head.

'Be a man,' he whispers. 'Just for once.'

'Fuck off,' I say. He's beaten me, and he knows it. Again.

'Right.' He gets up, flicks his cigarette into the fireplace. 'I'd better get going.'

'Where to?'

He taps his finger against his nose. 'Best you don't know. And don't tell her I was here.'

'Don't you want to see her?'

'And have her crying all over me because she's worried? No thanks.'

'I thought you loved her.'

He stands still, all six foot four of him. 'I do,' he says. 'I just don't want her to get involved.'

'She already is.'

'Not if you keep your mouth shut. You don't have to say anything.'

'Unlike you, I can't lie,' I say. 'She wants us to find you.'

'Not a chance.'

'You won't get far, not now.'

'Don't be so sure,' he says. 'I got away from them, didn't I?'

'So they'll come here and get her instead. I'm assuming it's those two blokes you took to Hall with you.'

He laughs. 'Ah, the simple world must be so nice to

live in.'

'Why the fuck do you keep talking in riddles?' He's too much like his sister, except she's not so aggressive.

For once he hesitates. 'Because the poor bastards are gone, that's why. Because they were my friends. Because I should stop wasting my time here and go.' He is torn, after all. He does want to talk to her, really. He shudders, pulls open the bottom drawer in the desk. 'Thank God for that.' He's got another phone in his hand, a wallet, and a passport. 'Insurance,' he says. 'I'm surprised she didn't check it.'

'I thought she had.'

'Never assume, mate, never. People never do what you think they're going to do. They're never as thorough as you.' He limps past me. 'Not a word to her.' His eyes glint, and his lips tremble.

'I can't promise.'

'Idiot. You're going to be the death of her.' He shakes his head.

'You are, you mean.'

'Don't meddle with things you don't understand,' he says, at the door.

'Where are you going?' I try again.

'Somewhere no-one can find me.'

'She will.'

'Sure.' And then he's gone.

I rush to the door, stand out in the rain, but his shadow's disappeared already, and there's no sound of footsteps. 'Bugger.' I run to the Bridge of Sighs in my bare feet; nothing. Then the other way into Second Court. All empty and silent. I should've stopped him somehow. Ha, but how? He's so much bigger and stronger than me. I turn, wet through by now, walk back to the room, feet slapping against the stones, close the door behind me. The smell of smoke has lingered, and there are small specks of blood over the floorboards. I get a towel from the kitchen, wet it, wipe the blood away. The floor is so dark she won't notice the few smears I've left.

In the bathroom, I wipe myself dry, rub my hair hard with a towel, strip, then stumble into the bedroom, exhausted, confused, lost. She's still asleep, just like he said she'd be, just like I knew she'd be. I climb in next to her, lie on my stomach, head on my left arm, facing her. I can feel the heat of her under the duvet, move closer to her, feel cold, so cold, start shivering, until my leg touches hers and her warmth runs into me and lulls me back to sleep.

The bed's empty when I wake. I'm too lazy, or tired, to move. That first moment after waking, when nothing matters, where memory doesn't exist, passes, and recollection sweeps over me. She comes into the room, a mug of coffee in her hand.

'He was here then,' she says.

'Who?'

'Simon. Don't play stupid.'

'He told me not to say anything, but I told him I couldn't lie.'

'I can smell the smoke.'

'I started again last night,' I say.

'Of course you did. I know you started again after the quake.'

'The rain kept waking me. I couldn't sleep.'

'You never could,' she says. 'But you're lying.'

I shrug. What else can I do?

'And you never were a good liar,' she says. 'Why didn't you wake me?'

'He was too quick.'

'For what?'

'Everything. He's always too quick for me to catch him.'

'I wish you wouldn't let him intimidate you.'

'I don't,' I say, still horizontal, regret how true her words are.

'What then?'

'He's just better than me, better prepared, I suppose. He seems to think about everything in advance.'

'Except you didn't manage to get rid of all the blood.'

Shit. 'What blood?'

'Oh, James, come on. I'm not stupid. And why are you trying to be loyal to him?'

'I'm not. I'm trying to protect you, not him. I don't want you hurt or worse.'

'Come on,' she says. 'You've got to be honest with me.'

So I tell her about it, about him, everything. While I sip my coffee.

'So where do you think he's gone?'

'I don't know.'

'That's no use.'

'I know.'

'And how can he say he's found Irvine?'

'I wish I could tell you.'

'You should've asked him,' she says.

'I tried.'

'You should've tried harder.'

'I was too shocked. I didn't know what he meant.'

'So he's not really found him?' she says, her face hard.

I say nothing.

'For God's sake! And he's taken his notes. And you didn't ask him about that gnomic scribble, did you?'

'Sorry.' I feel useless.

'No, I'm sorry. I should've woken up.'

'So much for this twin stuff.'

'I know he doesn't believe in it.'

'Then why do you?'

She looks at me from the foot of the bed. 'Because it's real to me.' She shrugs. 'And I was right, wasn't I?'

'I suppose.'

'You men.' She gets up. 'Go back to NZ, then, if that's what you want, if you don't want to find him.'

'I can't,' I say.

'What?'

'I can't fly on my own again.'

'Of course you can.'

'You still care more for him than for me.'

'Don't be ridiculous.' She sits back down on the bed, much closer to me now. 'I'm just pissed off I didn't see him, that I don't know where he is, that he's hurt and I can't do anything about it, that he cares so much less about me than I do about him.'

'That's the way he's always been.'

She nods. 'I know.'

'And still you've kept chasing round after him?'

'I've got to. No-one else will. It's my job to look after him.'

'He's a big boy now.' I don't tell her I think he was crying when he left.

'Sure.' She sighs.

'So what now?' I say.

She shakes her head. 'Wait.'

I sit up, cross my arms. The rain's stopped, sun in through the window.

'Hang on,' she says.

'I'm hanging.'

'Shut up.'

I lean back. My mind's blank. I haven't got a clue where we should go next. I'd just like to stay here, to be honest, to carry on fixing my love for her, to stop its waning.

She snaps her fingers. 'That's it,' she says. 'Of course it is.'

'What?'

'Buddhist monasteries. Somewhere.'

'Round here?'

'Maybe.'

'There must be hundreds in England,' I say. 'Why?'

'Where else would he hide?'

'And the dead guys?'

'Monks.'

'Aren't they all small and short?' I say.

'That's stupid.'

'Sorry.'

'Look it up, then,' she says.

I reach for my phone, type in *England* and *Buddhist monasteries*, click on the second hit I find. 'World Buddhist Directory,' I say. 'There's over five hundred hits.'

'There must be a way of narrowing them down.'

'Thirteen in Cambridgeshire, and they're not all monasteries.'

'Still. Would he go somewhere close?' she says.

'Not if that's where he got thumped, he wouldn't. And anyway, he wasn't exactly acting like a Buddhist.'

'He doesn't need to have become a Buddhist. He just needs somewhere to shelter, to find some sort of sanctuary.'

'What from?'

'Whoever or whatever attacked him.'

'Probably a jealous husband,' I say.

'That's flippant.'

I grunt.

'If we can't work out where he's gone, we're just going to have to go to Tibet,' she says.

'It's that simple, is it?'

'What else?'

'Go home, save what we can from the mess, start again somewhere.'

'And just leave him to his own devices?'

'Why not?'

'Don't you care?' she says.

'I do, actually, but I don't think he does. He doesn't want me, or you, to find him.'

Her phone interrupts us, a single beep, a text. She reaches to get it from the table next to her side of the bed, presses a couple of buttons. 'What the hell?'

Chapter 8

'What is it?' I say.

She just shakes her head, passes the phone to me.

U need 2 get out now. Just go. Don't look 4 me. Don't need u 2 help. All fine. Lv. Sx

There's no number to text back to or phone.

'At least he loves you back,' I say.

'Great.' She's trembling. 'It doesn't mean anything.'

I give the phone back to her. 'D'you think he's being serious?'

She shrugs, keeps staring at her phone. 'I've no idea. It's like I don't know him any more.'

'He's trying to protect you, that's all.'

'Protect me from what? And why do you keep siding with him? What did he say to you last night to make you like this?'

My turn to shrug.

'You don't think he killed those men, do you?' she says.

'No way.' I've got to tell her. 'I think he was crying when he left last night.'

'What?' Her eyes are wide open now. 'He doesn't do crying.'

I squirm. 'He said they were his friends. And I think that, deep down, he wanted to stay and see you, talk to you, tell you what's happening.'

'Oh.' She coughs that cough of sadness I've heard before. 'I'm sorry.'

'Stop saying you're sorry all the time,' I say. 'What are we going to do now?'

'We should probably do as he says. There's something he's not telling us.'

'What, and go home?'

She smiles and shakes her head. 'Let's get out of here, rent a car and drive round the countryside.'

‘A tour of Buddhism in Cambridge on your schedule, by any chance?’

‘Maybe.’ She jumps up, face still pale, eyes still wide. ‘Let’s go.’

Ten minutes later the room’s as tidy as it’ll ever be. We sling our backpacks over our shoulders. We wander through College, the paths drying out under the sun, the rain gone, the light unusually hot and bright for this time of year. We get to the main gate, walk out into the real world.

‘Didn’t you ever ask yourself why you lived behind these walls?’ she says.

‘Not really. It was weird at first, living inside history, but then I started to take it for granted. I think we all did. Why?’

‘It’s not something I’d have thought of if I hadn’t been here with you now, for the first time. Simon saw himself as being behind walls, because he always had most of his fun up in the mountains.’ Her voice tails away.

‘This was my home,’ I say. ‘He’s never felt that way, although he works here.’

‘Then why didn’t you come back here after the accident, when you’d healed?’

‘No-one understood. They all hated me.’

‘You’re wrong,’ she says. ‘They all love you here. They couldn’t stop telling me when I arrived. They talk about you all the time, and how sad they thought it was. It’s just that those climbers who hated you were the ones who shouted the loudest.’

‘Aren’t they the ones who count? They have the most influence.’

‘No. They’re just a bunch of self-indulgent, self-important snobs. They always have been. They were like that in Mallory’s and Irvine’s time. If you hadn’t gone to the right school, or made the right connections, you didn't have much of a chance. What was Mallory, after all? Just a teacher at some private school with friends in the right places.'

'But he was a brilliant climber, we all know that.'

'Yes, he was. But so was George Finch, and they chucked him off after one expedition because he was the wrong sort, because he wasn't all Empire, blah di blah.'

'D'you really think that was why?' I say. 'I thought that was just rumour.'

'I can't see any other reason. And he reckoned oxygen was the way to go when most of the old-timers reckoned that was cheating. Just like the Antarctic crowd in England thought Amundsen was a cheat because he used dogs.'

'You don't bear any grudges against the Establishment, then.'

She laughs. 'You know me. I'm an upstart. Death to the Commonwealth, up the Republic and all that.'

'You should've been an Aussie,' I say.

'Naah. They're not as honest as us Kiwis.'

My turn to laugh, mostly because I'm relieved she's so upbeat.

'And another thing,' she says. 'Irvine only got on the 1924 expedition because they thought he was a man they could experiment with and use; young enough and impressionable enough.'

'It didn't turn out like that, though, did it?'

'Too right it didn't. I reckon he ended up being the mainstay of it all, the one who held it all together.'

'Is that what Simon means in his note? Something that simple? I can't see why he'd get beaten up for that, and whatever else has happened.'

'It's got to be something deeper than that then,' she says. 'Simon wouldn't have written it down unless he thought he was really onto something no-one else has thought about before.'

'Like what?'

She shrugs. 'If I knew that, we'd know where we're going.' She stops walking. The streets are empty. February's not a tourist month. 'You didn't really need me, you know, when you crashed and burned. This place would've protected you against the people who tried to destroy you. Your college, your people; they'd never have heard a word said against you. You'd have been safe here.'

I shake my head. 'I've always needed you. It's not just the public hate; it's the being alone, the being afraid. That's why I hate it when you go away.' The wind is sour on my tongue, the sun vinegar. A choice. 'I don't mean to go on about it.'

'I know how you feel. I accept it. It's just difficult.' She starts walking again. 'Anyway, you're here now. You've made the first step.'

'What about the next steps? Just thinking about them scares me.'

'We'll take them as they come,' she says.

'If they come.'

'They will.'

I change the subject. 'There's another expedition planned for later this year, to find Irvine's body and his camera. To prove once and for all if they got to the top.'

'I know.'

'But Simon said he'd found him.'

'Maybe that's the point,' she says. 'Someone might be trying to stop him from telling, or trying to scare him off so they get there first.'

'You mean it could just be a case of professional jealousy?'

'More than that. Think of the money someone who found Irvine and the camera could earn, selling photos and books, lecturing. And the prestige, to have finally solved the mystery of Mallory and Irvine. Millions, James. And that's more than professional jealousy; it's a gold rush. People have killed for less.'

'What about Irvine's family?' I say.

'Would they be bothered? Does anyone care about them?'

'Don't you?'

'Of course I do,' she says. 'What those people did with Mallory, flashing pictures of his half-naked, bleached body all round the world, wasn't right. There's nothing wrong with trying to find them, but what they did with Mallory was grave robbery, really. And whatever they might say, I bet they did it for the money and the fame.'

'If you found Irvine, wouldn't you want to find the camera to get final proof?' I say.

'I'm not sure. I couldn't go rifling through the pockets of a guy who's been dead for nearly a hundred years just to prove a point. Let it stay a mystery.'

'But …'

'What?'

'I thought you wanted to know.'

'I do,' she says. 'But not at all costs. What would you do?'

'All I can do is think about Graham, and how he's still up there, without a grave, without anything.'

'Would you want someone to go through his pockets in a hundred years?'

I shake my head, bite my lip. 'I don't think I could do it, if I found Irvine. I'd just pile the rocks on top of him, give him some sort of bed, some sort of protection.'

'There's no morality in climbing now, you know. It's just every man for himself.' I forget how anti-women the climbing establishment still is.

'It was like that when Graham died. It's man against man, not man against nature.'

'She still fights back.'

'But she's getting weaker. There's no defence against technology,' I say.

'So there's nothing anyone can do about it.'

'I suppose not,' I say, think of how a satellite phone might have saved Graham. 'So, you think the guys from this new expedition are after Simon?'

'I didn't say that. But someone is. How many illegal expeditions go up there a year?'

'Dunno. There can't be many. It's much too regulated.'

'Once you're up on the mountain, who's going to stop you?' she says.

'And you think someone's got something planned, or that Simon went on one of these illegals, and found Irvine.'

'Something like that. How else do you explain all this?'

'I can't. I wish Simon would let us into his secret. We could help him, in some way.'

We've reached the market square by now.

'I'm starving,' she says.

'Then let's have breakfast. Anything in particular?'

'A full English would be good,' she says.

'The best place for that is near College.'

'Why didn't you say so sooner?'

'I'm not thinking straight. And I didn't know what you wanted.'

'Whoever says the best way to a man's heart is through his stomach obviously never met you.'

'Sorry,' I say. 'I just don't love food as much as you do. And that's not fair, because you can eat what you want and how much you want.'

'I'm just lucky,' she says, and turns on her heels. 'Let's

go. I need food.'

In the restaurant, coats hanging over the backs of our chairs, rucksacks chucked into the corner behind the table, we order big breakfasts. She'll probably eat most of mine, too.

'What does Simon actually care about?' I say, my mouth full.

'History. That's what. History and truth.'

'Why isn't he the same person to me that he is to you? And it's not just because you're twins. There's something else. He's such an arrogant git.'

'He always was,' she says. 'He's afraid to show he cares. He doesn't want people to think he's soft.'

'He's not soft, and he knows it.'

She shrugs, shovels another forkful of bacon into her mouth. 'If you'd have been here with him, if you'd have come back here after the accident, you might have got to know him better, you might have become friends.'

'What's that supposed to mean?'

She waves her fork at me. 'That came out wrong. I didn't mean you should've been here. I'm just saying that neither of you have ever given yourselves the chance of getting to know each other, not properly.'

I grunt. 'We're too far apart, him and me. I'm not sure it would've made a difference.'

She smiles. 'I think it would, and maybe the time will come.'

'When we rescue him?' I say.

'Maybe.' She puts down her knife and fork, leans back. 'I think I've changed my mind.'

'You're full already?'

She shakes her head. 'About finding these Buddhist places.'

'Why?'

'Well, he's not going to be there, is he? And if he was, we'd never find him. He's not that stupid or predictable.'

'What do you want to do instead?'

'I want to not listen to him for once, go back to his room, and sit there to see if something bad is going to happen to us.'

'Be bait, you mean?'

'Exactly,' she says.

'Are you mad?'

'I married you. Everyone thought I was crazy for doing that. And that you were.'

'Fair enough,' I say.

'What do you think?'

'It's dangerous, too dangerous.'

'Does it matter, James?'

'Death's sort of irreversible.'

'But we're away from home together for the first time.'

'That means it's ok to die, does it?'

'You're risk averse.'

'I always have been,' I say. 'Since then, anyway.'

'Now's your chance not to be. To make it up to yourself.'

The orange juice is cold in my throat. 'Everything or nothing, you mean?'

'Except for the fact I think you're being a bit over-dramatic.'

'You don't think it's dangerous, then?'

'I don't really care. I want to find Simon.'

'What you mean is that you want to find Irvine. It's not really just about Simon any more for you.'

'And that.'

'No matter what?'

'No matter what. As long as we're together.'

'And the house?' I say. 'I should have started sorting that out instead of coming over here.'

'It's replaceable,' she says. 'What counts is now, us,

being together. Not the future, not yesterday.'

'Do you want to drink to that?'

'Yeah,' she says, waves her hand at the waiter. 'Bottle of red, please.'

'I didn't mean with wine.'

'I know, but I did. It's like I've never known you before. You're alive.' She looks at me like she's never looked at me before, like she's never noticed me before.

'I'm not quite sure how to take that.'

'Then stop thinking about it, and just live it.'

'When this is all over,' I say.

'We'll be dead, or I'll be up the duff.'

I choke on my juice.

'You're an idiot,' she says. 'No two ways about it. You English are so frigging repressed. They must breed you that way.'

'Whatever you say.'

The wine arrives and we drink until the second bottle's empty, until all the words have run out, and I feel no more pain.

'Come on,' she says. 'Let's go.'

'I'd better get something together for the DB.'

'Who?'

'The Domestic Bursar, the guy you argued with about staying in Simon's room.'

'Oh, that boring little feller?'

'If that's what you say.'

'He was just a bit posh and difficult.'

'That's his job,' I say. 'It's nothing personal.'

'I suppose I shouldn't have sworn at him.'

'That might have been a good idea. And Simon being a bit more friendly with the people in charge.'

'That was never going to happen. It's not in his character.'

'I know that. You know that. The DB doesn't.'

She sways a little when she gets up. 'I suppose we

could just go straight to bed, couldn't we? And make a start?'

'You said not before all this is over.'

'I was lying, teasing you. Isn't that what women are supposed to do?.'

'We'll see,' I say. Am I really ready for this?

'You're getting cold feet.'

'No. I'm just a repressed, sensible Englishman.'

'Dickhead.' She slings her rucksack over her back while I'm paying and nearly knocks over the empty bottles.

'That's me,' I say, grab her by the elbow, and lead her back out into the sunshine before she can cause any more damage.

'Bugger, it's bright,' she says.

'That's what happens when you drink before noon.'

She shrugs. 'Good laugh, though.'

'Yes.' I put my arm over her shoulder. 'Have we ever had this much fun?'

'We must've done.' She pulls me into her, against the next vacant wall, kisses me. 'Mmm. You're such a nice man.'

I laugh. 'Thank you.' My stomach feels warm.

'You're welcome.' She pulls me along the road by my hand. I don't resist.

We get to the Porter's Lodge. I'm slightly swaying when I make out the cheque, stick it in an envelope, hand it to the porter.

'Good breakfast, sir?' he says and smiles.

'Too good, I think.'

'Impossible. You only live once,' he says.

'You could be right.'

'Have a good day, sir.'

When we get outside, halfway across the court, opposite the new library, she starts laughing out loud. 'They're so bloody polite,' she shouts. 'Couldn't he just have told you it was a little early to get pissed?'

'He could've done, but he probably thought it was best to be kind.'

'How many people ever get to experience this place?' she says. 'It's so remote from the real world. You and Simon don't know how privileged you are.'

'I do. I always have done. I just never appreciated it, and that's something different.'

'Pfft.' She shakes her hands at me. 'Some of us have had to work for what we've got.' Her hands are so thin, her forearms so strong. Made for the mountains.

'I do know.'

We walk on, through the courts full of echo, on ancient stones until we're stopped in our tracks. The shadows of Third Court are illuminated by a flickering light from Simon's room, an unnaturally bright orange. Before we realise what's happening, the window blows out, splinters everywhere, and we hear the crackle of history burning.

Chapter 9

Every year, just before the monsoons, they came down from the mountains, the few capable of adapting again to the lower altitude, and those who chose not to stay on the mountain forever. They climbed in silence, and always at night. It was an ancient ritual, passed on only by word of mouth. When it had started, none of them knew. They didn't have to. It was there. It existed. It had always been part of their truth, of their holiness.

Although the route was carved into its face by centuries-old markings, the mountain never gave of itself easily. No descent or ascent was simple, always a challenge to individual bravery and collective prayer, always a chance each of them took, to come away into their home valley alive. On their way down, they passed secret memorials to the fallen and the lost.

The procession reached the monastery before dawn. They carried no torches, no lights of any kind. The gates opened without summons, closed again behind the black-clad group in the valley's gloom. No-one saw them.

When the white men had first appeared, the monks tried to warn them off the mountain with tales of blasphemy and demons, but nothing could stop the explorers from trying themselves against the temper of the towering rock. The monks had benignly nodded their assent, knowing all the while that they had already reached the top, that they worshipped there every year, to celebrate Chenrezi's gift, to remember how he had been wafted by a sunbeam to the Holy Snows at the top of Chomolungma millennia ago.

'Did they succeed, Virya?' the Lama said to the leader of the returned.

'Yes,' Virya said, now in his orange robe. 'And they found the bowl.'

The Lama sighed. 'It had to happen. What did they do?'

'They buried it again, with some of their papers.'

'Did you move it?'

'We left it where they buried it. It's safest there.'

'They'll tell their people.'

Virya shook his head. 'They won't. They fell on their way down.'

'A tragedy,' the Lama said, his face pale. 'I wouldn't have wished that on them.'

'The one who worshipped here survived the fall.'

'And you took him back to the monastery?'

Virya nodded. 'He's been asleep for over a week, and there are no signs of him waking. He's getting weaker, and I don't think he wants to be without his friend.'

'Where is his friend's body?'

'On the edge of the Yellow Stones.'

'That's much too dangerous to reach,' the Lama said.

Virya nodded. 'We thought it best to try to save a life, not bury a lost one.' He didn't tell the Lama that he had tried to tip-toe his way across the brittle scales of the mountain to the body, that he'd only stopped trying when a shower of sharp slivers of rock had threatened to engulf him.

'You were right,' the Lama said. 'What will you do now?'

'I'll go back up with the novices tomorrow. Maybe Tara has managed to wake him by now.'

The Lama smiled. 'Your daughter has earned her healer's name quickly.'

'She's healed many on the mountain this year. We would have lost some of us if she hadn't been so gifted.'

'We always knew she was,' the Lama said. 'You should be very proud of her.'

'I am. And I tell her so all the time.'

'Good. You'll need to rest now if you're going back tomorrow.' The Lama paused, leaned closer to Virya. 'Don't you ever feel you want to stay down here with us?'

'I'm not sure I could,' Virya said. 'I've grown used to living up there.'

'I had to come back after two years. At first I thought I was a chosen one, but then it became so difficult, impossible, to live there. It's a great sadness to me.'

'You're more important to us down here. No-one could be better at dealing with the white ones than you. I couldn't fool them into believing we're afraid of the mountain.'

The Lama smiled. 'Maybe I'm a fool then.'

'That's not what I meant. I was praising you.'

'I know that. Just as I know I shouldn't really deceive them.' He prayed for forgiveness from the gods every day.

'But it's necessary. Who knows how many would have tried for the summit if it hadn't been for you?'

'I fear those days are over,' the Lama said. 'And what if someone else finds the bowl? Then everyone will know.'

'That won't happen for many more years now. They've grown sick of the mountain and its deaths,' Virya said. 'They'll leave us in peace now.'

'It's a shame so many have already died. That was never meant to be.'

'All mountains are dangerous, and they always will be.'

'They're an unrelenting temptation to those who want to conquer them.' The Lama leaned back in his chair. 'That's the way it will be forever.'

'It's not always a question of conquering. The one up there, the dying one, he just wanted to see the world from its highest place, not prove a point. It's their culture that wants to prove something.'

'Like those who would be our masters?' The Lama enjoyed these all too rare conversations with Virya, trusted him, appreciated his wisdom.

'Empires are all alike. The Chinese are no different to the English.'

'They all think they're superior to us, more sophisticated, stronger, and richer.'

'Those who lead them are hungry for power, nothing else. They don't understand that real power is the power we have over ourselves, not over others.'

'I still fear for the future. What will happen when we're gone?'

'The mountain will watch over us,' Virya said. 'No matter how difficult times become.'

'The bowl must be moved. It should be in the High Monastery, not on the summit. It will have to be carried to the summit every year for the celebration.'

'It may be too late now to move it.'

'Next spring then, at the latest,' the Lama said. 'Just in case others come.' He patted his friend's shoulder. 'Take care, Virya. I have a bad feeling about all this.'

The novices were nervous. Although they had trained for this day, although the last few years of their lives had been leading up to this, their faith allowed them a few moments of doubt before they threw on their dark, hooded cloaks, took their bags, and headed for the gates. Their training had involved praying, fasting, and climbing blindfold. But always in the safety of the monastery, where helping hands would catch them, where there was no unknown abyss, where no unseen crevasse could swallow them. And now, out beyond the walls, the reality of their calling waited. Some of them would never return.

The gates opened inwards without a sound. Above, the stars were sharp and clear into the night. The monks didn't speak as they moved out onto the desert of ice and frozen earth, into the never-ending wind. They had taught their feet to tread lightly, their bodies to be in balance, their steps soft. Mist rose from their mouths as they moved away, and the gates swung closed. They were on their own now.

Virya, always at the pace of the slowest of the ten monks with him, made sure they kept moving quickly enough to make their first camp before dawn came. They would hide in the meditation caves only they knew, that no-one else had discovered, that no-one else would find. He turned and looked back at the dark shadow of the monastery, now far behind. He smiled. This was the best way, to be always on the move, always going up.

The fires from the white men's camp shone across from the left of their route, subdued flickers, only an hour's walk away. He wondered if they had any idea that there was other life on the path to the mountain, wondered how much longer they would stay here now it was certain that their two companions were lost. They would have to go home, to their far-off country, and explain what had happened.

That first morning, their first of the five days they would spend climbing, the monks settled into their cave. The entrance was mostly obscured by boulders; the rest they covered up with white, rough material to which the snow would cling even through the stormiest of days. Their camouflage had always been this complete, to hide them not only from the new threat of the men from the West, but also from others in the East who persecuted them. They slept through the day, ready to move on again as soon as dusk had settled and the cold came. Five days without fire.

There were some alarms on the way, there always were. Virya had been doing this for over twenty years, and some of his friends had died on the mountain. He had mourned and rejoiced, because he didn't consider them lost. They were always here, with him, to guide him away from the obstacles at which they had faltered. And for some years now, he'd always led all his charges safely to the High Monastery. This year would be no different.

The cold was at its worst from the third day onwards. They had expected this, had learned not to resist the cold, but to let it into their bodies, to greet it as a friend, to draw energy from it, to welcome it, to let it become a part of them. This way their hands remained flexible, their bodies supple and strong. Their fingers could still read the mountain, the marks in the rocks their predecessors had left, even through the snow and the ice, even when the wind sliced the air into shards of glass. Their faith was not to fight pain, but to embrace it.

The procession had to take five days; that was the tradition, that was the proscribed way. It left them time to pray, to grow accustomed to their new life, gave their lungs time to expand into the thinner air, their breath to slow from the quickened beat the first day brought with it. It allowed them to meditate, to share new thoughts with their fellow believers, to become one with the mountain, to feel her heartbeat under their fingertips.

On the sixth dawn, they climbed up into the High Monastery, through the frozen crags where the sun never reached, along fissures in the rock so sharp their fingers began to bleed. Virya, the last to pull himself up through the narrow gap in the rocks, threw his hood back, pushed the counterweight into place above the sheer drop down the mountain's north face, and led his group up the steep steps, carved into the mountain by the first monks to discover this natural sanctuary.

Torches lit their way, warm yellow flames fixed to the

yellow and brown rock walls. Moments later they reached the Great Hall, filled with those monks whose duty it was to greet them.

'You kept to the agreed time, Virya, as usual,' the High Lama said.

'It's the only way to succeed, Tenzin Lama.'

'No faster, and no slower. The secret of reaching the heights.'

'That's what we were taught.'

'Our ancestors taught us well,' Tenzin Lama said. 'Now come and eat. Your fast is over.'

They all gathered around the stone table, stood for a prayer of thanks for safe travelling, then sat and ate in silence.

'Is there any news of the white man?' Virya said when they had finished.

'He's still alive, thanks to Tara,' Tenzin said. 'She hasn't left his side,' Tenzin said. 'We have to force her to break her fast. You know how stubborn she is.'

'She's like her mother,' Virya said. 'Stubborn and beautiful, with no regard for herself.'

'I'm sorry you have to be reminded of your loss every day.'

'Don't be. The mountain has her now. That's what she always wanted. I was lucky to have her as my wife for as long as I did.'

'We were all lucky to know her. Tara will be an even greater healer than she was.'

'Yes,' Virya said with pride. 'Has he woken up?'

'No. But he's not getting any weaker either. Not for the moment.'

'I'll go to her now.'

'She's expecting you.'

Virya walked along the winding corridors, some lit by the torches, some by a miracle of nature illuminated by natural light, until he reached the chamber where his daughter looked after the sick. He rounded the corner, saw her sitting by the white man's bed, holding one of his hands in both of her hands, head bowed, eyes closed, lips moving. He waited for her to sense his presence.

At last, she stopped mouthing her prayer. She turned round, her braided hair swinging with her, and lifted her almond-shaped eyes up to him. 'Father.'

'Tara.'

'I don't think I can heal him. I'm at a loss.'

'Tenzin said he was growing no weaker.'

'That doesn't mean he's getting stronger, though. I can't think of anything else besides what I'm already doing.'

'Is there nothing I can do?' He tried to reach out to her despair, and found he couldn't.

'He wants to be with his friend, out there on the mountain.'

'Then maybe you should let him go. Let him pass to the other side.'

'It's against my principles to do that.'

'Isn't it against your faith to resist the will of the gods? If you can't heal him, isn't it their choice what becomes of him?'

She shook her head, laid her hand on her chest. 'They are telling me to save him, to try to save him.'

'Then keep trying, even if it's only with the warmth of your hands.'

'Maybe he needs thicker air, maybe he can't live up here, not even for a short time.'

'We can't take him down, though,' Virya said. 'Not now. That would surely kill him.'

'I know.'

'Maybe sleeping longer will let his body get used to being up here. Perhaps it just takes his kind longer.'

'Maybe,' she said. 'But I'm tired.'

'Then let me sit here while you sleep.'

'You've got so much to do.'

'Another few hours won't stop me,' he said. 'It never could.'

'You should be sleeping after your journey. It's a hard climb, over and over again.'

'The older I get the less sleep I need.' He shrugged. 'I need to live every moment of this life if I can.'

'You're thinking about my mother, aren't you?'

Virya nodded. He always thought about her, every single day, the wife he'd lost on her first climb down to Rongbuk after Tara was born, blamed himself for letting her go, when they'd been full of the excitement of youth and parenthood.

'She was too weak,' he said. 'Still full of you, thinking of how she should look after you. She forgot to feel her way down the mountain.'

'You should stop reliving it. It doesn't do you any good.'

'I can't,' he said and touched his head. 'She's always in here, and I still miss her.'

'It makes me feel responsible.'

'It's not supposed to. And you're not responsible.'

She stood up, her shape narrow against the tapestries on the rock walls. 'Are you sure you're strong enough to sit here for a while?'

'I'm sure. There's nothing I'd rather do than help you.'

'I'll get someone to wake me in a few hours.'

'Sleep for as long as your body needs to.'

She walked up to him, put her arms around his waist, the top of her face below his chin. 'Thank you, Father.'

'We will heal him, daughter, we will.'

Virya sat down on the low stool next to Irvine's bed, wrapped his brown fingers around the white, scarred hand, lowered his head and began to pray, willed his strength into the dying man's veins.

Irvine's breath rattled up through his chest, his body convulsed and bent. 'George?' he coughed. 'Hold on. I'm here.'

Chapter 10

Suddenly sober, we recoil from the explosion. I rip my phone from my jacket, jab 999 into the keypad, shout into the phone, throw it back into my pocket. Alice is on her knees, her phone in her hand.

'What are you doing?' I shout.

'Trying to get hold of Simon.'

'There's no point.'

The flames grow fiercer, the heat dragged out across the court towards us by the cold. I hear sirens in the distance. 'How the hell?' The wind rips the words from my mouth. I race towards the heat, throw myself into the staircase opening, and drag the fire extinguisher off the wall and out into the open, hit the button, point it at the flames, my face turned away.

Porters arrive, two skidding into the court from the Bridge of Sighs, and two more sprinting in from the front gate. 'Use the fire extinguishers from the other staircases,' one of them shouts. Five of us are now trying to save Simon's room, the whole building, the old library opposite, stop the fire from spreading.

There's a siren close by now, loud over the sound of wheels on gravel. They've come through the back, right up across the Kitchen Bridge behind Simon's room. Firemen run through the arch, drag the hose along the red ground, shout at us to get away from the heat, arms pumping, facemasks on. Water gushes from the hose, splinters into the old room, all traces of patina and age and wisdom gone, all illusion of peaceful learning disappeared.

Alice is on the ground, across the court, her back against the wall of the library. She's crying uncontrollably, her body shaking, her face a white mask, her eyes swollen and closed.

'It's ok now,' I say, kneel down and put my arms

round her.

'What if we'd been in there?'

'We weren't. Simon saved us.'

'But who, who'd do this? What have we done?'

I shrug. 'I don't know.'

'There's no point trying to get to Simon, is there?' She's angry now, her eyes red with rage. 'We'll have to find who did this.'

'How will we do that?'

'We'll start at the beginning.'

'Which one? Here, now, or then, all those years ago?' The steam and smoke fill my lungs and the sky.

'Not Mallory, but Irvine, like Simon said. We've got to climb that mountain in Norway.'

'At this time of year? It'll be murderous.'

'Yes,' she says. 'Now, tomorrow.'

'You're mad.' I shake my head and shiver. 'I can't. No way.'

'You can. You'll do it with me.' She's on her feet now, her arms round me, her tears gone, strong again. 'You've always been able to do it.'

One of the porters comes over to me. 'You ok, sir? Madam?'

'We're fine.'

'Bloody lucky, you were,' he says. 'The coppers'll want a word, though, mind.'

'Then tell them to get a move on,' Alice says. 'We've got a plane to catch.'

He coughs to stop himself from laughing, then says, with a straight face, 'They're already at the Porter's Lodge, madam. I think you know the way.'

'They'll be bound to be coming this way,' she snorts. 'Let's go meet them.'

I follow her, after winking at the porter and shaking my head. Is it just we men who need this companionship of mockery?

'There they are,' she says, just as we walk into Chapel Court. 'Let's get this over with.' She walks up to the guy at the front, who looks too young to be employed. 'I think you were coming to see us,' she says.

'If you're the couple from Dr Young's room, yes,' he says calmly.

'What do you need to know?'

'Your names and address would be good.'

She gives them to him. I can't get a word in.

'And you say you left the room this morning?' he says.

I nod.

'Yes,' she says. 'And, no, we didn't set fire to anything before we left, and we didn't do any cooking and leave the gas ring on.'

'Your brother used to smoke in there, though, didn't he, miss?' he says.

'How would I know?' She raises her arms. 'And he's not been here for over a week.'

'I have my sources. Brother's a porter,' he says, looking at me. He turns back to Alice. 'No, so I hear. Missing, is he?'

Alice shrugs.

'You don't want to file a missing persons report, then?'

'I'm not his keeper,' she says. 'He's an adult, isn't he?'

He suppresses a smile. 'I suppose so. People round here don't seem to be particularly worried about him.'

'They're used to him,' she says.

'Quite. So, what were you doing back in College when you'd decided to leave?'

'I sort of changed my mind about leaving. I like it here too much.' She regains her composure quickly.

'And where are you off to now?'

'Oh, you know what we women are like, Constable. I changed my mind again and want to get to Stansted to get a plane.'

'Where to? Anywhere nice?'

'Does that matter?'

'I'd like to be able to get in touch.'

'But I'm married.'

The policeman blushes. 'I need to know where you are in case I need some more information, or if I've got something to tell you.'

'Oh.' She laughs. 'Haven't you ever heard of mobile phones?'

'I just wanted to make sure.'

'I don't know where we're going yet,' she says. 'I'm just a flibbertigibbety old Kiwi girl.'

He looks at me. 'Is she always like this?'

'Not all the time,' I say. 'Just now and again.'

'I trust neither of you will be driving.'

'Quite right, constable,' she says. 'We were just on our way to catch a cab. Anything else?'

'No,' he says, looks disappointed. 'Just keep your phones charged, please.'

She has this effect on most men. She melts them or bullies them. It helps being tall, I suppose, and beautiful. And clever. All the things that I'm not.

'Sure thing,' she says, shakes his hand. 'How nice to meet someone so efficient.'

He blushes again.

'Thanks for your help,' I say.

'Let's go, James,' she commands, and turns out towards the street. 'We'll be back,' she whispers. 'I can feel it.'

The taxi's already there when we get to the Porter's Lodge. We throw our bags into the boot, and get in.

'You don't think I was overdoing it, do you?'

'Men find it difficult to resist you,' I say. 'You could've gone a little easier on the poor boy. You made him blush.'

'You never blush, not at anything I do.'

‘That’s because I can never figure you out. It’s all way over my head.’

‘Even after all this time?’ She leans back in her seat, puts her head on my shoulder.

‘Even after all this time.’

‘Is that a good thing?’

‘Difficult to know, the state of mind I’m in. I suppose people might say it keeps a marriage alive.’

‘And, does it? Or are you bored of me, of us, of our marriage?’

I shrug. I don’t know what to feel or think. ‘It’s like I’ve been sleepwalking through the last ten years.’

‘You haven’t really. It just feels like it. We’ve had lots of good times. You’ve just had a lot to cope with.’

‘And you haven’t?’ I say.

’Only you. But nothing in my head. Nothing like what you’ve been going through.’

‘Things’ll be different from now.’

‘They already are.’ She doesn’t move her head. ‘Hey, it’s our first big adventure together.’

‘So it is. I hope I won’t let you down.’

‘Why would you?’

‘I might throw up on the plane again.’

‘At least you’ll be on the plane.’

I grunt.

She says nothing, falls asleep.

The sudden jolt of the car wakes me. I must have nodded off as well. I nudge Alice. ‘We’re here.’

She jumps up and out of the car quicker than me, able to switch sleep off like a machine. I pay the driver and get out. Alice hands me my rucksack.

‘Come on,’ she says. ‘Let’s see if we can get across there today.’

‘Where do we need to fly to?’

‘Tromsø’s the nearest airport, I reckon.’

We walk into the terminal, she striding ahead of me,

head held high, hair fluttering in the warm breeze coming out of the door. At least I'm not shaking this time. I catch up with her, walk next to her, feel her posture dragging mine up with it.

An hour later we have cheap tickets. We have to fly to Rygge, which is somewhere near Oslo, and then change for a flight up to Tromsø. It'll take a bit over four hours. And the flight's in two hours.

'That gives us enough time to get through Security,' she says.

'It won't take that long, will it? It took no time in Christchurch.'

'You're back in Europe, old man. Remember? And they're obsessed with security and stuff. Anyway, we can do some duty-free shopping.'

'You're off on an adventure and you want to go shopping?'

'Isn't that what girls do best?'

'I wouldn't know,' I say.

'Come on,' she says. 'You enjoy it, too.' She laughs. 'I do know.'

It only takes us half an hour to get through, in the end. Then she leads me off shopping, but not for what I expected. Instead, she gets us long johns and thick socks, gloves and balaclavas, everything we'll need to keep warm when we go climbing Irvine's Norwegian mountain.

We're sitting at the gate, waiting. It's almost too much for me. She grabs my hands, squeezes them tightly, feels the restlessness in them, strokes them, pulls them to her, takes a deep breath, over and over again, makes me slow my breathing to be in time with hers. At last it's time to walk down the metal ramp to the plane.

'You booked Priority,' I say.

'I thought it would be best, for both of us.'

'I should have done that. You think of everything.'

'I try to.'

'Thank you.'

'You're welcome, husband.'

'What a strange honeymoon,' I say. 'Ten years too late.'

'It was worth the wait.' She clings to me.

The temperature changes when we move into the cabin, warmer, drier.

'Choose your seat,' she says. 'Take your time.'

'Right at the back, by the tail. It's the safest.'

'That's where I always sit. Window or aisle?'

'Aisle. I may need to … '

'Quick getaway. I understand.'

'Do you mind?' I say.

'Why should I mind?'

'And I don't want to look down. Not yet.'

'It's fine, James, it really is.'

'We're strangers on this trip, aren't we?'

'The best kind of strangers,' she says. 'Strangers who love each other.'

She's right.

The engines raise their pitch. I close my eyes.

'Keep them open,' she says. 'You'll feel less out of control, like you know what's going on.'

'I'll try.' I'm sweating now.

'You do that.'

The plane starts rolling down towards the runway, turns at the end, faces back along the long strip. I can't see it, just feel it. She takes my hands again, pulls them into her lap. The howl begins. It's worse than when I left New Zealand or Singapore.

'I feel bad,' I say.

'Already?'

'Not that kind of bad.' I have to raise my voice over the engine noise.

'What then?'

'That I've not checked on any of our friends in Christchurch. I don't know what's going on.'

'They're all safe,' she says. 'I've been texting them.'

'And everything else?'

'Yes. Now just focus. We'll cross the Christchurch bridge when we have to.'

'What about the house?' The plane rises, the weightlessness grabs at me.

'It'll be fine. We'll deal with that when we get back. Let's just enjoy this.'

My stomach pitches. Space curves around me like a dark wall with no end. The cabin lights are off. I catch a glimpse of England swaying beneath us, outside the windows. The seatbelt lights click off. She lets go of my hands.

I rush to the toilet, holding on to the walls, slam the door shut, rip up the seat, throw up until my stomach's empty of the wine, of the Full English I shouldn't have eaten, until I think I can feel the acid eating into me. I can't do this, not even with her. I wipe my lips, rinse them with the water I can't drink, wipe my face, my sweaty, cheesy face. Finally pull open the door when I think I'm ready to face her. I drop into the seat next to her.

'Better?' she says.

'Not really. That was worse than before.'

'It'll take time. Nothing like that fixes itself quickly.'

'I thought I had it sorted.'

'You will have it sorted sooner than you think.'

'How can you keep believing?' I say.

'Because it's easy to believe in you.'

I close my eyes and see all my sins of omission. 'That makes one of you then.'

'Hmm.'

'Ladies and gentlemen.' The pilot's voice wakes me. I've been asleep for almost an hour. 'The weather in

Oslo is the worst they've had for forty years,' he says. 'We're not going to be able to land there. And the whole of southern Norway is covered by the blizzard. We're having to divert to Bergen.'

'Will he have enough fuel?' I whisper.

'He wouldn't be diverting there if he didn't.'

'Shit.' The panic rises through my weak knees.

'Calm down. It'll be fine.'

'That's easy for you to say.'

'Easy for you to believe, too. This isn't Kathmandu, not some rust bucket of a plane.'

'It can still crash, though, can't it?' I say.

'Everything can crash and burn,' she says, a deliberately harsh whisper. 'But this won't. There are things for us to do.'

'I wish I had your blind faith.'

'Kiss me.' She grabs me before I can react, puts her hand behind my head, grabs my hair, pulls my face to her face, her other hand on my cheek, a caress so gentle she must be an angel. 'You're mine, and I'll look after you,' she says when she comes up for air. 'I'll never let anything or anyone frighten or hurt you. I promise.'

My breath has slowed down again, though my heart's beating fast with her aroma, her taste, and my bitterness. 'What was that for?'

'For you,' she says. 'To calm you. To mark you.'

'No-one else would want me.'

'You'd be surprised,' she says. 'You never could judge women. You don't even notice the way some of them look at you.'

The cabin lights go out and the plane begins to shake. The seatbelt signs go on again.

'Ladies and gentlemen, we're experiencing some turbulence because of the storm down there,' the pilot says. 'Please stay in your seats. We should be through this in just over an hour, and then we've got clear air into Bergen, where onward transport will be arranged for you. Clear and cold up there, minus fifteen centigrade, but no blizzard.'

'See,' she says. 'There's always somewhere safe to go, always a haven for those who need it.'

I close my eyes, say nothing, squeeze her hand, breathe in through my nose. No nausea, not now. In fact, I'm hungry. It'll have to wait till we get to Bergen. There's lots that'll have to wait. We won't get to Tromsø today.

Chapter 11

'How the hell are we supposed to get there?' she asks at the info desk.

The guy behind the desk shrugs, looks embarrassed. 'You'll have to wait till Sunday, or try to get to Oslo.'

'In this weather? That's why we got diverted in the first place.'

He shrugs again. 'It's one of those things.'

Her rage radiates.

'Thank you,' I say to the guy in Norwegian. 'Come on,' I say to her, take her by the elbow, lead her away from the queuing crowd. 'There's no point in arguing the toss with him.'

'Why not? I'm cross, and I want to get to the mountain.'

'Because that's what Norwegians are like. They're natural pessimists and pragmatists. For them, everything's just the way it is. No point questioning it. Something'll always turn up.'

'Since when were you an expert on Norwegian culture?'

'It's one of the places I wrote a guidebook about. I spent a lot of time here before I met you. But not up North.'

'So you suggest we just sit tight here?'

'We'll get back in the queue and insist they give us a hotel in the town centre, not here on the airport. That way we can get to see a bit of the city while we wait.'

'Time's running away from us,' she says.

'I can't see any other option. Unless you want to drive up to Tromsø from here, and that'll take just as long.'

'Are you serious?'

'We'd need to drive round the fjords, in and out from the coast, lots of miles, lots of bends. We'd tire ourselves out.'

'If you say so.' She's still angry. 'Why can't something be simple for a change?'

'Because it never is, and you know it.'

'Well, I'm not talking to him again. You do it. You seem to know the lingo.'

'Only a bit of it.'

'I'm not waiting outside, mind. It's too cold for that.'

When we got off the plane, the hairs in my nose froze as soon as we stepped into the open air and walked across to the terminal. It's as cold here as I've ever known it, and it was a relief to get out of the cold into this overfilled shack of an airport, where heaven knows how many flights have been diverted to. Southern Norway's a mess. They've not even been able to get the trains to run, which is unusual in itself.

'Try to find a seat in the café, then,' I say. 'I'll come over to you when I've done.'

'Fine.' She's frowning.

'Alice.'

'What?'

'Don't be grumpy. Relax.'

'I'll try,' she says.

'Get yourself some hot chocolate.'

'It's too late for that. I'm going to get myself a beer.'

'You'll have to take out a mortgage.'

'You're joking.'

I shake my head. 'It'll cost you three times as much as at home.'

'Oh, well; when in Rome.' She smiles at me. It looks only a bit forced.

'I'll sort us out,' I say.

She disappears into the crowd. I rejoin the queue, relax into waiting without counting the minutes. *Just be patient.*

An hour later I've got vouchers for a hotel right in the town centre. I had to fight for them, but I've got them.

I go to find her in the café. She's sitting crushed into a corner, at a tiny table with one empty chair next to her.

'Ah, at last,' she says.

'At least no-one else had the same idea. Everyone else was asking for hotels as near to here as possible. Oh, and I've got tickets for the next Tromsø flight as well.'

'If it goes.'

'It will. The weather's moving south. At least that's what he told me.'

'Are you going to have a beer?'

'I'll help you finish that one. Then we'll get going. There's lots to see.'

'Like what?'

'Wait and see. On the other hand, you might just want to spend two days in bed.' I look at her. 'I wouldn't complain.'

'You're a fool.'

'I know.' I grab the beer and empty it. 'Come on, woman.'

We catch the bus into the centre. It drops us off near the hotel, according to the map. The wind blows right through my clothes.

'Should have put on that new stuff you got us,' I say.

'You were in such a rush.'

'I'm starving, for a change.'

'Then let's get to our room and eat.'

The hotel's on a busy junction, but it doesn't have any sharp edges. Its main corner, looking down onto the street and out across to the mountains, is an elegant curve, five storeys high, and long, sinuous windows on each floor.

'Bet we haven't got one of those,' she mutters as we hurry ourselves in through the glass double doors.

'We'll see.'

'Mr and Mrs Young?' the receptionist asks when we walk up the stairs to the desk.

'Yes,' I say. That was another bonus for Alice, not having to change her surname. Almost as much of a coincidence as one of my old ex-friends finding out his wife-to-be had the passport number after his.

'How'd you swing this?' she whispers.

'What?'

'They're expecting us.'

'I got the airport to phone ahead for us. Only reasonable, don't you think?'

She's grinning now. 'It *is* like a honeymoon!'

'I told you.'

She hugs me. 'Thank you.'

'No worries, mate,' I say, and see the receptionist smiling. I blush.

'Your keys,' the blonde girl says. 'You're on the top floor. The lift is over there. Enjoy your stay.'

'Thanks,' Alice says and rushes off to the lift.

We say nothing as we're pulled upwards. The lift door opens onto the usual suspicious peace and quiet of windowless hotel corridors. We creep along the carpet, looking for the room.

'Here it is,' I say, put the key card into the lock, push the door open. The room's warm scent wafts out of its darkness. Across from us, the panorama that is Bergen at night shimmers in through the thick, tall windows.

'It is,' she shouts. 'It is the top corner room.' She races in, throws her rucksack onto the floor, rushes across to the window, pulls the net curtain back. 'Oh, isn't it wonderful?'

'You're a child,' I say, stand behind her, put my arms round her waist, hands on her belly, my nose in the nape of her neck, taste the Norwegian cold and her perfume.

'I'm just excited. Aren't you?'

'Do you regret the last ten years now?'

She shakes her head, puts her hands over mine, still

clasped round her waist. 'No. If there's one thing I regret it's that I couldn't get you out of yourself before now, that I wasn't strong enough to think of something to push you forwards.'

'It's almost like you've invented this whole scenario with Simon.'

'Oh, yeah, and arranged an earthquake.' She's not really laughing.

'Dinner, my dear?'

'Where?'

'There's pizza places and posh places, steak places and fish places. Your choice.'

'I feel like some rare meat tonight,' she says.

'Steady.'

She elbows me. 'Don't be rude.'

'Sorry. I'm just happy.'

'What are those mountains?' She points out through the window.

'The seven mountains of Bergen. There's lots of history here.'

'So we are in Rome, really,' she says.

'It's not as cold there. It's not normally this cold here. It's supposed to have an ocean climate.'

'We can't have everything. It's warm enough in here. That gives us something to look forward to after dinner.'

Two hours later we're in one of the restaurants eating the rare steak she asked for. We don't talk of Simon, or why we're here; we just live the moment like it's the first one we've had together, like it's the first time we've been together as man and wife, like it's a new beginning.

On the way back, in the crisp night, we walk along the waterfront, hand in hand, the thick water, half ice, rising and falling against the tide walls. It's quiet; just the occasional car sidles by, drifts off into the distance.

The mountains surround us, dark against the moon.

'We could hike across those hills tomorrow, couldn't we?' she says.

'We could.'

'Do you want to? Or am I railroading you into something you'd rather not do?'

I stare up at the top of this valley, feel pulled towards those low peaks, feel like walking amongst the trees up there, to be free of the buildings, the people, to be free of the fears that have clouded my life since the day she found me. 'It would be a good test.'

'I'll look after you.'

'Maybe I won't need looking after, for once.'

'We'll see.'

'Yes, we will.'

'I love you,' she says.

'I love you, too.'

We slip into the warmth of the hotel, allow ourselves a glass of red wine, ask the receptionist where we can get supplies from for tomorrow. Then we go upstairs, into the dark light, without putting the lamps on, without closing the curtains, and lie in bed, afterwards, watch the mountains through the windows, watch the spectres of light and life flicker in through the glass, waiting for us, opening their arms to us.

The next day dawns bright and sharp, the air clear, clear like it never is in England or New Zealand. We get dressed, cram one rucksack full of all the warm gear we have, leave the other one empty for supplies.

'How long are you planning on being up there?' I say.

'All day, if we can.'

'The days are short here. Much shorter than most people think.'

'Let's take a torch,' she says.

'We should be able to get a couple of headlamps in the shop she told us about.'

'We'll do that then. We should be fine.'

'No risks, though,' I say. 'Please.'

'I don't plan on taking any.'

'However simple it looks. There are hidden dangers everywhere.'

'I promise. We won't be able to do all seven, will we? So we can take it nice and easy.'

'I don't think so,' I say. 'But we've got two days. We could go up again tomorrow.'

'Let's take it as it comes.'

We breakfast, shop, and then we're ready, wrapped up against the cold, gloves, long johns, hats, rucksacks on back. I feel odd, my boots heavy on my feet, my heart pumping, hoping I'll be able to do this.

'They're foothills, James,' she says.

'I know they are. I can't help being nervous.'

'And they've got wide paths.'

'I can see that.' We're standing in the marketplace with a map in hand. I do hate feeling like a tourist, hate being a tourist. But that's all we ever are, all of us, in this nomadic life we lead in the West, nothing but tourists in countries that aren't ours. And sometimes strangers in our own country, when we've been cast out by those who think they own us.

By lunch time we've reached three of the seven peaks. I'm surprised at how fit I must still be, never once out of breath. Although I'm sure she's been holding herself back, keeping the muscles in those marvellous legs in check, making sure I'm not pushing too hard, making sure I'm nowhere near any precipices, making it easy for me. I've not looked down once.

We're at the top of Mount Ulriken. There's snow underfoot, and some ice. There's a restaurant up here, but we just sit on a bench outside, unpack our food and drink, eat with our gloves still on our hands, stare out over the city.

'This is the highest one,' I say.

'Looks like it. How do you feel?'

'Fine. It's not like we're climbing anything, is it?'

'It's still high up,' she says. 'We've done well.'

'A foothill, like you said.'

'I'm proud of you,' she says.

'Why?'

'Would you have done this a couple of weeks ago?'

'No way.' *I wouldn't have loved you this much two weeks ago, because I'd given up.*

'See. You even had trouble driving over the pass to Lyttelton.'

'Don't remind me.'

'It's good, though, isn't it?'

I smile. 'Sure is.'

'Can we be bothered to do the other four?'

'I don't think the light will last. How about walking down in to the town and seeing what the light's like when we get down?'

'We could take the cable car.'

'Stuff that. We're here to walk me out of my head.'

She laughs. 'You said it. Ready?'

We get up and start down the trail. She makes sure I'm on the mountain side of her, nowhere near the drops. Our boots scrunch into the ground. We're halfway down when there's an unexpected gust of wind. It knocks her off her feet, off towards the steep slope. Automatically, she tries to throw herself away from the emptiness, only half manages, hands scrabbling in the dirt. Without thinking, I jump around to catch her, to pull her up, my head over the edge.

'Shit,' I shout. 'Hold on.'

She's back on the path now, panting, her eyes wide. I stand up, brush myself down. 'No danger of death,' I say.

'I know.' She looks at me in an odd way. 'I thought

you were afraid of heights.'

'I am.'

'Then …'

'I thought, at that moment, you'd gone.'

'No danger of death,' she says.

'I know,' I repeat. 'Maybe that's why I wasn't afraid. I don't want to lose you.' And I mean it, and I mean it forever, again, suddenly.

'Let's get back to the hotel,' she says. 'Last one down's a sissy.'

'You said no risks.'

'No risks.'

We slide and skid and laugh our way to the bottom of the mountain, with no thought of what might have been if we'd been on a bigger mountain. Better not to think of that. Because, sooner or later, she'll ask me to go back up again with her, up into the Death Zone, to look for Irvine, to find what Simon says he's found.

We do go up another of the seven hills early the next morning, but we use the funicular railway this time, to get to the top of Fløyen. Even though it's still well below freezing, it's hot out on the viewing platform up there, and we sit there for an hour, eating breakfast and drinking coffee, talking of everything and nothing.

'If you'd only just met me, would you still marry me?' I say, turn my face away from the open sea and the mountains and the city, and look at her.

She has her chin on her folded hands, her eyes on me. 'Yes,' she says. 'Yes, I would.'

'Why?'

'Because you're fun, you're clever, you're strong. Would you marry me?'

'On the spot.'

'Just because of my body.'

'No, not just because of that. Because you've got what

the Norwegians call sjel; you've got soul, you're unique. And, yes, you're beautiful. You'll always be beautiful.'

'Even when I'm eighty?'

'Even when you're eighty.'

'When I'm all wrinkly?'

'You'll have beautiful wrinkles.'

'And flabby?'

'You'll have gorgeous flab.'

'You're such a flatterer.'

'You said it.' I take her hand across the table. 'Would you really?'

'Yes,' she says. 'A hundred times yes. The last ten years haven't been as bad as you make them out to be.'

'What then?'

'Interesting. A challenge. A joy, for the most.'

There's nothing I can say to that.

We take the funicular back down, pack our bags, get a taxi back to the airport, in time for the mid-morning flight to Tromsø. It's pitch black there when we land two hours later, and there are metres of snow piled up alongside the roads.

'We should've booked a hotel,' she says.

'We did.'

Chapter 12

When we first get to the hotel, it doesn't feel like the right place. It looks just like a house, except brighter. There's a newspaper stand just inside the front door. I stop when I see the headlines. *To døde funnet på Jiehkkevarri.* I catch my breath, stare.

'What's the matter?' she says.

I pick up the paper. 'Hang on. This is too weird.'

'At least let me close the door.'

'Sorry.' I carry the paper with me to the reception desk. 'Shit.'

'Tell me then.'

'Let's check in first.' My hands shake as I hand the receptionist my card and our passports. His instructions to our room go in one ear and out of the other. I drag Alice with me to the bar. 'They've found two dead people on Jiehkkevarri.' They were foreigners, I tell her; that no ID was found on them, and that they'd been shot. Chinese, or something like that, apparently, but then the Norwegians don't care much about race.

'You don't think they're Simon's mates, do you?' she says.

'No idea. That's all it says. The police are clueless.'

'You don't think that Simon killed them?'

'Don't be silly,' I say. 'He told me they were his friends.' I try to recall exactly what he said about them, close my eyes, see his face again, sad and angry, aggressive and malleable at once. No, he couldn't have killed them. 'He said they were gone,' I say, my eyes open again. 'That's what he must have meant.'

'So he must have been here,' she says. 'He wouldn't know otherwise. We should go tell the police.'

'But we don't know for certain it's the guys Simon was with.'

'What are the odds?'

She's right, of course, but I don't want to go off to the police with a half-formed idea, with no idea at all, actually, about what's going on. And, no matter how much I dislike the man, I don't want to get Simon into trouble. Or his sister, for that matter, because that's what will happen. There's something odd about all this, something sinister which goes beyond anything Simon's capable of having conceived. 'I don't think it's a good idea to talk to the cops,' I say. 'All sorts of complications. Especially as we're not locals.'

She shrugs, changes tack. 'Is the mountain closed off?'

'It doesn't say anything about that. I guess we'll just have to find out when we get there.'

'But there'll be nothing there for us to find,' she says. 'It'll all have gone or been trampled on.' Her cheeks are red, and it's nothing to do with the cold outside, or the warmth inside.

'Calm down. They may have missed something. They don't know what to look for, do they?' And they don't. Simon's been and gone – if he was here at all, and that's that.

'I suppose not. But I can't help worrying now, can I?"

'Come on, let's get settled and eat.'

'D'you think we'll get up there tomorrow?' she says.

'If not tomorrow, then the day after.' I've got my fingers crossed behind my back.

'I can't wait now.'

'Neither can I, I suppose.' And I'm not shaking at the thought of it either, for a change.

'This'll be proper climbing, you know.'

'I know, I know.'

'Are you ok with that still?' she says.

'I think so. I'm a bit nervous, though, but then you know that as well.'

'I'd be disappointed if you weren't.'

We go upstairs. The room's small, but clean and

warm. We dump our bags in the corner.

'Do you want to see some of the night-life?' I say.

'I thought we'd try to go to bed early.'

'This is one of the most happening places in Norway, apparently.'

'What about getting sorted for tomorrow?' She sighs. 'I can't help being practical.'

'We'll ask at Reception, although I reckon it's too late to hire a car for tomorrow now. We'll have to do it first thing.'

'Even more reason not to stay out late.' She strokes the bed cover, smiles to herself, shakes her hair out of her face and turns to me. 'Sod it,' she says. 'You're right. Let's go eat and then let's have a party. It is our honeymoon, after all.' She gives me a long hug. All my doubts about us have gone now. *For now*, I doubt myself.

The receptionist confirms it's too late to get a car, suggests some of the cafes to us. It's too expensive in the restaurants, he says. When he asks us what we're doing here, we tell him we're off to Jiehkkevarri tomorrow.

'You'll need a guide,' he says. 'The glaciers are dangerous. There are many crevasses.' He doesn't say anything about the dead men.

'And where would we find a guide?' Not that I've got any intention of hiring one. Too many secrets to keep.

'There's a cabin in Lakselvbukt, about seven kilometres south of where the trail starts. The guy there can get you a guide, and you can stay at the cabin, too, if you want.'

'Have you got a phone number for him?' I say.

'Yes, sure.'

'Thanks.' I scribble down the number. 'I'll call him when we've found somewhere to eat.'

We do find somewhere, sit down, order. I call the guy

while we're waiting. He's called Birger. His English is much better than my Norwegian, as I find out when he changes to my language after my first sentence. After a couple of minutes, it's all sorted.

'He's expecting us at about noon tomorrow,' I say.

'But that means we won't get going till the day after.'

'It gives us time to make sure we've got the right gear. Or did you bring your crampons, just in case?'

'Course I did.' She laughs. 'I never leave home without them.'

'Very good.' I smile. 'And he said we could stay at the cabin for a couple of days if we wanted to. I said yes.'

'D'you think we'll need to?'

'You never know. And anyway, it might be fun, just you and me in the middle of nowhere.'

'We'll see.' She eats impatiently, voraciously, drinks the same way.

After dinner, we wander through the town. It's started snowing again, and the snow ploughs are out, keeping the streets clear for the drinkers. We pop in and out of bars, drink in some and not in others. But even I notice that our hearts aren't in this. We just want to get going, just want to start climbing, just want to test me and find an answer to Simon's riddle. So we drink one last drink and rush back to the hotel through the worsening snow.

It's time to wake too soon. Because we're so far north, the days are getting longer much more quickly than in England, much more quickly than they do in New Zealand when winter starts fading away. Not that there's any sign of winter fading here. The snow blows horizontally past our small window.

'Who's going to drive?' she says, still in bed.

'I'll do it. You obviously don't want to.'

'I didn't say that. It's just that they drive on the wrong side here. It's ages since you drove in Europe.'

'You've never driven in Europe, so it's definitely me who has to do it.'

'England doesn't count, I suppose.'

'No, it doesn't.'

'Fair enough.' She gets out of bed, walks to the bathroom. 'Stop staring,' she says.

'But you're gorgeous.'

'So you say.' She turns and disappears.

Breakfast done, we're off in search of cars and gear. The car's easily sorted out, and so's the gear, because here you can hire it. The only thing I decide not to hire is rope. I buy three new ones, along with new Karabiners, and a high-detail map. I don't want to leave this to chance. My heart's fast now. Time to drive.

We have to head south to get to Lakselvbukt. The fifty kilometres take much longer than they should. Sometimes the snow is so heavy I have to slow to walking pace. At one point I give up, pull over when I see a layby, and just wait for fifteen minutes. She says nothing, just huddles back in her seat, arms folded, eyes straight ahead.

At last, an hour after noon, we get to Birger's place, knock on the door, apologise for being late.

'Always the unpredictable weather,' he says, skin brown and rough, white stubble across his wrinkles. He must be at least seventy. 'It's too late for you to go out today,' he says. 'Bring in your things.'

He lives in the house next door, so we'll have this place to ourselves.

'We'll just drive down along the fjord to where the trail starts,' I say. 'To have a look at it.'

'Just don't start the mountain today,' he says. 'It's really not a good idea.' He hands me the keys. 'You have a guide?'

Alice and I look at each other.

'No.' I can't lie.

'But have you been on blue ice glaciers before?'

'Yes,' we both say.

'Then you know the drill, and you don't need a guide,' he says, his eyes twinkling. 'Good luck. I'll probably see you in the morning before you go.'

I close the cabin up, get into the car again. 'Come on,' I say to Alice.

'Why d'you think he smiled like that?'

'He must like you.'

'Stop being stupid. Be serious.' She looks at me. 'I'm not sure I like this new flippant James.' She laughs.

'Maybe he's glad someone's turned up who can actually climb mountains, not some summer tourist who doesn't know his arse from his elbow, and who doesn't understand blue ice.'

'That sounds more like it.'

We move slowly north, under the grey snow sky. It takes us half an hour to drive five kilometres, and we're still not there.

'What's the point?' she says. 'In this weather?'

'To do a recce. I want to know what I'm up against.'

'We won't see anything.'

'You don't know that. It could be clear over there.'

'Come on, James, look at the snow. Wouldn't it be best just to turn back and do it unseen tomorrow?'

'Just ten more minutes. If we're not there by then, we'll turn back.'

'I'm hungry and I'm tired.'

'Please.' I'm desperate to see this mountain, to get a picture of it in my head, to be frightened by it and to fight the fear overnight, and to beat it. It's the only way I think I can do this. It's not even a question any more of me thinking about her, or about Graham, or about heights and death. It's me thinking about me and nothing else. Just like it used to be.

'Fine.' She retreats into her seat even more.

I'm just about to turn round when the snow stops, and the clouds are ripped apart by whatever wind there is up there. We get a full view of the mountains.

'Jesus,' she says. 'That's amazing. I've never seen anything like it, not even in the Himalayas.'

I stop the car. We get out.

'See,' she says. 'That's the feature on the mountain there.' She points at the jagged rocks at the centre of our vision.

I look at the map. 'We've got the wrong mountain,' I say. 'Bloody Wikipedia's wrong. I should have known. That's not Jiehkkevarri, it's Holmbukttind. Jiehkkevarri's behind it. You have to climb this one first.'

'And this one's got the Everest step copy.'

'Yes.' I swear. 'The smaller one's the one we need to climb to follow Irvine.'

'Can you see any obvious routes?' she says.

'You tell me. I'm not an active climber, remember.'

'That big valley there, on the right, the one facing east, that's a possibility, but then we'd not be climbing the replica Second Step on the way up, only on the way down.'

'It looks like there's a massive glacier in the way anyway.'

'I don't think we can judge that from here,' she says.

'What about that narrow valley, to the left, the one facing northwest?'

'That's the one we really need to go up tomorrow, if we want to climb that Second Step on the way up. It's a lot steeper than the big valley, though.'

'We need to do it that way, though, don't we?' I say. 'There's no point otherwise.'

'If we want to put ourselves through what we think Irvine went through, yes. Although I don't think we can decide until we actually get to the junction of the two valleys.'

'We'd better set out at first light then. We might run out of time and light otherwise.'

'Agreed.' She grinds her teeth. 'Now, can we please go get some food?' She's almost shouting.

'Yes. Aren't you glad I persevered?' I turn away from the mountain, the images scratched onto my retinas, scraped into my memory, start playing the routes out already.

'Alright, smart arse.'

I avoid her play slaps, head back to the car, my head full of questions. What will we do tomorrow? Will we do it in one day? Why the confusion over the names? Why aren't there any police cars or tapes? Which route? Will I be strong enough? I want to do it now, not tomorrow. I might be weak again by then.

We get back, much quicker this time, eat in the local restaurant, go to bed early. Kiss and turn over. Too many nerves for passion. Too much adrenaline. Maybe that's counter-intuitive. She's snoring less than a minute later.

I can't sleep. I keep looking at the clock on my mobile, feel the tingling of my nerves under my skin, the night heavy around me, every movement an explosion of sound, not a whisper under warm sheets. After a while I've had enough. I get up, gather my clothes in an untidy bundle under my arm, tiptoe downstairs to where my bag is, grab my iron reserve of cigarettes, get dressed, and let myself out of the front door.

The taste of the cigarette is intoxicating. It's been such a long time. I lean against the wood pillar on the veranda, draw the smoke deeply into my lungs, for some reason don't feel the cold that radiates from the clear night, rest my head against the frozen wood, and look up at the stars.

‘Can’t sleep, eh?’ It’s Birger, appeared from nowhere, a pipe in his mouth, grey hair unkempt above his brown face.

‘You made me jump.’

‘Sorry,’ he says. ‘I thought you looked like a salmon out of water.’

‘I must be nervous about tomorrow.’

‘But you’re a climber.’ His look is full of questions.

‘It’s a long story, a very long story.’

‘Come over to my place and tell me about it then.’

‘I should be sleeping. We start early tomorrow.’

‘Det ordner seg,’ he says. ‘It’ll be fine.’

‘Are you sure?’

‘Oh, yes. On both counts.’

I follow him across the gravelly snow into his house. It smells of permanence and coffee.

‘Sit,’ he says, after leading me into the pine-panelled kitchen. He reaches up onto the top shelf. ‘Ever had akevitt?’

‘Too often.’

‘You like it, I take it, like all real people.’

‘Yes, unfortunately.’

‘Then let’s drink while you tell me your story. Let’s smoke, too.’

‘Is nothing forbidden in your house?’ I say.

‘Only not telling the truth,’ he says. He gets up again. ‘Wait. There’s something else we need.’ He opens one of the cupboards near the floor, pulls out a vacuum flask. ‘Kryddersild. Fish pickled in vinegar and herbs. Perfect. You ever eaten it?’

‘A long time ago.’

‘Good memories, then. Town folk don’t usually know it or like it.’

‘I suppose so.’ I remember some momentary friends, a cosy house set between rolling green fields, a tyre swing dangling from an ancient tree, careless afternoons and evenings full of laughter, kisses, and enormous mosquitoes.

He opens the flask, pulls entire tiny fish from it, guts them with a sharp knife, lays them in a porcelain bowl. 'Eat, drink.'

'For tomorrow you may die.'

'Any day. Enjoy what you have.' He grabs one of the fish, drops it whole into his mouth, and chases it down with a glass of the pungent yellow spirit. 'Now, tell me your story.'

So I tell him, tell him everything. I leave nothing out. He just sits there and listens, tops up my glass very time I've dragged down a mouthful of the potato spirit, feeds me raw fish, fresh bread, wordlessly, his green eyes on me all the while. And then I'm finished, and wrecked, and replete, in some weird and unexpected way.

'Good,' he says. 'There are too many climbers who don't tell their stories, who don't live them over and over again, who desert their dead comrades by never speaking of them.'

'It's the first time I've spoken about it, really, to someone else.'

'Except for your book.'

'What do you mean?'

He gets up again, crosses to the other side of the kitchen, runs his fingers along a shelf of books, pulls out a tattered copy. 'They sold it here, too. Very expensive it was.'

I sway on my seat. 'How did you know it was me?'

'I guessed from the photo. You look a lot older now.'

'Do you climb?' I say.

He shakes his head. 'Not any more. I'm too old.'

'Is that the only reason?'

'I'd have married if it hadn't been for the mountains.'

'Do you want to tell me your story?' He fascinates me,

so open and yet so secretive, so hidden, an old mystery.

'No, young man; I've told it so often it doesn't need another airing. Maybe when you get back.'

'I'll hold you to that.'

'If you remember, I'm sure you will.'

I look at the clock on the wall. Nearly three in the morning. 'I'd better get back.'

'How about one for the road?' He grins at me.

'I suppose I could.' Although I know I shouldn't.

'I wish you good luck for tomorrow. I hope you find what you want to find.'

'I'll need the luck, to climb and to find.'

'No you won't. Everything, everything's inside, in your head, in your heart. The good and the bad. The courage and the cowardice. All you have to do is choose.'

'And if I choose wrongly?' I say.

'I don't think you will. You feel ready now, don't you?'

'That's because I'm drunk.'

'No, it's not,' he says. 'It's because you want it so much, to be back up there in the mountains, because there's a secret you want to uncover, because you've been waiting for ten years to be sane and strong again.' He fills my glass and his to the brim with the pale amber spirit, lifts his up, and waits for me to lift mine.

I hold my hand in the air, shaking fingers around the glass. 'Thank you.'

'Skål,' he says. 'Lykke til. Good luck.' He tips the akevitt down his throat, thumps the glass back onto the table. 'Tomorrow evening, you and your beautiful wife will eat and drink with me, yes?'

'We'd be happy to.' I don't know what I'm saying. My tongue trips over my Norwegian.

'Good. Maybe I'll tell you my story then.' He gets up. 'Bring a rock back for me, from the mountains. I'd really appreciate that.'

'I'll try,' I say and stumble towards the door.

'Thank you,' he says.

Chapter 13

The next thing I know it's morning and Alice is pouring cold water over my head.

'What the hell did you do last night? I thought you were dead.'

'I couldn't sleep.' The alcohol and the fish congeal in my mouth. 'And Birger was still awake. So we had a drink or three.'

'You should have woken me. I'd have got you to bed.'

'Yeah. That's twice now I should've.'

She sighs. 'You can't blame me for this. It's self-inflicted, as usual. You never learn.'

'I'm not blaming you.' The room turns cartwheels. 'I know it's my fault. Sorry.'

'We need to go now.'

'What time is it?'

'Six.' She can't mask her anger or impatience. 'We should have gone sooner, really.'

'You're going to have to drive.' I'm still drunk. 'I can't.'

'You're an idiot.'

'I know that.'

'This is important for both of us, not just for me.'

'I know that, too.' At least I don't feel nauseous. 'But the old man insisted.'

'You can't blame him for this.'

'I'm not.'

'Get out of the frigging bed.' Ah, she's really angry. I knew she would be.

I stand up, unsteadily at first, then realise that maybe I'm not as drunk or hung over as I think. 'I need some food, though.'

'I got it all ready last night, remember. And you can't have any now. We'll eat when we get to the trail.'

'Fair enough. I'm sure I'll manage to hold out till

then.'

I shower very quickly. Hot water over my head does wonders, as usual. And not drying myself for a couple of minutes, so the chill air on my wet skin makes me feel even colder, wakes me up, sobers me up.

As we walk out of the door, he's there, Birger. He's got a plate in his hand. 'Waffles and sausages,' he says. 'I thought you might need something to see you on your way.'

'You're a stronger man, than me, old friend,' I mumble.

'Perhaps,' he says. 'Take it.'

'Thank you.' I put the plate on my knee. Alice drives. I eat. The hangover makes me feel alive, the waffles and sausage force their way into my gut, into my brain. By the time the mountain appears in the distance I feel almost human.

She stops the car. 'Thank fuck it wasn't snowing,' she says. 'You're an irresponsible bastard.'

'How many times do you want me to say sorry?' I've been saying sorry for the last ten years. It's time I stopped.

She shrugs. 'Let's get the gear.' She opens the boot.

'Should we use the skis?' I say.

'They might make us quicker.'

'Is that what we want?'

'I don't know. I always hate taking them with me if I'm going to climb. Unnecessary baggage.'

'Ok. We'll walk and climb,' I say.

'Are you sure?'

'Sure I'm sure.' I need the exercise. And we won't be needing skis on Everest, will we? Not that she knows I know that's where she wants us to go.

'We've got about two kms to get to the top,' she says.

'Is it really only that far? I thought it was further.'

'Ha ha.' Her voice is sharp in the clear air, travels to

the rocks and back.

I strap on my rucksack, gulp down another waffle. 'Come on, then. Let's go.'

She throws the car keys into the glove box, pulls her rucksack tight to her back. The sun carves shadows into her face. 'Ok. Here we go.'

We walk for over an hour before we get to the junction of the valleys. The air freezes onto my face, grabs my breath and carries it away to I don't know where. My eyes adjust slowly to the white, to the endless raggedness of the landscape.

'Time to decide,' she says when we get to the junction of the two valleys. 'Which valley do we take?'

'I don't think there's any choice, to be honest.'

'Why?' She's in her monosyllabic climbing mode.

'There's no point going up the main valley. It avoids the whole reason we're here.' I point at the jagged rocks straight ahead. 'We want to climb that, not take an easy western route to the top.'

'Ok.' She nods.

'And we can't really get past that glacier pushing its way down the valley. We'd be more than a day just trying to get on top of it.'

'Agreed.' She leans back, scans the route through her sun glasses, her eyes hidden from me.

'But we need crampons to go through the side valley,' I say. 'It looks really steep.'

We sit on our rucksacks to strap on our crampons. My heart begins beating too quickly again. This is where the real climbing starts. I'm afraid of making any mistakes. Even though I'm up for this like I'd never stopped climbing.

'It doesn't look too bad,' she says, bending down to do up the straps round her boots, her hair dangling in front of her face.

'That's easy for you to say. I haven't done this for a

decade, and you've never stopped.'

'Sorry.' She looks up, with her hand still on her straps. 'I didn't mean to be thoughtless.'

'It's ok. You're excited; that's all.'

'Aren't you?'

'Yes. Honestly.' And I am.

'Good.'

I look at the first part of the route. 'Make sure you're well-covered,' I say. 'There'll be no sun in that valley all day. It faces west and north. We'll not have any sun until we get to the step.'

'I hear you,' she says, her voice no longer that of a wife, but that of a climbing partner.

I breathe deeply, slow down my heart, surprised I can, and head off up the valley.

She follows. 'Since when were you leading?' she calls.

'Since I took the first step,' I shout over my shoulder.

'We'll see about that.' She speeds up and overtakes me.

'No silly games.'

'It's not a game,' she says. 'I don't like following, that's all.'

'Nor do I.' I'm next to her now.

'We'll do it together then.'

We're lucky. There are no clouds, and although we're in the shade, we feel the sun reflected from the ice fields to either side of us, see the rocks steaming where the sun manages to meet them. Our sunglasses shield our eyes from the incessant white. Two hours pass, and it seems we're still no closer to the traverse to what's become our Step now.

'Let's rest,' she says, as we come across a rock in the middle of our path that's not covered in snow.

'Struggling, are you?'

'I'm thinking about you, actually.'

'You don't need to worry about me.'

'Don't I?' she says. 'Maybe I've not been worrying about you enough.'

'Let's not go there,' I say. 'I feel fine.' And it's true. I turn to look back down into the valley. We have come a long way, although it doesn't feel like it.

'I was thinking about what's to come, too.' Her arm points in the opposite direction, up the mountain. 'It's even steeper from here.'

'We'll manage. It's still only a walk, not a climb.'

'I hope so.' She takes a huge gulp of her water. 'And I'm wondering why there's no sign of the cops having been up here.'

'It wasn't here they found them,' I say. 'Jiehkkevarri is over the top of the ridge and a good walk further up.'

'I'll forget about it for the minute then. Let's focus on one thing at a time.'

'I don't want to think about it either.' I drink, too, and find a sausage in my pocket, take huge bites.

'You're an animal.'

'That's why you married me, isn't it?'

She laughs. The crystal of it echoes around us.

'Don't start an avalanche,' I say.

'It's too cold for that.'

I screw the top back onto my bottle, lob it into my rucksack. 'You ready?'

'Yup.' She throws her pack over her back. 'How long till we get up there, do you reckon?'

'Two, three hours.'

'Lots of time for the daylight, then.'

'Yes.'

The climb from here's almost vertical. We don't rope ourselves together, because this is snow, not glacier. It's not easy going, although we're not that far above sea level. Well, one kilometre, which must be as far as we've come, isn't that far above sea level. Even so, we stop every twenty paces to catch our breath, to see if there's some other route that we could be taking. Down behind us, the lake shimmers in the sun.

It gets increasingly difficult for me to get going again after the 20-step rest. I get the feeling she's deliberately walking slowly, not to make me feel useless and pathetic. Her cheeks are red, her breath opaque out of her mouth, regular and even. My breath is ragged, transparent and irregular.

'Should I lead now?' she says when we're what looks like halfway to the ridge. She is still worried about me.

'I suppose I might let you, if you're really nice to me.'

'What's it worth?'

'A kiss?'

'That's easily arranged.' She puts her long arms round me. The waterproof, cold-proof material creaks, and our coats grate against each other. She kisses me, a proper kiss, not just a peck on the cheek. 'Will that do?'

The heat rushes into my face. 'Yes,' I say, wish I hadn't asked for the kiss, concentration broken.

She breaks trail in front of me, forgets I'm here, speeds up, until she's only a small black dot ahead of me as I laboriously follow in her footsteps, knee-deep, a crust forming in each step before I get there, because she's so quick. She's near the top of the ridge before she thinks to turn round and realises she's pushing me too hard. She turns and descends. We meet halfway to where she was.

'Sorry, James. I'm so sorry.'

'What about?' My breath comes hard.

'Running off.'

'It's what you do best.' I bite my tongue. Shit. 'I didn't mean that,' I say quickly.

'I know,' she says, more forgiving than I ever could be.

'I'm sorry,' I say. 'This is knackering me.'

'Do you want to turn back?'

'Don't be stupid. We've got a tent in one of the sacks, haven't we? So there's no issue.'

'That's not the point.'

'What then?'

'You; that's what the point,' she says. 'I don't want to spook you.'

'You won't. I'm just a bit out of shape, that's all. Come on; let's keep going. No lunch till we get to the top of this one.'

'Ok. On your head be it.' She turns and follows her own footsteps back up.

And then, before we know it, we're on the ridge. It's broader than it looked from down below, although the strafing wind's a challenge. We walk along it, to the right, north east, balancing on the crest of the range.

'Nearly there,' she shouts.

'Good,' I shout back. I wish I could just sit down and have a rest, but I mustn't be weak. I draw a deep breath, and then another. Nearly there.

It's in our faces, without us realising. It looks insurmountable, sheer rock carved out by time and wind.

'This is nothing,' she says, steps out of her harnesses, drops her rucksack on the snow. 'I can do that freehand.'

'Don't be stupid,' I shout.

'Just watch me.' And off she goes.

The sun is on us now. I watch it glint off her sweaty forearms, so much stronger than mine, constantly exercised.

She puts her left foot into the first hold she finds. Then her right. Then left, right, left, right. It's almost like she's swimming up the hill. Halfway up, she slows down, has to think about where she puts her feet, her hands. Melting water runs into her sleeves. She ignores it. Ten minutes later she's at the top of the Step.

'I told you,' she shouts down at me. 'Do you want a rope up?'

'No,' I shout back, start up myself, with my backpack still on, just to make me better than her. Before I start climbing, I fix a rope to her rucksack so she can haul it up when I'm done. The problem is, it's not easy for me. My fingers slip out of the handholds, my feet feel sluggish; it's like I'm climbing through treacle. I find a ledge a quarter of the way up, and rest.

'Come on,' she shouts.

'I'm coming.'

'Admit I'm better than you.'

'I admit it,' I call through the overhang.

'Then give up.'

'Never!'

I force my arms through the heat of the pain, force myself to climb again. I don't look down, afraid of what I might see, keep my face as close to the rock as I can, smell the earth on it, the damp, the cold, the frost, the origin of my species. My fingers ache, my arms ache, my legs, all of me. Push, push. *Alice.* I close my eyes, think of nothing but her, think of nothing but us together in bed, her eyes right up to mine, her smile, her hair. My hands begin to slip, and somehow I manage to grab hold of the next ledge, manage somehow to stay on the face. Then I come to the final overhang, and can't see a route, can't see where to put my hands. How did she find a way through this maze of rock? How did she skate through this conundrum? She made it look so easy. I stand there, my hands wedged into the rock, the sun on the back of my head, the water running into my sleeves, making me shiver, my breathing shallow, fast and harsh.

'Hang on,' I say. 'I'm working it out.'

'Relearning?' she says, just a few feet above me, but a life-time away.

'Don't tell me how you did it.'

'I won't. Don't rush.' And yet I can hear the impatience in her voice, the one good climbers have with those who try but can't succeed. I won't let her, or the mountain, beat me. My muscles start to burn, my breath ragged, sweat in my eyes. If I just … There, there, another handhold, just wide enough for two fingers. Pull, pull with one hand, push with my feet. Just one last bit of strength, please, body. Like a cork out of bottle, I go flying up over the edge and crash into the snow next to her, face down on the cold.

'Brilliant!' She jumps on top of me, pulls me over, covers my face in hot kisses. 'You did it, you did it.'

I laugh uncontrollably, without quite knowing why. I sit up, wrap my arms around the mad thin thing straddling my lap, hold her tight, as tight as I can. 'Oh God, I love you.' My breath is still ragged, the steam from my mouth wet in her hair.

'I love you, too.' She reaches over to her backpack. 'Celebration snack?'

'I think so. And water.'

'We can rest here for a few minutes.'

'How generous of you.'

She demolishes two biscuits, takes a huge gulp of water. 'Hang on,' she says. 'I've had another idea. Wait here.'

'What are you doing?'

She scrambles to the edge, turns to face me, gets down on her knees, pushes her legs out into the void. 'I want to do it again.'

'Are you mad?'

'Yes,' she whispers. She smiles, disappears out of view.

I crawl to the edge, put my head out over it, hold myself tightly to the ground, my insides coiled up after that climb with my fears made my fingers weak. There she is, hands and feet moving in unison and quickly, so quickly. As if it's no effort at all. She gets to the bottom in half the time it took her to get up.

'See,' she shouts. 'Not quite the Second Step, but close enough.' Her voice echoes in the stillness of the morning. 'Coming back up.'

She swims against the tide of gravity, hand over quick hand. I can hear her boots on the rock, the gentle touch of her fingers on the face, watch her gain height. She glides, first this way, then that, her eyes obviously faster than her hands, pointing them where she wants to go, not where the mountain wants her to go. She's in control. She's faster up than the first time, flinging her ponytail behind her, almost within touching distance of me now. She looks up, smiles with her eyes. And then she falls.

Chapter 14

Nothing ever happens in slow motion. Not falling in love, not falling out of love, nor losing your parents nor your friends. It's not like in films, not like in the recounting of memories. Life is sudden. She doesn't fall slowly. One second she's there, the next she's gone, and then she hits the ground, rolls over and over, and stops moving.

The scream doesn't even leave my chest. I turn, scramble down the mountain, I don't know how; half fall, half climb to the foot of the face, race across to where she lies in the snow. Some of it's red. I kneel down next to her.

'Alice.'

Nothing. I can't see if she's breathing.

'Alice.' Even more urgently now.

Blood leaks from her mouth. I'm afraid of moving her, gather some snow in my hands, drizzle it onto the exposed side of her face. No marks there. Her eyelid flickers.

'Come on, come on!' More snow.

A sudden intake of breath, and her body explodes into motion. She coughs and splutters, a fine spattering of blood flies up into the wind and back into her face. 'Shit,' she mumbles. 'That was stupid.' She groans as she sits up, wipes her face with her hands.

'You're bleeding.' And I'm shaking.

'I know.'

'Let me see.'

'It's my mouth, that's all. Split lip or something.'

'Let me check.'

'I'll be fine,' she mumbles.

'I'm not so sure. You're bound to have broken something.'

'No chance,' she says.

'Stand up then, and we'll see.'

'Can't do that yet. Still a bit dizzy. And pissed off.'

'How can you be pissed off? You could've been killed.'

'I'm pissed off because I fell. It shouldn't happen to me.'

'You're obviously out of practice. Like me.'

'Get lost.' Her speech is a bit slurred.

'You sound odd.'

'That's because my lip's hurting.' She spits out more blood, grabs some snow and stuffs it in her mouth. 'Bollocks.'

'That's not sterile.'

'Nothing is round here. It'll be fine. It's frozen. That's what matters.'

'You've probably got concussion. We should get down now and get you to a doctor.'

She shakes her head. 'Nope. My brain's still rattling round in there, as usual.'

'Do you have to be flippant?'

'What else should I be? I've never fallen.' She gets up. 'There. I'm fine now.'

'We're going back down then.'

'No! We've got things to do here.'

'Are you mad?'

'No,' she says, thickly. 'And I reckon I saw something on my freestyle descent that shouldn't be there.' She's pointing at an indeterminate spot on the face. 'I need to go have a look.'

'No, no way. That's really tempting fate.' I can't let her do that.

'And we've got to get our bags.'

'I can do that. You stay here.'

'Come on, James. I need to see what it was.'

'Then we'll both go, and slowly.'

She shakes her head again, scowls, then smiles. 'Ok.

I'll do it your way, for once.'

'And we'll look for an easier route back.'

'That route was easy.'

'So easy you fell.'

'Exactly. I must stop smiling at you every time I look at you. I must've lost concentration. '

'Is that what happened to Mallory and Irvine then?' I say. 'They lost concentration because the Second Step is so piss-easy?'

'That's not the same, and you know it. It's taller, and it's so high up there's hardly any air.' She bends down, picks up more snow, rubs it over her face. 'Ok, I'm talking crap. This one isn't a massively difficult climb, but it will have shown Odell that Irvine was much better than they'd thought he was. And to me that just proves he'll have been of much more use to Mallory than everyone seems to assume. And that they made it to the summit.'

'And fell on the way down?'

'Something like that. There's no other way of explaining it. But not on the Second Step. They fell further down on the way back, I'm sure of it.'

'So is this what Simon meant when he said he'd found Irvine?'

'I don't think so. It's just the beginning. Why wasn't Irvine's body near Mallory's? All those sort of things.' She sighs. 'Come on. Let's get back up there before we've lost so much time we can't get to Jiehkkevarri.'

'Is there any point getting there? We know it's this mountain we needed to see, not the big J.'

'I want to see if there's any sign of the cops or even just of the place those two men got killed.'

'That's a bit ghoulish, isn't it?'

'Yes,' she says. 'But it's necessary.'

We start climbing the wall. She puffs and pants a little, through clenched teeth. She's hurting, I can tell.

Halfway up, she diverts from the route she climbed first time round, moves across the face, finding new footholds, new handholds. She suddenly stops, held up by nothing more than her fingertips and her toes. Thank God I've found a wide enough ledge to rest on.

'I knew it,' she snorts.

'Stop messing about,' I say. 'Let's get to the top.'

'There's something here.' She stretches for whatever it is she can see.

'Leave it, Alice.'

'But I can just about reach it. Just a little further.'

'Do you remember *The Last Crusade*?'

'Eh?'

'The Indiana Jones film.'

'What about it?' The wind drags her words away. 'You're talking nonsense.'

'The girl reaching for the Holy Grail, and falling into the abyss?'

'Oh, shut up. This is nothing like that. She was a stupid, vain little Nazi moron.' She pushes up on tiptoes, leans across. 'There. I've got it. Come on, slacker.' There's laughter in her voice. It's the voice of an adrenaline junkie. And I'll never be able to cure her of the addiction. I don't think I want to. I realise now what I've been missing in my self-imposed hermit's life of fear.

When we get to the top, she rushes to our bags, grabs the water, pours half of it down her throat, sits down.

'What did you find?' I say.

'This.' She reaches into her pocket, pulls something out into her closed palm, holds her hand out to me, and unfurls her long fingers. A gold neck chain. 'It's Simon's.' She stares at me. 'Was he wearing it when you saw him? That's what I need to know.'

I'm non-plussed. 'I didn't even know he had one. I wasn't exactly looking at his jewellery when he broke into his room.'

'Try to remember. It's important.'

I close my eyes, try to visualise that night. It seems so long ago. I'm getting cold. It's too soon to tell her I can't remember, so I lie down on my back, keep my eyes firmly shut, and count to fifty. I sit up, shake my head. 'Nothing.'

'For God's sake, James,' she hisses. 'You weren't even trying.'

'I was doing my best.'

'You were moving your lips when you were counting, dickhead. Try again. From the moment you turned the light on.'

'Ok. I'll try this out loud. I heard a noise and didn't react at first. Then another noise. Got up in the dark, and looked for my boxers and a T-shirt.'

'How modest of you.' She's mocking me.

'I thought you wanted me to focus.'

'Sorry,' she says, rubs more snow over her swollen mouth.

'Then, a couple of steps to the door, open the door as quietly as I can. And I'm quite scared by now. I close the door behind me, turn the light on without thinking, because I don't know it's him. Then he asks me what the fuck I'm doing there, quote unquote. I'm surprised. Then, what then? Ah, his face is bloody, and so's his shirt.' I do close my eyes now. 'He's only wearing a shirt, a white shirt, blood all over it. Some buttons missing. Yes, that's it. It's open quite far down. I don't see a chain. No.' I open my eyes again. 'No chain.'

'So he was here with them,' she says. 'Why?'

'For the same reason we are?'

'Yes, but why with them?'

'God knows.' I shrug. 'And why wasn't he killed with them?'

'Whoever it was killed the two others, got hold of

Simon and tried to beat whatever secret he's got out of him.'

'But he escaped?'

'Yes,' she says.

'Then how did he get back to England without a passport?'

'Maybe it wasn't here they beat him up.'

'How would they get him back to Cambridge?' I say, stop myself. 'Oh.' The proverbial light bulb moment.

'What?' she says.

'Private planes.'

'You what?'

'There's an airport for private jets just east of Cambridge. That's how they could've got him back there.'

'How? What about airport security?'

'It's not so tight for private planes,' I say.

'You haven't been on a plane for ages.'

'I can't imagine it's changed. If anything, it'll have got slacker. All these rich bankers and the like.'

'Ok,' she says. 'So they kill the two guys here, grab Simon, cart him back to England, beat him up, and he escapes.'

'Yes. And they didn't realise for a couple of hours or so where he'd got to.'

'Then, when they realise, they come to his room, probably search it, find nothing, and torch it.'

'I reckon,' I say. It's all starting to make sense now. There's so much money at stake for anyone who finds Irvine, almost unimaginable money, and, what's probably more important, unimaginable fame. 'So where is he? Your turn to think.'

'Maybe he's somewhere totally unrelated,' she says. 'I'd never thought of that.'

'You mean we came out here for nothing?'

'Not entirely nothing. We found the step, and we

found his chain.'

'So, what are you thinking about that's totally unconnected?'

'Old girlfriends.'

'Why girlfriends? There must be hundreds.'

'Very possibly. But only a couple he's been in love with.'

'He's been in love?' I almost laugh. 'That's hard to believe.'

'Oh, yes,' she says. 'But these two dumped him.'

'You're kidding. Simon's been dumped?'

'Don't come over all superior,' she says. 'He's just a man.'

'Sorry. It just makes me feel a bit better about myself.'

'You're an idiot.'

'A repressed Englishman,' I say.

'So you keep reminding me.'

'And where are these two lucky and praiseworthy ladies?'

'One's in England, and one's in the US.'

'Ah.' Another dead-end. 'That's no good.'

'Yes,' she says. 'That could be a problem.'

'Do you know where they are?'

'Sort of.'

'What's that supposed to mean, exactly?'

'I only know where the one in England lives. I never even met the other one. He just told me about her.'

'Brilliant. We're clutching at straws.'

She nods. 'Come on. We need to push on.'

I look at the white ridge that leads to the real summit. 'Really?' I'm a bit tired of chasing my tail, and feel like we've learned nothing.

'The police might have missed something.'

'If they were ever up here,' I say.

'They had to get the bodies down somehow. They won't have asked someone else to get them, will they?'

'If you insist.'

'It looks easy from here.'

'It's bloody steep, that's what it is.' Just looking at it makes me feel tired.

'You've had steeper ones to climb. This is just a walk.' She gets up. 'Come on. I'll let you get pissed with Birger tonight.'

'I'd rather get pissed with you.'

'The three of us then.'

'Now that sounds like a good deal,' I say. And the warmth creeps into my body again, a warmth that could only come from her.

We rope up, something we should have done when she came back up the face the second time. I follow her. She's better than me, has been on God knows how many glaciers while I've been vegetating at home in Christchurch. We don't speak as we trudge on towards the top of Holmbukttind first, battered from all sides by the wind, then down into a valley of ice and snow, and then up again, along a fairly gentle slope, half in sun, half in shade, towards the top of Jiehkkevarri. It's hard work.

'We should've skied it.' I break the silence when we're about halfway up.

'No skis on Everest.'

'I'm not going there again.' Although I know I will.

'You may have to.'

'It'll take a lot more than letting me get pissed with Birger to get me there. This place doesn't scare me, doesn't remind me too much of the mistakes I've made.'

'There's nothing to be scared of on Everest,' she says. 'It wasn't your fault Graham died.'

I say nothing.

'Anyway,' she says. 'We need to find those girlfriends first.'

‘And how are we going to do that?’

‘We’ll see.’

The last few steps seem easy, somehow.

‘Yeah!’ I scream at the top of my voice.

‘And no sign of where these bodies were, or of the cops,’ she says.

‘They must have found what they needed.’

‘Who?’

‘The cops,’ I say.

‘Cops are usually unimaginative.’

‘And you’d know? Is there something you’re trying to tell me?’

‘Murder isn’t exactly common here or in NZ,’ she says.

‘What’s that got to do with anything?’

She shakes her head. ‘They’re not called plods for nothing.’

‘I’m sure some of them are anything but plods.’

‘I just don’t like cops,’ she says. ‘Let’s go explore.’

‘But I’m knackered.’ And I am.

‘Then wait here.’

‘I’m not letting you go off on your own again.’

‘Then come on.’ She’s getting impatient, which either means that I’m starting to be normal again, or that she’s tired of me being an ineffectual burden on her.

We circumnavigate the dome that’s Jiehkkevarri’s summit. There are no traces of anything here. No ski tracks. No blood. Nothing.

‘The weather’s not exactly conducive to leaving clues behind,’ I say.

‘There’s gotta be something,’ she mutters. ’I could do with something to dig with.’ She starts kicking at the snow with her boots. ‘Wait a minute.’

‘What?’

‘Did that paper say when they died?’

‘No. The bodies were frozen.’

'So let's assume it took them at least 24 hours to get Simon back to England.'

'That means they were killed at least a day before I saw Simon.'

'Which was when?' she says. 'I've lost track of time.'

'Just about a week ago.'

'And they found them when?'

'Three days ago.'

'So if Simon's mates dropped something the cops wouldn't have found it with the bodies.'

'Maybe not.'

'And if they were frozen, they'd have been where?' She looks around, reminds me of a cat, taking in scent through its half-open mouth.

'The paper didn't say.'

'It didn't have to,' she says. 'It'd have to be somewhere the sun doesn't get to much.'

'North.'

'Yes,' she says. 'Top marks go to the man without a split lip.'

'Over there.' I point.

'Well spotted.' She starts walking.

'There's nowhere up here for a sniper to hide.'

'You don't need to be a sniper if you're the one with the gun and the ones you're trying to get don't have one.'

'Fair enough. I hadn't thought of that.'

'Would it have been anywhere near the top, though?' she says.

'Probably. They would've relaxed having got to the top.'

'Simon never relaxes.'

'I'm not saying he did.'

'So let's find north and go down twenty metres,' she says.

We descend. The snow's undisturbed, just like at the

top.

'Bugger,' she mutters.

'Give it another ten,' I say.

'It seems pointless.' She sounds discouraged, keeps lifting her fingers to her lips.

'Just do it.' It's my turn to be impatient.

We go further down, carefully, on blue ice under the snow. I can feel it, slippery and malevolent, beneath my feet. Deceitful. She falls into a mini-crevasse. Only a metre. Hauls herself out without my help.

'This is fun,' she says.

'Yeah.' I'm not smiling.

A little further down, there's a tiny mound of snow, proud of the rest. 'There.' I point at it.

'Too obvious.'

'That's where the cops dug,' I say. 'Not where something might be lost.'

'So we look round here?'

'Downhill of it. If something got loose, it would've slid down.'

'Right down to the bottom of the frigging mountain,' she says.

'Not necessarily.'

'Ok. I believe you.' She paces gingerly down the slope. 'Here?'

'It's as good a place as any,' I say.

She kicks at the snow and starts digging with her hands, until she's dug a trench. Sweat drips from her face. 'Nothing.'

'Let me,' I say. We swap places. I kick at the trench walls, down towards the valley. It's cold here, without the sun. 'Fuck it,' I say, when my leg hits the hard ice. Kick it again for good measure. It gives this time. I kneel down in the trench and start to shovel out snow with my hands. Come up against something that's hard and yet gives. I scratch around its outline. 'That can't be right.'

'What?' She stands over me like a black-clad angel.

'It's shaped like a book.'

'Get it out then.'

'I'm trying.' I keep scrabbling at the shape with my clumsy gloved hands.

'Do you want me to?'

I shake my head. 'Nearly there.'

Finally, I get to it. It's much smaller than it felt to my foot. Probably because it's encased in ice. I pick it up. The whole thing's frozen. 'It'll defrost on the way back up.' I stick it inside my jacket, even though I'll get wet when it melts. Back at the summit, I pull the half-sodden mess out. It's a book alright, but it's not in English. I recognise the script, although I can't read it. It's a Tibetan prayer book.

Chapter 15

'Let me see,' she says.

I hand the book to her.

'How old do you think it is?' she says.

'I'd hate to guess, the state it's in.' I shrug. 'We won't know till we get an expert to have a look at it.'

'But why didn't the police find it? They must have searched this whole area, mustn't they?'

'It was probably already covered by the ice and snow when they got here.'

'You're right.' She turns it over in her gloved hands. 'I'll rip it if I try to open it. We'll have to thaw and dry it out when we get back.'

The light changes subtly, suddenly, and the wind strengthens. My cheeks are cold. Dusk, almost. 'It's time we started back,' I say. 'The light's going.'

'Don't you think we might find something else?'

'Do you?' I don't like the way the day is darkening. It only just started.

She shakes her head. 'I'm not even sure it's worth it. We've got the mountain, we've got Simon's chain, and we've got the book.' She puts it into her rucksack, gets up. 'Let's go.'

'Should we go back the same way we came?'

'Is there another way?'

I show her an easier route on the map.

'But that doesn't take us down to the car. We'll have to walk miles to get back to it.'

'It's safer, though,' I say. 'I like safe.'

She shrugs. 'I'm not sure we've got the time. We'll go down roped.'

'Ok,' I say. 'On your head be it.'

'We'll be alright.'

And we are alright. We get back to the car just as the last of the light fades. The air is frozen. Our breath grows a haze of life around the rigid wilderness around us. The inside of the car's frozen, too, and we sit there for almost half an hour with the engine on to defrost the windows, to make it bearable to drive without all our cold weather gear on. It's pitch black by the time we leave, but at least it's not snowing. I drive this time. The sight of the lights from inside Birger's house is a comforting one.

We get out, arms full of gear and rucksacks, let ourselves in to our house, revel in the warmth, in the artificial yellow light. I feel my body relaxing.

'Let me look at your face again,' I say.

'It's fine.' She stands under the light. 'I've just got a few scratches.'

'They'd have made you have stitches at home.'

'Well, it's a good job we're not at home then. All that fuss over nothing.'

'Maybe you should get someone to look at it tomorrow.'

'Don't be silly.'

There's a knock at the door.

'Ja,' I call.

Birger comes in. 'I heard you come back,' he says. 'All well?'

We nod.

'Well, that's not the truth,' he says and leans forward. 'What have you done to your face, girl? Let me see.' He takes Alice's face in his old hands, squints. 'You fell?' He shakes his head. 'I thought you were better than that.'

'I am,' she says. 'I just did the Holmbukttind Step once too often, without a rope.'

He steps back. 'Oh, that.' He grins. 'I do remember that.'

'How long is it since you were up there?' she says.

'A long time. I was young then.' He coughs. 'I have

something for your face,' he says to Alice. 'And for all the other bruises you must have. Did you find what you were looking for?'

'What?' she says.

'James told me he was looking for himself again up there, for his courage, and you for some sign of your brother.'

'You know Simon?' she says.

He shakes his head.

'He was there,' Alice says. 'We know it.'

'The first I knew about anyone being there was when they found the dead men,' Birger says. 'But I'd heard nothing, heard no cars, not anything, on those few days the police said they must have been on the mountain. I should have heard something. Maybe I'm getting old.' He shakes his head, irritated. 'Come, I'll feed you some decent Norwegian food. It'll be easier to talk over supper and beer.'

The three of us crunch our way across the snow to Birger's house. He opens the door, ushers us in, pushes the door closed quietly behind himself. The smell of cooking is heavy in the air.

'Don't you watch your cooking?' Alice says.

'No need. I know what it's going to do.'

'Pytt i panne,' I say.

'You remember,' he says.

'How could I forget? It's wonderful.'

'What are you two talking about?' Alice says. 'It's all double Dutch to me.'

'Smoked sausage, potatoes, onions,' Birger says. 'Throw it all onto a greased baking tray, put it in the oven and wait. We Norwegians are good at that.'

'That's it?' she says. 'Nothing more complicated than that?'

'Sit,' he says, grabs three beers from the fridge, his shadow dark against the pine-clad walls. 'The real finishing touch is this. Watch.' He takes six eggs from the tray next to the cooker, bends down to pull the tray out of the oven with his oven gloves, dark with the warmth and grease of endless meals in the past, stirs what's in the tray around with a wooden spatula, pushes the tray back into the oven. 'Count to a hundred,' he says, so we do. He pulls the tray out again, breaks the eggs quickly over the mixture, and hides the tray back in the oven's belly. 'Two minutes now,' he says, and turns up the heat. 'Plates,' he says, points at the pine dresser next to the fridge. 'Knives and forks are here.' He picks up his beer. 'Skål.' His voice is loud and strong into the silence grazing the outside of the house.

When the two minutes are gone, he opens the oven, pulls from it a steaming, sputtering, crisp meal, brings it to the table, puts it down on the cork mats already there. 'Ladies first,' he says, with that typical Norwegian habit of combing the *r* and the *s* together with a *sh*. 'Firsht,' he says again, savouring the sound.

We revel in the scent of the warm food, wait for him to serve all three of us, for him to sit down and take another sip of his beer. 'Eat,' he says, gestures at our plates with his fork, starts shovelling the hot food into his mouth, wrinkles working away around his lips.

'Were you expecting us?' Alice says.

'Sort of,' he says, his mouth full.

'Why?' She looks puzzled, not used to occasional kindnesses from strangers.

'I like you. You're serious people. You respect the mountains. You're not here to mock them.'

'But how did you know we'd be back today?'

'You had to be. You wouldn't have wanted to spend a night up there.' He chews another forkful. 'And you're too good to have to spend a night up there.'

'And if we hadn't come back?' She stares at him, her blue eyes hard into the green of his.

'I'd have sat outside all night and waited.'

'And then?' The edges of her mouth curve up, an almost smile.

He shrugs. 'I might've looked for my ancient ropes and crampons, somewhere in the dust up there, driven out and started climbing again.'

'There'd have been no reason for you to do that,' I say.

'Life isn't about reason,' he says. 'It's not about weighing up risks and deciding against them. It's about doing what's right. It's about not regretting what you do.' He looks at me now. 'It's about being true to yourself, grabbing a chance for happiness when you've got it. You might even find you're immortal.'

'What?' Alice says. 'That sounds a bit weird.'

'You're immortal, the two of you,' he says.

'How's that?' I say. He's mad.

He puts his hand on our book that's been lying on the table since last night. 'Something like this makes you immortal,' he says. 'Your words, your memories, your love, on these pages. You took your chance, you pulled life into your pattern, you didn't let it shape you.'

'And my ten years of fear?' I say, and shiver involuntarily. 'What about them?'

'Ach,' he says. 'What's ten years? You're a young man. You've got many, many years to come.' He empties his bottle of beer with a loud slurp. 'More?'

'Please,' Alice says. 'I'll get them.' She gets up, walks to the fridge, slowly.

'You're limping,' I say.

'You shouldn't sound so surprised,' Birger says. 'She could have died today.' His eyes are mournful.

'I know,' I say. 'She should be more careful.'

'No, no,' he says and smiles. 'More careless.'

'That doesn't make sense,' I say.

'Don't be afraid, don't ever be afraid again,' he says.

'It's fear that kills us, not what we're afraid of.'

Alice sits back down, hands out the beer. 'So, why didn't you ever marry?'

'I told James last night. I loved the mountains too much.'

'There must have been a girl around here who loved the mountains as much as you.'

'Oh, yes,' he says, leans back in his chair, his food finished. 'There was.'

'And?' Alice leans forward. 'What happened?'

'She was very beautiful, very strong, a bit like you, but blonde, not dark.'

'Did she die?' I say.

He laughs. 'No, no, nothing as dramatic as that. She was from Oslo, and came up one summer with some friends. A few years younger than me she'd have been.' He scratches his head. 'I suppose I'd have been about twenty-six then. I already had this place, because I loved being here so much.'

'And?' Alice says.

'And we fell in love and she stayed. For a year. We climbed all the mountains round here together.'

'So where is she?' I say.

He shrugs. 'I don't know. She hated the dark nights, maybe I should say the long dark night of the winter up here. Missed the streetlights of the big city, missed the tiny bit of daylight they get down there in the winter.' There's no hint of regret in his voice, and the bright light doesn't betray him.

'And that was it?' Alice says. 'Just like that?'

'I loved it too much here. I didn't have the heart to follow her down south.'

'But you were frightened for nothing,' I say.

'That's what I've learned,' he says.

'It's not too late,' Alice says. 'You could always find someone else.'

He laughs again, takes more gulps from his bottle. 'She'd be about seventy now,' he says.

'But you …' Alice says.

'I'm seventy-six,' he says, screws up his brown, haggard face. 'And I feel it.'

'And you've been here on your own since?' I say.

He nods, slams his bottle down on the table. 'If you've eaten enough we should get back to what we were talking about when you got back.' He shakes away the memory with an impatient nod.

'What have the police done with the bodies?' Alice says.

'They're still in the mortuary in Tromsø,' he says. 'You've got no chance of getting anywhere near them.'

'Why would we want to do that?' she says. 'I don't think there'd be anything there to help us.'

'No idea,' he says. 'I just thought you might.'

'I can't think of any reason to.' She takes the small book from her pocket. 'I think we found what we need.'

'What is it?' Birger says.

'A prayer book, I think,' I say.

'Did you read it?' he says.

'No,' both of us say. 'But it doesn't matter.'

'Could I have a look, please?' he says.

Alice gives it to him, places it gently in his hand.

'Why did you never go to Everest?' I say as he turns the book over and over.

'I'm afraid of flying,' he says, and doesn't even look at me, though there's a fleeting smile on his face. 'You'll need to dry this slowly, not on a radiator or by a fire.'

'We will,' Alice says. 'Is there any other way they could have got to the mountain, not through here?'

'The other valley, round the back; that easy route you obviously avoided,' he says, his eyes still on the book. 'But I should have heard, even from here.'

'They probably used a silencer on the gun,' I say.

'I don't mean the shots,' he says. 'I mean the cars or whatever.' He shakes his head. 'I am getting old. And I don't like it.' He hands the book back to Alice. 'It's from Tibet,' he says, casually.

'How do you know?' she says.

'I studied the place and its culture when I couldn't persuade myself to fly out there. It looks like one of their holy books in miniature.'

'Would you be able to translate it if we managed to get it open?'

Birger shakes his head. 'Not tonight, not in a month. There must be at least three hundred pages there.'

'Maybe there's something for every day of the year,' I say.

'I don't think the Tibetans worked on a year with 365 days,' Alice says.

'They did,' Birger says. 'Their months were different, that's all. And they measured their time by natural events, like the monsoons and such.' He gets up and fetches three more bottles from what seems like an inexhaustible supply of beer in his fridge, stands them on the table. 'And it looks so precious, too fragile to just be opened by us now. Maybe a museum.' He shrugs, sits down again.

'But they were carrying it around with them,' Alice says. 'So it can't be that valuable.'

'Maybe we should go to the police,' I say.

'No, no,' Birger says. 'You'd never see it again. And they wouldn't do anything about it anyway. It would disappear in the system.'

'What about solving the murders, though?' I say.

'Ah,' Birger says. 'They think they've done that, so the paper today said.'

'Eh?' Alice says.

'They're saying now it was a suicide pact.' He laughs.

'A simple practical solution, so typical of my fellow Norwegians.'

'No mention of Simon?'

He shakes his head.

'They found a weapon, then, did they?' Alice says. 'They must have some sort of proof to say it was suicide.'

Birger nods, holds up his hand. 'Two.'

'I don't buy it,' she says.

Birger looks at me.

'She doesn't believe it,' I say.

'Oh,' he says. 'Neither do I. But I still wouldn't go to the police. There's no point. It would just make everything complicated and you'd be stuck here for an age.'

'What if they know we're here?' I say.

'Who? The police?' Alice says.

'No. Whoever did this. Whoever set fire to Simon's room.'

'I don't think they know about us,' she says. 'When Simon sent that text to warn us I don't think he was saying they were after us, just that his room would be the first place they'd look for him.'

'So why torch it if he wasn't there? That seems unnecessary.'

'They didn't know he wasn't there, did they?' she says.

Birger coughs. 'Maybe they were looking for this.' He picks up the tiny book. 'Maybe that's what they want.'

'You mean they didn't realise it was under their noses all along?' I say.

'Exactly,' he says. 'You see, everyone over-complicates things, and ignores the most obvious answers. Not just good people, but bad people, too.'

'Maybe whoever had it on them stamped it down into the snow without being noticed,' Alice says. 'That's why it was so far down.'

'And they let themselves be killed for it?' I say.

'If it was important enough, precious enough, yes,' she says.

'Mountain people,' Birger says. 'They know honour.'

'What makes you say that?' I say.

'It's the only thing that makes sense to me,' he says.

'People from the Tibetan mountains?'

'People from any mountain,' he says. 'But probably from there. Buddhists. Special people.'

'Maybe we don't need to find Simon after all,' I say. 'We need to find out who's after him instead.'

'It would be easier to find him and ask him, you know,' Alice says. 'And so we can give him that back.'

'You think that's the key?' I say.

She shrugs. 'It's got something to do with all this. And it's not just a souvenir.'

'How soon do you need to leave again?' Birger says.

'Why?' she says.

'Let it dry out overnight,' he says. 'And then maybe we can just open the first page and read what it says without doing too much damage. If you keep it in your bedroom tonight, it may be dry enough tomorrow. You can bring it over after breakfast.'

'Sounds like a good idea,' I say.

Alice looks uncertain. Her twin bond working again. She scratches her head, undoes the hairband, redoes her ponytail. 'I suppose one more day won't hurt.' She leans back in her chair. 'Any more beer?'

'Sure,' Birger says.

'I'll be back in a minute,' I say. 'I just remembered something.'

I'm back in less than a minute, my fingers coiled around a promise. I walk up to Birger, unwrap my fingers, and let the stone roll onto the table.

'A part of Holmbukttind,' I say. 'I did promise.'

Chapter 16

Birger takes the stone in his wrinkled hand, weighs it, smiles, puts it back down without a sound. 'Thank you. I thought you'd forgotten.'

'He wouldn't forget,' Alice says. 'He never forgets. That's his problem.'

'I understand,' he says. Picks the stone up again, tosses it from one palm to the other, looks at her. 'And how do you feel now?'

'Fine,' she says. 'There's no need to fuss.'

'Do you have any arnica?' he says. 'It might help a little, bring those bruises out more quickly.'

'I forgot to get some before we came.'

He gets up, walks to a cupboard on another wall of the cavernous kitchen, pulls out a tiny green glass jar with a white lid, filled with minute tablets.

'Do you live in this room?' she says. 'It's like everything you need's in here.'

'No, no.' He laughs 'I spend most of my time in here, yes, because it's cosy and comfortable, but I use the other rooms, too.' He hands her the bottle. 'Here, take two tablets now.'

'And two more in half an hour,' she says.

He smiles at her. 'Yes. Even though they tell you to wait two hours. You need to work on that bruising.'

'I daren't look,' she says. 'I'll get changed in the dark tonight.'

'Isn't that what the English expect of us foreigners anyway?' he says.

'I say, old boy,' I laugh. 'I'll check her out later.'

'More beer?' he says. I think he could drink any bar dry and still be standing.

I look at Alice.

'One more,' she says. 'Just the one. I'm exhausted all of a sudden.'

'You might want some akevitt,' Birger says. 'It'll take away some of the pain.'

'After what it did to James last night? I don't think so.'

'It'll warm your bones,' he says. 'Help the healing.'

She looks at him, smiles. 'You sure?' When he pulls a face, she laughs. 'Ooh, that hurts.'

'Akevitt and beer it is then,' he says. 'I'll not force you to have more than one.'

'What about the washing-up?' she says.

'That can wait.'

'I'll put all this crap in the sink,' I say. 'At least it's out of the way then.'

Birger nods, gets the akevitt from yet another cupboard. Alice limps alongside him, grabs three more beers.

'What will you do now?' Birger says.

'How about letting you try to translate some of this?' I say.

'Have you got any tweezers?' Alice says.

Birger looks puzzled.

'Pinsett,' I say, motion with my fingers.

'Oh, ja. Sorry, yes.' He pulls a drawer out of table. 'I use them for ticks sometimes. In the summer. If I can't find this.' He gets the special tick pincers out.

'But you keep them in the same place,' Alice laughs.

'Old men, you see,' he says. 'We keep our things in safe places. What do you want them for?'

'I want to try something.' She reaches out for the book. 'Maybe the first page is dry enough by now.'

'You're determined to go tomorrow, aren't you?' I say.

'No, I just want to find out what it says. Don't worry. I'll be careful.'

'I'm sure you will,' Birger says, watches her long fingers, flawless fingers, pick up the book, put it back down close to her.

She bends forwards so her eyes are level with the book, runs her fingertips across its dark cover. 'Leather?' she says.

'Could be.'

'Why's there no writing on it?'

'Can't you feel any unevenness?' he says.

'No. It's totally smooth.'

'That's unusual. The books normally have an inscription on them. I thought it might have faded and left just the shapes.'

She holds the book still with her left hand by its spine, leads the tweezers down towards it slowly, tries to lift the front from the rest of the pages. The tweezers slip off. She grunts. Starts again, slips off again.

'It's still too damp,' I say.

'You'd think it would just fall open,' she says.

'Nothing's that simple,' I say. 'Maybe you should wait.'

'I can't,' she says. 'I don't want to.'

Birger raises an eyebrow. 'Patience, girl. Here, let me try. You're shaking. You're in shock. You just don't know it.' He takes the book, puts it in the cupped palms of his huge hands and sits still.

We say nothing for ages. He doesn't move. Alice and I drink our beer. The silence is almost reverential, an act of worship, although I've never believed in any gods. Even if I did, further back than I can remember, I lost any faith when I fell on that mountain, that monster.

'Maybe that will have worked.' He wakes me from my daydream.

'What?'

'The warmth of my hands. I only just thought of it,' he says. 'Let's see.' He blows hard into the pages now. 'No moisture in a sharp breath.' He blows again, the tweezers in his hand now. 'Yes.' It's an exhalation of relief and exhilaration. 'There are some reading glasses here somewhere,' he says. 'In a drawer at that end of the table.'

I rummage where he tells me to, until I find an old pair of horn-rimmed specs, battered frame and scratched lenses. I hand them to him.

'You'll need to put them on for me,' he says. 'I don't want to let go.'

I take a step behind him, manoeuvre the glasses over his ears, push them down onto his nose. 'Ok like that?'

He nods, lowers his face. 'Hmm. How odd. What does that mean? Hmm. Yes. Oh. Ah, now that's interesting.' He mutters away to himself like this for a few minutes, as if he's forgotten we're here.

'What?' Alice says.

'Shh,' he says. 'Just a minute. Is that possible?' He looks up. 'There's pen and paper somewhere, too. Sorry to keep asking you to find things.'

This time Alice finds what he needs. She tries to hand it to him, but he shakes his head. 'I'll read. You write it down. But we'll need to double check this in the morning.'

'Go on,' she says. 'I'm ready.'

'Forgive me if I don't get it right med en gang.'

'Straightaway,' I translate.

'Yes, that's it,' he says. 'Ok. Ready?'

Alice nods.

'I've never heard of this before,' he says.

Alice starts writing.

'No, sorry, that's not part of it. I just thought I knew all the writings of the Tibetan monks. Here we go.' He coughs. 'The Thin Air Sutra.' He shakes his head. 'What can that mean?'

'If we write it all down, maybe we can work that out later, like you said,' Alice says, her face young and impatient next to his granite, ancient brow.

'That's true,' he says. 'I forgot. So, it says The Sutra of Thin Air.' He coughs. 'We climbed until we found a haven, until we were weak enough to become strong again. We were called when the land rose from the water and grew up into the holy snows. The thin air feeds our lungs, illuminates us, makes us wiser than the heavy air of the lowlands. We take the cold into our bodies when we climb, and become a part of the mountain. We are the mountain.'

'Is that Everest?' Alice mouths at me.

'Wait,' Birger says, almost a command. 'There's more.'

'We will always climb, always live here. We are the guardians of the Holy Mother's secrets, and these are our prayers, written into the thin air of her many summits.' He sits back, takes his glasses off. 'That's all there is on this page.'

Alice looks through her scribbles, repeats it all. 'It is Everest,' she says. 'It has to be.'

'Of course it is,' Birger says. 'There can be no doubt about that.'

'But,' I say.

'But what?' she says.

'How can it be? The English were the first to get to the top.'

'The sherpas helped them,' Alice says. 'And Hillary was a Kiwi, don't forget.'

'A New Zealander,' I say to Birger who's looking at me helplessly.

'So they're just talking figuratively?' I say. 'Like the book's a fable or something?'

'Rombuk's in the thin air,' Alice says.

'Yes, but this sounds like it's higher. It's hidden and it's on one of many summits.'

'Everest's only got one summit,' she says. 'It's got to be no more than poetic licence.'

'The licence of faith,' I say.

'What?' Birger says.

'A lie dressed as literature,' I say.

'Not from mountain people,' he says.

I look at him, say nothing, shake my head.

'So what does it mean?' Alice says.

'What does any written word mean?' Birger says. 'Is it invention, or is it the truth? We never know. The thing is, poets speak the truth more often than historians; writers speak the truth more easily than politicians. This could be real, although ...'

'Although what?'

'Although I can't believe that anyone could live in those heights,' he says. 'Even now, climbers still need oxygen to survive up there.'

'The Death Zone's not called that for nothing,' Alice says.

'No,' I say, unwanted memories on the march.

'So what are you going to so with it?' Birger says.

'Dry out the rest of it and get you to translate at least a few more pages,' I say.

'We're going to find Simon,' Alice says at the same time. 'He obviously knows more about this than any of us.'

'That's like looking for a needle in a haystack,' I say.

'We've got two possibilities,' Alice says.

'And one's thousands of miles away. Craziness.'

'So let's start with the closest,' she says. 'In England.'

'Even finding her would be a miracle.'

'I've got her address,' she says.

'Why didn't you say so?'

'I was going to, but I never got round to it.'

'Where is she?'

'London,' she says. 'At least the last time we were in touch.'

'And how long ago was that?'

'Couple of months.' She takes her last mouthful of the

bottle.

'Ready for some more?' Birger says.

'Oh, why not?' Alice says. 'Is it time for more tablets yet?'

He looks at his ancient watch and nods.

'Good.' She opens the glass bottle, tips more pills into her mouth. 'Cheers.'

'Akevitt time,' he says, the last word two syllables in Norwegian.

'Do I have to?' she says, pulling a face as if she had tasted something sour.

'Just the one.'

'Ok then,' she says.

I've seen her drink whisky. I lost that contest.

'Ooh. Nice,' she says. 'Why haven't I had this before?'

'Careful, I say. 'It's addictive. And you can't get it easily in England or NZ.'

'Thank God,' she says, drains her second glass. 'It's brain death, I reckon.'

'Or wisdom,' Birger says.

'What did you do when your girl went back to Oslo?' Alice says. 'I can't believe you've been here alone ever since.'

'Here ever since, yes,' he says, measures his words. 'Not always alone, though.'

'That's something, at least,' Alice says.

I enjoy watching the two of them feed from each other, as if they'd been friends all their lives, as if they'd been born at the same time, were the same age, as if their souls had met before.

Birger smiles. 'Some of them have been much younger than me. But they've all loved the mountains.'

'Have any of them loved you?' Alice says, the akevitt taking hold.

'Maybe,' he says. 'Maybe so. It's hard to know.'

'And you, have you loved any of them?'

'Oh, I've been in love with all of them,' he says. 'How couldn't I have been? I've been a lucky man.'

'And none of them ever wanted to stay?' Alice says, surprised.

'Some did, for a little while, but it gets lonely up here, and love doesn't enjoy solitude for very long.'

'That's sad,' Alice says, eyes glistening.

Birger holds out his arms. 'Not really. We have good times. And then they go, and I cannot follow. And then I live my life alone again. I enjoy being on my own. I can do what I want. I can walk when I want, sleep when I want, eat and drink when I want, and drink as much or as little as I want.' He throws back a glass of akevitt. 'I can sit outside all night without anyone calling me to come inside, without anyone telling me I should be doing something less interesting. I can sleep on the porch all night in the summer, with the sun on me, warming my old bones.'

'And that makes up for being alone?' she says. 'I don't think I could do that.'

'We're not born to be with other people,' he says. 'Living with someone else is a life of compromise, a life of balancing yourself against someone else's self. It's not always comfortable; not for long, anyway. And silence, girl, silence is like gold; precious and full of secret light.' He leans back in his chair. 'You two are lucky, to have found each other. If there's any sadness it's that I've not been able to overcome my fear of travelling far from here.'

'Maybe you should try now,' she says. 'James has.'

'He's a young man.' It's like I'm not here. 'I'm too old to change.'

'How do you know?' she says. 'When was the last time you tried?'

'I've lost count of the years,' he says.

'Maybe we'll be able to persuade you,' I say, to remind

them I'm still here.

'I doubt it,' he says. 'I'll see out my days here, content in myself.'

'What if I said you could translate the whole book if you came?' I say. 'Just sit in a room in England and work through it?'

'I'd be away from my mountains,' he says. 'You could just leave it here with me.' He winks.

'I can't do that,' Alice says. 'It's too important.'

'I know it is,' Birger says. 'I was joking.' He shrugs. 'But then we Norwegians have no sense of humour.' He laughs out loudly. 'I need a smoke.'

'Let's sit on the porch then,' I say. 'We've got warm clothes.'

'Only for a little while,' he says. 'I don't want you young people to fall asleep and freeze to death out there.'

'We wouldn't.'

'It happened to some youngsters in Tromsø,' he says. 'They decided to climb up the ski jump when they were drunk, and fell asleep up there. The next morning, all but one of them were dead. And it was only autumn.'

There's an uncomfortable silence.

'That makes it even less likely that the Thin Air Sutra's the truth then,' Alice says. 'How could a bunch of monks in rags survive near the top of Everest?'

'Faith does strange things to your body,' he says.

'You believe that?' she says. 'You believe?'

'I have faith in something I can't understand,' he says. 'It's not, how do you say, touchable, but it's there. It's primitive, barbaric, to say nothing's there. We can still do what we want, even if something's watching over us.'

We sit outside, wrapped in our climbing gear, Birger in a thick jacket and a blanket. He smokes a pipe, while I smoke another one of my iron reserve cigarettes.

Alice sits there, immobile, her face turned in the direction of the mountain, that insignificant foothill of a mountain that almost killed her.

'I'll sleep on it,' Birger says as my cigarette crumbles and the embers in his pipe die. 'I'll tell you tomorrow if I feel brave enough to come with you.'

When we wake the next morning, he's disappeared, his house unlocked and empty, as empty as the space on Alice's bedside table where she put the Sutra of Thin Air.

Chapter 17

The drive back to Tromsø is less than comfortable.

'Why did we ever trust him?' Alice says.

'I still do,' I say, stare at the road.

'He nicked off with the book.'

'Is that really what you think? You got on with him as well, you know.'

'No sign of a break-in or a struggle.' She sighs, sounds disappointed. With herself or with him, I don't know.

I shrug. The car slithers on the icy road. 'It's easy to cover up that sort of thing.' Brake, counter steer, foot off brake. Instinct. Nothing more. The white is black.

'What do you think happened then?' Her voice is harsh.

'They came back, what with losing Simon and the book.'

'Unless they've got Simon again, and tortured him, and he told them.'

'I don't think he even knows about the book.'

'He must do.' A shrill complaint.

'Even if he does, I don't think he knew that the two monks had it with them.' I am trying to be sensible.

'What'll happen to their bodies, do you think?'

'If no-one claims them, they'll just get an anonymous burial.'

'How long before that happens?'

'I don't know.'

'We'll come back.'

I grunt. 'I don't think we'll be in time. And anyway, I don't know if I'll be able to fly again.'

'What?'

'I keep thinking this must all just be temporary, that the fear will come back, that I'll go back.'

'Stop being negative.'

'I'm trying.'

She scrunches herself into her seat. 'Can't we get a move on?'

'Not unless you want a thousand quid fine for speeding.'

'Who in their right mind would have a fifty-five mile an hour speed limit?'

'People who live through 9-month winters.' The car hiccoughs again over an unsalted slab of ice. 'See what I mean?' I'm getting cramp in my hands from the effort.

'Wake me up when we get there,' she says, and closes her eyes. I'm on my own again, empty road ahead of me, glad the conversation's done.

As soon as we get to the hotel, she's out of the car, and up to the room. It's undisturbed, or so it seems. She shakes her head. 'It doesn't make sense, for him to disappear with the book. And if they came and took it, how come we didn't wake up?' She drops heavily onto the bed. 'I suppose it didn't help that we were tired and half-drunk.'

'There's no point thinking about it any more,' I say. 'It's happened. Let's just get out of here and get on the first plane back to England. I want to see what this ex of Simon's has got to say for herself.'

'He'll be there,' she says. 'Don't you worry about that.'

'You're setting yourself up to be disappointed. You can't be sure he'll be there.'

'I can feel it.'

'We'll see.'

We check out, and walk to the car.

'Let's get enough cash out in the town centre to pay for the flights,' she says.

'Why?'

'They can trace credit card transactions.'

'Oh, come on, they can't be that sophisticated, these people. They'd have to be influential beyond measure to do that.'

'You still think they're are small-time criminals?'

'Well, they're not government agents, if that's what you were thinking.' I sound ridiculous, and I know it. I'm out of my depth. We're out of our depth.

She slams the car door shut, like she knows what I'm thinking. 'We don't know that.' Her eyes are dark.

'It's just a bit over the top, that's all.'

'Sorry.' She curls up in a small ball, tucks her long legs under her, closes her eyes, and sighs. 'I just feel very exposed.'

'I'm sorry.' I reach across to her, stroke her ankle. 'We'll get the money before we go to the airport.'

'Thanks,' she says, sounds tired.

When we've taken the car back to the hire place, we wander across the car park in between the piles of snow on either side, stamp the snow and grit off our boots before we walk into the terminal building. It takes me an hour to get flights back down south, but no connecting flights to England. At least we're flying to Oslo, so there'll be plenty of choice.

'I'm so annoyed about the book,' she says, does up her seatbelt, looks out of the plane window. 'I should've put it under the mattress. How the hell didn't we hear whoever took it?'

'We were drunk and tired.' I don't mention the spectacular pattern of bruises which had erupted all over her body by the time we went to bed.

'So he got us drunk deliberately, and snuck in with his spare key.'

'He was as drunk as us,' I say, and shake my head. 'I still don't believe he did it.'

'If I catch whoever it was, I'll kill 'em.'

'Steady.'

'Well, they're obviously bastards.'

'Very focused bastards.'

'You don't think it's those Yanks who are going to

look for Irvine in the autumn, do you?'

'That's a difficult question,' I say.

'Good, old-fashioned British evasion.'

'I'm confused about everything, to be honest. Let's just see what happens.'

'At least I've still got those notes I made.'

'If Birger did steal the book, maybe he just made up what he was telling you.'

She closes her eyes. 'I'm looking at him while he's reading it,' she says quietly. 'No, he didn't make it up; he was just as surprised as us at what it said.'

The engines get too loud for us to talk. I close my eyes, swallow, deeply, search out her hand, squeeze it tightly, ever so tightly, until the plane levels out and we're at 35,000 feet. When I open my eyes, I wish I hadn't thought about the height we're at, so I close my eyes again. That helps a little, and I don't need to grab for the sick bag.

'James.' I hear her calling from far away, claw my way back to consciousness. I must've fallen asleep.

'What?'

'You were shouting,' she says.

The people in front of us, and behind, are staring at me.

'Sorry.' I feel my ears going red.

'You ok?' she says.

'I think so. I must've been dreaming.'

'I'm not even going to ask what about.'

'I can't remember anyway.' I ignore what's around me, swallow against the urge to vomit. 'How far are we from Oslo?'

'Twenty minutes.'

'Thank God.'

We're back in the air an hour after we touch down. There were a couple of standby tickets for Heathrow, and not having any luggage always helps.

I stay awake this time, let Alice sleep, watch her breathing. Her hair is ragged, some of it hanging down over half her face, almost touching her nose, hiding her black eye. Her lips are still swollen and split. As the plane drones its way across the North Sea, I stroke her hair, her face, feel the heat in her cheeks, those cheekbones burning. I look out of the window without thinking, see only early evening clouds and my reflection. I wish this was all over, wonder what's happening in Christchurch, what we'll do with the house when all this madness has ended and we've stopped travelling again. Wish myself into her, a part of her forever, with no need to keep running, no need to keep blaming myself; wish myself somewhere safe.

Alice doesn't wake until the tires hit the runway. Even then, she doesn't wake with a start, but with the controlled elegance she always has, that impression she gives of always being in control of her body, of not wasting energy on the unnecessary, an economy of movement, an ethereal gracefulness.

'Good,' she yawns. 'Thanks for letting me sleep. Let's let all the other losers get off the plane first. Don't fancy getting crushed in the rush.' She laughs. 'They'll all have to wait around for their luggage anyway.'

We sit there holding hands for ten minutes, then get up and stroll to the front of the almost-deserted plane. She stretches as she walks, her bones cracking, keeps yawning. Our footsteps are muffled by the carpet, grow louder as we leave out onto the metal gangway.

'So what's the address of this woman?' I say. My voice echoes in the bare corridor.

'West London somewhere.'

'D'you think you can be more precise?'

She digs her mobile from one of her combats' many pockets, turns it on, stops to lean against the wall. The screen illuminates her face. The black eye makes the rest of her face look unnaturally pale. 'Eaton Place,' she says.

'So, couldn't you just have called her if she's in your phone?'

'I haven't got her number.'

'Couldn't we have called directory enquiries?'

'I don't know her surname either.'

'Jesus. So you're not exactly bosom buddies.'

She shrugs. 'I've never been that organised. You know that.'

'S'ppose.'

'Come on,' she says, puts an arm round my shoulder. 'Come on, oh weary traveller. We've got lots to do.'

I shake my head.

We walk through the terminal, against the traffic of people heading for their gates to escape the dreary English weather, fat raindrops sliding down the huge windows overlooking the tarmac, planes huddled as near as possible to the buildings to stay out of the rain. I'd forgotten how wonderful it can be to travel light, to move in the opposite direction of the crowd, to walk upright and without fear. I look at her and smile.

'I used to love doing this on my own,' I say.

'I know.'

'Then I lost it.'

'I know that, too,' she says.

'And then I found you.'

'Actually, I found you.'

'You know what I mean.'

'I'm being silly,' she says, squeezes my hand. 'I want you to be happy; I've always wanted you to be happy. It's all I ever hoped for.'

Out through the green channel, along the fake marble floors, towards the blue and red of the Tube. We buy tickets with cash, then down the escalator to the platform. It's still warm here, no taste yet of the awful weather outside. We've been almost hermetically sealed since we left Oslo. Modern life's hermetically sealed. No-one's in touch with nature any more. No-one's in touch with themselves any more. Rush, greed, rush. Maybe that's what it was, when they all ganged up on me. Not just being judge, jury and executioner, but an envy of the beautiful consolation I'd found, of the way I seemed to have come out of that disaster better than anyone else. And Graham still foetally frozen in that cave on Everest.

'I should go back to bury him,' I say.

'What?' She can't read my mind, obviously.

'Graham.' The train rattles its way through the tunnel.

'You want to go back to Everest?'

'You want me to go anyway, don't you?' I say. 'Isn't that what all this is working up to?'

'I …' She catches her breath. 'Yes, of course.'

'I might break down.'

'Me, too.'

'I might go crazy.'

'So might I.'

'I can't see either of those things happening,' I say.

'Then why should they happen to you?'

I look at her, put my hand under her chin, kiss her as gently as I can. 'I suppose there's no reason to think they will.'

'Mmm.' She smiles, breathes a deep breath. 'You may kiss me again.'

'People might start talking.'

'Then let them talk.'

'And staring.'

'Let them stare,' she says.

'Do you still love me?'

'Would I want you to kiss me if I didn't?' She pulls her head back. 'Yes, I do love you.' And then she kisses me again.

'You do realise Eaton Place is really posh, don't you?' I say.

'And?'

'So Simon's ex - what's her name by the way?'

'Miranda.'

'So Miranda must be quite wealthy.'

'I don't know. He met her at some book launch at the Victoria & Albert Museum.'

'Simon at the V&A? At a book launch?'

'Why not?'

'Well, just, well.'

'You're an idiot.' She punches me.

'Next you'll be telling me he likes flower arranging.'

'No comment.'

We get off at Sloane Square. My stomach's rumbling. We've not really eaten today.

'I'm starving,' I say.

'Let's get this done first,' she says. 'We can worry about food later. There's bound to be a burger joint round here somewhere.'

'You might be struggling.'

'Whatever.'

'Do you know how to get there?' I say, trailing through the crowds after her.

'GPS is a lovely thing,' she calls back to me.

'Slow down. What's the rush?'

'I can't slow down. I want to see my brother.'

We're getting soaked. The rain shows no sign of stopping.

'I preferred the cold and the snow and ice,' I say.

'Me, too. But we'll be out of it soon. It's just round the corner here.' Her voice is a vapour trail.

The houses are all white, creamy white, so consistently uniform. It's impressive and annoying at the same time. I suppose they're all run by the same management company.

She turns right, then left, stops in front of a row of tall, terraced houses, front doors protected by canopies supported by white pillars. 'Here we are,' she says, walks in under the canopy out of the rain, looks at the row of gold door bell buttons, ten of them, the highest number at the top. 'Damn,' she says, looks at her phone. 'I've only got the house number, not the flat number.'

'Great joy,' I say, look up. 'Wonderful.'

'It's not my fault.'

'Why not try the middle one?'

'There isn't a middle one. It's an even number, Dumbo.'

'Five or six, then. You decide.'

'I can't.'

'Stop being stupid,' I say. 'I'm getting cold.'

'Ok. An odd number it is then.' She presses the gold button with the Number five on it, waits, stares at the camera at the top of the button plate.

'Hello?'

'Is Miranda there? This is …'

'Alice, is that you?'

'Yes.'

'Come in, come in.' The door clicks open. 'Second floor,' the voice calls.

The staircase is carpeted, clean, warm, the banisters polished a rich, dark brown. Everything oozes wealth and comfort. Tasteful, framed reproductions on the walls. I follow Alice up the stairs, can't stop myself from staring at her bum. I start sweating.

'Nearly there,' she says. No echo in this opulence.

We get to the second floor. There's a closed door straight ahead. A door opens in the hallway to our left.

'Alice.' The voice is even more gravelly than it sounded on the intercom. 'Come in. It's been ages.' The woman whose voice it is isn't much over five feet tall, skinny, highlighted hair. She must be in her fifties.

Alice bends down to kiss her. Must be Miranda's mother. 'Hello, Miranda,' she says. 'And *you* can drag your jaw off the floor,' she says to me.

'What?' I hold my hands out.

'This must be that husband of yours I've heard so much about,' Miranda says. She holds her hand out to me, as if she's expecting me to kiss it. She's wearing a pearl necklace, tight, pleated trousers. 'Didn't Alice tell you that Simon has a weakness for more mature women?' She winks at me. 'How nice to meet you, dahling.' She kisses me on the cheek.

We walk into the flat, all wooden floors, rugs, high ceilings.

'Here,' Miranda says. 'Just plonk all your stuff on the floor. I'll take your coats to the bathroom; they'll dry there.'

We take off our shoes while Miranda fusses, slide our way carefully from the entrance hall into the huge living room, no reproductions on the wall, just what look like originals, and a massive sofa with lots of cushions.

'Sit, sit,' Miranda says. 'Make yourself at home.' She sits down on the other huge sofa. 'Now, what can I do for you?'

'I thought Simon might be here,' Alice says.

Chapter 18

Miranda crosses her legs, smoothes the creases from her trousers, lays her hands flat on her knees, and says nothing.

'He's running from something or somebody,' Alice says. 'I thought he might come here to be safe.'

'Does he want your help?' Miranda finally says.

'No,' I say. 'Anything but.'

'He needs it, though,' Alice says.

'What makes you say that?' Miranda says, crosses and recrosses her legs.

'He can't cope on his own,' Alice says.

'I saw him just over a week ago in Cambridge,' I say, 'And he'd been beaten to a pulp, or something like that. And then he texted Alice and told her to back off.'

'How strange,' Miranda says, pushes a stray hair behind her left ear.

'You don't know where he is, then?' Alice says.

Miranda rubs imaginary specks of dust from her trouser legs. 'Well,' she says.

Down the corridor, a door opens and closes. Footsteps. We all look towards the sounds, know what we'll see.

'You're a bloody awful liar, Miranda,' Simon says.

Alice gets up, runs towards him, throws her arms around him. 'I've been so worried.'

'Calm yourself,' he says, and pushes her away. 'Why can't you listen to what I tell you?'

'Tell me what's going on, and I might.'

'It's got nothing to do with you,' he says. 'And it's dangerous.'

'I know,' Alice says, stays standing, crosses her arms. 'You shouldn't always assume I'm useless, just because you're older by fifteen minutes.'

'Oh, do leave it, and sit down.' He sighs, and drops

onto the sofa next to Miranda. 'I told you not to get involved,' he says. 'You're still my little sister.'

Alice sits down again, right next to me, her heat seeping through my trousers. 'But we *are* involved, Simon.' She raises her arms. 'Do you know how close we were to getting blown up with your room?'

'I told you to get out,' he says. 'Wasn't that enough?'

'And we did, thank you. But we went back.'

'That was bloody stupid.'

'Only because you didn't tell us what was going on. If you'd have stayed instead of disappearing again in the middle of the night, if you'd have shared with us, we wouldn't even have been near the place.'

'And I'd have been dead,' he says. 'For certain.'

'Just explain things to us.'

He folds his arms, unfolds them, runs his hands through his hair. 'I can't.'

'Do you know where we've been?' Alice says.

'How could I?'

'We've been to Holmbukttind,' she says.

'The police found the bodies,' I say. 'They claim it was a suicide pact.'

'And?' he says, hands fidgeting. 'What's that got to do with me?'

'We found your chain.'

'So I've been there, too,' he says.

'But why?'

'I could ask you the same,' he says, his voice level and accusing.

'Probably the same reason you and your dead mates went,' Alice says. 'Because Irvine had been there.'

'You do realise they'll have followed you here,' he says. 'Miranda's in danger now, too. And this isn't a safe place any more. How did you find me, anyway?

'I just thought this would be the first place you'd come if you were in trouble.'

'There's more to it than that,' Miranda says, and tries to suppress a smile, unsuccessfully.

He shoots a glance at her. 'You're impossible.'

'We're back together,' she says, pulls his unwilling hand towards her. 'He could never resist me.'

'Why's he so horrible to everyone else then?' Alice says.

'He's got a serious personality defect,' Miranda says. 'That's why I threw him out in the first place.'

'And now?' Alice says. 'What's changed?'

'I didn't stop missing him. And he needed me to look after him when he turned up a week ago. He was worried about you, you know.'

'I give in,' he says. 'I can't cope with being fussed over and interrogated.'

'So you're going to tell us everything?' I say.

He starts to sneer, changes his mind, leans forward, intertwines his fingers. 'I suppose so, but quickly. We need to get out of here.'

'I'll pack then, shall I?' Miranda says.

Simon nods. 'You'll have to find somewhere to go, my love,' he says, unexpectedly gentle.

'I'm coming with you.'

'Don't be ridiculous. You won't like living in a tent.'

'There's got to be a first time for everything,' she says. 'And I can't stay here.'

'Fine,' he says. 'Fine.' Always so impatient. Like his sister.

'Come on then,' Alice says. 'Spill the beans.'

'Where do you want me to start?'

'Why did you say you'd found Irvine?' I say.

He rubs his hands together, clenches his fists, red creeping into his face, an agitation about him I've not seen before. He opens his mouth, closes it again, purses his lips, opens his mouth again, struggles to form the words, fights to find the right words, to find the will and courage to speak. 'It's not easy to explain,' he says. 'You'll think I'm mad.'

'Go on,' Alice says. 'Try me.'

'I don't think he died when Mallory died.'

'A few days later, you mean?' she says. 'Two or three. He can't have lasted any longer than that.'

'Unless he was found and taken somewhere.'

'What?' Alice snaps.

None of us say anything. Alice and Simon stare at each other, unflinching. Miranda and I wait for them to break the silence. They wait for each other.

'That's impossible,' Alice says, giving in. 'You can't be serious.'

He shrugs. 'Why?'

'There's nothing to suggest it, nothing at all, not in any books, not anywhere.'

'So why hasn't his body been found?' Simon says. 'Why's everyone so sure he died at the same time as Mallory?'

'You think he climbed off the mountain and just disappeared?' she says. 'And didn't go back to his family?'

Simon shakes his head again. 'There's something else,' he says. 'Something I don't understand.'

'And what's that?' she says.

'These mates of mine, as you call them; they weren't just sherpas, they were monks. And they told me …' He stops himself, like he's said too much already.

'What did they tell you?' Alice is almost begging him to speak.

'They said that there's a secret up there, on the mountain, near the top.'

'What sort of a secret?' She's the impatient one now. I can imagine her stamping her feet in a minute if he doesn't just keep talking. Her fingers scratch at her trousers, her breaths short and sharp.

‘A place, a special place,’ he says. ‘That’s where I think Irvine is.’

‘You don’t think he’s still alive, do you?’ I gate-crash their conversation. ‘You of all people believing this Shangri-La crap?’

‘Oh God, no.’ He laughs when I’d been expecting him to be angry because I’d shot my mouth off without thinking. ‘All that immortality stuff is just that – stuff. Nothing mystical about this. All I thought was that if there’s a special place up there, then maybe he lived a few years longer.’

‘In the Death Zone?’ Alice says. ‘That’s crazy.’

‘I don’t know where,’ he says.

‘Didn’t they tell you?’ she says. ‘If you were such good friends?’

‘They wanted to, I think, but didn’t dare,’ he says. ‘That’s what it felt like, anyway.’

‘Why?’

‘So that I wouldn’t be able to tell anyone. So they wouldn’t be breaking some code of theirs.’

‘Wouldn’t it have been easier for them not to tell you anything?’ Alice says.

‘There’s some funny stuff going on up there. And I saved their lives, once.’

‘When?’ Alice says. ‘You never told me.’

Simon rolls his eyes. ‘I don’t have tell you everything.’ He takes a deep breath. ‘It was a couple of years ago. They fell into a deep crevasse. I got them out.’

‘That sounds a little simple.’

‘There’s no need for any detail. I got them killed in the end, really.’ He covers his face with his hands, shakes his head. ‘It was my fault.’

‘But who killed them?’ Alice says. ‘And why?’

‘That’s the point,’ he says. ‘I don’t know. I don’t know who’s chasing us, me.’

‘Have you heard of the Sutra of Thin Air?’ Alice says.

'You what?' he says, his face blank.

'You haven't, then, obviously,' she says.

'I have no idea what you're talking about.'

'So you weren't on Holmbukttind to bury it?'

'Whatever it is. No. The boys just said they wanted to go there, because that's where Irvine started his serious climbing, where Odell finally decided he ought to go on the expedition.'

'What happened when you were up there?' she says.

'Aren't you going to tell me?' he says. 'You seem to know everything.'

'Don't be ridiculous.' She's almost shouting.

'I'd heard there was a cabin for rent near the mountain, but we decided we didn't want to do that, so we camped out near the fjord, and never went anywhere near the town.'

I start to say something, but Alice puts her hand on my leg and makes me stop.

'You didn't hear or see anything unusual?'

Simon shakes his head. 'We started off early the next morning, when it was still dark. Used our headlamps to find the way. And we made good time. Winged it up that step, too, unroped.' His eyes are alive and excited by the happy memory. 'And then we went on to Jiehkkevarri.'

'Why?' Alice says. 'The step was the important bit, wasn't it?'

'Well, they'd explained to me that Odell and Irvine had never made it to the top because of the weather, and that they wanted to make it to the top for Irvine.'

'Ah, that figures,' she says. 'And then?'

'We were at the top, heard a sound like a skidoo coming from the other side of the mountain. Didn't think anything of it, really. I turned to see what was going on, and the next minute, there's a bunch of masked people, and they get the boys.' Tears start down his face, but he refuses to sob. 'And … and, well, you know. I tried to make a run for it, made it as far as down that step, more falling than climbing, ripped myself open, but there were more waiting at the foot of it. I couldn't fight them all.'

Miranda puts her arm round him.

'Your boys buried something in the snow before they were killed,' Alice says as gently as possible.

Simon lifts his head. 'What?'

'The Sutra of Thin Air. It's a prayer book, or so we think.'

'Have you got it with you?'

'Erm,' Alice says. 'We did have it, but we lost it again.'

'Jesus,' he says. 'And you say I'm ridiculous?'

I tell him what happened.

'And you've no idea where this Birger guy is now?' Simon says.

I shake my head. 'Where did they take you when they'd got you?'

'They must've had a chopper somewhere, because that's what we flew in to start with,' he says. 'And then a plane that smelt very clean. I was blindfolded all the way. But I do know we landed at that airport near Cambo and taxied into a hangar.'

'Weren't there any security checks?' I say.

'They'd chucked me into a freight box at the back of the plane,' he says. 'And I couldn't move when I heard the customs folk come on board. Trussed up like a turkey, I was.'

'So how did you get away?' Alice says.

'Well, they were kicking shit out of me, tied to a chair, asking me where the book was, where the place was. … I suppose that must be the Sutra … I kept telling them I didn't know what the fuck they were talking about, because I didn't, thank fuck. And then they untied me, to do some real damage, I suppose, and I thought what the hell and just started head-butting them and all sorts of stuff.' His face grows red with remembered anger.

'Why didn't they shoot you?' I say.

'Because they still think I know more than I do, I think.'

'So why kill the other two?' Alice says.

'They knew the boys would never talk.'

'I guess so,' Alice says.

'Just read me the bit of the Sutra you've got,' he says. 'It might mean something to me.'

Alice gets the paper out of her pocket, reads it out loud, puts it back in her pocket.

'See,' he says. 'A secret, special place.' He repeats the words soundlessly. 'And it's the Western psyche that changes it all into something mythical, mystical, into this dream of immortality, the cup of youth and all that bollocks, when they're just talking about a holy place they've found, like all mountains have holy places.'

Alice raises an eyebrow. 'Since when have you been into this holy stuff? I thought you were a man of the world.'

'It's not religion, really, you know,' he says, his eyes clear and unblinking. 'It's a faith in nature and in your own strength. That's all it is. What we have inside us.' He puts his hand on his heart and sighs. 'And let's not dissect it all now. What it actually is is irrelevant.'

'So what's all this funny stuff happening on Everest?' I say. 'All that stuff you were talking about.'

He raises an eyebrow, nods almost imperceptibly. 'Rongbuk got robbed, then sherpas started to go missing. But no-one's ever found them – or their bodies.'

'But people need permits to get up there,' I say.

'We all know there's illegals up there all the time,' he says. 'And there's no way of knowing if they've been sanctioned by the Chinese government to intimidate the Tibetans.'

'Is that what you think this is?' Alice says. 'Chinese government?'

He shrugs. 'It'd make sense, wouldn't it? They really don't like this Western sympathy for Tibet, and this constant banging on about restoring independence and human rights.'

'Were they Chinese, then, these people who got you?' Alice says.

'Difficult to say. They never took off their masks, and they spoke accentless English.'

'Great,' Alice says. 'Another dead end.'

'Sorry,' he says. 'I can't help that.'

'So it's either the Yanks or the Chinese out to get you,' Alice says, regardless.

'Or a rogue third party,' I say.

'Thanks for making it simpler,' she says. 'This is crazy.'

'I don't think it's the Americans,' Simon says. 'Holzel might be misguided and obsessed, but I don't think he's malicious. And he's not got the resource to organise the expedition and mobilise people with guns and helicopters and skidoos.'

'That just leaves the Chinese and the rogues, then,' I say.

Simon nods. 'Looks like it.'

'Hey, I think that's the first time you two have agreed on anything,' Alice says.

'The exception to the rule,' Simon and I say, at the same time.

'Oh God,' Simon says. 'Better not let this become a habit.'

'What now, then, dahlings?' Miranda says, her hands busy with her hair. How she's going to survive roughing it, I don't know.

'Tibet,' Simon says. 'No other choice.'

'Tonight?' Alice says.

'Well, as soon as possible,' Simon says. 'But we have to get out of here.'

We all get up.

'How exciting,' Miranda says, trots off.

Simon raises his eyes to the ceiling, mouths a *sorry* at Alice.

'It'll be fine,' she whispers back.

'I hope so,' he mumbles.

Miranda's back again, with two rucksacks, obviously packed to the top. 'I'm ready,' she chirps. 'Let's go.'

'How organised of you,' Simon says.

'I was thinking this might happen, so I'd had most of our things washed and pressed ready to go,' she says.

'I think you're going to have an interesting experience,' I say.

'Good,' she says. 'Life's been boring these last five years without Simon.'

We're about to open the door to go, when Simon stops us. 'Leave your mobiles here,' he says. 'They can probably trace them, even if they're switched off.'

'Bugger,' I say. 'Why didn't I think about that?'

'Because you've only just re-joined the planet,' he says, without malice. 'No offence intended.'

'None taken.'

'Put them in the safe,' Miranda says, pushes a button on the side of the sofa she was sitting on, and a hole appears in the floor next to it. A keypad appears, and she punches in a few numbers. The door opens. She grabs a couple of small boxes, puts all our mobiles in. 'There.' She pushes the door closed, pushes the button again. 'All safe. Bombproof, in fact.'

'Why?' I say.

'One of the ex-husbands left me a lot of expensive jewellery,' she says. 'And it seems quite glamorous having a safe in the floor.'

'Can we stop the chit-chat?' Alice says.

'Sorry,' I say.

Miranda just laughs. 'Oh come on, dahling. We've got to have lots of fun if we're going to get killed.'

'You're mad,' Alice says. 'Stark-raving bonkers.'

'I know,' Miranda says. 'I should have married Simon when he asked me. I'd have been much better at this with more practice.'

We walk down the stairs without putting the lights on, get to the door.

'Let me,' Miranda says, pushes her way past the three of us to the door, and opens it. 'Did you come in a four-wheel drive?' she says, and shuts the door quickly.

'We walked from the Tube,' Alice says.

'Well, then they're here already,' Miranda says. 'I've never seen that car round here before.'

'Can you be sure?' Alice says.

'I'm sure,' Miranda says. 'Let me think.'

'Are there any cellars in this place?' I say.

'There were, but they converted them to basement flats ages ago to make more money,' Miranda says.

'So we can't get out without them seeing us?' I say. 'Dammit.'

'There is one possibility,' she says. 'Hang on.' She turns round and goes up half a flight of stairs, knocks on the door of Flat 1.

'Oh, hello, Miranda,' a male voice says.

'Listen, Charles, dear thing,' she says, her voice at its gravelly seductive best. 'I've got a bit of a problem. There's one of my stalkers outside, and I'm trying to take my friends out to dinner. We couldn't by any chance slip out through your back door, could we?'

'You should get in touch with the police, you know, old girl,' the voice says. 'You do have such an effect on the male of the species.'

'I will, I will,' she says. 'But the table's booked for in

fifteen minutes, and we really are rather in a hurry.'

'Of course,' Charles says.

We all rush past the portly Charles. Miranda obviously knows his flat well. She finds the back door, pulls it open.

'Why have you all got ruck …' Charles stutters.

'I'll explain tomorrow, dahling,' Miranda calls. 'Thanks ever so.'

The door slams behind us.

'This way,' Miranda whisper-shouts. She power-walks to a pink four-wheel drive. 'I hate having to walk round to it,' she says. 'That's why I know where Charles' back door is.'

'It's a bit conspicuous, isn't it?' I say.

Miranda laughs again, a deep laugh. 'The worse your taste appears to be, the more people ignore you,' she says. 'Jump in.'

Once we're all in, she gets the engine running, turns left, then right, towards Sloane Square. 'They won't even know we're gone,' she says. 'Just can't get the staff nowadays, whether you're Chinese or American, or whatever.' She pushes a button and the radio comes on. 'Right, let's enjoy this drive to Heathrow before we have to start slumming it. It's so exciting.'

Chapter 19

Simon turns round to me, smiles sheepishly, scratches his head. He's about to face the front, when his face changes. 'Shit. They're on to us.'

'They don't know we're in the car,' Miranda says. 'Calm down.'

'They'd have stayed outside the flat if they didn't know. They'd still be waiting.'

'Oh God,' she says. 'What about Charles?'

'Too late to worry about that,' Simon says. 'Put your foot down.'

'That won't work,' she says. 'Not on its own. Hold tight.'

The car leaps forward, wheels screeching, swerves to the left, past a familiar red and white sign.

'It's a one-way street,' Simon shouts.

'I know,' Miranda says. 'Good, eh?'

We hurtle down the road, weaving through the oncoming cars.

'Just enough room, this one,' Miranda laughs. 'I've done this once before, just for a laugh.'

'Will you concentrate on driving?' Simon shouts. Is he scared?

'I am,' she says, laughing. Cars pass by either side, horns blaring, lights flashing. 'It's much more exciting at night time.'

'Yeah,' he says.

'Are they still behind us?' she says.

'Yes,' he says. 'But they're losing ground.'

'Jolly good.' She rips the wheel to her right. The car jumps over the pavement into another road. Radio Three's still playing, something by Mozart, I think. 'We're going the right way this time,' she says. 'Off West we go.'

'They're still there,' Simon shouts.

'One more right,' she says. 'Here we go.' She sways with the car. 'And left again. Any sign?'

'No, I don't think so,' Simon says.

'You really are mad,' Alice shouts.

'A girl needs some entertainment,' Miranda calls over her shoulder. 'I'll think of some back way to get us out of here. But not on the motorway. It'd be too easy for them to catch up.' She ducks down over the steering wheel.

Simon's still looking out through the back window. 'I can't see anything now. I think you've done it.'

'We're not out of it yet,' she says. 'But you lot need to talk. Let me worry about the road.'

'Have you actually got an Everest permit, Simon?' Alice says.

'Not really,' he says.

'In other words, no.'

He keeps turning round. 'It doesn't matter. We'll just do an illegal. The North route's not very popular anyway. They can't just haul tourists up that way. There's still some proper climbing on that side.'

'And what if the Chinese get wind of it?' I say.

'They won't.'

'Just like they didn't know we were going to visit you at Miranda's?' Alice says.

'You don't know they're Chinese,' Simon says.

She grunts. 'I don't like not knowing, so I'll settle for them.'

'Stubborn old cow,' I say.

'That's me.'

'How the hell are we going to pay for this?' I say.

'Travellers' cheques,' Miranda says. 'I've always got a stash on me.'

'What do you do?' I say. 'For a living?'

'Nothing, really. I married a rich man who died before he could divorce me,' she says. 'Not that his death had anything to do with me.'

'We'll pay you back when we're done,' Alice says.

'Don't worry about that now.'

'What about times?' I say, look at my watch. 'It's gone seven.'

'It doesn't really matter what time we get there,' Simon says. 'We'll just catch a flight to anywhere and think on tomorrow. We need to get out of the country tonight, though.'

'What about visas?' Miranda says, her slow voice a counterpoint to our hurried exchanges.

'We can get limited ones at the airport,' Simon says. 'And then just go AWOL.'

'Won't they try to find us?' I say.

'We'll be long gone by then,' he says. 'And once we're on Everest, they won't bother.'

'You've forgotten about supplies and other such insignificant things, dear brother,' Alice says, her eyes shining.

'Rongbuk,' he says. 'We'll get them there.'

The traffic's thinned out now, more coming into London than going out. The lights of the cars shimmer in a chaotic pattern, moving, stopping, moving, shaking.

'How odd not to be going out in town for the evening,' Miranda says, more to herself than us.

'You can always just drop us off at the airport if you're losing your appetite for adventure already,' Simon says. There's hope in his voice, and concern.

'Don't be silly,' she says. 'I'm just reflecting. I want this as much as you do.'

'No sex in tents,' he says, laughing.

'I'm sure we'll manage,' she says.

'I'm not quite sure how to take that.' He leans back in his seat.

'Any way you want, dahling, any way you want,' she

chirps.

'How much further?' I say. 'I'm lost.'

'About half an hour if the traffic's kind,' Miranda says.

'And then?' I say. 'When we get there?'

'I will go and find us a flight. You three will go and get a couple of satellite phones, bought without a name, of course, and with six hours prepaid talk time on them. And then we'll get on a plane. Any other shopping we can do wherever we stop over.' She doesn't sound quite so dippy anymore.

'What's it like to be a kept man?' Alice says.

Simon shrugs, turns away, puts his hand on Miranda's shoulder.

'Won't they cotton on to us leaving the country when our passports are scanned?' I say.

'It's a chance we have to take,' Simon says. 'I've got my second passport here. Same name, just a different nationality.' His silhouette shrugs. 'There's no other way.'

'None of that fills me with confidence,' Alice says. 'Underprepared, overpsyched, and hunted.'

'Oh, I wouldn't worry, Alice,' Miranda says. 'You know what his motto really is – the more often I get into trouble, the more often I get out of it.' The whine of the engine slows to a whirr. She winds the window down. 'I need some cooler air. And I hate the air con.'

'I still can't believe I'm doing this,' I say. 'What if Simon's right and I am a wimp?'

'Ignore what I said last week,' he says. 'It was the heat of the moment.'

'And all the other times before that?' I say.

'The heat of envy.'

'What?'

'All twin brothers are in love with their sister and hate it when that sister falls in love with someone else,' he says.

'Your transformation into a non-shouty person is quite disturbing,' Alice says. 'I never hated any of your girlfriends.'

'You're probably better balanced than me.'

'You're talking sense for once. I can't remember the last time you did.' She laughs.

'Oh, fuck off,' he says.

'That's more like it,' Alice says. 'Now shut up and let me sleep till we get to the airport.'

I close my eyes as well, feel more nervous and fearful about this trip. So many uncertainties. What if I can't hack it up there? What if the same happens that happened to Graham and me? Sometimes I think, I know, even, that it was my fault he died, that I should never have agreed to go up there with him.

The sound of the traffic lulls me away from my morbid thoughts, rocks me into a half-world of irregular sounds, quiet then louder, whoosh and past. I think I hear Simon and Miranda mumbling to each other, but I can't be sure; it could just be me dreaming, imagining, escaping. The only constant now, the only constant there's ever been, is Alice's warmth next to me, keeping me sane and safe. And then I'm gone and all is silent.

Not for long. The car stops.

'You lot get out here,' Miranda says.

We're in front of Terminal 4.

'Come on. Chop, chop,' she commands. 'I'm just going to dump this in short-term parking. I'm sure whoever it is who's chasing Simon won't think we're the extravagant types. They probably don't understand extravagance. I'll meet you inside. I won't be long. You go and see what flights there are. We should be able to get something to Delhi, Hong Kong or Bahrain. And then we'll see from there.'

The doors slam. I'm still in a daze. My heart's starting

to beat too fast again.

'Just act normal,' Simon says.

'I am.'

He shakes his head, some of his old arrogance back. He grabs me by the elbow. 'We're going to do this,' he says through gritted teeth.

'I know we are,' I say. 'Just don't assume it'll be easy.'

'I'm not assuming anything.'

'Good,' Alice chimes in as we push our way into the busy terminal hall. 'We need to have a plan.'

'I've got maps of where I think they fell,' he says.

'Oh, by the way,' Alice says. 'I forgot to ask you. What did you mean when you wrote that stuff about Irvine on the piece of paper we found in the books?'

'Just what I said before, really,' he says.

'There must be more to it than that,' she says. 'Something you worked out that makes you think he survived the fall.'

He brushes her words away with his big hands. 'Later. Let's sort out these flights first.'

The terminal isn't as full as it would be during the day, but it's busy enough. The lights are bright, and there's a constant buzz of people talking, interrupted by the occasional shout or laugh. I pull my coat tighter around me.

'Come on, James,' Alice says. 'It's not too bad. Once we're on the plane, you'll be fine.'

'I'm fine,' I say. 'I just hate crowds.'

'That comes from living at the end of the world,' she says. 'Christchurch isn't exactly the most accessible city on the planet.'

'But I like it.'

'What's left of it,' she says.

'It'll survive. It's got to.'

'I hope so. Because I love it, too.'

'There's a flight at half past nine,' Simon says. 'I

reckon it'll start boarding in about fifteen minutes. Nothing after that, by the looks of it.'

'Where's Miranda?' Alice says. 'We're cutting it a bit fine.'

'If we miss the Asian flights, we'll just have to fly to Spain or somewhere else in Europe first,' Simon says.

I look round. 'How do we know they're not here already?'

'We don't,' Alice says. 'But then they don't know where we are, either.'

'They'll have a good guess at us trying to get out to Everest.'

'But they won't know for sure. And they might think we're going to Gatwick, or somewhere else.'

'I suppose.' I'm not convinced, and this cloak and dagger stuff doesn't suit me.

'Look at it this way,' Simon says, trying to smile. 'What would you rather be doing, trying to talk to insurance companies about your house, or having an adventure, however difficult it might be for you?'

'Do I have to choose?' I say. 'Joke.' I hold up my hands.

He shakes his head. 'Come *on*, Miranda.' He's getting agitated.

I'm the first to see her, weaving her way gracefully through the crowds. She's waving bits of paper at us from a distance. 'Come on, dahlings. I've got the tickets already.' She runs the last part of the way, throws herself at Simon. She's like a teenager. 'Now, I think congratulations are in order, but you can save them until later. We need to get to the gate in the next thirty minutes.'

'And how are we going to do that?' Simon says. I thought I was the only miserable git of our group.

'Fast-Track, of course, dearest,' she says, leads the way towards the security barriers. 'I got us First Class tickets.'

'What?' Alice says. 'That must have cost a fortune.'

'Only a small fortune,' Miranda says breathlessly. 'No big deal.'

'So where are we flying to?' Simon says.

'Delhi Indira Ghandi,' she says. 'Just over eight hours flying. And then half a day in the airport.'

'Shit,' he says.

'Don't be silly, Simon. It'll give us lots of time to go shopping. And lots of time to talk. Won't it?' She smiles. I wouldn't like to get on the wrong side of her. She knows what she wants, pretends to be vacuous.

'I suppose,' he says and bows his head.

'You get bored much too easily,' she says. 'It's time you grew up.'

He laughs. 'The next thing you'll be asking me to marry you.'

'You're not scared of following my first husband, are you?'

'In what way?' he says.

'To the grave, of course.'

'I'm not rich.'

'That was below the belt,' she says. 'I didn't marry him for his money.'

'Sorry.'

'Don't be. Right, passports, please. Quickly. Open on the photo page.'

We hand them over.

'Leave this to me.' She strides ahead, smiles at the security guard. 'Hello. How are you?'

'Fine, madam. You?'

'In a bit if a hurry, actually. Last-minute decision.'

'Holiday, is it?'

'No, no. Just a shopping trip to Delhi. I need a new sari for a friend's wedding. And *they* need new clothes.' She looks down her nose at us.

'Oh.' He doesn't know what to make of her.

'We're not rushing you, are we?' she says.

'Not at all, madam.' If he had a cap he'd be doffing it. 'The gate's not far. Have a safe trip.'

'Oh, thank you so much. How nice of you.'

She wafts past him, lets herself be patted down by the female security guard, waits impatiently as we get patted down, too. 'We must hurry, dahlings, or we'll be in all sorts of trouble with the Raj.'

'You'll be fine, Madam,' the guard says. 'Five minutes to the gate, max. You'll just have to do without the duty-frees.'

'I don't drink anyway,' she says, smiles. 'But they do.'

We all pile towards the gate. I start running.

'There's no need for that, James,' she says. 'They'll wait for us.'

When we get to the gate, everyone's still sitting, waiting.

'Come on then, kidlings,' she says, walks to the girl at the desk. 'Miranda Howard and guests. How do we get on?'

'Just follow my colleague,' the girl says. 'We're all ready to board you.'

'Thank you so much,' Miranda says, minces along the corridor, across the clanking metal and into the plane. 'Upstairs,' she says. 'Let's make sure we get comfortable.'

Once we're in our seats, she orders two bottles of champagne. 'We'll have a glass before we take off,' she says. 'I find the bubbles go well with the excitement of leaving the ground.'

I sit down. All this space around me feels very odd after the economy flight to Norway, the waiting in the cold outside Christchurch airport.

'Cheers, all,' Miranda says. 'Here's to a lovely shopping expedition.'

We clink glasses, drink deeply from the thin-stemmed crystal. The alcohol slows my heart down, as does Alice's hand on my leg.

'That's much better,' Miranda says when no-one's around for a moment. 'We don't need to deprive ourselves of life's pleasures just yet, do we?'

Chapter 20

Irvine's scream echoed through the passages of the High Monastery, reached Tara just as she was about to go into her room. She turned and walked, as quickly as she could, back to the sick man's room.

'George,' Irvine called again, sitting up, eyes open, but unseeing.

'Calm,' Virya said. 'Your friend is safe.'

'Father,' Tara said, quietly. 'Let me.'

'Even words in his language won't make him rest.'

'I'll calm him down,' she said, took Irvine's massive hand from her father, intertwined her thin fingers with those of the climber, murmured words Virya couldn't make out, hummed a gentle tune. Irvine stopped shouting, struggling, began instead to rock back and forth. Tara stroked his face with her free hand. 'See that shelf over there, Father?' she said.

Virya nodded.

'The middle jar, please bring it over to me.'

Virya lifted the jar from the shelf, returned to his daughter's side.

'The water bowl,' she whispered. 'Put it on the bed.' She hummed again. 'Now open the jar, pour two of the tablets into my free hand.'

Virya did as she asked.

'Now please go and stand behind him. He's not really awake, but his pulse is racing, and he needs this medicine if he's to live.' Still holding Irvine's hand, she sat on the bed next to him, next to the water bowl, reached up to his mouth, stroked his scabby lips, put the tablets in his mouth, reached for the water, and fed some to him.

Irvine swallowed the tablets without a struggle, gulped down the water, opened his mouth for more, which Tara gave him. He stopped swaying, sat still for a moment, and then collapsed onto the bed, Virya's hands guiding him gently down. His breathing was deep and regular, his face soft and unmoving.

Tara stood up, closed her eyes and took his pulse. 'He'll sleep now, for about two days.'

'You can read my mind.'

'No,' she said. 'It was obvious you'd ask.'

'Will he survive?' There was an undiscovered caring in his voice.

'I hope so. But it's not certain. I shouldn't have left him.' She shook her head, took a deep breath, stared at the sleeping man.

'I'm sorry.'

'It's not your fault. You're not a healer, you're a preacher. I just didn't expect him to react so violently.' She stroked Irvine's motionless hand, more in hope than in conviction.

'I think he felt you leave,' Virya said. 'He must know you saved him.'

She smiled and blushed. 'Then he's definitely recovering.'

'But you mustn't carry the entire burden yourself.'

'I don't have a choice. I can't let him die when he wants to live.'

'I'll bring your bed in here,' he said.

'I can't sleep when I'm looking after him.'

'I can sit here while you sleep. At least that way you won't be gone. I'll wake you if anything happens. Agreed?'

She nodded. 'Was it wrong of me to rescue him?' She was close to tears.

Virya shook his head. 'Why would it be wrong?'

'It's a burden to the monastery,' she said.

'No, it's not. We have everything we need. One more mouth makes no difference. The mountain gives us all the warmth we need. The supplies we have are enough until after the monsoons.'

'And when he wakes?'

'We'll see,' he said.

'He'll want to go home.'

'I know. But that can't be avoided.'

'Won't he give us away?'

'I don't think so.'

'Why?' she said. 'How would he be able to stop himself from telling his people about us?'

Virya reached across to her, took her hand. 'You worry too much, ask too many questions.'

'Tell me why you think he wouldn't give us away.'

'When I was at Rongbuk, I was told he'd worshipped at the statue of Buddha.'

'Does that matter?' She was puzzled. There had been white men before who had worshipped there.

'He thought he'd not been seen, but a couple of the lowlands monks followed him. They said he'd prayed loudly, in our language, and that his words were wise beyond his years.'

'Did they tell you what he said?'

'They couldn't remember the exact words,' Virya said.

'What did they remember?'

'He prayed to the mother of the earth, and asked her to guard and guide him and his friends. He asked her not to think badly of him that he was going to try to get to the top, that it was his duty to his family, that it was his will to reach the summit even if it was the last thing he did.'

'She must have listened to him, because he did get there.'

'Then why did he fall?'

'I think it must have been his friend who fell. Otherwise we'd have found two bodies.'

'Maybe you're right. It's a shame one of them had to die.'

'We should try to find his friend's body.'

'That's too difficult.' He hated having to tell her it was impossible to challenge the mountain again.

'After the monsoons.'

'Is it worth it?' he said. He didn't want to risk his people's lives, would try to dissuade her.

She wouldn't give in, although she felt his thoughts. 'We can at least cover it with stones and say a prayer.'

'The wind will move the stones after a while.'

'We'll see,' she said. 'The monsoons may be late this year.'

'I'll go and get your bed.'

'Father?' she said as Virya was about to leave the room.

'Yes?'

'Thank you.'

'You've nothing to thank me for,' he said, turned and left.

Tara sat on the bed again, next to Irvine, touched his now still face, ran her fingers through his hair, clean and long. It was the first thing she'd done when they'd brought him back here, washed his hair. She closed her eyes, bowed her head, spoke out loud. 'Please Mother of the Earth, please spare him. He meant you no harm. We can save him, together.'

When Virya came back, a few minutes later, he found Tara, asleep, her head on the climber's bed, her hand tucked inside his hand. He covered her with a rug, quietly built her bed against the wall under the shelf of medicines. He sat next to her, listened to her and the Englishman breathe, almost in unison, stayed there, unmoving, all night.

When he sensed Tara waking, Virya got up and left the room. He didn't want to embarrass her. And he needed to sleep. The journeys to the lowlands were taking more and more out of him. Soon, he knew, he'd have to stop his travels down, and spend the rest of his life up here without visiting Rongbuk. He shrugged. At least he'd been climbing for longer than anyone else in living memory.

And then it happened, what she'd been waiting for. On the evening of the second day after she'd given him the pills, Irvine woke. She was watching him, saw his eyes move under their lids, his cheeks twitch, his lips part.

'Water,' he said.

'Here.' She lifted the bowl to his lips.

He pushed himself up onto his elbows. 'Is this heaven?'

She smiled and shook her head. 'No, just a monastery.'

'There are girls in monasteries?' His lips were still cracked.

'A few.'

'You speak English. I didn't expect you to speak English.'

'My father taught me.'

He took a deep breath. 'Where is this monastery?'

'High up.'

'I'm back in Rongbuk?'

She smiled again. 'Higher than Rongbuk.'

'That's impossible. There's nothing beyond Rongbuk.'

'I'll explain when you're better.'

He looked at his hands. 'No frostbite?'

'You were lucky. We found you in time.'

'And George? Where's George'

She shook her head. 'There was no hope for him.'

His eyes filled with tears.

She reached out to him. 'I'm sorry.'

'It should've been me,' he said. 'I was the novice.'

'It could have been both of you.' She stroked his hands again, loved how they felt, how they dwarfed hers. 'You almost died, too.'

'What do I do now? What can I do?'

'Get better,' she said. 'You can't decide until then.'

'How did you find me?' The flood of words would not stop. He was reincarnated. 'Were you looking for me?'

'No.' She shook her head. 'I happened to see the moonlight reflect on your hair just before darkness came. You'd lost your hat.'

'You were on the mountain?'

'I'm always on the mountain,' she said. 'It's where I belong. It's where I live.' Her mouth formed the words gently, without haste, her lips red and soft.

'But that's an impossibility.'

'Not for some of us.'

'How old are you?' he said. 'Maybe I shouldn't ask.' His eyes searched for hers, found them, held them, grief and interest mingled into one colour.

'Nineteen.'

'Three years younger than me,' he said. 'I still can't believe it.' His lips were dry again. 'I can't think.'

'Drink,' she said. 'You must drink all the time.'

He took deep gulps of the water this time, held the bowl in his shaking hands, then handed it back to her, wiped his mouth. 'How long have I been here?'

'About two weeks. A long time for one of your kind.'

'I've slept all that time?' His eyes were wide open now, searched the room. 'And you've looked after me?'

She nodded. 'Your body needed the sleep. You were almost dead when we found you.'

'I have so many questions.' He sighed, his face limp again, marked by tiredness.

'Tomorrow,' she said. 'Ask tomorrow, and I'll try to answer them.'

He looked at the clothes he was wearing, then around the room. 'But who?'

'I did.'

He blushed. 'But …'

'I'm a healer,' she said. 'I've seen it all before.'

'And your name?'

'Tara; the one who saves.'

He repeated her name slowly, and smiled.

'And yours?' she said.

'Andrew, but they called me Sandy.'

'Sandy.' Her voice was a singsong. 'Is that right?'

'Perfect.' He smiled.

'You must sleep now. You need more strength to survive.'

'I need …' He grimaced.

'Do you think you can walk?'

'I'll try.' He slowly swung his legs over the edge of his bed. 'You're not big enough to support me.'

'I can try. Lean on me.'

'But you're tiny.'

'Come.' She was much stronger than she looked, not only because she climbed, but because she practised, every day, the art of grounding herself to her mother earth, because, as often as she could, she would get the men to try to push her over, and remained standing through her will alone, her feet anchored into the soil, into the stone, into the heart of the mountain.

They took a few uncertain, slow steps, stopped.

'It's more difficult than I thought,' he said.

'It will get easier.'

She led him out of the room, walked along the narrow passage until they came to a small chamber. 'I'll wait here,' she said. 'Call me if you need help.'

He shook his head. 'I'll be fine.'

She was almost ready to go in to him when he came out.

'Sorry,' he said. 'I didn't mean to concern you.'

'Your body needs more time.'

'I'll sleep now.'

'Good,' she said, led him carefully back to the room.

He looked across at her bed. 'You've been sleeping in here?'

She nodded.

'Why?' There was nothing but purity in his glance, in his question.

'We all thought you'd die. I didn't want you to. And if you were going to, I didn't want you to die on your own.' She looked at him. 'And every time I left the room, you became restless and started calling out your friend's name.'

'Thank you,' he said. 'You're very kind.' He climbed back into the bed, lay down. 'Very …' He was asleep again.

'You've done well, Tara,' Virya said from the door.

She turned quickly. 'You startled me.'

'Sorry. I didn't mean to. Will he be able to survive up here?'

'I don't know,' she said.

'Does he know where he is?'

'Not exactly. I evaded his questions.'

'I've spoken with Tenzin Lama. He thinks we should tell the Englishman where he is, and give him the choice of leaving.'

'Really?' she said.

'He believes the same as I do, that this man is honourable, that he'd do nothing to give us away.' They sat down on her bed together.

'Why do we fear being given away so much? Wouldn't it be easier to let the world know we live up here?'

Virya shook his head. 'I wish it was that easy.'

'Isn't it? The secrets weary me sometimes.'

'You're a strange one, you know. You are so wise, so all-knowing, and yet there are some things you don't yet understand.'

'I'm still only a child.'

'No, no,' he said. 'You're a woman. And you are destined to be one of the greatest lamas there have been.'

'Me?' She pointed at herself with her long, thin fingers. 'No.'

'Believe me,' he said. 'It's true. You belong up here.' Virya hugged his daughter. 'I'd be afraid for you, if you tried to go down into the lowlands, afraid of losing you.'

'That's just because you lost my mother.'

'No.' He shook his head. 'It's not because of that. It's because, when I'm down there, I hear so many things about the world. And the English, they're no better than the Chinese or any of the others. They fought a war in their part of the world in which millions of people died, a war that lasted for four years.'

'That's not his fault, though.' She looked at Irvine, caressed his shape with her eyes.

'No,' he said. 'I didn't say it was. I'm trying to explain why we have to keep ourselves a secret. There's something else, too.'

'And that is?'

'How easy do you think people will assume this mountain is to climb if they find out about us?'

'Will they really think it's so easy anyone can climb it?'

'They'll not understand that any normal person would still need to bring heavy air with them to survive. They'd invade us to find out how we do it. They wouldn't accept that only very few are born to live at this great height, that most people would die up here in a few days.'

'And yet you and Tenzin Lama are prepared to let him go if he wants to. How can you trust him so much when you don't even know him?'

'You've sensed it, too, Tara,' he said. 'You know

already he's an honourable man, that he'd do anything to preserve the sanctity of the Holy Mother. He would have given his life for his friend, would have given his life to be on the summit without guilt.'

She said nothing.

'And we all know that he and his friend buried the singing bowl again, that they chose deliberately not to take it away with them when they could have robbed us of our most holy symbol.'

'Yes.' She got up, crossed the room to the sleeping Irvine, looked at his peaceful face. 'I don't think I want him to leave.'

Chapter 21

This isn't like a plane at all. It's more like a living-room, restaurant and bedroom in one, miles above the ground. Which is probably why none of my fears materialise. I've never flown First Class before. As soon as we've taken off, an army of stewardesses swarm out to us, start taking orders for dinner, plying us, at Miranda's beckoning, with more champagne. I even start enjoying myself, and forget what might be ahead of us.

The food smells like it's freshly-cooked, but then I'm no judge. It's served up like in a posh restaurant, and it looks posh, too.

'Nosh,' Alice says, and that's all she says, because she starts stuffing her face in that endearing, untroubled way of hers. 'It's just fuel,' she says, when she notices we're all staring at her. 'No room for manners when all you're doing is fuelling up.'

'You're impossible,' Simon says. 'Disgusting.'

Alice sticks her tongue out at him from her half-full mouth. 'You can hardly talk,' she says.

'I've got manners,' he says. 'Very good ones.'

'When it comes to eating food, maybe,' she says. 'Not in much else.'

'I just don't suffer fools gladly.'

'That's what everyone says who's got a superiority complex.'

Simon glares at her. 'I thought we were going to do this my way,' he says.

'I don't remember agreeing to that. We'll do it the right way.'

'What is the right way?' I say.

'Any way that gets us out of there alive,' she says.

Miranda sits there, a smirk on her face, says nothing.

'If you mean we should allow ourselves to

acclimatise,' Simon says. 'There's no time for that. We just go in and out.'

'You're not giving yourself long enough to find him,' Alice says. 'You can't expect to find something on the first day on the mountain. Not like when they found Mallory.'

'No,' he says. 'That's true. But we haven't got time to engage in siege tactics and spend weeks and weeks out there.'

'So we'll just fly in to Kathmandu, get a bus to Rongbuk and start climbing the next day?'

'You're being extreme again,' he says. 'I reckon we spend one night in Kathmandu ...'

'If we can find anywhere to stay,' Alice says.

He frowns. 'One night in Kathmandu, and then we'll drive to the monastery at Rongbuk. Well, when I say drive, I mean drive to one day's walk from it. Drop the car somewhere and walk through the night.'

'What?' I say.

'I don't want anyone following us if I can avoid it.'

'Fair enough,' Alice says. 'And then?'

'We get close to the monastery, then wait again till it's dark, and then we go in.'

'Will they let us in?' I say.

'They'll be expecting us,' he says.

'Are you a Buddhist now then, Simon?' Miranda says.

He squirms. 'A little, I suppose.'

'You're either one or you're not,' Alice says. 'You can't have it all ways, not in matters of faith. Not like the rest of your life.'

'I see the attraction of it,' he says. 'They are kind and gentle people, and they're my friends.'

'That makes you a sympathiser, not a believer,' Alice says, scrapes the last morsels of her main course into her mouth.

'That'll do me,' Simon says. 'And the China thing gets

my goat.'

Miranda shrugs. 'Horses for courses.'

'You say you agree with the invasion and occupation?' Simon says.

'Oh, God,' Alice says. 'Here we go.'

Miranda looks at Simon, smiles again. 'Don't take it so seriously,' Simon,' she says. 'All I mean is that some nations still believe territory is everything.'

'They're just trying to annexe the last symbol of a pure faith,' he says.

'The mountain's not so pure any more, though, is it?' Miranda says. 'It's a rubbish tip, full of empty oxygen bottles, dead people, and shit.' She spits out the last word. 'Not exactly an idyll, is it?'

'No, it's not,' he says. 'You're right. But it still has a hold over people's imagination.'

'You mean it still has secrets and mysteries,' Alice says. 'And it's easier to access than the Antarctic. And that's not exactly mysterious any more when you can fly to the South Pole as long as you've got the dosh.'

'There was talk about building a hotel on the South Col at one point,' I say, back to the mountain.

'There was talk of clearing all the crap off the South Col as well,' Simon says. 'But that never happened.'

'It will happen one day,' Miranda says. 'Taking the rubbish off and building a hotel. And some day they'll build some sort of pressurised funicular to the top. Mark my words.' She's serious, all of a sudden.

'That would be awful,' Simon says, puts his hand on her knee.

She puts her hand on his. 'Yes, it would be. Why couldn't we just leave the world as it was?'

'If we did that, we wouldn't be in this plane now,' Alice says. 'And James and I would never have met. And …'

'And you couldn't go travelling all the time,' I say.

'I …' she starts, but stops, looks at me, eyes wide open, blue gems sparkling.

'I wasn't …' I say.

'I know.'

'If Mallory and Irvine had come back, maybe the mountain wouldn't have become so mystified,' I say. 'There'd have been no ghosts to chase, no need for so many people to die trying to get to the top.'

'Oh, people would still do it,' Alice says. 'Not everyone goes up there to find Mallory and Irvine. They think it's a status symbol of sorts, think it's an extreme sport, when we all know the fattest bastard could get up there if he's got enough manpower and oxygen to support him.'

'It's the sherpas who are the real adventurers,' Simon says. 'But they get no recognition, just enough money to be well-off within their context. And yet they're so much stronger, so much more resilient than the so-called mountaineers.'

'Tougher than you?' Alice says.

'Hell, yeah.' It's the first time his Kiwi accent really comes out. Years in Cambridge have mellowed it to a slight nuance rather than a mark of nationality. 'I'm not sure I believe it when they say sherpas never started climbing in the Himalayas before the white men arrived.'

'Interesting,' I say. 'But why would they suddenly become subservient to the white man?'

'Because his empire was all-powerful. And now they're servants to the Chinese. Some things never change, and colour makes no difference at all, in the end, does it? Murderers are murderers.'

'I didn't know you were a revolutionary,' Miranda says.

Alice looks at her, mouth open.

'I'm not, really,' he says, blushing.

'You are after my money, then?' she says. 'To redistribute it?'

'No. I don't even think about your money.'

'A champagne socialist?'

'No.' I've never seen him this embarrassed.

'An opportunist?' Miranda says.

'That's more like it,' he says.

'That's ok then,' she says, laughs, and ruffles his hair.

'You're weird, Miranda,' Alice says.

'Not really. What do you think I am?' She leans back in her seat. 'I'm the same as him. That's why I love him.'

'I thought opposites attract,' Alice says.

'Only sometimes. There's more friction between likes. And that's a hell of a lot more fun,' Miranda says.

'Anyway,' Alice says. 'So we get to the monastery, and they put us up and feed us for a while.'

'A couple of days, no more,' Simon says.

'You're mental.'

'And then we do an alpine ascent along a line someone's never done before. Five days supplies and oxygen max.'

'But I've never even climbed in the Himalayas,' Miranda says.

'I thought you could stay at the monastery.'

'With a load of smelly blokes?' she says.

'Actually, they have nuns up there as well,' Simon says. 'And not all Tibetan monks or nuns have to be celibate.'

'I've never heard that before,' Miranda says. 'You'd trust me with them, then?'

'I'd trust you with anyone.'

'We'll see,' Miranda says. 'I might surprise you all and be a natural mountaineer.'

'You're reckless enough,' Alice says.

'Thank you, my dear.'

'So what line were you thinking of?' Alice says.

'Between the Central North Face route the Russians took in 2004 and the Norton Couloir.' He leans back in his chair, folds his arms, grins inanely.

'You must be bloody joking,' she says.

'Nope.'

'Why the fuck would you want to climb up that route? It's one of the most dangerous ones there is.' The veins in her neck bulge.

'Perhaps that's why.'

'But it isn't, is it?' I say.

He shakes his head. He's gone from being an aggressive idiot one minute to looking like a vulnerable, hurt child.

'Why then?' she says.

'I've always had this stupid feeling that Irvine totally lost his bearings when he tried to get back to Camp Six after Mallory fell.'

'Eh?'

'I don't think he's anywhere near where they found Mallory. … I reckon he went west instead of east in the darkness, felt his way along the face, towards the Norton Couloir.'

'And then? People have climbed up there and found nothing,' she says.

'They've not been looking properly. Or they've died.'

'You think he fell down the Norton?' I say.

'No. I reckon he found some sheltered space with the stars over him. And that's the special place the boys were talking about, and the one those people are trying to find.'

I open my mouth, but Miranda beats me to it.

'I don't understand you climbers, never have,' she says. 'One minute you're all emotionless about death, the next minute you get all poetic and teary about how one of you might have died. Death's never pleasant.'

'You've never been at high altitude,' he says. 'It's so easy just to close your eyes and drift, to forget you're cold, that you're dehydrated, not getting enough air into your lungs. You're just tired, so tired; nothing means anything any more, and life down in the valleys seems pointless, something it would be so wonderful to escape to, just to sleep.'

'That's not the point,' she says sharply. 'You seem to accept it as inevitable that you'll die, or one of your mates will die, and talk about it with … no, I was going to say stoicism … and that's not it at all. You talk about it without any emotion attached to it whatsoever – there, cold fact. It's hard and heartless. And then, now, you almost start crying when you're talking about Irvine. Why?'

He shrugs. 'I don't know. Maybe we just pretend to be hard.'

Miranda looks at me, at Alice. 'Oh, shit, sorry, you two, didn't mean to …'

'That's ok,' I say. 'It's something I think about a lot.'

'It stopped you climbing, Jim, mate,' Simon says.

'Let him finish,' Miranda says.

'Because I felt responsible,' I say, feel Alice's hand creeping into mine. 'How many times do I have to tell you?'

'For God's sake, I wasn't getting at you,' he says. 'I was just saying.'

'You know how many friends I've lost?' I say.

'Yes, I do,' he says. 'And I can understand you, I really can, because I have, too. I just …'

'What?' I snap.

'Don't take this the wrong way, but sometimes I think you're too clever to be a climber, too much of a sensitive intellectual. You analyse it all too much. Accidents happen, not just on mountains, everywhere. Thick idiots like me just suppress it all, ignore it, the fear, the regret, the dying.'

'Thus spake the Cambridge professor,' Alice says and claps sarcastically.

'You know what I mean,' he says. 'You should know better than most. I might be clever, but I'm not an intellectual. I don't analyse feelings, I analyse geology, and I hate doing that. It's just a job, most of the time. I like being out on the mountains, and I'd be out there all the time if I could afford it.'

'You'd be able to if you married me,' Miranda says.

'Is that a proposal or a deflection?' Simon says.

'Maybe a bit of both.'

'You mean that, deep down, under all that sneering arrogance and bravado and womanising you miss the friends you've lost?' I say.

'Of course I do,' he says. 'But I can't afford to think about it, because the fear would stop me from climbing, too. I'd have thought you'd see that.'

'I see it now,' I say. 'But you've been such a tosser that I'd never bothered even thinking about you as someone worth analysing.'

'I guess that makes us quits,' he says. 'Being taken apart in front of my wife-to-be and my sister by my brother-in-law. Humiliated in public.'

'You should be an actor,' I say. For some reason, I hold my hand out to him, wait for him to shake it.

He looks me in the eyes. 'Are you serious?'

I nod.

'Ok.' He puts his huge hand around mine, squeezes hard, keeps staring right into me. 'Mountain men together.'

I nod.

'How nice,' Alice says, a slight mocking tone in her voice. 'Now, let's get back to where we were. You want to do that crazy route because you think Irvine's somewhere at the top of it.' She closes her eyes. 'I can't see it somehow.'

'I'll do it alone if I have to,' he says.

'No chance, you bastard,' she says, and there's that greedy fire in her eyes again, desperate to be climbing, to be on the mountain, that mountain, the Holy Mother. 'I'll be there with you.'

'That's three of us, then,' I say.

'I'd better give it a whirl then, too,' Miranda says.

'I don't think so,' Simon says.

Miranda just ignores him, doesn't even look at him, knows he won't be able to stop her. She makes me smile, so different to what she appears to be.

'And what will you do if you find Irvine?' I say. 'Desecrate his resting place, like they did Mallory's?'

'They say they didn't,' Simon says.

'Oh, they can say what they want,' Alice says. 'Whatever it was, it wasn't nice. I'm not so much against them having gone through his pockets, but flashing pictures of his body all round the world; that was bad.'

'You're right,' he says. 'It was awful, and greedy. They could've done the whole book, the whole documentary, and just excised the body shots.'

'You think the body shots got them extra cash?' Alice says.

'Probably. Anyway, I *will* look for the camera if I find him.'

'And take pictures and write a book?' Alice says.

He shakes his head. 'If the camera's even there, I'm going to give it back to his family.'

Chapter 22

The three of us sit there, mouths open.

'You weren't expecting that, were you?' Simon says.

'Er, no,' Alice says.

'Well then,' he says.

'Hang on,' she says, 'Have you told anyone else that you're planning to risk your life just to take an old camera back to England?'

'Just to take … ?'

'I mean, could that be why you got kidnapped?' she says.

'Bloody hell. I hadn't thought of that,' he says.

'You're such a dickhead,' she says. 'Now think who you could have told.'

'Why would I tell anyone?,' he says. 'I only spoke to the two dead boys about anything to do with Irvine.'

'What about when you were pissed?' she says. 'Climbers' pubs and all that.'

'Oh.' His face drops. 'I wouldn't remember that, would I?'

'You still drink enough to lose your memory?' I say.

'It's the only thing I do well.'

Miranda coughs.

'Well, almost the only thing,' he says.

'Be serious,' Alice says. 'This could be important.'

'Like I said, I can't remember telling anyone, but, to be honest, I've been keeping it secret for such a long time I don't think I'd have told anyone even when I was pissed.'

'So let's assume you only told those two poor boys,' Miranda says. 'How did you tell them?'

'Letter, phone,' he says.

'They have phones in a monastery?' Miranda says.

'Times are changing. They help, helped, with so many expeditions they needed to be available. Mobile phones.

When they were in Kathmandu.'

'So someone could've listened in?' Alice says.

'I suppose so.'

'Or intercepted your letters.'

'I guess,' he says.

'An unlimited circle of suspects, then,' Alice says.

'Borders on the almost unlikely, though,' Simon says.

'It's still possible, isn't it?'

'Is it worth thinking about?' he says. 'Let's face it, they're probably on their way there by now as well.'

'If they haven't already got people on the ground,' I say.

'It doesn't matter,' he says, grimly. 'There'll be a fight when we get there, regardless. That's what's bound to happen. Someone else wants that camera.'

'And they want to get there before you or Holzel,' Alice says, hands working overtime, in her hair, on the table, intertwining. She hits her forehead with the palm of one of her hands. 'How stupid we've been. We'll lead them right to it.'

'Of course we will,' Simon says. 'That's part of the plan. And then just a little push over the edge, and it'll be sorted.'

'You'd kill for the camera?' I say.

'To save it for what it's intended, yes,' he says. His face is taut, his cheekbones prominent, his eyes dark. 'They'd do the same to me. They've already done it to my friends.'

'Aren't you afraid?' Alice says.

He shrugs. 'What's death but the start into something else, something greater?'

'I thought you were a cynic.'

'Maybe I was,' he says. 'Not any more.'

The stewardesses come and take everything away. We drink one more glass of something alcoholic. My brain feels fried and fuzzy. The cabin lights are dimmed, then turned off. It's dark now, just the occasional flicker light from the galley. Our seats have turned into beds. I cover myself with my blanket, lie on my back, eyes wide open. I sigh, because I think no-one will hear it.

'What is it?' Alice whispers.

'Oh, everything and nothing.'

She reaches across to me. 'Tell me.'

'I'm worried about letting you down.'

'You'll be fine.'

'I'm not in a good enough shape for this.'

'You're not unfit.'

'It's the North Face,' I say. 'It's much more difficult than the stroll up through the South Col. And the mad line he's chosen.'

'He knows what he's doing.'

'That's what worries me. I don't want to hold him back.'

'You won't. He won't let you. You'd not rather stay in the monastery, would you?'

'No chance,' I say. 'I guess he's right about death.'

'In some way, I suppose he is. But there's a lot to look forward to after this.' She squeezes my hand. 'This'll be the last climb.'

'What?'

'I'll stop after this.'

'You don't have to,' I say.

'I want to.'

'Why?'

'You know why.'

'You could regret it,' I say, stretch to catch some of her scent. 'You'd be a long time not climbing.'

'I don't think I will.'

'You really want to be a mother?'

I feel her nod. 'And you a father?'

'I reckon.'

'We could always take them climbing with us.'

I laugh under my breath. 'That's your cunning plan, is it? To get the kids to persuade you to start climbing again?'

'Maybe,' she says. 'Not for ages yet, though.'

I grunt, revel in this warmth, in this togetherness.

'G'night,' she says. 'I love you.'

'I love you, too.'

She lets go of my hand, turns over.

I'm asleep within seconds, and the next thing I know, the cabin lights go on and it's time for breakfast. It always seems strange to me that we sleep in transit, in our travelling clothes, something we'd never dream of doing at home. And on the mountains, of course, we'd not change for weeks. Lovely.

Over breakfast, we don't talk much. Where everything was just so much talk last night, even as we flew out of Europe and down into Asia, the mountain and its possibilities are so much closer now, so much more real. I struggle with my food, while Alice just gorges but says nothing, her eyes down at her plate. Miranda looks skinny and drawn, black bags forming under her usually clear eyes. Simon just looks tired, preoccupied and very unshaven.

'Just an hour or so now,' he says, finally, wiping his mouth with his sleeve, just like his sister does.

'And then half a day of waiting,' Alice says.

'There's gear to be bought,' he says. 'We're going to have to get out through passport control and catch a cab to the nearest place we can get hold of the stuff from.'

'Far, is it?' I say.

'Depends on the traffic,' he says. 'Things have changed a lot since you last came this way.'

'Why don't you three stay at the airport, and I'll go get the gear,' Miranda says, the slang sitting uncomfortably in her throat.

'No, we'll all go together,' Simon says. 'I'm not happy about us being split up now.'

'Fair enough,' I say. The sun breaks through the cloud and suddenly I feel like eating.

Stepping out of the plane's like walking into a warm shower, although it's not as hot as the last time I was here, over a decade ago. March isn't the hottest month, but already the temperature's up in the twenties.

In the air-conditioned terminal, Simon's by the far the tallest person.

'Bloody difficult to keep you hidden,' I grumble. 'Can't you bend your knees or something?'

'Funny,' he says. His face says differently.

'What if they're already here watching?' I say.

'They'll not dare do anything now. If they've got any sense, they'll just follow us at a discreet distance, even on the mountain.'

'If they can climb,' Alice says.

'They can climb alright,' he says. 'How else would they have caught up with us in Norway?'

'And where's the Sutra?' Alice says. 'And Birger?'

'God knows,' I say.

'We'll come across them soon enough,' Simon says, and I'm not sure who or what he means.

Miranda gets us out of the airport, finds us a taxi in the madness that is this place. Simon throws himself in next to the driver. 'Rajendra Place,' he has to shout above the din.

'Yes, sir,' the driver says. 'The climbing shop, yes?'

'Yes,' Simon says. 'How d'you know?'

'You look like people who'll be wanting things from there.' He looks down at the controls. 'You going to Everest?'

'K2,' I say without thinking.

'Early season,' the driver says. 'Monsoon winds aren't near yet.'

'We like a challenge,' Simon says.

'The ladies, too?' the driver says.

'Oh yes,' Miranda says. 'We like the excitement.'

It only takes us half an hour to get there. The city passes us by in a whirl of colour, and the tension of not knowing who might be following us. That takes the edge off being somewhere I know, somewhere I used to know. When we stop, I don't know where we are. It could be anywhere.

'Wait for us?' Simon says.

'Very busy here. I can drive round and come back for you. How long?' He's just bargaining.

'An hour,' Simon says, hands over a wad of rupees. 'Don't forget, an hour.'

'I'll be here,' the driver says, zooms off in a haze of exhaust fumes.

'Come on,' Simon says. 'Lots to do.'

'What do we need?' Miranda says.

'Snow suits, ropes, crampons, stoves, gloves, goggles, ice axes, karabiners, headlamps, descenders, belayers …'

'Sleeping bags, tents,' I say. 'Pitons, helmets.'

'The whole shop, then,' Miranda says. 'In an hour.' She looks up at Simon. 'You could have given me a bit more time.'

'Your sort of shopping's back at the airport,' he says. 'You can indulge yourself there, can't you?'

'You say the nicest things,' she says. 'I'll enjoy this, too.'

An hour later we've got a huge pile of stuff.

'This isn't going to fit in the cab,' I say.

Simon runs to back of the shop, rips rucksacks from the display. 'We'll stuff most of it in here,' he says.

'We'll need to get suitcases at the airport,' Alice says. 'And check them in.'

'No, we'll just get another couple of ruckies,' Miranda

says, walks leisurely to get them, walks slowly back. 'Here we are.' She gets a fist full of travellers' cheques out of her handbag, spreads them out on the counter and starts to sign them.

'Enough, enough,' the guy at the till says, hands her a handful of notes in return.

Miranda gives him a load of them back. 'Thank you very much.'

He bows to her, smiles.

We pile out of the shop, our backs heavy with new gear. A car horn beeps at us wildly. We throw the stuff in the boot, heap the rest onto ourselves on the seats, and we're off back to the airport.

'That wasn't so bad,' Miranda chirps.

'No,' Alice says. 'Thank you.'

'Oh, don't worry about the money,' Miranda says. 'It's nice to spend it on something useful for a change.'

'I can't imagine what it must be like, to have so much money you don't know what to do with it,' Alice says.

'I wake up some mornings and can't quite believe it myself,' Miranda says. 'But then something like this happens, and I know there is a reason for it.'

Alice shakes her head.

The rest of the day goes much more quickly than I'd anticipated. We follow Miranda around the shops, where she buys nothing much, actually.

'What will I do with it, anyway?' she says when I ask her about it. 'I'm not exactly going to take a designer handbag up Everest with me, am I?'

Instead, she ends up buying all the chocolate bars she can find, and other confectionery she reckons won't freeze when we're up there. 'We'll all need to keep our blood sugar up, won't we?'

'I won't disagree with you,' Simon says, steals one of the bars from the bag.

'Oi,' she says. 'They're not for now.'

'Sorry,' he says, his mouth full. 'I couldn't resist.'

'I think I should have one, too,' Alice says. 'I need to eat as much as I can before we get out there.'

I grab one, too.

'You're all impossible,' Miranda says. 'I shall abstain.'

'No need to be a martyr,' Simon says.

'You'll be sorry if we're three bars short at the end,' she says. 'And don't think I'll share my last bar with you lot if we are.'

We all collapse in a heap laughing.

Amidst the jollity, I look up at the board, see our flight on there, *Kathmandu*, smile, and realise I'm happy, for the first time in a very long time. I put my arms round Alice, my hands on her belly, my head in her hair, turn her round, give her a long, slow kiss, let the noise and hustle fade away, lose myself in her embrace, feel time slow and fade, too, until it's only her and me, static, at the eye of the storm, solid, as we've always been, rocks in a sea of manic mankind.

'Steady on, children,' I hear Miranda say. 'This isn't your honeymoon, you know.'

'But that's exactly what it is,' Alice says. 'We never had one ten years ago.'

'Oh.' Miranda blushes, purses her lips, wipes something out of her eyes, turns to Simon. 'Too soon for us, I suppose.'

'Here we go again,' he says. 'There'll be plenty of time for that when we get back.'

'Maybe the Lama will marry us,' she says.

'Not sure that would be legal in England,' he says. He puts his hands on his hips. 'Is that really what you want?' He towers over Miranda.

She looks up at him, leans into him, her head on his chest. 'Yes,' she says. 'It's what I always wanted.'

'We'll do it then,' he says. 'We'll do it.'

She hugs him. 'You dear boy,' she says. 'You'll have

lots of money when I'm dead and gone.'

'We'll see about that,' he says. 'We might spend it all well before then.'

For the hour before we have to go through security, we wander around aimlessly, not saying much. I feel the tension rise in my stomach, my muscles tensing, my shoulders stiffening. The others look like they're having the same symptoms.

'It's normal,' Simon says. 'Even guys who've climbed all the 8k metre summits say so. The closer they get, the worse it gets.'

'That's reassuring,' I say.

'It is,' he says. 'Because if we didn't have nerves, we'd fall off the first obstacle we came across.'

At last, it's time to board. This will be our last taste of comfort for come time, our last sense of real warmth, even though it's much less luxurious than the flight from London.

'Just over an hour and a half,' Alice says.

'I know,' I say through gritted teeth.

'Are you ok?' she says.

'Yes, just, you know.'

'I know.' She sighs. 'It'll be fun, you know, this …'

'Our honeymoon?'

'Yes,' she says and smiles broadly. 'Exactly that.'

'I'll look after you,' I say.

'That's my line.'

And then we're up and away. I don't look down. I never look down.

Chapter 23

Tara couldn't get to sleep that first night after Irvine woke up. She lay in her bed on the other side of the room, listened to him breathe, watched the solitary candle flicker slowly, reaching for more air, air it could never find. She turned to face the wall, closed her eyes, tried to think of nothing, to clear her mind, to become empty and just be. She didn't succeed. She got up again, padded across to where he lay, facing away from her now, his broad back immense in the yellow light.

'What if you're not who we think you are?' she whispered. 'What if you go home and betray us, and send legions of your men to come and find us?'

He didn't move. 'I won't,' she thought she heard him say.

The candle guttered and went out. She felt her way to where she would sleep.

The next morning, Irvine woke first. He levered himself onto the floor, walked to her shape by the wall, lowered himself down onto the ground, and leaned against her bed, not understanding where he was, what he was doing.

She stirred, turned over, her hair on her face. 'You're awake,' she said.

'Of sorts. I keep thinking I'm in a dream.'

'You're not. This is real.' Her face was next to his, her breath warm on him. 'How do you feel?'

'My body? Much better. I should be dead.' He looked away. 'My mind? I should be dead. George is the one with family.'

'There's no explaining fate.'

'There'll be no explaining to his wife either.'

'She knows by now,' Tara said softly.

'Messages can't travel that quickly, not from out here.'

'I mean she'll have felt it, the moment it happened,'

she said, feeling the unknown woman's pain.

'And live in uncertainty until the message does reach her.'

She shook her head. 'She'll be certain now, just unbelieving of her intuition. All of you from the lowlands have forgotten who you really are. You've forgotten how to use your minds.'

'Is that why I'm here? To learn to live properly?'

'How would that be?' she said.

'Why else would you have saved me if not to teach me?'

'I saved you because I had to, because it's my duty to try to save the dying.'

'It's a shame you couldn't have saved George.'

'I wasn't out there then.' She remembered what she had seen, the gruesome reality of shattered death, of a destroyed, white body. 'None of us were.'

'Out there? Where? Where are we really?'

'Can't you guess?' She couldn't tell him.

'I can guess, but I need certainties.'

'Why?'

'I need something to hold on to,' he said.

'Is that why you prayed to our gods? Why you asked for forgiveness?'

He laughed. 'Is there anything you don't know?'

'I don't know you.'

'You talk to me as if you do.'

'I've spent the last weeks with you, but you've only sleep-talked at me, not with me.' What she felt was beyond words. She could tell no-one.

'Is there a difference?'

She sat up now, brushed her hair away from her face, and her scent away from him. 'Of course. Delirium doesn't make us tell the truth.'

'Perhaps it does.' He got onto his knees so his face was next to hers again. 'When we're conscious we make up so many things about ourselves, paint pictures of ourselves we think others want to see.'

'So were you painting when you were praying, when you thought you weren't being watched?'

He shook his head. 'I suppose not. But your gods didn't believe that, did they? Otherwise George would still be alive.'

'That's a very simple way of looking at it,' she said. 'Accidents happen.'

He turned away, and she watched his body shake. She touched his shoulder, bent him back to her with her gentle palm. 'My mother died on the mountain.' Her breath was a shard.

He said nothing, blinked away his tears.

'I can't remember her.' She put her hands around his face. 'I can't remember her.' Her thumbs wiped at the wetness under his eyes. 'But my father can. Every day. And I miss someone I never knew, someone I have no memory of.' She let him go. 'Is that easier?' Her body became slack.

'I'm sorry,' he said, his whole being drawn towards the unknown. 'And I can't answer your question.'

'I didn't expect you to.'

He coughed. 'And I can't believe we are where I think we are, because I can breathe much more easily here than at Base Camp.'

'We're higher than there.'

'We can't be.'

She shook her head. 'I'll show you.' She got up. 'Come.'

He pushed himself onto his feet with a gasp.

'Are you sure you're strong enough for this?' she said, hoped he was.

'Just bone ache,' he said. 'I'll be fine.'

'Stay close. I don't want you to get lost.'

'I'll be right behind you.'

They crept out into the passage, past the small cubicle he'd used the day before, along low corridors, through tall halls, rights and lefts at junctions he would never remember, down rough stairs carved into the stone, around corners which nature had shaped.

'It's getting cold.' He shivered.

'We're close.' She stopped and turned to him. 'Are you sure you're alright? I'm not walking too quickly, am I?'

He shook his head.

'You must be very special,' she said.

'How?'

'To be so alive. To have the strength to survive and breathe our air.'

'You all do.'

'There aren't that many of us.'

'That sounds sad.' The question in his voice lit the gloom.

'It isn't supposed to. Not everyone can live up here. We aren't all born the same.'

'What do you mean?'

'There are some born in the lowlands who can climb, and they have always climbed.'

'Like the sherpas, you mean?'

She nodded.

'But?' he said.

'They aren't always the ones who can live up here. Of those who choose the faith and who come to the High Monastery, only a few are strong enough to live here for a long time.'

'How long before you can tell?'

'Less than ten days. And you've been here for more than fourteen.'

'So I am a chosen one?'

She leaned against the wall of the sloping corridor. 'Perhaps.' She felt so weak in his presence, wanted nothing more than to tell him everything.

'How will you know?'

'Do you want to be one of us?' It was a question she knew she shouldn't be asking.

'Does that mean I can never go back?'

'Oh, no,' she said, her eyes on the rock behind him, unwavering. 'You have a choice. You have a choice now. When you're well enough, you can go home, as long as you swear not to tell anyone about us.'

He put his hand against the wall next to her. 'Why?'

'It's complicated.'

'Explain.'

She shook her head. 'Not now. This isn't the time.'

'When then?'

'When there's time, when you're really better.'

'I bow to your judgement.' He relaxed, the tiredness of being close to death softening his harsh outline.

'All I want is for you to live to be old.' She touched his arm, pushed it away. 'Whatever your faith.'

He nodded, stood up straight again. 'Lead on.'

They walked for what seemed to him an age, and to her a fragment of a second, because the path was so familiar to her. At last they reached the Great Hall, where novices and returners were always welcomed. It was freezing cold, and the echo of its silence almost unbearable for her, who always dreamed of climbing down the mountain, of finding her way to the lowlands, where she wanted to heal and to preach.

She stopped. 'Look,' she said, pointed down at a small, wooden trapdoor in the ground. A thick cord of rope protruded from it. She bent her knees, grabbed the rope and pulled open the door.

'Dear God,' he said, and knelt down by the abyss.

'Careful,' she said, touched his shoulder.

He stared down at the bare rocks, dropping away into the nothingness, almost all the way to the foot of the mountain, a seemingly impossible climb, scarred by snow and ice, the wind sweeping remnants of white up into the air, whistling in through the open door, grasping at him. And beyond, as far as his eyes could see, the other peaks of the range, the world, not in miniature, but in relentless actuality, so far away, yet looking close enough to touch. He wished he was a bird, to soar from this eyrie out across the rock needles, out and away, down into the green lowlands he could just see or imagine, away, away to the rivers and the warmth, to his friends, to his sister, his mother, his father, to tell them he was still alive, to tell them he would never see them again, that he had found where he wanted to be. He turned to Tara. 'I want to stay.'

'Don't decide yet,' she said. 'It's too soon. Think of what you'll miss.'

'I miss it already. That's why I can never go back.'

'Come away,' she said, pulled at him gently, until he followed her command. Closed the door, shut the wind out from the hall.

He got to his feet, towered over her.

'You're crying,' she said.

'That's what normally happens when I'm sad,' he said.

'Why?'

'I don't think I could ever live down there again.' He was telling the truth. He felt it in his hands, his scarred but mended hands.

'Let's walk,' she said.

'You don't rush anything, do you?'

'We can't rush at this height,' she said. 'And we don't believe in being hasty. You should heed that.'

'It's difficult not to follow impulse. Especially when it feels so right.'

'You must learn not to.'

'Is that really what you think? Is that what your faith teaches you? Not to follow your heart as soon as it speaks?'

She tripped. He caught her by the arm.

'That's not what I mean,' she stuttered. 'I don't want you to ruin your life.'

'You don't like it up here, do you?'

'That's not it,' she said. 'I'd like to be down there, too, that's all.'

'And they won't let you go?'

'My father won't.'

'Why not? What is he afraid of?'

'He doesn't want to lose me like he lost his wife. He thinks I could be the great lama of the High Monastery.'

'A woman?' He regretted the words as soon as the left his mouth.

'We're all equal,' she shouted at him. Her voice boomed up and down the tunnels.

He blushed. 'Sorry. I shouldn't have said that.'

'That's where our faiths are different,' she said. 'Yours won't accept women as equals.'

'I've never thought about it. I've never had to think about it.'

'Maybe you should.'

He settled into a gentle rhythm alongside her, up the slopes, down the valleys of corridors. 'Maybe you can teach me.'

'Maybe.'

'Please.'

'And then?'

'I'll still want to stay.'

'Won't you miss your type of woman?'

'I don't know what my type is.' He'd never spoken to anyone like this.

'One who doesn't contradict you, one who asks you no questions, lets you do what you want.'

He laughed as they walked back into his room. 'I

don't think that's what I want, not at all.'

'You could live without women?'

'If I had to.'

'Do you really believe that?'

He shrugged. 'It's better than being dead.' He sat on his bed. 'I'm tired now.'

'Drink.' She handed him the bowl of water.

'How do you get all these things?'

'The Holy Mother provides.'

'Is it really that simple?'

'There are mysteries and miracles we shouldn't question.'

'Yet you want to go down.'

'Only to tell everyone about the miracles.'

He emptied the bowl. 'Is that what you were doing when you found me?'

'Trying to get down?'

He nodded.

'No.' She smiled. 'The opposite. I was giving thanks.'

'Thanks for what?'

'Once a year, we celebrate how our first god was carried up into the Sacred Snows.'

He stared at her, waited.

'We were on our way to the summit when we heard your screams.'

'You climb at night?'

'It's the only time we climb.'

'But that's madness.'

'There are signs carved into the rocks,' she said, couldn't understand his questioning.

'It's still mad.'

She stood in front of him, arms crossed. 'We were on our way to the ceremony, which we were duty-bound to celebrate at sunrise. Then we heard you. And then I saw your hair, gold in the dark.'

'And what did you do?' His breath rushed out of him,

however much he tried to keep calm.

'We climbed down to you and saw the snapped rope. Two of us came back here with you. I went back up, because tradition demanded it.'

'Why?' He tried to touch her, but she moved away. 'Why you?'

'I am the one who sings to the gods. And when we got there, we found the holy ground disturbed.'

'I thought it was blasphemy to climb the mountain.'

'That's what we tell everyone to keep them away.' She knew she was saying too much, but she wanted to tell him everything.

'And George?'

'We couldn't find him at first, but then we saw his body. He was dead as soon as he fell.'

'Why didn't you try to reach him?'

'The Yellow Stones are too dangerous.'

'But it was light by the time you got to the top.'

'I couldn't risk sending anyone into the Yellow Stones. There are no markings there. They're dangerous in light or dark.'

'So you came back here and left him out there.'

'What would you have done?'

'I don't know.' And he didn't, his doubts clawing at him. What would George have done? 'Maybe I'd have tried to see if he was still alive.'

'If he had still been alive, he would have been calling out for you. We heard nothing, and we saw no movement.'

'Can I go and look for him?'

'Not now,' she said. 'You'd die.'

'What have you done with the bowl?'

'We buried it again,' she said. 'Like we always do.'

'Aren't you worried that my friends will come to look for me?'

'They've left the mountain already. They waited a few

days, until they were convinced you were dead.'

'I don't blame them.' He buried his face in his arms.

'I'm sorry,' she said.

'You have nothing to be sorry for.'

'You're upset.'

'There's one thing I don't understand,' he said. 'Why do you lie to us?'

'It's a necessary lie, to protect the Goddess Mother.'

'And let us die for a lie?'

'The mountain will always be dangerous. We've lost many friends to her.'

He raised his head, looked at her, through her. 'And you still celebrate?'

'This life is only one of many. We - we must keep the tradition.'

'Why?'

She shivered. 'Because it's the only way we can survive; to give thanks to the god who first led us here, who showed us that we, of all people, can survive the heights and the cold and the thin air.'

'Incredible,' he said. 'What a price to pay for believing.'

'How can you question our faith?' She walked away from him, her robes a shadow on her skin.

'I'm not questioning it,' he said, dropped to the ground, followed her, touched her shoulder. 'I think it's amazing.'

She turned to face him. 'You're not angry?'

'I can't be.'

'What about your friend?'

'He lived for the mountains,' he said. 'I don't think he would be sad to die here.'

'Only sad to die.'

Irvine nodded. 'There was much he wanted to do.'

'In the next life, maybe.'

'He's still far away from his family.' His breath rasped

into a harsh echo, against the walls of the cave.

'Souls know no boundaries.'

'Is that what you're hoping for?'

'I haven't thought about that,' she said. 'I'm still young.'

'No-one's too young to die.'

'I know,' she said. 'Next year I'll be as old as my mother was when she died.'

'Are you afraid?'

She shook her head. 'How could I be? I serve the gods. I am happy.'

'Except for yearning to go down.'

'Yes.'

'Maybe you will, one day.'

'Who knows?' she said. She took his hand, led him back to his bed. 'Let me get you some food. And then you must sleep. Tomorrow, we'll find you a chamber away from here, where you can reflect on your own.'

'And then?'

'You'll have to decide what you want to do.'

'I want to stay here with you,' he said, pulled her hand to his lips and kissed it.

Chapter 24

Kathmandu is a warren where old and new mingle along dusty streets. We try to merge into the crowds as soon as we leave the airport, try to cover our tracks even if we're not sure anyone's following us. That's after Simon has managed to get us visas for China. He refuses to hire a car at the airport, instead hires a car from some back-street operator with Miranda's cash, a four-wheel drive, false name, no questions asked. We ignore the temples and the histories, and head out into the traffic jams and the heat, along the high valley, rising into the thinner air of its upper reaches.

At first, on the road north, after we've beaten the traffic, after we've extricated ourselves from the convoluted streets of this overcrowded city, Simon drives slowly, teeth clenched, one hand on the gear stick, the other on the wheel, never going over fifty, never risking getting anywhere near the speed limit, windows down, the air sticky in through the doors, watching his mirror, the dust on his brown face.

'You don't think they're tracking us now, do you?' Miranda says from the passenger seat at the front, the seat she bagged as soon as we got to the car.

Simon doesn't answer, the sun on his grim face, pushing onwards, slowly.

'Talk to me,' she says.

'It doesn't matter,' he says. 'Let's just get this first bit done. I'll be happier when we've got across the border.'

'Why?'

'They'll search us,' he says. 'We'll have to empty our bags and answer a load of stupid questions. We're just tourists, right? On the way to Lhasa via Everest Base Camp. No stop-offs or anything else. Right? No mention of climbing.'

'What about all the gear?' Alice says. 'If they search us

they'll cotton on, surely.'

He brings the car to a sudden stop at the side of the road, cars whizzing past us. 'Shit. I hadn't thought of that.' He gets out, drags the rucksacks, all the gear, out onto the ground. 'Where can we hide it?'

'Won't they search the whole car?' Miranda says.

'Not if we're lucky,' he says. 'Let's stuff it into the spare tyre.' He pulls everything out of the sacks, stuffs it into the cavity under the car where the huge spare sits, pulls the interior wall coverings off, pushes sleeping bags into the voids, closes them up again. 'Fuck 'em.'

'We'll really be stuffed if they find that lot,' Alice says.

'They won't,' he says. 'And we can't think that way.' He distributes the clothes into the rucksacks, fluffs them up, to make them seem full. 'We'll stop in the next village and buy some stuff we don't need, to make us look like tourists.' He jumps back into the driver's seat, revs the engine, and we're away again.

We don't reach the next sizeable village for a few hours, dull, interminable hours, always an eye out behind, always waiting for someone or something to leap out at us from the trees, still lush and green here, growing up to the top of the steep mountains around us. He stops at Dhulikhel, late in the afternoon, grabs some provisions from the general store there, liberal with Miranda's travellers' cheques, and stuffs them into the bags. He still isn't smiling.

We almost feel our way along the narrow and winding roads, the bends growing tighter and tighter, the ravines more and more steep, until, at last, we drive in Kodari, the last town this side of the border. It's plastered into the abrupt sides of the abyss that marks the end of Nepal, a mess of wood and concrete, a mass of ramshackle, labyrinthine buildings, an eastern Gormenghast, towers at least six storeys high, leaning out from the walls of the valley, almost dropping into the river that marks the frontier, thinning forests behind them.

With no more than an hour's light left, we reach the so-called Friendship Bridge, and wait to cross. The car rolls slowly forwards, in queue.

'Out,' the guard says.

We pile out of the car.

'Where going?' he says.

'Lhasa,' Simon says.

'Climbing?'

'Maybe on some of the rocks on the way.'

'Everest?'

'No way,' Simon says. 'Too dangerous. Don't wanna get killed.'

'We kill you if you lie,' the guard says, smiles, hardly old enough to be out of school. 'I check car now.' He puts his machine gun on the front seat, crawls round the car, pulls the seat covers off, crumples them back on, works his way through to the boot, and bangs on the window to be let out. 'You ok,' he says. 'But if you lie …'

'We wouldn't lie to you,' Simon says.

'The others, no talk?' the boy says.

'We talk, alright,' Alice says. 'Just got nothing to say. He's our boss.'

The guard shrugs. 'Do as he say, then.' He moves on to the next car.

We slowly get back into ours. He turns just as Simon starts the engine. 'You lie, you dead.'

'Fuck you,' Simon says, under his breath, gets the jeep moving, at walking pace, across the bridge.

And then we're into China. We follow the road slowly, through Zhangmu, modern compared to Kodari, the town it faces across the river, only the bridge joining it. Neat terraces of houses, entirely fashioned from concrete, tiered into the mountain, stretching almost to the top, where there's still no snow, where the trees still reach for the sky, dark blue, almost purple by now.

'Don't look back,' Simon hisses when Miranda moves.

'But it's so beautiful,' she says.

'Just don't.'

She puts her hand on his thigh. 'Calm down, dear,' she says. 'They won't do anything now.'

He laughs, a bitter snarl. 'They'd do anything, just to prove they're in charge.'

'They won't,' she says. 'We're not their own. They'll only pick on their own.'

Alice raises an eyebrow. 'What do you mean?'

'That's what genocide is, isn't it?' Miranda says. 'Like the thin line between love and hate. Picking on those closest to you, those who are almost like you, but not quite. And that's why they threaten you, that's why they've got to oppress you.'

I cough. Hidden depths, or what?

'Where did you come up with that?' Alice says.

'In my head,' Miranda says, and smiles. 'You're all so wrong about me, you know. I *can* think for myself.'

There's an awkward pause, just the rattling of the car and what sounds like a half-shot suspension.

Miranda laughs. 'Oh, stop being such stick-in-the-muds,' she says. 'It doesn't matter to me that people think I don't have a brain. I suppose that's half the fun.'

'You're an odd one,' Alice says.

'That's why he loves me.' Miranda smiles, blows a kiss in Simon's general direction, faces the front again.

Outside, the chaos of cars and livestock and lorries goes on, as we push our way slowly northwards. It's a confusion of centuries, a chaos of time.

'A couple more miles,' Simon says. 'Then I can put my foot down.'

'Aren't you going to rest?' Alice says.

'No chance,' he says. 'I'm going to drive through the night. And then we can rest up in some shade somewhere, some track somewhere.'

'And after that? You make it sound much too simple.'

'We'll get to Rongbuk tomorrow night.' He wipes his forehead. 'You worry too much.'

'Have you texted ahead?' she says, the greying greenery passing by her in slow motion.

'Don't be ridiculous,' he says. 'Not a word from this end. They'll be expecting us. I know it.'

'You're mad,' Alice says. 'They don't even know we're on our way.'

'They'll know, alright,' he says. 'You wait and see.'

The traffic eases with every yard we cover, almost clears entirely when we reach the boundaries of the city. The engine revs.

Miranda puts her hand on Simon's leg again. 'Not yet,' she says, quietly but firmly.

He takes his foot off the accelerator, slows the car. 'What do you mean?'

'Wait a while,' she says. 'Just take it easy, until there's even less traffic.'

'But …'

'Trust me,' she says. 'You'll attract attention if you head off like a loony now. We're just tourists, remember.'

'Ok, ok,' he says, grits his teeth, cheekbones harsh into the rapid dusk. 'But not for much longer.'

'Just another hour,' she says. 'Just another hour. And then you can be as impatient as you want.' She takes her hand off his leg, leans back in her seat, closes her eyes. 'We'll get there soon enough.'

More traffic falls away, the road ahead almost clear now, climbing mercilessly up into the steep. The broad leaves of the forest die away, replaced by the narrowness of pine needles and their trees. The last light of the sudden dusk curls their shapes into indistinct patterns, folds sharp edges into soft shadows. And then they're gone, because we're heading beyond the tree line, passing snow drifts, at first occasional heaps of white by the side of the road, then gradually lengthening into glistening patches in the last light. The peaks grow higher, and the whiteness at their tops hints at deep snow and reminds me of Norway, reminds me of the mad crevasses of Everest. And then night falls, a vicious, sharp-toothed darkness, a suddenness of black that buries the increasing desolation of these unforgiving heights.

Simon doesn't put the headlights on, just the sidelights. The car swerves and skids along the hairpins.

'You're a fucking head case,' Alice shouts when the rear wheel shoots over the edge. 'You're going to kill us all before we even get there.'

'Relax,' he says. 'It's better than being shot.' His teeth glisten through the darkness. It's the first time he's smiled since we left Kathmandu.

We fall silent again. Through the windows, we glimpse the occasional light, drifting by us without name, without description, without certainty, shapeless, ethereal, nothing but a blurred pinprick.

The hooded lights of the car pick out a sign on the road when we're nearly past it. *Nyalam.* It's seven hours since we left Kathmandu. Simon stares at the road ahead.

'Put your headlights on,' Alice says.

'Not yet,' he says.

'Come on,' she says. 'We're nearly thirty miles from those idiot guards.'

'Not yet, I said.' He's almost shouting. 'Let's get up into the mountains first.

'You mean we're not high up yet?' Miranda says.

'Why? Have you got a headache?' he says.

'No. I'm just bored. No countryside.'

'You're impossible.' I hear him smile. It's an odd thing, to be sitting in a car with an old enemy and liking him. I relax into the feeling, comfortable with it, sure he'll not be an enemy again.

'I'm just being me,' Miranda says. 'You know, the impatient one of me.'

'Another hour,' he says. 'Quote, unquote. I know this place.'

'But you sound tired.'

'One more hour,' he says. 'And then someone can take over and use the headlights. Honestly.'

We're through Nyalam by now, leaving the houses and dim lights behind, a short respite from the ceaseless rise into the landscape. The road races ahead, steep and turning, harsh and unrelenting. I stare out of the window, watch the occasional skeleton of light flicker past me. I've read about this road, wanted to write about it, wanted to live it, but never dreamed to be here, not after my fear and humiliation. I shiver.

It wasn't always this easy, if this serpentine tarmac can be called that. The black tarmac has erased the memory of the landslides that used to confront travellers every five hundred yards, that used to destroy the road and make progress almost impossible. Travellers could be delayed here for days, or weeks. And now we glide our way across the new tarmac, almost effortlessly. The Chinese built this. Was it to make their war easier, or to attract more people to what they think of as theirs? And in that rational part of me I see what it's for; to annoy the Indians, to boost trade across that ragged border, to bring more money in. Greed is a universal fertilizer.

The wind starts, at first scratching at the sides of the car, then knocking on its windows, and pushing it this way and that across and back over the road.

'Fuck,' Simon says.

'Pull over,' Miranda says, just as Alice opens her mouth. 'I'll drive from here.'

'You don't know the place.'

'So? It's dark. It could be anywhere. Just point me in the right direction.'

Simon stops the car. There's nothing in front or behind us, just the dark. He slips across to Miranda so he doesn't have to get out. She pushes her slimness through under his bulk and drops into the driver's seat.

'Just follow the road,' he says. 'And then we'll be where we need to be.'

The handbrake clicks out, and we start the climb again.

'Where?' Miranda says.

But Simon's gone, snores into the void from the passenger seat, head lolling towards the window, misting it up when it touches the growing coldness outside.

Miranda shrugs. 'Follow the road,' she mutters. 'Follow the yellow brick road to the beast. Ha.' Her laugh is natural, not strained. 'I do so love an adventure.'

In London she'd driven like a manic, but here, in the dark, in the unknown, she drives steadily, humming to herself, relaxed in the driver's seat, head erect on that long neck, eyes wide open. The car rocks, rocks me to sleep. I don't wake up again until I feel Alice stir against me, until the car pulls to stop, and it's light again outside. We're parked up next to the stone wall of row of square houses, flat roofs, withered shrubs growing their spindly way over the top of the wall.

'Where are we?' I say.

'Just a few miles from the Pang La Pass,' Simon says, still curled up in the passenger seat, voice rough from just waking.

'Not far then,' I say.

'Nope. Forty miles or so.'

'What you planning on now, then?' Alice says.

'We'll hang out here for most of the day,' he says. 'There's no point in going any further just yet.' His eyes are hollow and his voice thick. He needs more sleep, just like we do. Not that he's admitting it.

'When do we go on?' Alice says.

'We'll drive up onto Pang La just before the light goes. We should be able to dump the car somewhere and then walk.'

'And where are you going to dump the car, as you so eloquently put it?' Miranda says.

'There's a little village about ten miles north of the monastery,' he says. 'We can hide it there.'

'Is there any point in that?' Alice says. 'Won't whoever wants to find us have found us by then?' That game she plays with me, where she knows all the answers before she's asked the questions; is she playing that game with her brother now?

'There's always a point in keeping something hidden,' he says, and doesn't even sound irritated by her constant questioning.

'Wouldn't it be better to have the car near by?' Alice says.

'That's a bit of a double-edged sword, isn't it?' Miranda says at the same time.

Simon ignores Miranda's spiked question, and looks at Alice, the slightest of smirks on his face. 'It would look a bit odd for the same car to be parked in the monastery for weeks,' he says.

'Weeks?' Miranda says. 'Weeks? You said you wanted to do this quickly.'

'A couple of weeks will be quick,' I say. 'If we live.'

'Ever the optimist, eh?' Simon says, grins a boyish

smile.

'Life and soul of the party, that's me,' I say.

'Are you all feeling ok, by the way?' Simon says.

'Why, shouldn't we be?' Miranda says.

'We're up at almost 5,000 metres,' he says. 'Thin air. I thought you might be struggling with the altitude.'

'I'm obviously much better at this than you thought,' she says, and folds her arms. 'We'd better keep drinking lots, though.' There's a certain proud bossiness in her voice, like she's always known better than us.

'While it's easily available,' Alice says. 'We'll soon be melting snow for it.' Are they trying to keep up with each other to impress us?

We down a bottle each of water, grab some of the food out of the rucksacks. It's getting cold in the car. Miranda turns on the engine.

'Time to get some extra clothes on,' Simon says.

By the time we've finished our food and wrenched ourselves around inside the car in mad contortions getting the warm clothes on, the sun's high in the sky.

'Come on,' he says. 'Walkies.'

'I thought you wanted to be inconspicuous,' Alice says. 'You're so bloody contrary.'

'It'd be conspicuous not to get out and have a wander.'

The four of us walk through the village. There's not much to see except the mountains, the odd yak or three, the dust road in and out. The wind is a knife, even here, though not as ragged as it would be on Everest. But we can't see it yet, still hidden as it is by the mountain ranges in between.

'You'll see it soon enough,' Alice says, her arm through mine.

'What do you mean?'

'You keep looking south, like you're trying to find something.'

I shake my head. 'Sorry.'

'What for?'

'For being so predictable.'

'I'd worry if you weren't,' she says.

'Predictable?'

'Looking for Everest.' She smiles.

We get back to the car. Simon gets behind the wheel.

'Don't I get a go?' Alice says. She's not joking.

'On the way back,' he says.

She shrugs. 'You're going to kill us before we get there.'

'I'll sleep some more when we get there,' he says, without even turning round to her. 'It's not long now.'

And then we're off again, along a bumpy road, more of a track, tyre marks almost the only sign that it's a track at all, that it's going somewhere. We don't talk, like we're all waiting for what comes next. There isn't a cloud in the sky, and the car climbs and climbs, zig-zag, zig-zag. The wind batters it at every turn.

Out of nowhere, it's there, the cairn that marks the highest point of the pass, prayer flags attached to the pole that rises from its centre, ragged flags streaming away in the wind. Simon stops the car, and we get out, push the doors closed against the gale. The cairn's base is covered in smaller stones and bones, offerings to the gods. Miranda bends down, picks up one of the stones, kisses it, puts it back at the very top of the pile, turns and looks across the mottled green and grey valley.

At first, I daren't follow her gaze, afraid of how the view might affect me. But there's no avoiding it, and I'm drawn to it, no matter what my fears and memories are. I lift my eyes, follow the flight of thin air, away, up from the green, up to the splintered rocks, the snow, the ice, the massive pyramid, that distinctive shape from whatever angle you look at it, that plume racing away from the needle-sharp summit, that place I wanted so much to reach, that immovable mountain, Chomolungma, Goddess Mother of the Earth.

Chapter 25

'Are you ok?' Alice says.

I just nod.

'Are you sure?'

I nod again, breathe in deeply, notice the lack of oxygen for the first time, tense, and try to relax. I walk away, back to the car. 'Let's just get on with it.'

The last of the sun strafes the layers of stones on the North Face, paints the cold stones a warm colour, the detail too sharp for this distance to make sense to the naked eye. The others come back to the car, get in, shake off the cold. Alice sits next to me, her cool cheek against my hand.

'Are you sure you really want to go all that way?' Simon says to Miranda as he starts the car.

'That's what I'm here for,' she says. 'You can't get rid of me that easily.' She's not even bothering with the innuendos any more; she must be serious. Judging by her face, she is.

By the time we get to the village Simon was talking about, it's almost midnight. The way here was nothing but light and abrupt darkness, the rush of the wind, and me in some kind of trance, not paying attention to who said what or what was said.

Simon kills the engine, lets the car roll almost soundlessly down the hill into the village, no sign to be seen anyway, turns the wheel, and lets it glide to a stop behind what must be some sort of barn. It seems deserted, this place, only the occasional barely visible flicker of light from one or other of the houses, if that's what you can call them.

We jump from the car, push the doors quietly closed, pick our gear out from the spare tyre, fix our head torches on.

'Hang on,' Simon whispers. He pulls a tarpaulin from

the back of the car, drapes it over its shape, fuzzy in the yellow light of the torches, fixes it to the bumpers at either end.

'Where did you get that?' Alice says.

'It came with the car.'

'You knew what you were looking for,' she says.

'Of course I did,' he says. 'Illegals need to hide their transport all the time.'

'They knew you'd be doing an illegal?' Miranda says, sounding uncomfortable with Simon's vernacular.

'Sort of.'

'What if they give you away?'

'No names, no pack drill,' he says. 'And, anyway, if they give us away, they give their whole operation away with us.'

'I suppose so.' Miranda shrugs and turns to go.

Simon catches her up. 'Let me lead,' he says. 'It's not going to be child's play, this walk. You still ok? Enough breath?'

'Yes, Simon,' she says. 'I'd tell you if I wasn't.' There's an edge to her words, an impatience, an insolence. She doesn't want to be treated like an idiot any more, however well she plays being one.

He shakes his head, trudges off ahead. The light of his torch meanders over the hard ground.

We follow him, the dry cold on our faces through our balaclavas, though our neck gaiters, a pervading cold I remember and find hard to resist, a slow cold, a gentle killer. And we're not even on the mountain yet. I put my head down, push one foot in front of the other, try not to show any weakness to any of them, make sure I'm at the end of our column of four, match my pace to myself, not to that of the others. Do they forget about me, or am I just really slow? I lose their lights until I'm stumbling around behind the cone of yellow my torch throws onto the ground ahead of me.

We don't stop to rest, push on up the slopes, through what feel like one all-consuming abyss after the other, unyielding ground under our feet, and what sounds like the clatter of our boots echoing around the valley. Outside the reach of our torches, there's nothing but blackness, deeper than darkness, more absolute than the darkest of black inks. Beyond the light is a void. I try to ignore it, try to keep my eyes on the broad track that will lead us to the monastery. I cannot bear to think of anything else, can't think of the last night I spent here, on the skating slopes of Everest, clamped to a wall of rock, dying, and a dead man next to me, stiff as the ice that took him.

Closed eyes are no good. I stumble over a small obstacle I could have avoided if I'd been looking. I open my eyes again, see the others' lights ahead of me, seemingly within touching distance. They move away, flicker and dance in the night. I shorten my strides, try to quicken them, to catch up with the other three. It doesn't work. There's a weight on my chest, one I haven't felt for over ten years, an unknown, unremembered, pressure. God, if my body needs more oxygen now, what will it need once we're on the mountain, just touching distance away across the valley, not brooding, not glowering, but watching, seeking, licking its hungry lips at the prospect of more prey?

'Relax.' I can't decipher the soft voice next to me, don't recognise the gentle touch on my elbow, keep plodding on, ignore it.

'James. Stop.'

I try to take another step. My feet won't move. I am weak. 'Go on without me,' I say, a rasp from my throat.

'It's in your head,' she says, the invisible goddess. 'You're fine. Pulse ok. Breathing ok.'

'Liar.'

'Stop, for fuck's sake, dickhead.' A different voice this

time, not gentle, not forgiving. A god, a man. Whatever.

'Leave him, Simon.' She's defending me, whoever she is.

'I knew we shouldn't have brought him.' That horrible voice again. Disappointed beneath the impatience.

'Piss off. Just give me a minute.' I think I'm shouting, but I don't know. My voice sounds muffled.

My legs are collapsed under me. 'Breathe, James,' she says. 'It's your mind. You're fine. Just ignore him.'

My eyes swivel slowly, try to focus on the voice, my body like a drunk man's. I stop breathing, for a second. Try to focus. Oh, there she is. Black hair, skinny face, skin yellow from the light. I know her.

'Sorry,' I mumble. Reach out to her.

'You're imagining things,' she says, holds out both hands to my starving fingers. 'This is only the beginning.'

'I can't help it,' I mumble.

'You'll beat it. Take your time.' She passes me a bottle of water. 'Drink it all.'

I watch my gloved hand reach for the bottle, as if I were separate from it, see the yellow fingers grab at it, miss at first, then take a firm hold, bring it to my mouth.

'The lid,' she says.

The glove unscrews the lid, comes towards my mouth again, pours mouthful after mouthful into my scarred throat. The cold liquid draws a trail of blue through my body, fills me with new strength. I get up. 'Let's go,' I shout.

'Shut the fuck up,' Simon hisses. 'Do you want everyone to know we're here?'

I don't feel drunk any more. 'You shut the fuck up, wanker,' I say. 'We're on the same side, fuckface. Now get your arse in gear.' I lead off, although I've never been this way before.

Simon sighs, chunters into the snow, catches me up, overtakes me. 'I lead.'

'Fine,' I say. 'Doesn't bother me.'

I follow. He leads. I don't know how. I am a lost soul in this echo. Our lights stumble against a mud wall, skid on to black gates, enormous above our heads, too high for me to measure. A single rap and they open. Soundlessly. The cold grabs at me, along with handfuls of barenesses. We're there, we're here, we're where we need to be. The gates close behind us. There is nothing. I wake up in a bed of cotton, bereft of clothes.

'Are you ok now?' It's only Simon and me.

I nod. 'I don't know what happened.'

'It's probably your mind and a bit of altitude sickness.' His face is open.

'Already?'

'It happens.' He nods. 'You know it does.'

'I'm sorry.'

He shrugs. 'No worries.'

'Are you still going let me come up with you?'

'There's no choice. No question. I can't do it without you.'

'What did they say?' I nod towards the door.

'Nothing. You know what they're like.'

'I didn't mean the girls.'

'Neither did I.'

I push the cotton away from my nakedness. 'On we go, then.'

He doesn't take his eyes off me. 'Tomorrow,' he says.

'Why not now?'

'We all need to rest.'

'Because of me, you mean.'

'No, not at all. We do need to take a breather. I was totally and utterly fucked last night.'

I pull on some clothes. The sun is harsh through the window. 'You mean they're all in my state.'

'No. You're the worst.'

'But the others are struggling, all of a sudden,' I say.

'Didn't you expect that?'

'I didn't know what to expect.'

'Where's Alice?'

'Downstairs,' he says.

'What's she doing?'

'Finding out what's been going on.'

'What does that mean?'

'They think someone else has already gone up.'

'Someone they don't know?'

'Someone they don't know.' His hands are restless on his knees. There's something he's not telling me, and his face is pale even against the white walls. This place feels like no place at all, a void.

'You want to go now,' I say. 'And not wait.'

'Yes,' he says. 'Although I know it's the wrong thing to do.'

'Then go.'

'I just told you I can't go without you and Alice.'

'I thought you did this sort of thing on your own all the time.'

He looks out of the window, almost directly into the sun. 'Not this sort of thing exactly.'

'But if you think it's important.'

'Nothing's more important than another man's life,' he says.

'But you didn't stop climbing, all those years ago.'

'You hadn't even got onto the mountain when I got to the top.'

'I suppose not,' I say. 'There are so many details I choose to forget.'

He gets up, sits on the bed. 'Are you sure you want this?'

I nod. There's nothing else I can do.

'Then do as I say. Rest. One day. Sleep as much as you can. Drink as much as you can.'

'Why are you so much stronger than me?'

'I'm not,' he says. 'We're just different people, that's all. Nothing more than that, and nothing less.' He gets up. 'Do you promise?'

'Send Alice up,' I say. 'I want to talk with her.'

'I'll see what I can do.'

'You're lying, aren't you?'

'What about?' he says.

'Her having breakfast.'

He blushes. 'Not really.'

'What's that supposed to mean?'

'She *is* having breakfast.'

'But?'

'Just not here.'

'What?'

'Just not here.'

'Where then?'

'Somewhere on the way to the mountain,' he says. 'She was gone when we all woke up. She's gone up on her own.'

'Why the fuck didn't you wake me any sooner?' My heart quickens, and I feel hot all over.

'Because you were rough as shit. Because she left me a note telling me not to.'

'Why? She doesn't even know what she's looking for.' I stare at him. 'And since when have you listened to her?'

'She's looking for Irvine. That's all she needs to know. She took my maps.'

'That's comforting.'

'There's nothing we can do,' he says.

'Fuck off. We can head out now.'

He shakes his head. 'There's one other thing.'

'What's that?'

'The people who went up before her.'

'What about them?' I say.

'They had guns, or so the monks say.'

'And they didn't try to stop them?'

'Without weapons?'

'I suppose.' I say. He knows these people so much better than I do.

'And they had someone with them, someone who wasn't armed.'

'How do they know all this?'

'They were watching.'

'And did nothing?' I say.

'They can't.'

'They won't, you mean.'

'They can't. It's against their faith.'

'That's bollocks.'

'It's not, actually.'

'You sound like me.'

'That, mate, is totally irrelevant.' He paces across the room, a caged warrior.

'So who was this other person?'

'An old bloke,' he says.

'What?'

'A white man with a climber's colour, that's what they said.'

'Birger,' I say. I miss the old man's company, for some reason, think of those couple of nights at his place as a time of sanctuary. I'm relieved I was right to trust him.

'Probably.' He's impatient, worried, doesn't focus his eyes on anything, as restless as everything about him.

'When was that?'

'A couple of days ago.'

'Did he have the book?'

'They didn't say.' His fists clench and unclench. 'They

wouldn't say much. Do they even know about that book?'

'They must be hiding something,' I say.

'They're always hiding something. They don't want strangers to know their secrets.'

'Is that why you do know some?'

He half-shrugs, twists his body away from me, almost as if to evade me, my questions. 'There's no answer to that.'

There's nothing more he'll tell me, is there? Nothing of all the things he does know, the things that brought him here, despite or because of me or Alice. I get the feeling he'd like to stay here forever, become one of them, never go home. But something stopped him, is still stopping him, otherwise he'd have been living here for years.

'Miranda, she didn't hear anything then?' I say.

'She found the note, but she was out cold when Alice left.'

'Brilliant.' Trust Miranda to sleep through. Mind you, I probably would have, too.

'There's nothing we can do,' he says.

'We can go now.'

'When the sun's at its strongest? You know better than that. That's a death sentence from the start.'

'We can walk up to Base Camp.'

'Don't be stupid. We'd get spotted.'

'And she hasn't?' I spit. 'And they haven't?'

'Not by anyone but the monks.'

'So why didn't they tell us she'd gone?'

'They thought it was our plan.'

'Great plan. Skinny woman on her own against big mountain and men with guns.'

He laughs an empty laugh, but says nothing.

I'm dressed now, stare at the empty snow outside. 'Come on, Simon. Let's go. No point waiting.'

He stands at my shoulder. 'What about Miranda?'

'Let her come if she wants.'

'She'll die.' His voice shakes a little.

'Do you care?'

He hesitates. Looks at me, at the mountain out through the window, back at me. 'Probably not.'

Chapter 26

'I thought you wanted to marry her,' I say.

'I do.'

'But?' I'm confused. It's like he can't make his mind up about anything, not being here, not Miranda, not Irvine, nothing.

'She annoys me. Especially wanting to lead and all that.'

'Married people always annoy each other. You can't have everything your way all the time. You have to compromise.'

'That's for wimps.' He bites his mouth closed, cheeks working. He looks frightening.

'Not in all things, just in occasional things,' I say, put my hand on his shoulder. 'She loves you, you know.'

'I love her, too.'

'Then make her stay here while we go on up.'

'That's a double-edged sword.'

'And saying you don't care if someone dies isn't?'

'Let's leave it,' he says. 'It's not really important right now.'

'You really want to leave it till tomorrow to go after Alice?'

'I don't see what else we can do. I don't know how she plans on surviving up there without proper provisions.'

'This is crazy.' I shake my head, lost in it all. Why does everything have to get so complicated?

We're down the stairs now. I feel in surprisingly good nick, my fit or whatever it was last night considered.

Miranda is sitting at the table, head in her hands. Simon walks up behind her, puts his hands on her shoulders. She shrugs them away, turns round to her. Her eyes are red. She's crying. 'You don't want me here, do you?' she says to him, soft, harsh words into the silence. 'I know you don't.'

'I do,' he says. 'But –'

'I'm sorry about yesterday,' she say. 'But you can't always have it your own way. You don't always know better.'

'That's what I hate.'

'But you'll have to get used to it. If not with me, then someone else.'

'Maybe no-one else,' he says.

'You'll be lonely all your life. Doesn't that scare you? I've been alone all mine, and it's awful.'

Simon opens his mouth.

I raise my hand. 'Look, I'll let you two sort this out in private,' I say. 'I'll just go for a gentle walk in the courtyard.'

'Don't leave the monastery,' he says. 'Whatever you do.'

I nod, push my way out through the door, into the sun. It's surprisingly warm, and my madness from yesterday seems an age away. I go down some stairs, put my feet into the grey dust. I feel the mountain watching me, from beyond the walls of this place, feel myself drawn to it, turn my head, and stare at what I can see of it. The plume's still raging from the summit, thrown out westwards by what must be horrendous winds up there. I sit on the steps, keep looking up, the sun in my face. I close my eyes.

'You're the dead man, aren't you?' It's a voice from nowhere, slightly tinted by geography.

I open my eyes and look at the monk sitting next to me. 'What do you mean?'

'You were dead on Chomolungma, and then she found you, the lady who left during the night, and brought you back to life.'

'Yes,' I say. There's nothing else to say.

'It's dangerous up there,' he says.

'I know.'

'But only if you don't believe.'

'Don't believe what?' Am I going to get another lecture on the sanctity of faith, of the mountain, and how only true believers will succeed, and on how foolhardy I was, then, when Graham was still alive and I'd done nothing wrong. I smile against my instincts.

'That you'll come back down, that you'll be protected.'

'Gods, you mean?'

He shakes his head. 'Not just gods. People.'

'I thought you believed only in your gods.'

He smiles, a slow, gentle, knowing smile. 'The gods might understand everything, but they can only reach us through the people who live with us. Was it coincidence that brought the lady to you?'

'Some would say so.'

'What do *you* say?'

This is freaking me out, making me feel more than a little uncomfortable, but there's no way I can back out of this conversation now, nowhere for me to wander off to. 'I don't know. Sometimes I think it was meant to be.'

'You loved her before you went onto the mountain.'

'Yes.' And I did. I realised it then, and I realise it again now. It's the years in between that I wasn't quite so sure. What happened then? Why did I almost hate her? I don't hate her now. I want her with me always.

'So it was intended,' he says, bends forwards to look into my eyes. 'But you said nothing?'

'No.'

'That's because you didn't believe it then, not totally, I'm sure.'

'How easy is it to believe in love?'

'Or how difficult? And in the gods?' He leans back, hands behind him on the stone steps. 'It's not supposed to be easy.'

'And my friend?'

'Ah.' He leans forwards again, puts his arm round my shoulder. 'You mustn't blame yourself.'

'So I should blame the gods?'

His hand grasps me tight and hard. 'We can't blame them for accidents.'

'That's a good excuse for them,' I say.

'It's not an excuse, my friend. It was meant to be. Otherwise your love was not meant to be. Equal measures.'

'That makes faith very difficult. That's probably why I've never been able to figure out if I believe in God, or in any gods.'

'Faith is difficult,' he says with a sigh. 'It's easier not to believe.'

And not just in faith, I think, and change the subject. 'Have you been up there?' I say.

'Maybe. Maybe not.'

I laugh. 'You mean you won't tell me.'

'I mean I don't know.'

'I don't know if I'm capable of doing it.'

'You are,' he says, his hand still on me. 'You're blessed.'

'After last night?'

'That was the last of your death and guilt, your soul vomiting.'

'You have an explanation for everything.'

'So do you. Just different ones, negative ones.' He looks up at the summit, squints. 'You can get there. Although the top isn't that important.'

'What?'

'It's what you learn on the way up and down,' he says. 'Not what you see when you get there. It can blind you.'

'Is that a parable?'

'I think so. There is always a way there, and always a way back. In all things.'

'Who are you?'

'Oh, just a monk.'

'Are you all this wise and impenetrable?' I say, and mean it.

'I'm not sure that's a compliment any of us could accept.'

'I'm not sure I can wait to follow her.'

'Go tonight. We can lead you. Tell Simon. He has helped us so often.'

'He never struck me as the kind of man to be particularly helpful.'

'We all wear masks. It doesn't make our real feelings any less true.' He gets up. 'Eat. Drink. Rest. Until tonight, or the next night.' He walks up the steps and disappears into the building.

I stay where I am, wondering over his words. He had an odd presence, all-consuming, almost, an inescapable aura. Weird. I close my eyes again, let the sun drain into my face, until it gets too hot, until I grow tired again. Back inside, it's cool, and I fill up with water and whatever else I can find. Simon and Miranda are nowhere to be seen, so I go back to bed.

No matter how hard I try, I can't dream, not of success nor failure. My sleep is undisturbed, no flashing pictures of Graham, or of Birger, or of Alice. It's ten o'clock in the evening when I'm woken.

'Food,' Simon says. 'Lots of it. Then we walk out.'

'Good. You don't want to wait till tomorrow night, then?'

'No. I think we're all ok now. You?'

'I've never felt better to be honest, however odd that sounds.'

'It doesn't sound odd at all.'

'Is everything alright with you and Miranda?'

He shrugs, then nods. 'How do you ever know? How have you managed to stay married for so long?'

'I don't know. Compromise, like I said. Your sister putting up with me.'

'It sounds so, so …'

'Boring? Normal?'

'Yes.'

'I suppose it is. But then this isn't. And every once in a while, something happens to make you realise it's not boring, not normal, but the best thing ever.'

'Thanks,' he says and hugs me, then pushes me away, embarrassed.

'That monk outside, earlier, he said some pretty weird things.'

'That monk, for your information, is the Lama.' He's smiling now, a broad smile where nothing else matters.

'What? I thought they wore, like, costume and stuff.'

'Obviously not.'

'Oh God.'

'What? You didn't say anything stupid, did you?' he says.

'Nothing but stupid things.'

'I bet you didn't. He's a cool bloke, eh?'

'I understand some of what he said better now.'

'Shouldn't make a difference who said it, Jim. They're all equal. The one deemed most wise by the others is the lama.'

'It's beyond me,' I say. I can't imagine that happening in our so-called civilised world.

'You'll understand soon enough,' he says.

'Like you do about relationships?'

'Maybe.'

It's midnight. We have as much as we can carry, and there are ten monks with us. There are no torches, nothing to light our path, nothing that might draw the attention of the Everest tourists settled at Base Camp. We stand in the courtyard of the monastery, looking up the steps to the guttering candles next to the doors into the main building. The lama is on the steps, this time with the addition of a cloak. He leans forwards into the wind.

'Take them safely to where they need to be,' he says. His voice carries without him raising it. 'Keep them close. Remember what calls you, what calls them. Remember that we are the first climbers, that we carry, always, the burden of history and wisdom on our shoulders. Remember, forever, the Sutra of Thin Air, which is what guides us.'

The Sutra Of Thin Air? So they do know it. Why didn't they say something last night, when we arrived? Maybe I was too out of it to remember. I turn to Simon. He looks as puzzled as me, raises his shoulders in a wordless shrug.

'No life is worth losing,' the lama continues. 'You are their guides, not their saviours. The gods will decide their fate. You must lead them, but you don't have to follow them. They know enough to make their own decisions. Now go, and meet your destiny.' He raises his arms, casts what sounds like a blessing in Tibetan onto our bowed heads. Then he turns away, walks back into the warm through the doors. The torches go out, I don't know how. We are in darkness.

'Come on.' Simon grabs me by the elbow, his other hand on Miranda's back. 'Ignore the dark. Your eyes'll get used to it soon enough.'

I look at Miranda. Her face is taut. Age pulls at her. But she doesn't look worried. Maybe there is no such thing as total darkness. The gates open, just wide enough to let us out in single file. I hear them close behind us, a surreptitious yawning of well-greased hinges, made to keep secrets.

This procession, madness in itself, I think, moves forward in silence. I start to understand. We'll be taking a longer route to the base of the North Face, to avoid Base Camp, to make sure we'll not be spotted. But I don't understand how we'll have enough provisions to get up the mountain, never mind the top. *The top isn't that important.* What did he mean? Why didn't he tell me he was the lama?

Apart from a few stumbles, we move forwards rapidly enough. After almost two hours, the sky lights up on our left, a flickering yellow song into the sky.

'Base Camp,' Miranda whispers.

'How do you know?' Simon says.

'I'm not a stupid girlie, that's how,' she says. 'Keep walking.' End of conversation.

We walk for two nights, an unremitting slog across moraines, across ice, along what feels like a detour designed to avoid any chance of being spotted by anyone else attempting the mountain. During the day we all hide in small caves which are so well-hidden I would have walked past them. There's precious little talk, just the certainty that we're gaining height, that the air's getting rarer, that we're getting closer to where the serious climbing starts. And still no sign of Alice.

I can feel the mountain even without seeing her. She has a gravity of her own. She guides the winds, touches the valleys that reach to its base, rules the ground, the air, the skies, the darkness, the moon. She is the mother of everything around her, living and dead. I pray for forgiveness, forgiveness for doubting, forgiveness for what I'm about to do, for ever blaming her for Graham's death, for wanting her levelled to the ground in revenge for my best friend's death. She doesn't answer. The wind pushes along the ground of the valley, round the boulders, troughs and rises. It soars to the mountain and up her flanks. I can see, imagine, the path it takes to the very top of her, and the power with which it lifts snow from the summit to fly that white pennant from the top of the most famous pyramid in the world. I don't close my eyes. I don't listen to the wind, don't hear the whistle of it, not the murmuring of the monks as we finally reach, dawn again just starting to build, the base of this immense mountain, the feet of their goddess, the starting place for all final adventures of man, a place from which we have to stretch and reach out into the sharp rocks.

Where is Alice? Shouldn't we have caught up with her by now? I guess not. She's at least a day ahead of us. Where? Why? Doesn't she love me enough to have waited for me? The monks pull us into a cave in the side of the mountain, tell us to sleep, to keep our voices down, ply us with drink and food, let us wrap our sleeping bags around us while they lie down on the freezing ground with no protection but their robes.

'What the fuck?' I say.

'They do this all the time,' Simon says.

'You've been up with them before, then?' I say.

'Sort of.'

'You're as secretive as they are.'

'I've just heard it tell that they can bear the cold better than we can.'

'So all this crap about the English teaching them to climb is just that; a pile of shit?'

'Yes. In a word.'

'Jesus.' I should have guessed, I suppose, that the Empire builders and slave traders of England would have shaped history for their own benefit and glory. I've been too busy looking into myself to look at what's going on around me.

'Toute écriture est réécriture,' he says.

'All writing's re-writing. What's that supposed to mean?'

'History's nothing but the rewriting. What people make up. What they want people to hear. None of it's true.'

'So now you tell me. So World War II never happened?'

'Very funny.' Not that he laughs. 'You're being too literal. What I mean is that we don't know anything unless we've been there ourselves or it's independently verifiable.'

'The scientist-philosopher. Wonderful. It doesn't get us any nearer to Alice.' And that's where I want to be, need to be.

'Oh, but it does,' he says.

'How?'

'There's no way she'll have taken the route I wanted to do. Not on her own. She'll rely on what's known, pragmatist that she is.'

'But she's got your maps,' I say.

'They won't necessarily mean anything to her.'

'So what will she do?'

'She'll choose some route that's been done loads of times before. There'll be fixed ropes and pitons. Somewhere she can fix herself to, a path well-trodden.'

'But she won't want to bump into anyone either, so she'd need to stay away from those.'

'Maybe,' he says, his face grim. 'But I don't think my route can be done by someone on their own. You'd need at least two people.'

'What if she found someone?' I say.

'Don't be stupid.'

'Did you count all the monks when we got to Rongbuk, and again when we left?'

'That's … .' He coughs. 'Shit. That's perfectly plausible.'

'See.'

'Oh, shut up, you two,' Miranda says. We'd almost

forgotten about her. 'Just sleep. It's obvious they …' She inclines her head towards the monks. 'They have a route in mind already and we won't have a choice. Just sleep and see where they take us. Alice can look after herself. She's not the kind of girl to go off without making sure she'd be safe.'

'But she hasn't got any fucking oxygen,' Simon says.

'She obviously doesn't need it,' Miranda hisses.

'Everyone needs oxygen up there,' I say.

'That's what our minds would like us to believe,' she says.

'Are you mad?' Simon says.

She giggles. 'To be here with you, yes. To think that, no. Messner and Habeler did it ages ago, and Stangl got from Camp III to the summit in less than 17 hours, and without oxygen. And Odell spent weeks up high without oxygen in 1924. So there.' She turns away from the two of us.

'Ok, ok,' Simon says, rolls his rucksack over to her. 'Sorry.' I hear him kiss her.

'That doesn't make it any better, though, does it?' I mutter and get the feeling I'm talking to myself and the gloom.

Chapter 27

Tara didn't pull away when Irvine kissed her hand. Instead, she smiled. 'What does that mean?'

'What do you think?' he said, released her hand slowly, sat back.

She shrugged.

'It means I want to be here, with you.'

'You rush all things, don't you?'

'It's a part of me I can't change.'

'That's the easy way out,' she said. 'You haven't even asked me if I'm in love with anyone.'

'It didn't cross my mind.'

'That's a very selfish way of looking at things.'

He didn't move, looked straight at her, and then down onto the ground. 'Yes, it is.' His lips were a straight line. 'I've got a lot to learn.'

'There's nothing wrong with emotion, and everything wrong with emotion without thought.'

'How can I apologise?'

'Move to your new room tomorrow, and spend some time alone.'

'I don't think I could bear to be alone.' He wanted to reach out to her, take her hands in his, but didn't dare.

'It's a lesson we all have to learn.'

'Why?'

'Because we'll all be on our own at the end.'

'You were there at mine,' he said.

'But it wasn't your end, was it? That wasn't your fate, not then.'

'But George's?'

She nodded.

'That's cruel.'

'You don't just want to stay here to go back out there to find him, do you?'

He shook his head. 'That would be foolish.'

'That's what I was going to say.'

He folded his arms over his chest. 'And what do I do on my own, up here, in this impossible mountain?'

'You learn to live like we do. You learn to speak our language.' She stared at him, challenged him to contradict. 'That's what you must do.'

'Even if I decide to go back down, after all?'

'Are you changing your mind already?' she said. 'Because things aren't as easy as you were hoping for?' Her voice accused him.

He shook his head. 'No. Absolutely not.'

'I envy you the choice,' she said, almost reached out to him, but wouldn't allow herself to.

'Are you allowed envy?' he said.

'Envy is a small sin compared to others.'

'Aren't there any big sins in such a small community?' he said.

'Such as?'

'Murder, jealousy, faithlessness?'

She smiled. 'Those are all easy ways out, the ways of your world maybe, but not ours.'

'That's a very harsh judgment on a world you don't know.'

'But it's true.' Her tone was sharp. 'We know more here than you might think. And understand more than you might want us to.'

'I underestimate you, obviously,' he murmured. 'But there are wars here.'

'At the foot of the mountain, true. But that's not our world. *This* is our world.' She put her hands on her chest, then spread her arms to encompass the heart of the mountain. 'Now sleep,' she said. 'There's still much in you to heal.'

The next morning, they moved all his things to another chamber, not far away.

'You must grow familiar with your surroundings,' she

said. 'I don't want you to get lost. And I don't want you to go near the door onto the mountain.'

'Why not?'

'Because you'll be tempted to climb out and look for George before you're ready, no matter what you've promised.'

'So I'm your prisoner?'

'No, you are your body's prisoner. In a week you'll be free, if you live slowly enough. And then we'll take you back down if you want us to.'

'Would you come down with me?'

She shook her head and smiled. 'No. I have to stay here, for now. We are all of us, this family of believers.'

He looked at his worn clothes, piled neatly against one of the walls, then looked down at himself, the plain robes he'd been given. 'Will I need those old things?'

'If you go down, yes.'

'They'll ask me how I survived.'

'You'll be able to make up something.'

'They won't believe me.'

'The more impossible it seems, the more they'll believe it,' she said.

'I'd never expected a holy person to be such a cynic.'

'I don't understand that word.'

'A famous writer in my world once said a cynic *knows the cost of everything and the value of nothing*.'

Her smile was hesitant.

'Very simply, a cynic is someone who doesn't believe anything good of the people or things around him.'

'Oh,' she said. 'But that's not me at all.'

'I can see we both have a lot of learning to do.'

She started by teaching him the Tibetan words for all his western possessions, and then, at each meal time, she made him repeat after her the words for all the different foodstuffs they had, all the provisions they brought here year after year, dried and stored, and ground and cooked.

'How no-one notices you is beyond me.'

'That's why we travel at night. And this place is well-hidden and inaccessible to anyone who doesn't know how to follow the mountain's marks.'

'I hope you'll teach me that, too.'

'Slow down.'

He raised his hands. 'I will.'

Within a few days, he could speak some simple sentences, ask the health of the other monks who smiled at his concentrated efforts to make the words sound real when they came from his mouth, who were amused and bemused to have a yellow-haired giant living with them, who humoured him and made him welcome. Virya greeted him each day like a son, a big smile on his face, a gratitude Sandy was still alive.

'You faith is so gentle and flexible,' he said to her at the end of the week.

'Faith should come from the heart, not from the head,' she said, opposite him, across a low table in his room.

'And yet you are ruled by traditions.'

'If our hearts didn't tell us to keep the traditions, we wouldn't.'

'It's not blind obedience, then?' he said.

'Would we be as bending as we are if it were?'

'I suppose not.'

She reached into a pocket in her robe, pulled out a small book, a tiny rectangle of old paper sheets, bound untidily, and put it on the table between them. 'This is what guides us,' she said.

'What is it?'

'It's *The Sutra of Thin Air*.'

'A bible?'

'Something like that.'

'Is that the original?'

She shook her head. 'That's too fragile to be held now, too old. This is a copy.'

'It looks very old, though.'

'The first one is ancient.'

'And this one?' he said.

'It's hundreds of years old.'

'I won't be able to read it.'

'I'll read it to you.' She smiled at him.

'And translate it?' His face pleaded with her.

She nodded.

'Why?'

'You need to decide what to do.'

'I know,' he said. 'What does your father think I should do?'

'That's not important. We can't make other people's choices for them.'

'What do you think?'

'I can't make your decision for you.'

'You already have.'

She blushed. 'That's not what I meant. You don't know me. You can't …'

'I can't what?' he said.

'You can't know what you want of me now.'

'Can certainty not be born suddenly, in an instant? Does it have to come with years of understanding?'

'That's a question I can't answer.'

'Read to me.'

Her blush didn't disappear. It grew, instead, as she read and translated, with a fragile voice, in broken sentences, and still it sounded like a song to him, her voice not an echo against the walls, but a tapestry of syllables.

She put the book down, closed it, looked at him. He couldn't look away. She put her hands on the table next to the small volume, veins raised under the skin, long fingers unmoving.

'It's beautiful,' he said.

She nodded, but said nothing.

'Am I supposed to make my decision based on those few words?' he said.

'Do you understand what they mean?'

'That you've been here forever, and that you'll be here forever.'

'We're not immortal,' she said. 'There is no eternal life here.'

'I understand that.'

'My people have been here forever.' She sat up tall.

'But?'

'But there are fewer of us as the years wear on. And there will be fewer in the future.'

'Unless?'

'Unless we take the word to the lowlands, unless we have more monks coming to Rongbuk.'

'Your father doesn't agree with you, though, does he?'

'Oh, he knows we need more of us up here. But he doesn't think that to go and preach in openness, to reveal that we live here, is the best way for us to find more followers.'

Irvine shrugged. 'There's nothing I can say.'

Silence. She looked at him without emotion.

'Are you this difficult with everyone you heal?' he said.

'Not everyone is like you.'

'I'm different?' His eyes were alight.

'Everyone here has already chosen their path. You haven't.' Her voice was level. 'And you haven't considered everything.'

'Oh, but I have. There was a woman, before I came here …'

'I'm not sure I should know this.'

'But you must. She was married, yet she still wanted …'

'Enough. That's your life, not mine.'

He leaned forwards across the table. 'You have to know this, understand this. That's why I prayed in your temple. That's why I climbed this mountain. That's why I'm here.' Irvine's face was taut with anger, regret, pain, urgency.

Tara leaned back, pulled her hands from the table.

'You're so distant,' he said.

'I have to be.'

'She, she wanted to keep me, to stay married, because he had money, to stay rich, to pay for me to be her … to be with her, but she wasn't, she wasn't, would never have been …'

'Faithful?'

He nodded. 'So I finished it, some time before we came here. I wanted the purity of the mountain to see what I could make of life, not to see what life could make of me. And when I didn't get my chance, to start with, to try for the summit, I didn't collapse. I thought it was some god's way of telling me that I wasn't ready yet, that I should learn more, that I had to become a better man.' His breath was ragged now, more than at any other time since he had woken from his injuries.

She reached out to him, could not, this time, stop herself from putting her hand on his. 'Enough. You're making yourself worse again.'

'I have to tell you the truth. You have the right to know.'

'I am no-one. Healers aren't gods.'

'That's the first line of the next page, is it?'

She shook her head, and reached for the book.

Gods are not healers.
The healing comes from the heart of those called.
Healing rides on the thinnest air.

'Do the words change whenever you want them to?' he said.

'It's not a magic book, nor a book of spells,' she said. 'It tells the story as it is, as it was.'

'Why are you afraid of me?'

'I'm not,' she said.

'Do you love someone else?'

'No.'

He didn't smile, just put his hands on the table, palms up, said nothing.

'Very few of us get married,' she said. 'Virya and my mother were an exception.'

'But it's allowed?'

She nodded.

'So … ?'

'What?'

'Do you love me?' The question took even him by surprise.

'How would I know?'

'Do you want me to leave?'

She shook her head, lips clamped together. This time she didn't blush.

'So why does it feel like you're trying to make me go?'

'I don't want your life to become one of regret.'

'How could I regret?'

'You might have fallen in love with anyone who healed you,' she said.

'Maybe. But I don't think so.'

'How do you know?'

'Because my heart tells me. Because it's not the height that takes my breath away. Not any more. It's you. Not just your beauty, not just the way your hair sways when you walk, how it follows the movement of your body; not just your eyes, nor the sound of your voice. No, it's much more than that, something words can't say, something I can't grasp into your language or mine. I cannot imagine not being married to you.' He stopped marking each syllable with a fist against his chest, put his hands on the table again, fingers curved up.

'Should a woman marry the first man she thinks she loves?' she said.

'I can't make that decision for you.' He smiled at the closing of the circle of words.

'I won't let you tell me what to do.'

'I won't.'

'I won't let you compare me to other women.'

'I won't.'

'There have been no other men.'

'If there had been, I wouldn't care.'

'There are my gods. I am already wed to them in spirit.'

'I would expect no less.'

She put her hands down next to his, deliberately avoided touching him. 'This isn't an easy life.'

'I know.'

'There will be no way back.'

'To the lowlands?'

'To anywhere. If we marry, it's an unbreakable bond.'

'As all marriages should be.'

'I will have to talk to Virya,' she said.

'Don't you want me to?'

'We're all equal, remember.'

'Is this what you want? I will go if you want me to.'

She shook her head. 'No. Don't go. Stay.'

They let their hands meet, palm over palm, warmth into warmth.

Chapter 28

A sleepless day. I twist and turn on the hard ground, can't close my eyes, can't close my ears, hear Simon's snoring, and the silence from the others. The monks sleep like robots powered down. My eyes, accustomed to the dark caves by now, see them lying on their backs, rigid, arms folded over their chests, all identical, all in a row, of a kind. I daren't get up, even when I'm desperate for a piss, even when I'm so impatient in my sleeping bag that I want to walk through these rows of sleeping men and women and wake them, shake them awake, ask them where we're going, why we're doing everything in the dark, how we're going to catch up with Alice. And the most amazing thing is that Miranda sleeps just like the monks; soundless, on her back, motionless, a smile on her face.

The light at the entrance to this overhang fades, just as I'm about to fall asleep, tired of all this waiting. One of the monks stands up, woken by I don't know what, walks along the line of sleepers, touches them lightly, until they're awake, upright, eyes bright in the gloaming. He needs longer to wake Simon and Miranda, but when they, too, are on their feet, wide awake, he stands in front of us, gestures with his hand to make us drink and eat, leads the way out into the serrated wind, no lights again, shows us where the handholds are for the first step up the face.

'Why no lights, not even here?' I say.

'Secret?' Simon says.

They all turn to us, hands on lips. No talking, just follow, is what it means. I shake my head.

'You can do it,' Miranda whispers, close behind me, until we're separated, each one of us sandwiched between monks, so they can help us, I suppose. I shouldn't complain, I guess.

The dark grows more dense. I can't see my hand in front of my face. A pair of warm hands grabs mine, leads them into holds I wouldn't even have seen in the light, pushes me up the sharp rocks. A pair of hands from above pulls at me. I can sense they're doing this for all three of us. Why?

This relay lasts for what seems like an age. I look down and see, in the furthest distance, the flickering lights of what I take to be Advance Base Camp, imagine the climbers there milling around, waiting for what they think is perfect weather. The wind snatches at me, tries to pull me from the mountain. I have a silk rope around my waist, a flimsy lifeline. It feels like nothing at all, a tenuous link to the real world, to the solid ground we're leaving. I understand now why we've got no torches. If I can see the Advanced Base Camp fires this clearly, they would be able to see us, here, trying to scale the mountain in the dark.

And then the lights are gone, as if someone had switched them off. The wind howls around my ears. My hands struggle again against the wall of rock, slip and grip. My face is up against the mountain again, the cold drifting from the rocks. I feel my breath, hot and fast, as I inch my way up. This is an impossibility, I want to shout, scream, feel like pushing myself off the face into the darkness all around me. Are we even on the right path to find Alice? Where is she? Is she thinking about me, or just about what's up there, above our heads, looming unseen in the blackness, waiting for the sun to come up again, in God knows how many hours more.

I want to rest, but I'm not allowed to. The mute monks keep pushing and pulling us, keep driving us up along the route they've chosen. I've lost all my bearings, wonder if Simon has, despite his familiarity with the mountain, but I can't get anywhere near him, can't call to him, can't ask him. The unfamiliar breeds fear, and my shaking, cold hands are an insecure hold. The gale, unrelenting, feels its way into my clothes, despite their modernity, despite their so-called weatherproofness, and chills me to the bone, showers of snow blowing into my face, melting, trickling down under the hood, the neck gaiter, the layers of material that are supposed to protect me from the cold. I start shivering all over, can't control it, cough and pant, try to stop for breath, can't, put one foot up ahead of the other, brief pause, then on again, always on again, up and up, a hell of ice and pain and fear and loathing.

When we stop, I still have no idea what time it is, or where we are. There's no sign of the sun yet, although it must be close. We all squeeze into yet another hiding place, I suppose, hidden from any binoculars that might start scouring the mountain face when the light does come. We sit, melt snow, drink as much as we can, force whatever food they give us into our mouths, although we don't feel like eating. No-one feels like eating up here.

'Are you sure these are the good guys?' I say to Simon.

He nods, tears at his food with bared teeth, looking as if he's enjoying it. 'Trust them,' he says, his mouth full.

'But where are we?'

'The North Face, somewhere.'

'Thanks for being so specific.' My heart's racing again. I try to slow my breathing down, but the air's so thin I can't.

'Relax,' he says.

'That's easy for you to say. What about the bloody oxygen?'

'We're nowhere near the Death Zone yet. They'll have carried some up ahead for us.'

I shake my head. 'I wouldn't bet on it.'

He shrugs. 'We'll see.'

Miranda's sitting with us. Her carefully-constructed hair style is long gone, and she looks younger with it all dishevelled. She smiles at me. 'I'm finding it difficult, too, James.'

'But you've never been on a mountain before.'

'Not here, maybe,' she says.

'Is that another secret you've been keeping from us?' I say.

'Not from me,' Simon says.

'Am I the only one who doesn't know about all these things?' I say.

'That's because you're in a world of your own,' Miranda says, gently. 'And that's not a bad thing. It's as if you're unsullied by the real world.'

'That doesn't feel good to me,' I say. 'It makes me sound naïve.'

'There's nothing wrong with that,' she says. 'It means you're pure.'

I smile and shake my head, crawl into the sleeping bag. I've stopped shivering.

'What?' she says when I look at her again.

'Which mountain?'

'The Eiger,' she says. 'That's where I first met Simon.'

I smile again. 'What would we do without the mountains?'

'Live longer?' she says.

'Mmm,' I say. I feel sleepy, and my throat's hurting.

Simon's snoring by now.

'I always think climbers have a secret death wish,' she says.

'Why?'

'Why else would they do what they do?'

'To prove something?'

'No need. The proof's there already.'

'What?' I don't understand her.

'Nature is greater than we are, and always will be.'

'So why did you climb the Eiger?' I say.

'I didn't say I climbed it.' She giggles.

I shake my head. 'The train.'

She nods. 'But it made me want to climb.'

'And here you are.'

'All those years later.'

'Do you really love him?'

She nods again. 'I'm afraid so.' She wraps her arms around herself. 'Although he's such an arse.'

'I suppose he's a bit of a grower. He's growing on me.'

'After ten years of dislike.'

'That was mutual,' I say, and wish it hadn't been. It seems like lost time now.

'I think he's getting quite fond of you, too.'

I take an enormous drag of water out of my bottle. It sears my throat, and I cough. I try to suppress it, but that only makes it worse. I sit up and try again to stop, hand in front of my mouth.

'Are you alright?' she says.

'Fine, I'm fine,' I say. Cough again. 'It'll pass.' It stops. 'Better get some sleep.'

'Yes,' she says. 'See you later.'

'I'm not going anywhere.'

'I guess not.'

I turn over, wipe my mouth again with the back of my hand. It comes away sticky, and even in the weak light I can see the red across my pale skin. I pull my glove back on, drag the top of the sleeping bag up over my head and fall asleep, forget about the pain and the blood.

When I wake up, everyone else is still asleep. I crawl out of my bag, tiptoe across to the opening onto the mountain face. The wind is worse than ever, and it's snowing. It's a whiteout. I can see nothing for the swirling drift. Even so, I push my head out into the wind, crane my neck to look upwards. The flakes blow into my open eyes. I try to blink them away, hope for a break in the blizzard, the clouds, so I can see something, anything, that will help me work out where exactly we are. I'm about to turn away when the wind drops, when a rip opens in the curtain of clouds. I can see about a hundred metres either way, for a brief instant. Dear God, we're in the Norton Couloir, that gash ripped into the mountain from just below the summit pyramid all the way down to the glacier to the west of the North Col. Jesus wept! This is madness.

I stumble back to my bag, throw myself into it. This is an impossibility. If we've come this far already, why haven't we caught up with Alice yet? I start shivering again, even with all my clothes on, curl up, and still it won't stop. I reach for the water bottle beside me, open it, and put it to my mouth. It's frozen again in the short time I've been out of my bag. Shit, shit, shit. I'm forgetting all the rules. And then the headache starts, a crashing pain that bleeds through my skull, like rivers of lava down the sides of my head, hot, melting my thoughts and my soul. I close my eyes.

'Come on, James,' Miranda says, mouth right next to my ear. 'We've let you sleep as long as possible, but we need to go.'

'Just leave me,' I say, half asleep.

'You know we can't do that. What about Alice?'

I jump up, shivers down my spine, needles in my head still, eyes half-open. 'Yes, yes, of course. Sorry.' I snatch up my gear, stuff it into my rucksack. The monks are staring.

'For fuck's sake, Jim, just calm down,' Simon hisses, grabs my arms, forces them down by my sides. 'You'll fuck everything up.'

I drop onto the cold, hard ground, take deep breaths.

It's like nothing's coming in. 'Sorry.'

Simon hands me his thermos. 'More tea. Drink it all.'

'What about you?'

'I've got another two bottles.'

'I'm just worried about Alice.'

'She's a better climber than he is,' Miranda says, steps in front of him, sits down next to me. 'You shouldn't worry.'

'But I know something's wrong.'

'We'll find her,' she says. 'I'm sure she's got some people with her,' she whispers. 'It'll be fine.'

I finish the thermos, feel like a different person already, warm again and no shivers, and the needles blunting. 'Thanks. I need to be stronger.'

Simon laughs at me. 'No, just more organised and less emotional. We all know what the risks are.'

'Exactly,' I say. 'That's why I want her here with me, not out there, on her own, or with God knows who.'

'We'll get there, mate. We'll catch her up, today. I promise.'

'Don't make promises you can't keep.'

'No,' Miranda says. 'Don't. I'd never forgive you.'

'I'll marry you when we get back down to the monastery,' he says.

'Will that be legally binding in England?' she says.

'I don't know. As long as it's legally binding in my head.'

'We'll have to do it in England, too,' she says. 'Imagine the party we could have.'

'Whatever you say.' He winks. 'It's your money, anyway.'

'Come on,' she says. 'We've got to go.'

The monks are all smiling. Strange how we've not had any real interaction with them, like they're keeping themselves consciously apart from us.

'Why don't they talk to us?' I say, just as we walk

towards the darkness.

'I don't think they want to risk becoming too attached to us, and vice versa,' Simon says.

'You're becoming sentimental,' Miranda says. I just think it.

'I'm different out here,' Simon says.

'Maybe we should stay here forever then,' she says. 'And screw the English wedding.'

'You'd miss London too much.'

She shrugs.

'Come,' the oldest of the monks says, the first time he's spoken. 'It really is time. Difficult climb now.' You mean it wasn't difficult before?

For some reason or another, Simon hugs him. 'The most difficult part.'

The monk nods, pushes his way out.

Our crampons clatter across the rock as we slide out onto the ice and snow. The blizzard hasn't stopped. I'm beyond asking questions, but our leader answers my unspoken one. 'We have to climb, even if the weather is bad. Keep away from others.'

'But only two people have ever got up by this route. And one of them got killed on the way back down.'

'This is our way,' he says. 'It must be.'

'Fair enough.' I still can't believe we're doing this, in a blizzard, in the dark.

It's steep here, cracked and rotten ice under the fresh snow, dangerous in the light, never mind the bitter darkness. Progress is slow, hard on legs and arms. The monks carve half-decent steps into the snow with their ancient axes, push onwards, without a word, a spiralling track upwards into the nothingness, with unremitting focus and concentration. I can't see them, can only hear the faint, dull beats of their step-cutting. At least there's the chance to rest every five paces or so as we move upwards. A tug on the rope and we move; at the next tug, we stop and wait, recover our breath. Another tug and off we go again. It's unlike anything I've experienced before, unlike anything I'll experience again. No more mountains after this, I keep thinking. Children and all the new worries they will bring, but no fear of falling into an abyss the bottom of which I cannot see.

And then, out of nowhere, after who knows how many hours, not long till dawn, a sudden, low shout, and the indistinct voices of the monks up ahead, an unexpected chatter, a murmuring, an unholy dialogue in a language I can't understand.

Chapter 29

'But you're like a son to me,' Virya said. 'And my son can't marry my daughter.'

'But I'm not your son,' Irvine said. 'And Tara isn't my sister.'

'Is this really what you want?' Virya said to Tara.

She nodded, not timid like she had been at first with Irvine, but standing upright, her eyes glistening with the fire which made her the healer she was.

'He hasn't blinded you with his white man's ways?' He used his own language, but Irvine could sense his meaning.

She shook her head, smiled, and spoke English. 'He's more like we are than they ever could be.'

'And nothing I say will make you change your minds?' He rubbed his hands together, to stop them shaking.

'No,' she said.

'No,' Irvine said. 'But I will go if you want me to, if you find this insufferable.'

Tara looked at him, slowly, painfully.

'I respect you, Virya,' Irvine continued, in his broken Tibetan. 'And I would never wish to hurt you.'

Virya stood up, walked across to Irvine, grasped him by the shoulders, and pulled him into a hug. 'You do me too much honour,' he said. He stood back, at arm's length, still holding on to Irvine. 'You've shown me much respect by learning my language. Thank you.' He turned round, wiped his eyes, faced them again. 'And you're willing to pay the price?'

'Never to go down again?' Irvine said. 'Yes.'

'And Tara? You always wanted to go to the lowlands, and I wouldn't let you.'

'They've come up to me with Sandy,' she said. 'And our children's children will go there, I'm sure.'

'Perhaps,' Virya said. 'There is one more thing I

would like to do before you marry.'

'What?' Tara said.

'Are you strong enough to climb again?' he said to Irvine.

'I think so.'

'Do *you* think so, Tara?' Virya said.

'It depends on what you want him to do,' she said.

'I want to take him to the top again. I think it's time we brought the bowl back down here. I've got a feeling there will be more attempts at the summit, and soon.'

'We can save George's photo of Ruth, then,' Irvine said.

'I thought you'd like that.'

'But isn't the bowl meant to stay there?' Tara said. 'What about the tradition? It's been there for hundreds of years.'

'Times are changing,' Virya said. 'I thought you'd understand that, of all people. We can't lose the bowl. We were lucky that Sandy and George are such honest men.'

'You're right,' Tara said. 'We'll just have to start a new tradition, the carrying of the bowl skywards.'

Virya smiled. 'Yes, Tara Lama.'

She blushed. 'You can't say that! What if Tenzin Lama hears?'

'That's what he wants anyway,' Virya said. 'When the time comes.'

'But it's not up to just him,' she said. 'Everyone here has a say.'

'I don't think any of them want anyone but you to be Lama,' Virya said.

'And is Tenzin Lama happy for Sandy to bring the bowl back with you?'

'He is. All three of us will go.'

'Which three?' she said.

'The three of us,' Virya said. 'It seems the right thing

to do.'

'But he's never climbed in the dark,' Tara said.

'He'll have to learn.'

'When do we go?' Irvine said.

'The sooner the better,' Virya said. 'The monsoons will be here in just over a week.'

'Can we look for George?'

'Not this time,' Virya said. 'It's too dangerous. We don't want to lose you just when we've found you and healed you.'

Irvine clenched his fists, unclenched them, jaw working, took a deep breath. 'I understand,' he said. 'I really do. I just hate the thought of him lying out there, all alone, all uncovered.'

'He may not be on the mountain any more,' Tara said gently. 'His body could have fallen all the way by now.'

'Then there'd be nothing left of him,' Irvine said. 'Just shreds for the birds.'

Virya nodded. 'Sorry.'

'Better to be realistic,' Irvine said. 'But I will still look for him, next year.'

'I hope you do,' Virya said.

'And I'll come with you,' Tara said.

The following evening, they crept out into the dark, climbed down through the door onto the sheer face of the mountain, traversed to the East, into a mighty gully of snow. There was hardly any wind, and the cold was gentle on their faces.

'A good night,' Tara said. 'Perfect for climbing.'

Tara and Virya wore their usual black cloaks, and Irvine one specially-made for him, to fit his uncommon stature, the hood hiding his bright hair from any light the half-full moon might throw into the mountain's cavernous crevices.

'There's lots of time,' Virya whispered. 'No need to hurry.'

The white crunched under their feet as they moved slowly, carefully, upwards. Irvine felt at home here, back amongst the snows, the rocks, the welcome gravity of height, a part of nature, of what surrounded him. He'd never felt comfortable with climbing as a challenge, a battle, wanted it to be he and nature that reached the summit together. George had felt that way, too, he thought, not as obsessed as people thought he was with conquering peaks. He'd been in love with the mountains, that's all, the higher the better, the further away from humanity's inhumane grasp the better.

They stopped after a few hours, only a slightly less steep part of the gully.

'How do you feel?' Virya said.

'Good,' Irvine said.

'You have a great gift,' he said.

'Do you think there are any other white men like me?'

'There are great people everywhere,' Virya said. 'I should think there are. They just don't know it. They are too bound by the way in which they live. And that goes for those among our people, too.' He pointed out into the black speckled with the crystal stars. 'I'm sure there are men and women down there who could live and climb with us. They just don't realise it. They haven't been given the chance to feel what we feel, to be called to this great task of happiness.'

'Is that what you call it?'

'I don't feel happy anywhere else. Up here, I can be who I really am. I can be true to who I am. Nature guides me.'

'How do you find your way in the dark?' Irvine said.

'We feel our way,' Tara said. 'With our hands, our feet, our bodies. The mountain has moulded us. There are marks in the rocks only we know, shapes we've come to understand. It's the same path every time.'

'Even when the snow covers her?' Irvine said.

'Even then. If anything, the snow makes some of it easier. Shapes grow more distinct, and the white gives more light.'

Irvine shook his head. 'I have a lot to learn.'

'It will be simple for you,' she said. 'You're born to it.'

'We'll see about that,' he said. 'There's a long way to go.'

'None of us are perfect,' Tara said. 'Some of us die here, as you know, and it's through no-one's fault. It is just what happens. The mountain will always be dangerous.'

'Life will always be dangerous,' Irvine said. 'There's death in all things, just as there is life.'

'Yes,' Virya said, got up. 'Let's move on.'

They picked themselves up, Irvine resisting the temptation to kiss Tara. He felt so light, so full of all good things. He couldn't believe that just three weeks earlier he'd almost frozen to death not far from here, had lost one of his newest and best friends, would have been dead, too, had it not been for these amazing, secret people whose faith he had long admired from afar without knowing its real secret, who were teaching him the very essence of their faith, letting him into the very centre of their beings, making him one of them.

As they climbed, he felt the steam of his breath drift from his mouth, over his face, and up towards the summit, to become part of the plume up there, or so he imagined. This was the perfect way to climb to the summit, sheltered, almost in every direction, from the wind, from uninvited watchers. He felt safe, in between Tara, who was leading, and Virya, whose presence he felt behind him at every step. And yet he didn't feel like a passenger, not someone they were dragging upwards beyond his abilities. He felt a part of them.

They came to the top of the gully, where the snow petered out, and steep rock took its place, where they had to push through deep crevices, up onto the Northeast Ridge, where the wind started to blow at them from the other side of the mountain.

'I recognise this place,' Irvine shouted. 'It's the Third Step. That's what George called it, anyway.'

'We call it the Final Leap,' Tara shouted back. 'Where our faith is rewarded.'

Irvine grinned in the dark. To be here again. The grin faded. Why hadn't George picked this route, why had he gone across the ridge where they'd been battered by the wind? But then they hadn't known any better, either of them, had they? It had seemed easiest to attempt the ridge with its less steep approaches, to place camps on the more level parts of the mountain, to rest at the North Col, before gradually, too gradually perhaps, pushing up towards the very top of it.

He watched Tara, in the reflected light of the snow below, a lithe shadow against the glistening rocks, marvelled at her strength, how much more easily than George she moved upwards, not swimming against the current, but floating, her pulling and pushing almost unnoticeable, her cloak rippling in the wind, her arms and legs moving so quickly, and yet so slowly. If George had been brilliant, she was unbelievable. She was pulling him up with her, not physically, but in spirit. It was so easy to follow her, to move along the same line she took, to feel his hands melding into the rocks, no cold, no wind, no pain, no effort, really, to just be one with the Mother Goddess. Because she was her. That's why he loved her, he realised. That was why he'd fallen in love so quickly, with such absolute certainty.

At last, they reached the final summit ridge, back on snow, the night black and red against the white. From here, it was no more than a walk up to the summit. They walked in a line, three black cloaks, three kindred souls. Tara took his left hand, Virya his right, as they picked their way up, up, up, to the highest point in the world.

And then they were there. The wind dropped. Silence surrounded them. They stood still, for a moment, heads bowed, the curve of the mountain graceful against them. He thought of George, of Ruth, of Odell, of Norton, of Arnold, and of Peter Lunn, of Norway, of all the people he would miss, who wouldn't know he was still alive. The tears froze on his cheeks. And then he looked at Tara, hood down now, the braid of thick hair down her back, her cheekbones so proud, so perfect, her back straight, her body tight through the cloak blowing against her, and knew he wouldn't miss his old life for long. And he thought of how he would now always be close to George, how they would never be parted, their souls together on this mountain of all mountains. He looked at Virya, his hands clasped together, his lips moving in a silent prayer of thanks to his gods, his faith rising from his as a warm glow. And he knew he'd made the right choice, knew his new life was here, could be nowhere else. This was where he would live forever, until his time did come, until he either fell from the mountain or fell asleep forever in his bed, with Tara at his side, and the silence of the High Monastery around him, until all things were complete.

Tara kneeled down on the snow, pushed at the snow with her bare hands, parted the ground and reached into it. She pulled the smooth, brown, wooden box from the ground, placed it carefully next to her, filled in the hole with earth, snow and ice.

'She will grow into the void,' she said. 'She's always growing.' She opened with box with one touch, didn't struggle like Irvine and Mallory had to find a way into it. 'A final song to bring it back to the Monastery,' she said. 'We'll put everything into its place when we get back down.'

She took the bowl from the box, put the lid back on it and stood up. The bowl in both hands, she raised her arms to the sky and started to sing.

Irvine had never heard her sing before, not realised how her smooth voice could reach the depths of the valleys, and then soar higher than even this place. It was from another world, the sound she drew from within her tiny body, a lament, a celebration, a song full of sadness and reflection, joy and ecstasy. Her shadow was tall in the half-light, and when she stopped singing he felt bereft, and swore he could feel the mountain sigh beneath her feet.

'That is the most wondrous thing I've ever heard,' he said.

'It's what I was born to.'

'It's like her mother's voice,' Virya said. 'Exactly like her mother's voice.' He turned away and looked into the void of the distance.

Tara opened the box again, packed the bowl into the prayer flag, closed the box, wrapped it into the cloth contraption that worked as a rucksack, and wound it around her, under her cloak. 'We should go down again,' she said. 'Dawn is only a few hours away.'

They walked down the ridge, followed their frozen footsteps through the snow, let themselves drift down the face with arms and legs working with the mountain, found their way back into the gully of snow, lowered themselves down the steep slopes, facing away from the mountain and looking into the abyss in front of them, until they reached the point at which they had to traverse back into the centre of the face, into the huge fault in the mountain that hid the entrance to the High Monastery.

The sun was just below the horizon of peaks out to

their right. The yellow stones started to gleam in the morning light. They checked their rope, made it tight, and, on tiptoe, moved across the hidden steps back into the mountain.

Inside, she put the box onto the table in the main hall, opened it, pulled out the flag and the bowl, and, finally, Mallory's photo of his wife. 'Keep it safe,' she said to Irvine.

'I will,' he said. 'And the bowl and the flag?'

'Tenzin Lama will decide where they are to be kept,' she said.

'And you and me?'

'Tomorrow night,' she said. 'Virya has arranged for us to be married tomorrow night, just as I wanted. Before the monsoons come and we can't go outside.'

Chapter 30

The sounds are confused, a chaos of words. The monks rush back down this break in the steepness, push the others to one side, questions spouting from their mouths.

'A black-haired woman,' I hear.

'Two more of ours dead,' I hear.

My head sinks down, until I focus on nothing more than my unwieldy boots and crampons in the snow.

'Just where the traverse begins,' is something else I hear, before the first of them reaches me. 'Your wife,' he says. 'In the snow. Blood.'

I rip off the ridiculous silk bond, that smooth nothingness that bound me, back and front, without making me feel safe. I sprint across the uneven slope of crisp, new snow, or whatever counts as a sprint up here, ignore the gravity pulling me into the valley, rush to the limp shape on the ground, etched into the ice, throw myself onto my knees.

'No, oh, please, no.' It's Alice, snow on her face, her nose white with the frost, unmoving, prostrate on the ground, hands bare. And through her clothes, through her thick parka, through the hole in it, blood, frozen, dark, black red, a pool around her, from her abdomen, from where we wanted to grow our children, and her face transparent with death.

'Is she breathing?' I scream. 'Get some light here! Who cares who can see us? They already know we're here.'

'Just do it!' Simon's next to me now. 'Fuck. How bad is it?'

'I don't know.' I put my hand under Alice's head. 'Light!'

One of the monks, Ryokan I think his name is, kneels down next to me, turns on a small torch, the yellow light suddenly fierce in my eyes.

'Alice,' I say, try to feel for a pulse in her neck. At least there's no blood from her mouth. And then I see it, in the pale light, a narrow stream of sepia steam from between her lips, rising from her, like her soul leaving her body. 'She's still alive,' I scream, and the sound rolls down into the valley and echoes back up. 'Alice, for God's sake.'

'Let me,' Ryokan says gently. 'I'm the healer.' He unbuttons her coat, feels around her stomach, one hand above, one below. 'The bullet's gone right through her,' he says. 'But she's lost so much blood.'

'How long since it happened?'

He shrugs. 'I don't know.' He scratches his head through his black hood. 'But we've been catching them up. They'll have been climbing in the daylight. Five or six hours, maybe.'

I hear sobbing behind me. Simon's sitting in the snow, head in his hands, shaking, Miranda next to him, her arm around his neck, mouth by his ear. I can't hear what she's saying.

'We need to get her back down,' I say. 'That's the only way we'll save her.'

Ryokan shakes his head. 'She'd definitely die.'

'What are they doing here?'

'They must have found us.'

'What?'

'We're close to what they want to find,' he says, resigned.

'You're talking in riddles.'

'Later,' he says. 'I need to fix this first.'

Alice starts to moan as he rips open the layers of clothing under her coat. I nearly throw up when I see the hole, the ripped skin and flesh where the bullet has destroyed her body. He grabs something from behind him, pulls out a prayer flag, and binds it around her, tight, so tight her taut skin wrinkles under its pressure. She screams.

'Do you know what you're doing?' I shout.

He nods, grits his teeth. 'This is all I can do here. We need to wrap her up in more clothes.

'Oxygen, we need oxygen,' I say. 'Why the fuck didn't we bring any?'

Simon crawls across to me. 'I've got one small bottle, for emergencies.' His face is scratched, his eyes desperate, his breathing ragged and fast, ice clinging to his skin.

'Why the fuck didn't you say?'

'I've not been thinking straight.' He pulls the red bottle from his rucksack. 'Here.'

I fix the mouthpiece to the bottle, put it over her mouth and nose, turn the valve, gently, not too much. Then the picture flashes by me, how she knelt by me, all those years ago, when I was almost gone, when I was an hour away from death, when she gave me her oxygen, when she gave up her dream, just to let me live, to stop me joining all those unsuccessful, forgotten climbers, those who'd tried and failed. How she gave up her life for me, really, to drag me down from this mountain, and gave me something new. Now's my time to repay her.

I hear her breathing, pulling the heavy air into herself. After a couple of minutes, I pull the bottle away from her. I grab my thermos, open it, bring the steaming rim to her lips, pour, gently, ever so gently, tiny droplets of it, onto her lips, into her mouth. She's so white, almost a ghost already. 'Please, God, please.'

Ryokan looks at me. 'All our gods.'

I say nothing, don't understand why I'm not crying, why I'm not panicking anymore, why I'm standing on a steep snow field above a 3-mile abyss and not afraid anymore. I want her to live. I need her to live, or I might as well jump off the mountain now and let my body be torn apart by the fall. Without her, there's nothing.

She pulls away from the thermos. 'Hurts,' she says.

'You need more.'

'I can't.'

'You must.'

'Too late.'

'Stop talking rubbish.'

'Tired. Cold.' Her head falls back onto the snow.

I rip off my outer layer, cover her in it. 'What now?' I say to Ryokan.

'We're two or three hours away,' he says.

'What from, what the fuck from?'

He turns round, looks at the other monks, looks at Simon.

'Simon,' I shout. 'What the fuck's going on? Do you know what he's talking about?'

Simon doesn't move, lifts his head so slowly it's as if he daren't look at me, as if he daren't speak. And then he nods.

'What?' I'd hit him if I could, thrash his face into oblivion. 'Why didn't you tell us?'

'I couldn't risk it,' he says. 'Just in case you got caught, too.'

'What is it?' I say. 'Tell me, for fuck's sake.'

'A monastery,' he says. '*The* monastery.'

I gasp. 'You didn't even tell Alice, you bastard. This is all your fault.' I step across to him. He cowers, does nothing to defend himself. But I can't hit him, can't take my rage out on him.

'I know,' he says, almost inaudibly. 'I'm sorry.'

'Have you been there before?' I say.

He shakes his head. 'They didn't need me to help them up here before. And they wouldn't tell me how to get there.'

'You fucking idiot,' I scream.

'You weren't meant to be a part of it. Not you, not Alice. I tried to keep you away.'

There's nothing to say. I turn away from him, kneel back down next to Alice.

The other monks come across. Ryokan gets them to move Alice away from the frozen blood, away from the other bodies. 'A lot of the blood's from the other two,' he says. 'Head shots. Close range.'

'How do you know all this?'

'Just because we live away from the world doesn't mean we don't learn from it.'

The monks pull long pieces of cloth from behind their backs, fashion a big type of sling, slide Alice into it, take the oxygen bottle from me, fix it in next to her, fix the mouthpiece to her face. Ryokan crouches next to her, pulls part of the sling over his head, over his shoulder, then pulls himself up, Alice now lying against his back. It's only now I notice that he's at least a foot taller than the other monks, and broader.

'We've got to keep going,' he says. 'The others will need help, if they're not dead already.'

'The others? What others?' I say. 'Talk to me, please.'

'You'll see,' he says. 'The most difficult part is to come. And we have no guns. Rope up to me and follow.'

He trudges upwards, back bent. I keep pace, behind him, watch Alice's shape loll in time with his steps. What else can I do? The others follow. Everything is in slow motion up here. Five steps, rest, five steps, rest. Soon, we're resting after every three steps. I need oxygen, but there isn't any. We're all going to die. I can feel it, and it fills me with a kind of strange hope. Maybe it will all be over soon, all the uncertainty of life, the madness of trying to understand what's in my head and in others'. I lose myself in the calmness of those thoughts, find it odd to have been afraid of death, of loss, to have been afraid of heights. Nothing matters, does it? Not really. All we fear is ourselves.

Two hours later, and we're down to one step, rest, one step. The sky is growing lighter. Ryokan raises his hand, stops.

'We've lost too much time,' he says. 'The light's almost here.' He turns to Simon, Miranda and me. 'We have to traverse from here.'

The mountain is no longer just a shadow. Dawn transforms it into an obstacle of real rock, into something somehow more tangible than the presence it had in the dark.

'Traverse?' Simon says. 'You must be kidding. Which way?'

'West,' Ryokan says.

'Towards Hornbein?' Simon says. 'That's impossible.'

'It can be done.' Ryokan looks across the snow, out into the dark rocks. 'The only problem is that they'll be able to pick us off one by one at the entrance if they're in there already.'

'In where?' I say.

'The High Monastery, where we live.'

Simon's face drops, and my legs turn to jelly.

'What?' Simon says. 'You're mad. You can't live up here all the time, surely.' His face shows me he's telling the truth. He thought it was just a monument now, not a living monastery.

'That's why they've come,' Ryokan says. 'I think that's what they've been looking for. And if they've got the Sutra of Thin Air, they'll have found the way.'

'Why kill your two mates, then?' Simon says.

'And Alice?' I say.

'The sutra doesn't make it obvious unless you're close. They'll have forced our friends to speak. They did. I saw it.'

'How?'

'I looked at their bodies. Death was a gift after that.'

'So why didn't we hear anything?'

'Silencers, I should think,' Ryokan says, a thoroughly modern monk.

'God, what have they done to Alice?'

'I don't think they intended to kill her. She must have tried to protect the others.'

'That's not what I mean,' I say.

'I don't think they'd burden themselves with rape now they'd come this far,' he says, with a smooth-faced honesty I hate and admire.

'So what now?' Simon says.

'We need to get Alice inside. We can heal her there.'

'And if they're already there?' Simon says.

'We don't have a choice.'

'But you said they'd be able to pick us off at the entrance.'

'That's why one of us needs to go ahead and check,' Ryokan says. 'And it has to be me.'

'Why?'

'Because I know this place better than any of you.'

'What about your mates?' Simon says.

'Better even than them. I was born up here,' Ryokan says.

'Dear Lord,' Miranda says. 'Incredible.'

'We can't wait till it gets dark again,' Ryokan says. He crouches down, lays Alice softly on the snow. 'You need to check for bleeding,' he says. 'And give her lots of tea and change the dressings. I'll be back as soon as I can.'

'Shouldn't one of us come with you?' Miranda says. 'At least you'll be roped then.'

He shakes his head. 'I've done this on my own before. And I don't want to put any of you in any more danger. I can move more quickly alone.'

'But you've got nothing to defend yourself with,' I say.

'I've got my hands and my faith,' he says. 'That's enough.' He nods. 'Take care of her. She will survive if we can get her inside.'

He stands up straight, turns, and walks across to where the snow ends, where the striated rock begins, and disappears into the gloom. Silence replaces him. We flatten the snow, huddle in a circle around Alice, don't speak. I kneel next to her, brush her hair away from her pale face. She opens her eyes.

'Still alive,' she grimaces.

'Yes,' I say.

'Just.'

'More than just.'

'Thirsty.'

I feed her some tea. She drinks more of it this time. Closes her eyes.

'Better?' I say.

'Pain, down there.'

I check the dressings. They're saturated. I'm going to lose her, aren't I? I get more cloths from the monks, but I don't change the dressing. I tie the new one on top of the old one, tight and thick. Her face contorts, but she stops herself from screaming.

'Are we there yet?' she says.

'Where?'

'The High Monastery.'

'So you did know about it.'

'Only because they were talking about it.'

'Who are they?'

She tries to catch her breath. 'I still don't know.'

'What?'

'Prayer flags over their gear.' She looks puzzled.

'Not Holzel or the Chinese then?'

'No. Can't figure it out.'

'9/11?'

She shakes her head.

'What?'

'I don't know,' she coughs. 'More tea.' She gulps it down, gasps for breath. 'English, I think. They argued about hurting others.'

'Not American?'

Her low voice is insistent. 'English.' Again she shakes her head. 'Sleep.'

'No, don't sleep, not now. You mustn't.' I'm frightened for her again. I thought she seemed better.

'Tired.'

'Stay awake.'

'Can't. It's time.'

'No, no, Alice, it's not. Stay with me, stay.' I rub snow into her cheeks.

'Cold,' she says. 'Too cold.' She smiles. Blood seeps out from between her lips. 'I love you.' Blood on her chin. I wipe it away.

'I love you, too. … Alice.'

She closes her eyes just as Ryokan emerges from the shadows.

Chapter 31

Irvine was on the mountain again, crouching, leaning into the wind, the full moon his guide. Ten years since he and Mallory had reached the top, only to lose it all on the way back down. He'd been on the face so many times since, looking for his friend's body, but he'd never managed to find it. After a few years, he'd given up, and let his grief flow out into the rocks every time he touched them with his bare hands.

Today was no different. He loved the feel of the rock under him, the sway of the black cloak across his back, the sense that he was in control, that he had the gift of floating up the mountain now, that he could do so without trying, without having to fight any weakness in his body. Tara had healed him well, taught him well, and now he was one of them, one of the monks of the High Monastery, had been gifted a happiness he would never have expected.

The wind was whipped into a gale from the gentle breeze it had been when he'd climbed out of the door a few hours ago. Time to go back. He turned to look at the summit, hoped the weather wouldn't take a turn for the worse, wanted the next night to be cool and calm and bright. He shrugged, felt his way down the face, each unevennesss of rock familiar, each nook and cranny of the mountain signposts back to what was now his home. The wind pounded and howled at the rocks around him, whisked the snow up into a fog of white. The plume around the head of the Goddess Mother would be immense when the sun rose.

A few more handholds brought him to the entrance of the Monastery. He pushed his way in through it, out of the wind, and into the warmth of sanctuary. He brushed the snow from his cloak, pushed back his hood, stamped his feet. His footfalls echoed through the hall as he made his way to his married chambers, excited, as always, at seeing Tara again, even after only a few hours away. But then they took nothing for granted, none of them. The mountain chose to give or take, and could take at any moment, and no matter how safe they felt, no matter how in control they might feel, accidents could and would happen.

The chamber door made no sound as he pushed it open. The room had a scent all of its own, that mingled fragrance of male and female, mixed now with something even sweeter, the essence of a new-born, a gift six months before, finally, after many years of tears and doubt and prayer. Irvine bowed his head as he moved into the room, a greeting for his family. Virya, in the far corner, with the child on his lap, and Tara, busy as ever, reading the Sutra of Thin Air, finding new ways to interpret it, Tara Lama as she now was, had been for the last four years. They still missed Tenzin Lama who had gone to sleep one night and not awoken, whose wisdom had lasted almost eighty years.

Dawa, as they had called their son, loved Virya, coiled his tiny hands around his grandfather's fingers, made singsong noises, smiled and giggled. Virya had been rejuvenated by the boy's birth, a joy to soothe the grief for his wife he'd carried around with him for too long. They all turned to Irvine now, as he sat down beside Tara.

'There may be a blizzard coming,' Irvine said.

Tara shrugged. 'We've done the ceremony in them before.'

'I know,' Irvine said. 'I just prefer the clear sky.'

Virya laughed. 'Some of your western ways have remained, then. It's not for the beauty we have the ceremony.'

'I know.' He rubbed his chin. 'But it's the one thing that frightens me still, the whirling snow.'

'It may not turn out that bad,' Virya said. 'You know they come and go.'

'I wanted to take Dawa with me tomorrow to watch his mother. But I can't do that if the weather's bad.'

Virya nodded, ran his fingers through Dawa's incongruous golden hair. 'No, that you can't risk.' He leaned back, breathed deeply. 'It will be fine. I know it will. The boy's first ceremony. It has to be.'

'Will you never tire of reading the Sutra?' Irvine said, reached out to Tara, put his arm around her.

'No,' she said. 'I want to find new meanings in it for this new age. It opens my mind.'

'Your energy amazes me.'

'This life is short,' she said. 'I must get as much done as I can. None of us will ever know what tomorrow brings.'

'Yes,' Virya said. 'Although we all hope it will bring good things.' He took Dawa from his knees, got up and carried him across to Tara and Irvine. 'I'll leave you now. There's much for me to do. And for you.' He kissed his daughter, put his hands briefly on Irvine's shoulders. 'I'll meet you in the Great Hall tomorrow.'

Irvine put his hands on Virya's. 'Thank you.'

'He's young again,' he said to Tara when Virya had left.

'It's the boy,' she said. 'It's all he wanted, really. He's even more certain now than ever that we'll not leave this place, not go down into the valleys, and give the monastery away.'

'He doesn't trust us?'

'Oh, he trusts us alright; it's impulse he doesn't trust.'

'Just like you didn't,' he said.

'A woman can be wrong occasionally.' She smiled.

'But a lama?'

'I wasn't Lama then. I wouldn't have become Lama without you.'

'You would.'

She shook her head. 'It's what Virya wanted, but without love I would never have had enough wisdom. Knowledge, perhaps, but not the wisdom that comes with knowing a lover.'

Irvine blushed.

'Don't be embarrassed,' she said.

'I find this uncompromising honesty still quite difficult. In England we always had to hide everything for fear of offending.'

'There's no room here to hide anything, and no need to. Why lie, when everything's best out in the open anyway?'

'I know you're right.'

'You're one of us now.'

'I know that, too.'

'What were you doing out there today?' she said.

'Just re-treading old paths, sharing my thoughts with the mountain.'

'Thinking of George?'

He nodded.

'I'm glad you gave up searching for his body. The Yellow Stones are too dangerous, too fickle, the dark side of the Goddess Mother.'

'I realise that now. I just wish, sometimes, that we'd known there was a better way to climb her.'

'At least George died after getting to the top.'

Irvine looked across to the photograph of Ruth he had fixed to the wall. He nodded. 'That is something, yes.' He got up, walked to the old pile of clothes in the corner, rummaged in the pockets, pulled out the old camera. 'There are pictures of us on here,' he said. 'Such a shame we can't get them.'

'Your memories are more important,' she said. 'I'm sure you can remember his face when you got to the top.'

'Yes,' Irvine said. 'And his kindness in letting me step up first. That's more important than anything else. I still don't know why he did that.'

'I should think he recognised that you're a very special man, that he saw in you what I saw then, what I see now.'

'I'm not perfect.'

'I'm not talking about perfection. I'm talking about humility and strength.'

The next evening, they all met in the Great Hall. Prayers were said, Tara intonating them with her deep, smooth voice, words dragged from the pit of her stomach, words flashing from her, unprepared, unrehearsed. Words of instruction, inspiration, revelation.

One by one, they dropped out of the door of the monastery onto the rocky traverse. Irvine was one of the last to go, Dawa wrapped tightly to his chest, swaddled in warm, black cloth. Two monks remained, as always, to watch over the monastery, to keep it alive.

The blizzard hadn't materialised, and the late night was still. The procession picked its way east across the layers of stone to the snow, then upwards towards the final pyramid. The reached the summit just as the first rays of the sun exploded onto it. Tara Lama, in her ceremonial robe, bent forward to take the singing bowl from Virya, placed it on the ground in front of her, unfurled the prayer flag from inside it, handed one of its ends to Irvine, who handed it on to the next, until a flag circle formed around the very top of the mountain, and Tara in the middle, taller than any of the others, on the very highest pedestal of the world.

'The cycle has completed again,' she said, out into the frost, the biting cold. 'We have lived another year, in the most inhospitable of places. We have sown our seed, and it has grown. In this circle of flags, we remember those who have been, those who are now, and those who will be. Raise your arms in praise of them.'

They all raised their arms, flags in hands. The silence was complete, with even the wind dumb and rested.

'This is the pole,' she said, 'the top of this revolving planet. This is its highest point. All that is moves through us, more strongly than it moves through the unpeopled poles of north and south. The sun meets us here the soonest, breaks the clouds first, casts its warmth sooner than anywhere else.' She picked up the bowl. 'It sings to us, wakes us from our silences and meditations. The Earth revolves around it, without knowing, without understanding. We are the guardians of all that lives. And though we may not be immortal, our song is, and so is the Goddess Mother.'

The monks bowed their heads, let out a collective hum, from deep in their throats, a low, constant note, which crept across the snow and rolled gently down the slopes to the edges of the mountain. She struck the bowl with a small leather mallet, drew from it a single, high note, a flickering, fleeting sound. And then she sang. The song had no words, was rather a manifestation of consciousness, a physical expression of what makes a soul, a pure prayer. As the last note faded away, out towards the lower neighbouring peaks of the range, the sun reached its full strength, and illuminated the summit in all its glorious colours.

Chapter 32

'She's dead.' I shout at Ryokan through my tears. I want to kill him.

He runs the last few yards, drops into the snow beside her, fingers on the side of her neck. He shakes his head. 'Not yet,' he says. 'Let's go; now.' He goes to pick her and the sling up, bends his back, ready.

'No,' I shout. 'No. Enough. I'm doing that, should've been doing it all along.'

'You're not strong enough,' he says.

'I will be.' If I fall off, at least we'll die together. I can't live without her, don't want to.

'Whatever you say.'

I crouch down, put my arms through the looped cloth. He helps. She seems diminished, weighs nothing, and I can't feel her breathe through the thickness of my parka. My heart races, and I struggle to catch my breath.

He moves back towards the rocks. 'They don't know about the second entrance,' he calls over his shoulder. 'They didn't notice me creeping up right behind them.'

'What?'

'No more talk; we need to move.'

The other monks gather round him, as if they know what to do, form a group, ropes ready. When we reach the rocks, they've already decided which order we'll go in. He points straight ahead.

'That's the traverse to the main entrance,' he says. 'To get to the other one, we need to climb up first, and then across.'

'I don't know what the hell you're talking about.'

'You will,' he says.

'That's what you keep telling me.'

He shrugs.

'And what about Miranda? She can't do this.'

'Yes I can,' she says. 'Simon will lead me. I'm not useless.'

Ryokan and I are roped together.

'We go first,' he says.

'Yes.'

'When we get into the mountain, silence,' he says. 'We need to take them by surprise.'

'Go on, then,' I say, feel stronger for the weight on my back, dare a look down the side of the mountain. Nothingness stares back at me.

We start across the traverse. Rough rock bites into my hands. I've taken my gloves off so I can feel better where I'm going, what I can hold on to.

'No fixed ropes,' he says and skips on to the face. It looks like he's floating up the mountain without any effort. 'Look at my feet, not my hands.' He's out into the mist.

I pull myself in the same direction as him. My feet miss their first mark, and I only just manage to cling on to the mountain. My breath catches in my throat, my heart beating up into my mouth. I grit my teeth, feel my jaws clutching at each other, my face hot with the effort and the scathing cold. Up we go. This isn't as easy as it looked.

'Keep going,' he says.

'I am.'

'Not far.'

I don't know how much time has passed when we start moving across instead of up. Alice is growing heavy on my back. My head is pounding, keeps lolling out into the abyss. I have trouble keeping my eyes open. Oh, just to slide off into oblivion. But I can't. Not after all this. Not with her depending on me. And with God knows what waiting for me up ahead. I turn my head and see them all following us, in a straight line, with nothing below them. Miranda's face is a revelation.

It shows no fear, just realisation, amazement at where she is and what she's doing. Ice clusters around her eyes, a white monobrow. The rest are black shapes on the rock.

There's a roar down below. At first I want to look down to see what it is. But then I remember. The wind's coming to get us. There's a storm somewhere down there, working its way up to us. We need to get away from it. God, how much further?

'Three more steps,' Ryokan calls. 'Then we're there. The top chamber.'

I only just have the energy to nod. Nothing more. I need to breathe, need lungfuls of air, air that's not here. How can they do this? How can they be up here?

And then we're there. My muscles burn from my ankles up to my shoulders, a continuous, uninterrupted line of pain. Just as I want to give up, we're into a crevice where the wind doesn't reach, where there's a man-made darkness, slats and rows of wood. He pushes at them, and they give inwards, and we fall into a dry, snow-free, wind-free tunnel, slide down towards a pale light, yellow and warm.

Ryokan is out of the slide first, up onto his feet, puts his finger on his lips, unropes himself.

'What about Alice?' I whisper.

'One second,' he says, tip-toes towards the light, waits. He turns to me, hand aloft, thumb in the air, gestures me towards him. 'It's clear here. Bring her down.'

I half-crawl, half-walk towards him, jump the final two feet into some sort of cave, hewn from the rock, somehow warm.

'Lay her down on the floor,' he says. 'We'll come back for her.'

'I can't leave her on her own.'

'You're going to have to,' he says. 'We need to get rid

of them first.'

'How did you know about this?'

'My great grandfather was an engineer.'

'Not a monk?'

'That as well.' He pulls the hood from his head, reveals dark blond hair, short-cropped, strange against his Asian features.

'Who was he?'

'Can't you guess?'

'Not Sandy?' I think he'll start laughing.

'Yes, Sandy,' he says. 'He lived here, made this escape route, because he feared exactly what's happened.'

Simon has rushed up to us. 'He didn't die with Mallory?' He clenches his fist. 'I knew I was right.'

Ryokan frowns and shakes his head. 'I'll tell you everything later. Now let's work out how to deal with those bastards.'

'I didn't think monks swore,' I say.

'Only when we have to.'

'But they've got guns.'

'We'll deal with it.' He turns, shoots a few words in Tibetan at his fellow monks, then says, in English. 'Miranda, stay here. Look after Alice. Simon and James with me and the boys. If we're not back in an hour, we'll be dead, and you'll be on your own.'

'Fine,' Miranda says. 'But I'll get annoyed if you don't get back ahead of time.' She claws at Simon, betrays her real feelings, snatches at his mouth with her lips.

'Quiet now,' Ryokan says. 'I have an idea.'

We steal along stone passages until we hear raised voices.

'All I want to do, High Lama, is protect you from the Chinese.' An English voice, sharp, angular, male.

'And you show your protection by killing defenceless monks?' Birger.

'That was unfortunate,' the voice says. 'It's not what

I'd ordered to happen.'

'That's too easy to say,' Birger contradicts.

'They'll be punished in due course, those who disobeyed me.'

The echo of his voice peters out. Birger says nothing. Nor is there a voice from someone who could be the High Lama.

'Someone you know?' I whisper to Simon.

He shakes his head, tries to push his way past me. I stop him, lean against his now feeble limbs, against his heaving chest. He stops moving, head bowed, tears dripping to the ground, lifts his hands to his face, covers his eyes.

Ryokan shakes his head at his men, points them down two passage ways opposite each other, lifts both hands, fingers spread wide.

'I beg your forgiveness, High Lama, for those deaths.' That voice again. It could cut through rock.

I push forwards, not thinking, look round the corner. There's the man, tall, facing away from me, still in his climbing gear, short hair, bulky coat bright red in the gloom, and draped in a bright prayer flag.

'You needn't ask my forgiveness.' An old voice, strong. 'But can you forgive yourself?'

The unknown man scratches his head. 'I think so.'

'Then why don't you tell your friends to put away their guns?' Birger says. 'The same guns they used in Norway and out there.'

'I still feel like I need protection,' the man says. 'Who knows who might try to surprise us?'

'No-one knows we're here,' the High Lama says. 'Not the Chinese, nor anyone else.'

'They'll find you some day,' the cut-glass voice says. 'That's why I'm offering you protection.'

'And what's in it for you?' Birger says.

A red-coated shrug. 'Maybe I'll learn how to live up

here.'

'Only the chosen ones can live here,' the High Lama says. 'And the chosen ones don't kill.'

'Nor do I.'

'You make it too easy on yourself,' Birger says.

The man walks to one side, and my view clears.

Birger's sitting at a table, his face more creased than ever, all the ruddiness gone, all that tan replaced by a deathly pallor. He looks sad, confused and tired. And next to him what must be the High Lama, proud, unperturbed, almost relaxed.

'And what about that beautiful woman they shot out there?' Birger says.

'That was an accident. She shouldn't have tried to get in the way. Maybe she'll live.'

'Isn't that what you call collateral damage?' Birger says.

The man shakes his head. 'You don't know who I am, do you?'

'I don't care who you are,' Birger says. 'You're a murderer, and I don't trust you.'

'What you think is actually unimportant, although your command of English is quite remarkable, even for a Norwegian. I want to hear what the High Lama thinks.'

The monk sits up even straighter, an odd smile on his face. 'You want something more than to give us what you call protection,' he says, slowly. 'What is it?' He rubs his chin. 'If you're looking for immortality, which all you westerners believe lies in any Himalayan secret, you are sadly misguided.'

'I know there's no everlasting life here,' the man says and stops pacing, finally sits down opposite Birger and the High Lama. 'I don't believe in pathetic little myths. I'm a businessman, after all.' He puts his hands on the table. 'So let's negotiate.' He puts his hand into his coat pocket and pulls a small package out of it. 'This must be worth something,' he says, unwraps the parcel and puts what was in it on the table.

It's the Sutra we found in Norway. I have to bite my hand to stop myself from gasping.

'You can read it, then?' the High Lama says.

'Of course,' the man says. 'I'm an educated man, after all. I went to the same university as Irvine.'

'That makes no difference,' the High Lama says. 'Irvine never killed or threatened anyone.'

'I'm not threatening you.' He taps his fingers on the closed, fragile book. 'And I know that this isn't the original.'

'And you want the original in exchange for protecting us.' The High Lama's words have an edge to them, a precision odd to hear from someone who has probably never left this country.

'No, no,' the man says. 'That's not quite right.' He leans back. 'I did say we'd negotiate.' He licks his finger. 'There are some business people who thrive on publicity. I don't. I might be one of the richest men on the planet, but I don't parade myself to the world, not when I don't have to.' He picks up the book, opens it, gently, turns the pages with obvious respect. 'How about ten of my men permanently up here with their guns and other gadgets, and ten million pounds a year. And you don't even have to give me the original Sutra. I'll just know it's safe here and that it belongs to me. Let's just call me John Smith.'

Birger leans forwards, is about to say something, when the High Lama pulls him back. 'We don't need your money or your protection,' he says, softly. 'No-one will find us, not the way you have.'

'Oh, please,' John Smith says. 'Someone will, some day soon, some climber or the Chinese, or Irvine hunters. You don't understand the real world. I do.'

And then he reels off the name of some Stock Exchange quoted company and how he's been on the highest mountains on every continent, and that not even his wife knows about his adventures.

The High Lama looks unimpressed, inclines his head in a knowing, patronising way. 'They are not trophies, these mountains. They are holy. Getting to the top is not enough if you learn nothing from it, if all you've done is pull yourself up on the end of someone else's rope.' He stares at Smith, whom I can see trembling. 'And, by the way, I went to Oxford, too.'

Smith shakes his head, laughs. 'How amusing.' The laugh sounds anything but real.

The High Lama ignores him. 'If someone does find us with peace in their hearts, they are always welcome,' he says. 'Fate will have chosen them.' He puts his elbows on the table. 'And it has happened before. And some people choose to stay here, and some decide to leave.'

'And they've not given you away?' The man sounds incredulous.

The High Lama shakes his head. 'We trust them, and they don't betray that trust. Can you say the same of yourself and your men?'

Smith laughs. 'I don't think you're comparing like with like,' he says. 'They're probably not driven like me, not as successful as me.'

'But they're happy,' the High Lama says.

'Teach me how to live up here,' Smith says. I see his back stiffen, wonder what his face is telling the High Lama and Birger.

'The gods have made our bodies special,' the High Lama says. 'There have been monks here for too many centuries to count, men and women who can live in this thin air.'

'I have read the book,' Smith says. 'I do know. But I don't understand how.'

'None of us understands it,' the High Lama says. 'We just accept it. Some can do it, some can't. Some might call it something as simple as faith.'

'Rubbish. That's just a myth made up by people who aren't strong enough to believe in themselves.'

The lama shrugs. 'That's a sad view to have. And even less reason to want to protect us.'

Smith gets up, takes a few paces, and sits down again. I wish I could see his face. 'I've tried to believe. I wish I could believe.'

'This isn't the way to do it,' Birger says. 'Through force.'

'What would you know?' Smith sounds angry. 'You've never been here. You don't believe. You're a nothing. And you're scared of flying. Pathetic.'

'So even now you can't persuade yourself to be kind, to forget your world, and to accept ours as it is?' the High Lama says. 'I think our negotiations must be at an end.'

'I don't think so,' Smith says and pulls a pistol out of his pocket. 'If I can't do it with money or my obvious penitence for those deaths, I'll just have to do it this way.' He points the gun at the High Lama. 'Where is the original Sutra?'

'I'll take you to it if you put your gun down, and tell your men to do the same.'

'I won't fall for that one,' Smith says.

'Then you won't see it.'

'Do you really want to die?' Smith says.

The Lama shrugs. 'No-one will tell you if you kill me.'

'But I want the book. And I'm offering you safety. Don't you understand?'

'What you don't seem to understand is that we are already safe, that we don't need you, that the book stays here, that it's owned by the mountain, not by us. The world outside has no bearing in here.'

'Where the hell are the others?' Smith seems suddenly distracted, barks at the two short-haired men behind the table. One of them shrugs.

'Go find them. I'll deal with this.' He gets up, points the gun at Birger, then the Lama, then Birger again. 'I don't want to do this,' he says. 'But I will if I have to. I don't know why you don't understand, why you won't take my money.' He leans across the table, pushes the muzzle of the gun even closer to the two old men. I see it shake.

Ryokan pushes past me, stares at the entrance to the chamber, nods at something I can't see, and rushes into the room, shoulder-charges Smith, and with the same movement hurls himself into space and at the man next to the lama, headbutts him, and somehow manages to land on his feet.

For a second I freeze, and then I charge into the room after Ryokan, screaming at the top of my voice, swinging my arms and fists at whatever gets in my way. My vision blurs red with rage, the images scatter across my eyes. And then all hell breaks loose.

Chapter 33

There are gun shots far off, and the screaming of what sound like a million voices. I am kicking at some lifeless mass on the floor in front of me, my fists flailing at some other white face to my left. And I'm still screaming, still shouting, because they killed Alice, my Alice, just when we'd planned to start again. And my hate knows no bounds, and my rage is unconfined.

A horde of black-hooded monks sprints into the room, forms a circle around Ryokan, who is standing upright, blood smeared across his face, his blue eyes, in their Oriental sockets, burning, illuminating the gloom that is this place. And then, all of a sudden, there's silence. No-one moves, nothing moves. My vision grows sharp again, everything back into focus.

On the floor, motionless, is Smith. Simon's on his knees next to him, his hand on his neck. 'He's still alive,' he says. 'Worse luck.

Birger stands up, shakily. 'It's good so,' he says. 'We can talk to him later.'

'Alice,' I shout. 'We've got to get Alice.'

Ryokan steps out of the circle of monks, throws off his cloak, lets it fall to the ground. 'She's already in the best place for her.'

'Oh no, oh God, oh God.'

'Not that, my friend,' he says, takes hold of me. 'Where my great-grandmother looked after Sandy, in the healer's chamber. She'll survive, with prayers and a bit of luck.'

'I need to see her.'

He nods at one of his monks. The hood falls away from the guard's face. It's a woman, with similarly golden hair. 'My sister,' he says and smiles a smile that soothes me.

I follow the woman along what seem interminable

corridors. Finally, we arrive at a small hole in the wall. She lets me past her. 'Please,' she says.

Alice is spread out on a raised block of stone that looks almost like an altar. I see her chest rise and fall. A robe covers her, of purest yellow. I pull it to one side. A bright white bandage covers her wound, her belly covered in sweat. I kiss the bandage, softly.

'You took your time,' she says.

'I was busy.'

'Makes a change.' Her voice is so weak.

'How?' I clutch at her hand. 'You're so much stronger than me.'

'She saved me.' She nods, almost imperceptibly at the woman. 'Jetsun Dolma; that's what she's called.' She closes her eyes.

I sit down on the floor. I'm exhausted. The woman sits next to me.

'Do you want me to explain?' she says.

'I won't remember.'

'Good.'

'Oh.'

'This is meant to be a secret place,' Dolma says.

'It's a bit public for that at the minute.'

'Ryokan, he's too much of a warrior.'

'Yes, I thought he was a bit handy for a monk.'

'I don't understand.'

'A bit too violent, a bit too good with his hands.'

'Oh, I see,' she says. She coughs, quietly. 'Sandy lay on this bed. And they fell in love, Sandy and his healer. Tara, she was called. My name, that's a different form of her name.'

'They're not still alive, are they?'

She shakes her head. 'They've been dead for a long time. Unfortunately.'

'So they married?'

She nods. 'The same year she found him on the

mountain, almost dead.'

'And then?'

'My grandfather was born almost ten years later.'

'That's a long time.'

She shrugs. 'These things take time. Maybe it's because Sandy wasn't from here. Maybe his body took that long to really get used to being here.'

'People don't survive up here.'

'We do.'

'And then?' I say.

'My father was born when my grandfather was thirty.'

'And you?'

'I'm twenty-nine of your years old.'

'And Ryokan?'

'Thirty-two.'

'Have you ever been down the mountain? Or do you all have to stay up here all the time?'

'We've been down a lot,' she says. 'Things have changed since the old times.' She wipes her eyes. 'Tara and Sandy never went down.'

'So you know everything about the mystery of Mallory and Irvine?'

She nods. 'It's not a mystery to us.'

There's the scuffling sound of boots in the passage outside. I jump up. Simon and Miranda, Ryokan and the High Lama stumble in.

'You need to sort him out,' Ryokan says to his sister. 'I think he's in shock.'

'Put him on the other bed.'

'What about Birger?' I say.

'He's coming,' Simon says. 'Under his own steam. Stubborn old bastard.'

'That's him,' I say.

'Sorry I was wrong,' Alice says, from behind me, awake again.

I rush to her, bury my face in her hair. 'I thought you

were dead.'

'So did I.'

The Lama sits on the other bed, his breath too quick. Dolma says something to him. 'He needs to sleep for a few days.'

The old man laughs, stretches his hand out to me, says something.

'He likes to sleep,' Dolma says. 'Because he's celibate, he says.'

I can't help but smile.

'He'll be fine,' Dolma says.

'What about Sandy?' I say. 'What did you do with his body?'

'Does it matter?' Miranda says. 'We're alive. That's all that matters.'

'I'm obsessed now,' I say.

'I thought that was my job,' Simon says, static in his bloody footsteps.

'You want to know as well, don't you?'

'Yes and no,' he says, leans against Alice's bed.

'But you're where it started,' I say.

'And now it's finished.'

'What about taking the camera back to his family?'

He shrugs.

Dolma gives the Lama something to drink from an ancient-looking bowl. She lifts her head and looks at us.

'You know English very well, don't you?' I say.

'Yes. I spent a couple of years in Kathmandu.'

'I don't understand it,' I say. 'We're in the Death Zone. We should all be dead, and so should you.'

'Our faith keeps us alive,' Dolma says. 'The first line of the Sutra says it all. It can't be explained.'

'Tell me about Sandy. Have you got any of his things left?'

'James,' Simon says. 'Leave it.'

'I can't.'

'Until Tara became High Lama, we only kept the bodies of the high lamas,' Dolma says. 'There aren't many.'

'She's still here?'

'She was the first High Lama to marry. So we kept her and Sandy.'

'Did they die many years apart?'

'A week,' she says. 'She couldn't bear to be without him.'

'How long ago?'

'Before I was born.'

'How long before?'

She frowns. 'In your years, twelve.'

I try to work it out. 'Eighty-two. Thirty-one years ago. Didn't he ever want to go home?'

'No. He loved Tara too much. From what I've heard, they swore to her father that they'd never leave.'

'All that time. He'd have been eighty.'

'Is she really still here?' Simon says.

'Yes.'

'We'll show you later,' Ryokan says. 'Let's tidy up first.'

Birger stumbles in through the door. 'English bastard,' he says, lips thick with bruises. 'And you're to blame, young man.' He shakes his fists at me. Stops. And smiles. 'You should never have chased up that mountain.' He sits on the floor. 'I could do with some akevitt.'

'There's some whisky somewhere,' Ryokan says.

'Shh,' Dolma says. 'We're not supposed to have that here.'

'It's only medicine,' Ryokan says.

'And you're ill all the time,' she says.

'Only sometimes.' He gives the bottle to Birger.

'We need to go back down,' I say. 'We can't stay here for as long as these special people.'

'Two days,' Dolma says. 'Then you can go, and we'll just have to trust you.' She stands next to Birger, runs her fingers through his hair.

'I'm not going anywhere,' he says. 'I think I'll stay here and take my chance.'

I say nothing. Love needs no explanation.

Later, much later, the monastery cleared and bloodless, I'm lying next to Alice on her bed, when Ryokan and Dolma come in.

'It's time,' Ryokan says.

'What for?' I say.

'You wanted to see Sandy.'

'What?'

'Come and see him.'

'Can I come, too?' Alice says.

'Are you strong enough to get up?' Dolma says.

'Yes.'

'So come.'

We walk through the passages without a word. It feels like we're going up.

'What did you do with that man and his guards?' I say.

'The guards were dead, so we threw them off the mountain,' Ryokan says. 'The four of them will be scattered to the winds now.'

'Doesn't that make you feel bad?' Alice says.

Ryokan shrugs, looks across at the High Lama. 'Sometimes it can't be helped, when we have to defend ourselves, our lives, this mountain. I didn't want them to die, but …' He looks at the lama again. 'They would not have spared us.'

'And Smith?'

'He's still unconscious. Maybe he'll wake up and not know what he did. I don't think he can go home.'

'What if he wants to?'

'He won't,' Dolma says. 'I don't think he'll know who

he is.'

'And what if he's not one of the chosen ones?' I say. 'What if he can't survive up here?'

'The irony is that I think he is one of the chosen ones,' Dolma says. 'His sleep seems natural. But his memory will have gone, because his head was hit so hard. Perhaps he'll become a good person now. Perhaps he'll become one of us.'

'I hope so,' Ryokan says.

We turn a corner, and there are Simon, pale and haggard, and Miranda, cheeks rosy.

'I can't do this,' he says.

'You can go down tomorrow,' Dolma says.

'So why's Miranda fine?'

'Maybe she's like Sandy; just made for this place.'

Simon looks at Miranda. 'You don't want to stay, do you?' he says, looking weaker and more desperate than I ever thought he could.

She shakes her head. 'I want us to be together.' She takes his hand, kisses it, serious for once.

The passages grow colder as we move upwards.

'How do you keep warm in the winter?' Simon says.

'The mountain is warm,' Ryokan says. 'When you go down inside her. She's a natural giver of life.'

'Weird,' Simon says.

'It saved the lives of our forebears,' Ryokan says. 'I don't think that will change.'

We come to a dead-end. A huge boulder blocks our path.

Ryokan pushes against the wall beside it. The rock rolls away, with a groaning sound.

'You mustn't touch anything,' Dolma says, her voice sharp. 'This is the holiest room of this place.'

We walk into the hush, so cold it's tangible. Our collective breath rises.

'Come,' Ryokan says, and leads us onwards, along

another passageway. Then he stops.

'Here,' he says, and takes a step back.

Cloaked in a red robe, her face flushed as if she had just come in from the mountain, there's the body of a woman, not withered by age or death or pain, a thick braid of black hair extending down to her waist, a woman so beautiful I'm not surprised Sandy would have fallen in love with her. She looks alive, real, like she's about to get up from her bed and greet me.

And next to her, robed in yellow, his arms across his chest, lies Sandy. His face is wrinkled, laughter lines around his eyes, eyelids down, a vision of calm and happiness, not much different to the photos I've seen of him, just a lot older.

'He was happy then?' I sniff.

'Oh yes,' Dolma says. 'The happiest days of his life, he said.'

'And the camera?' Simon says.

Ryokan reaches under the stone shelf on which the bodies lie, pulls something out. 'With his clothes from when Tara found him.' He hands the Vest Pocket Camera to Simon. 'He always said he wished he could have the pictures from it. To remind him of George.'

'How do you know?'

'My father told me. Sandy was a legend here, too. The only westerner ever to become one of us.'

Simon weighs the camera in his hand. 'What now?'

'I don't think you should take it with you,' Miranda says. 'Whatever you intended when you started this.'

'But … but, doesn't the world need to know?' he says.

'Isn't it enough that you know?' she says.

He looks at her, cradles the camera to his chest, then hands it back to Ryokan. 'I suppose it will have to be.'

Epilogue

8th June 2024, Jiehkkevarri, Norway

We're at the top of the mountain step Irvine climbed before he went to Everest. The day is bright, the sky blue, and the wind mercifully kind.

'Funny to think this is where I fell over a decade ago,' Alice says, her arm in mine, as we both stare out into the distance, at this Norway that's our home now. 'And you thought I'd died.'

'I was afraid.'

'So was I.'

I swallow. 'Not as afraid as when you were bleeding out on Everest, though.'

'No.'

The memory is heavy on both of us. It's because of that we've never been able to have children. But she didn't die, we didn't die. We survived. And that's good fortune enough, though it doesn't seem like it on our darkest days, of which there have been many. We'll both carry our mountain injuries forever.

And yet here we are, to remember Irvine and Mallory, 100 years on from the day they were last seen, by the world outside the High Monastery, at least. It's still not been discovered, its secret still safe, even in this over-connected world we live in now.

We get occasional letters from Birger who appears to be happy with Jetsun Dolma, as unlikely a couple as any we might ever have imagined. He signed his house in Lakselvbukt over to us when it became obvious he wouldn't be coming back. Some loophole in the Norwegian law, apparently, as long as we carried on renting out the house next to where he lived. That old kitchen table with the drawer in it remains as it was, and his junk is still in it.

Alice gets down on one knee, opens the rucksack, pulls out the two plastic flutes and the bottle of prosecco, and uncorks it. The fizzing merges with the gentle wind. It's an indulgence, we know, but it's worth it, not just to celebrate that we live here now, and always will, but to celebrate anyone who has ever looked at a mountain and wanted to climb it, not because it's there, but to escape from themselves into themselves, to be a part of nature that politicians and industrialists are doing their best to destroy.

Talking of which, the mysterious businessman didn't forget who he was, and disappeared. He didn't make it to the foot of Chomolungma. His family sold his empire and gave almost all the proceeds to charity. There was a rich irony in that.

Simon never climbed again. Like us, he and Miranda couldn't face living in an England that became more and more restrictive by the day, so they moved to Greece, from where they travel around the world, travellers' cheques still always at the ready. We have no idea where they are from one moment to the next, because they're even more disconnected from the world than we are.

'Cheers,' Alice says as our plastic glasses touch. 'I love you.'

'I love you, too.' Her lips are delicious in the cold.

'To Sandy and George, and everyone else,' she says, and lifts her glass skywards.

I grin and do the same.

THE END

Historical Notes

This novel is of course a reimagining of what might have happened to Mallory and Irvine on Mount Everest in 1924. However, I have changed neither the historical time line nor any biographical details.

The facts remain that Odell last saw the two men close to the summit on 8th June 1924, and that they were never seen again. Mallory's body was found in 1999. The picture of Ruth he had taken with him was not in the effects the search party retrieved from his body. Irvine's body has never been found. The location in which Holzel thought it might be was searched quite recently but nothing was discovered there.

There have been any number of peer-reviewed scientific papers which have found that the physiology of those living near Mount Everest, and of sherpas climbing the mountain, differs from the physiology of so-called lowlanders to such an extent that it would be possible for them to live in the Death Zone.

The starting point for *A Fear Of Heights* was my belief that Mallory and Irvine reached the summit. What I was focused on were the people and the mountain, not mountaineering techniques nor hugely detailed accounts of the 1924 expedition. I was drawn to Irvine's story not just because his body has never been found, but because, for most people, he's an unknown, just a name forever associated with Mallory. Mallory, on the other hand, has always been a legend, could be said to have been one during his life-time.

I have also always been fascinated by the mountains, by climbing, by the stories behind the ascents and the not ascents. And, as a writer, it has always been the personalities, the people, which have interested me more than the dry facts. The list of mountain books I've read in my life so far is too long to reproduce here (and I probably can't remember them all). But, in terms of influence on me and my life, *Die Weisse* Spinne stands head and shoulders above the rest.

My main references for this endeavour, though, have been:

- *Fearless On Everest: The Quest For Sandy Irvine*
    - Julie Summers;
- *Ghosts Of Everest*
    - Jochen Hemmleb, Larry A Johnson, Eric R Simonson, William E Nothdurft;
- *The Mystery Of Mallory and Irvine*
    - Audrey Salkeld, Tom Holzel;
- *The Wildest Dream: George Mallory*
    - Peter & Leni Gillman.

This just leaves me to say, as with all my historical fiction, that this book, this story, is just that, a work of fiction. It is intended to pay tribute not just to Mallory and Irvine, but to each and every mountain, to each and every climber, and, most importantly, to the sherpas.

R, Norwich, April 2024

One final note – apologies to my alma mater for blowing up a part of the historic Third Court, at the time of writing still Professor M's set, where I spent many fruitful hours (or fruitless, depending on whom you ask) as an undergraduate.

Printed in Great Britain
by Amazon

43633186R00192